Sorority Sisters

Sorority Sisters

CLAUDIA WELCH

BERKLEY BOOKS, NEW YORK

THE BERKLEY PUBLISHING GROUP
Published by the Penguin Group
Penguin Group (USA) Inc.
375 Hudson Street, New York, New York 10014, USA
Penguin Group (Canada), 90 Eglinton Avenue East, Suite 700, Toronto, Ontario M4P 2Y3, Canada
(a division of Pearson Penguin Canada Inc.) • Penguin Books Ltd., 80 Strand, London WC2R 0RL,
England • Penguin Group Ireland, 25 St. Stephen's Green, Dublin 2, Ireland (a division of Penguin
Books Ltd.) • Penguin Group (Australia), 250 Camberwell Road, Camberwell, Victoria 3124, Australia
(a division of Pearson Australia Group Pty. Ltd.) • Penguin Books India Pvt. Ltd., 11 Community Centre,
Panchsheel Park, New Delhi—110 017, India • Penguin Group (NZ), 67 Apollo Drive, Rosedale,
Auckland 0632, New Zealand (a division of Pearson New Zealand Ltd.) • Penguin Books (South Africa)
(Pty.) Ltd., 24 Sturdee Avenue, Rosebank, Johannesburg 2196, South Africa

Penguin Books Ltd., Registered Offices: 80 Strand, London WC2R 0RL, England

This book is an original publication of The Berkley Publishing Group.

This is a work of fiction. Names, characters, places, and incidents either are the product of the author's
imagination or are used fictitiously, and any resemblance to actual persons, living or dead, business
establishments, events, or locales is entirely coincidental. The publisher does not have any control over
and does not assume responsibility for author or third-party websites or their content.

PUBLISHING HISTORY
Berkley trade paperback edition / June 2012

Library of Congress Cataloging-in-Publication Data

Welch, Claudia, (date)–
Sorority sisters / Claudia Welch.
p.   cm.
ISBN 978-0-425-24743-3 (pbk.)
1. Female friendship—Fiction.   I. Title.
PS3623.E46215S67   2012
813'.6—dc23   2012002081

PRINTED IN THE UNITED STATES OF AMERICA

10 9 8 7 6 5 4 3 2 1

In memory of the Exclusives who have passed on.
You are not forgotten.

And to all Exclusives everywhere,
no matter how you met or what you call yourselves,
hold each other fast.

ACKNOWLEDGMENTS

There wouldn't be a book if not for the Exclusives. First and foremost, because she remembers all the things I had forgotten and never tired in answering any question I had, thank you, Captain Grace Sheehan, USN, Retired. Grace was my touchstone during the writing of this book. In addition, my deepest thanks to DiMarco, Friend, Les, Junkin, Gief, Shartel, Higgins, Wiggins, Rust, Read, Chapman, McCarthy, Brooker, and Helen. It's been almost forty years and you still make me laugh like no one else can.

This is a work of fiction. The Exclusives, *my* Exclusives, are not.

There would not have been a book without my daughter, Morgan. She begged me to write it. I am thankful that I listened to her.

Thank you to my agent, Dominick Abel. He encouraged me to follow where my heart led, assuring me that he would walk by my side no matter where we ended up. I could not have taken a single step of this journey without him.

Nothing at all would have happened without my editor, Kate Seaver. Even on a Saturday morning, she'd answer my emails. It doesn't get better than that. Thank you, Kate, for believing in this book and in my ability to write it.

Leslie Gelbman, your vision and your enthusiasm lifted me up and carried me along just when I needed it most.

To everyone else at Berkley, thank you. I try not to be high-maintenance. I suspect I fail more often than I succeed.

To my fellow goddesses, thank you. That I am still a goddess, I owe to you.

To the Biaggi Bunch: I'd lose my mind without you. Thank you for always being there.

⋅ To my son Paul, thank you for being my in-house tech. Not a single attached file would have been sent without you. To my son Daniel, thank you for being as obsessed with character as I am.

Finally, Tom, you have the worst life I can imagine: you are married to a writer. I have the best life I can imagine: I am married to you.

Sorority Sisters

Karen

Whenever someone finds out that you're in a sorority, they want to know if there's a secret handshake. Turns out, there is.

It hadn't been my idea to rush a house. Just saying the word *rush* sent a coil of terror into my gut where it rattled ominously. Sorority girls . . . Aren't they stuck-up?

Aren't they universally pretty?

I'm not pretty. According to my mom, my looks are "interesting." We all know what that means.

I'd been at the University of Los Angeles for a year, a perfectly fine freshman year where I'd lived in Birnhaven dorm, all women, a nice cafeteria on the ground floor; gotten good grades; found a nice boyfriend; and still my mother wasn't satisfied. It's not that she's one of those difficult mothers; it's just that she has certain ideas about nearly everything and she holds to them extremely firmly.

The thing is this: my mother made me do Rush. She said that after a year at the University of Los Angeles I ought to have more friends. She said that coming from outside of California like I did,

(I'm from Connecticut), and with ULA being a huge private university in the middle of downtown Los Angeles (though I couldn't swear there is a "middle" of Los Angeles; it's kind of a sprawl), I needed something smaller, some way to make female friends that will last me a lifetime.

My mother has always been very big on the idea of female friends. She's kept every friend she ever made, starting with Carol, who lived across the street from her when she was four, to Dottie, who lives across the street from her now. I'm not that great at making friends. I usually have one or two for a few years; then we drift apart and I make one or two more. It doesn't bother me that I have one friend to my mom's thirty-seven (I'm estimating low), but since she insisted that I join a sorority, I guess it must bother her. I wouldn't mind having more friends, but is joining a sorority the way to do that? My mother thinks so. Since she wasn't in a sorority, I'm not sure why she thinks so, but after fighting with her about it all summer, and then finding out she mailed in the necessary paperwork to make sure I was a part of Rush before I'd actually agreed to it . . . the short version is: she won. My mom always wins. She fights dirty. Anyway, I went through Rush, which wasn't as bad as I thought it would be. In some ways, it was actually fun. Anyway, now I'm a Beta Pi pledge. Whatever that means.

Tonight is Presents: the pledge class of 1975. There are twenty-six of us. I wish we all looked like scared rabbits, which I'm sure is how I look, but some of the girls are laughing and talking with friends in the mob that is surging into the Beta Pi living room.

The mob is composed mostly of college guys—frat guys, I think.

Presents, accent on the first syllable—don't ask me why—is a slightly horrifying, slightly barbaric, completely degrading ritual that I didn't know anything about until I did Rush and pledged Beta Pi. Now that I'm a pledge, I get to stand under a thin poster-board placard with my name on it so that the world at large, and fraternity guys specifically, get to look me over. Maybe jot down my name for future reference. Maybe chuckle derisively.

As an introduction to sorority life, it's not great, but what can I do about it? Keep my chin up and hold on to as much dignity as I can manage. But I'm definitely going to tell my mom about *this*.

Looking at the other pledges standing under their signs, all of us in white formals (the symbolism is *so* subtle), I'm helpless to resist making comparisons. They're a nice-looking bunch of girls, though only two or three are truly gorgeous. It's mostly the old routine of pretty face and so-so figure or something slightly off with the face but the body is good. I'm in the face-is-slightly-off group, in case I was too coy earlier. My body is good, not that I can take any credit for that. I hit puberty at twelve and have had pretty constant male attention since then. I'm not complaining. Who would?

"Why don't we just wear bunny ears and get it over with?"

I look to my left and snort in companionable misery.

"I've got a bunny tail pinned to my underwear," I say. "I'll be ripping my dress off in half an hour. I'll give you a two-minute warning, okay?"

She chuckles and I read her placard. Laurie McCormick. I'm Karen Mitchell. We've been alphabetized as well as categorized. The frat guys seem to appreciate it; it has to make sorting through us later so much more convenient.

I wish they had placards.

I may not be very good at making and keeping girlfriends, but I have no trouble at all making and keeping boyfriends. Which, during high school, may have been the problem with the girlfriend situation. My mother said as much once or twice (I'm underestimating), but what am I supposed to do about it? Give up guys?

Laurie McCormick is one of those blue-blood types, the type who looks like she grew up around horses and sailboats. She has light brown, streaky blond hair, long and shiny, and light grayish blue eyes. She's thin and has nice skin. Those are the positives. If I'm going to be brutally honest about her looks, her teeth are a little crooked and her hair is a little stringy. But she has the cutest nose I've ever seen. I have a thing for noses. I've never liked my nose, but then, I'm not crazy about my whole face.

"Rip it off now," says the girl to my right. "That should be fun to watch."

I glance right. Ellen Olson. She's blond, tanned, and has light aqua-blue eyes. She's a girl of the red-blooded variety. Not perfectly beautiful, but pretty enough not to have to worry. She's definitely higher on the scale than being interesting-looking. That's how my mom *and* my grandmother describe my looks: interesting. I don't start these conversations, believe me, but I can't ignore them either. She's my mom. There's just no ignoring your mom.

"You first," Laurie McCormick answers. "Why don't we watch them do it to you?"

Ellen smiles crookedly and shakes her head. "Hey, just kidding." Ellen has a truly fantastic smile.

We're supposed to stand politely, not talking, not flinching in embarrassment when some guy looks you over like a suit he's buying, studying your name like it's a math problem he can't quite get. It's worse when they don't come to check you out at all, or, if they do, they shake their heads and move away fast, or they laugh dismissively. It happens. In fact, it's already happened to me. Twice.

How did this tradition start, and why? Did the Beta Pi pledges of 1890 find it any less humiliating? Maybe back then, the guys

were gentlemen, and instead of taking notes, they were introducing themselves. It's slightly better to imagine it that way. Not
much, but some.

"She seems to be having fun," Ellen says, an olive-branch
statement. I accept it. I follow the direction of her gaze, as does
Laurie.

Diane Ryan. She's smiling at the guys, talking to them, drawing them in. She doesn't have to say much. She's got long black
hair, brown eyes, and a nice figure, a little pear-shaped, but nothing grotesque. She's sexy, and she's throwing it all over them. They
like it.

The thing about guys is that they're very predictable. They
like certain things and they like those certain things to distraction. I had that figured out by the time I was fourteen, and I'd had
a pretty good idea about it at twelve. I didn't *do* anything about it,
not much anyway, but I had it figured out.

I'm not pretty, but give me a half hour with 60 percent of the
guy population and I can somehow get him to name that tune.
I don't why, I don't even know how, but I can. Sixty percent give
or take.

I'm not easy. It's not that, though I think the parents of my
various boyfriends thought that. Maybe it's that the guys think
I'll be easy, but then, why do they stick around when they find out
I'm not? I've never been able to figure it out. I try not to think
about it. Naturally, I think about it all the time.

Diane Ryan? I get why they're swarming around her. She's
giving it off, that sign or that scent that guys stumble after. She's
doing it and she knows she's doing it. She's obviously enjoying
herself while she's doing it, which isn't exactly in the best of taste.
It's okay to enjoy it—you'd be a fool not to—but no one's supposed
to be able to tell. I got that message from my mom.

One of the girls down the horseshoe line shrugs, shakes her head, and lurches out of the line and out of the room. Missy Todd. Has it been an hour?

"I guess she's had enough," Laurie says.

"Gutsy move," Ellen says, watching Missy Todd until she's out of sight.

Whether it's been an hour or not, the chapter president smiles and shows the guys the door. They leave shuffling, acting reluctant, which could be seen as a sign of good manners, a compliment of sorts, in a very generous interpretation. After all, every sorority on The Row is presenting their pledge class tonight. They have eleven other pledge classes to grade, rate, and sort. It's such a convenient arrangement for them since the fraternity and sorority houses are all on one street less than a mile from campus, maybe less than half a mile; I've never measured it. It's a short bike ride away; that's all I know. Anyway, since all the houses are on the same street, it's called The Row.

It's a bit intimidating. All these huge houses, mansions really, lined up, their front yards scrubby with struggling grass from all the bikes parked there. ULA is a bike-riding school. If you live off campus, you ride a bike to get to it. Walking is too dangerous because it's too slow.

I never came to The Row during my freshman year. It was way too intimidating. If you don't belong on The Row, then you should stay off The Row. Or that was how it seemed to me, living in Birnhaven, eating in the dorm cafeteria. Sorority and fraternity people seemed like people from another world, the world of The Row and exchanges and drinking beer on the lawn on Thursday afternoons, getting a head start on the weekend.

Am I one of them now? Will I fit in? Do I want to?

Why ask me? Ask my mom.

After the living room clears of everyone who's not a Beta Pi, there's a lot of aimless milling around, and the noise level rises like a tide. Holly Clark comes over and we look awkwardly at each other for a few seconds.

"I'd better get this dress off," I say.

"Sure, if you're ready," Holly says.

It's her dress. I didn't have a long white gown of my own and so she let me use hers, which was pretty sweet of her. Holly is probably four inches taller than I am, so she pinned the dress up along the seam under the bust; otherwise I would have tripped over the hem. I'm the shortest one in my family, and no one in my family is what you'd call tall.

Maybe that's why the guys didn't seem all that impressed with me. I'm wearing a long dress that doesn't really fit me and certainly doesn't show my figure off. I pay a lot of attention to what I wear. I figure most girls do, but I'm really inspired not to look like Quasimodo.

I wonder how my picture is going to turn out.

A photographer took a picture of each of us before Presents started, standing in our white gowns, holding a bouquet of white and yellow flowers, standing on the stairs leading from the foyer to the second floor. It's going to look like a bridal photo.

The symbolism of that is hard to shake.

What is a sorority? A marriage mart? Brides for sale?

Not at all what my mom had in mind. I don't think.

I want to get married. It's not that. I've wanted to get married since I first realized that men and women got married. I think I must have been about five. I've had a boyfriend since the second grade, not the same one, obviously, but one right after another, and sometimes more than one at a time. I don't go into a relationship intending to cheat; it just happens.

Considering that my intentions are good, I've never felt overly guilty about it. I've never gone out with a guy who was dating someone else. That's a firm policy and I don't break it. It's just that when a guy pursues me like I'm the last word on womanhood, it's hard to resist. Plus, the old relationship was on its last legs; we were both getting bored or lazy. It was time to move on. That's what I've decided, thinking about it as often as I have.

I've been dating Greg Hall since November of my freshman year and I haven't cheated on him. That's if you don't count Christmas vacation when I went back to Connecticut and went out a few times with my old high school boyfriend. You'd also have to ignore the two—no, wait, three—dates I went on over the summer. With three different guys.

I was home for three months! What was I supposed to do with myself for three months? Besides, two of the guys were just accidents. I never even saw them again after meeting them while out with my high school friends. According to my mom, what Greg doesn't know won't hurt him. Since I was in Connecticut and he was in Washington, it didn't hurt him.

I love Greg. I do. I want to marry him and he wants to marry me.

So, we'll get married after we graduate. And I'll wear my own long white gown and carry a bouquet that doesn't remind me of scrambled eggs.

The house is quieting, the sounds of female voices subduing, hushing, as the pledges leave. Not all sorority sisters live in the house, and no pledges do. I live in an apartment over a few blocks and two blocks behind the house, just off of Adams, about ten minutes on my bike. It's dark now and I'll be riding fast. In fact, I want to leave with the bulk of the throng, no matter where they're going. There's safety in numbers, which they make a point of telling you at freshman orientation.

"Thanks again," I say, handing Holly the dress on its hanger. "I really appreciate it."

"No problem. I'm glad we could make it fit," she says.

We walk back into the hallway together, a big crowd of pledges at the door, laughing as they walk into the night.

"Bye," I say. I don't want to leave alone. LA is no place to be alone.

Holly smiles and waves, already walking up the stairs to put her dress away.

I hurry down the brick steps, find my bike, unlock it, relieved to see that others are unlocking their bikes, struggling in the dark to see the dials, going by feel alone. We ride down The Row together, not talking, not knowing one another, but somehow bound together by Presents, by virginal white gowns and a scrambled-egg bouquet, by having just pledged a sorority together, individually, yet linked now. We share the most fragile of bonds, the bond of humiliation beneath the shadow of our names on a placard, the bond of rushing a house and finding a place in it.

It's not much of a bond, but it's something.

I stay with the pack, our bikes whizzing through the night, for as long as I can. I split off and pump furiously down the middle of darkened streets, holding to the center where the streetlights overlap. I get to my apartment building, lugging my bike up the long stairs to the gate. Greg is waiting for me, and he wraps one arm around my waist and with the other he holds my bike while I press myself full against him, arms around his neck.

Home.

I open the gate and we walk to my apartment, ground floor of a two-story stucco building, facing the kidney-shaped pool, a bed of lush philodendrons forming a green barrier between my front door and the pool. It's all very old-school California, like something out of a Joan Crawford movie; I love it. It's dark inside as I unlock the door, which is a relief. I'm rooming with a girl I barely know; Ingrid was looking for a roommate, I was, we had a mutual friend, and here we are.

"Were you waiting long?" I ask, turning on the overhead light.

"Maybe ten minutes," Greg says, grabbing me from behind, his arm around my waist, kissing the back of my neck. The back of my neck is very easy to get to; I have very short hair. When nearly every other girl my age is wearing her hair as long as it will grow, tumbled hot-roller curls, loose and glossy, my dark brown hair is nearly crew-cut short. Why? My mother thinks short hair suits me. You know what? She's probably right.

"What took so long?" Greg says.

"I don't know. I had to change," I answer. He waited for me. I feel both glad and guilty.

"Where's Ingrid?" Greg asks.

"Dunno," I say, slipping out of his grasp to pull the cheap drapes closed, then facing him again.

Greg is nice-looking in a very boy-next-door sort of way. He's dark-haired, blue-eyed, and six feet tall. We've been dating since November 22 of our freshman year, and he is my third college boyfriend; college really is the mother lode of cute, available guys. Greg is not in a fraternity and has no plan to rush one. I think it's because his family can't afford it, not that he'll admit that. Greg's father is a high school gym teacher and his mother is a secretary for a realty office in Washington. He's at ULA on scholarship. He's the only one I know who is, not that he ever talks about it and not that it matters. He mentioned it once, when I first met him, but since then, not a word.

"How was it?" he asks, shoving his hands deeply into the pockets of his beige cords. "Lots of frat guys, I guess, looking you over," he says.

I don't say anything. I just stare at him, hoping it will pass. He gets like this sometimes. He really hates the whole sorority-fraternity thing. It took me by surprise at first; when I wrote and told him my mom had signed me up for Rush, his first letter back to me was vitriolic and intense. And long. Seven-pages-of-block-letters long. I wrote back explaining again how my mom was *making* me do it, which is true enough, but what was there to be so angry about? Why hate something you don't know anything about? To be honest, that kind of bothered me, but I got over it.

"How can you stand stuff like that?" he says.

It strikes me again that Greg has never been to The Row, or to Presents, and so, even if he has sort of hit the nail on the head, he did it by accident, striking blind. It might be an *accurate* assessment, but it's not really a *fair* one.

"It was okay. You could have come," I say, walking toward him. He wraps me into his hug, a blanket of safety surrounding me, shutting out his anger.

"With all those frat guys? No way," he says just before he kisses me.

I'm going to marry this man. We'll be happy and have two kids and live a Technicolor life in the suburbs. He'll be a great husband. He'll work hard and have a good job and he'll be a devoted father to our kids.

He pulls back from our kiss and I press my face against his neck. "Do you think I'm pretty?" I ask as his hands slip under my shirt and move up to cup my breasts through the whisper-thin fabric of my bra. He unhooks my bra with ease born of practice.

"Yeah," he says, thumbing my nipples.

I can't help wondering where Ingrid is and when she's coming back. Greg lifts my shirt over my head and sticks a couple of his fingertips into the waistband of my pants. He's looking at me expectantly. I make myself stop thinking about Ingrid.

"I love you," I say, wrapping one leg around him.

"Me, too," he says, unzipping his cords.

Hey, I've been dating him almost a year and we're in love. We're going to get married. I'm not easy. I'm really not.

Going to exchanges is getting a little old. I mean, I have studying to do and Greg to keep happy, and he is *not* happy about all this fraternity stuff. I didn't get home from the Eta Epsilon Tau exchange until after eleven, which might not have been a problem except that I'd told him I only had to stay for an hour. Since it started at eight, he was pretty mad that I stayed longer than I had to. It was definitely a case of what he didn't know wouldn't hurt him. The trouble was that I'd told him too much, he *knew*, and he was therefore hurt.

My mom really has a gift.

"I have a test tomorrow. This is going to be a short night for me. How about you? Are you going to stay long?" Ellen says.

I look down at Ellen. She's sitting on the arm of the couch on the long wall of the Beta Pi living room, looking up at me. I'm standing because I'm wearing a dress that wrinkles under a hard glance. Ellen's eyes are an amazing shade of blue, almost an aquamarine. She's pretty, but she doesn't really act like it. Not like Diane Ryan. Diane knows she's a fox and she acts like it. Ellen just seems to ignore it. It's all very weird. If I were gorgeous, I would definitely know it and act like it.

"Probably not," I say. "I'm getting tired. I think I need a night off from all this playing. I'm out of shape."

She laughs and recrosses her legs. Ellen's wearing black pants, very snugly fitted through the hips, with a pale blue blouse tucked in. A narrow black leather belt at her waist and a thin gold chain at her throat complete the outfit.

"Do you know any Rho Delts?" she asks.

I shake my head. "I don't know anyone on The Row."

"Same here. Have you met anyone you liked?"

I met an EE Tau I sort of liked at an exchange, but I haven't seen him since, and I did kind of look. "I have a boyfriend."

"Is he in a fraternity?"

"No."

"Planning to rush one?"

"No."

Ellen nods, her brows raised a bit. "How's he feel about all this?"

"He's okay with it," I say. He is, basically. Mostly because we don't talk about it. Greg just sort of refuses to talk about it, and really, it's probably for the best. What could I say to make him feel better? Ignorance is bliss, right? "Do you have a boyfriend?" I ask.

Ellen chuckles. "No. Not that I wouldn't mind one."

"You haven't seen anything that rings your chimes at any of these exchanges?"

"Well," she says, rearranging her gold necklace so that the clasp is at the back of her neck, "the free beer's not bad."

"God, I thought you'd be there by now and I'd have to walk in alone," Laurie says, hurrying through the doorway at my back to stand next to me.

"That would have been bad," I say.

"Yeah, if you miss attendance," Ellen says, "the whole evening goes down as a no-show."

"I haven't missed an exchange yet," Laurie says, "and I'm not missing this one."

"Going for a perfect attendance record?" I ask.

"Why not? I could stand a little perfection in something," Laurie answers, running a hand through her hair, fluffing it out. "Does my hair look okay? I tried a new shampoo."

"You look great," I say.

And she does. She looks fantastic. Her hair is shiny and straight and full, a long fall of golden highlights flickering through the light brown color. Her makeup is very natural, just mascara, blush, and pink lip gloss. She's wearing a pink blouse and skintight jeans, a woven leather belt at her waist, and small gold hoop earrings.

"Do you really think so?" Laurie asks, looking at me, her glance sliding briefly to Ellen before returning to me. "My jeans are so tight I can't sit down without passing out."

"Don't sit down," Ellen says, her eyes twinkling. "It's worth it. You look tiny."

She really does. Her hips and waist look the width of a straw, her shirt flowing smoothly over her ribs and bust without a bulge.

"How'd you get them on?" I ask.

"I laid on my back and pulled the zipper up with a pair of pliers. My roommate hoisted me off the bed."

"God, I am so doing that," Ellen says, her eyes alight. "What are you going to do when you have to use the bathroom?"

"I'm not. I'm not going to be able to drink anything."

Ellen leans back against the couch cushion with a groan and closes her eyes. "There goes that plan."

"You really look great," I say. "If you need a bathroom buddy, I'm there for you."

"Thanks," she says. "You look great, too."

"Sure I do. In my dress." I'm the only one in the room wearing a dress. I want to kill myself.

"It's a nice dress!" Laurie says.

"Yeah. Nice."

Ellen starts laughing. "Shut up. You look great, Karen."

"I think it will all be a lot easier when we all live in the house and I can take a survey before I put on my underwear," I say.

"You do underwear surveys?" Ellen asks. "What kind? All kinds? Even the slutty kind?"

I look down at her, straight-faced. "Define *slutty.*"

Ellen roars with an abrupt bark of laughter. "Come on! Give me a survey! I want to do a slutty survey!" Half the room looks at her. At me. At her again. The pledge trainer frowns in our direction.

"Geez, give the poor kid a survey before she passes out," Laurie says, grinning.

"First question, second attempt: Define *slutty,*" I say. "Visual aids are allowed, though I advise you to unzip with discretion. If such a thing is possible."

Ellen bursts out laughing. You've got to love a girl who laughs from her belly like that.

"Here they come," says a voice from the front of the room. The cigarettes get put out; we stand up, file into the foyer, laughing and talking. Then out we go, flowing down the steps of the Beta Pi house, across the struggling lawn and down the sidewalk, into the night and the joys of another fraternity exchange, this time with the Rho Delts. Since the Rho Delta Pi house is way down the block, we have a lot of time to talk before we get there.

"So, you're not looking," I say to Ellen.

"I'm not looking, but I'm not blind," she says.

Actually, I could say the same about myself. But I won't.

"Laurie's not looking either," I say.

"I'm not?" Laurie asks. "Please tell me I'm not blind."

"Hey, four exchanges," I say. "I've watched you. You're polite, you mingle, and you get out. You don't act like a girl who's looking."

"As long as I don't act like a girl who's blind," Laurie says, tapping her pack of cigarettes against her thigh as she walks. Laurie never goes anywhere without her cigarettes, the lighter pushed down in between the wrapping and the cellophane. Laurie's fingernails are always painted, and her hands are delicately shaped with long slender fingers. She looks good smoking, and you can't say that about very many people. Me? I've never smoked. Oh, I tried it for a while when I was twelve, but I never liked it. "But just for the record, I'm looking. I just don't see anyone who's worth looking at and I can't be held responsible for that."

"Blame them, definitely," Ellen says. "They can't cut it. EE Taus, Upsilon Chis, Phi Sigs. What's the scoop on the Rho Delts? Are they hunks or dogs?"

"I'll let you know in fifteen minutes," Laurie says. "Let's just say that, since hope springs eternal, I have hope."

"An optimist," I say. "I'd never have guessed. What about you, Ellen? Any hope for the Rho Delts?"

"I'll tell you after fifteen minutes and a beer or two," Ellen says brightly. "Hope gets real springy after a few beers."

Me? I'm not looking, but . . . you know.

Ellen

"The free beer is the best part of fraternity exchanges," I say. We're not even halfway to the Rho Delta Pi house and the guys who are escorting us are staying at the front of the pack; Laurie and Karen and I are bringing up the rear.

Karen looks askance at me. Laurie looks down at her feet.

"Come on," I say. "Free. Beer. That's got to be unanimous."

"I can't stand the taste of it," Karen says.

"I've seen you drinking beer at every exchange," I say.

"I was faking it, just trying to be polite," Karen says.

"Laurie? Do you fake it, too?" I ask.

"I'm not polite enough to fake it," Laurie says. "No manners at all, I'm afraid."

"God, why did you join a sorority if not for the free beer?" I ask.

"My mom made me," Karen says. "I'm glad she did, though."

"I wanted to make friends," Laurie says. "I barely made friends with my dorm roommate last year; she's in the marching band. They practice all the time."

"Yeah? What'd she play?" I ask.

"Clarinet. She practiced in our room when she wasn't marching with the band. She didn't like an audience when she practiced either, so I spent a lot of time in Darvey Library. It was one of the reasons I wanted to join a sorority."

"No sorority girls in the Spartan marching band, huh?" I say.

"Something like that," Laurie says, smiling at me. Laurie's got such a quiet look, so composed, even when she's smiling. I should probably take a lesson, but I don't think being composed is ever going to be in my repertoire. "Why did you join a sorority?"

Why'd I join a sorority? One reason was that it annoyed my dad, Ed. Being in a sorority is expensive and Ed's footing the bill. He can afford it. Besides, it's good for the old guy to spend money on something other than his weekend deep-sea fishing trips and redoing his orthodontic office every five years. But I'm not going to share that tidbit while walking down The Row on the way to a nice alcoholic buzz. "Besides the free beer? That's easy. My freshman roommate, who did not play the clarinet, practically had her boyfriend living with us last year. Yes, I know it was against dorm rules. No, I didn't say anything."

"Why not?" Laurie says.

"I chickened out," I say. "But any girl who's sharing a twin bed seven feet away from mine is beyond shame anyway."

"We're here," Karen says. "Time to look cute and friendly."

"Easy for you to say. You're built cute and friendly."

"And you're built for plague and pestilence?" Karen says, laughing.

"I wish," I say. "More like whole or skim."

My bust is massive, disgustingly bovine. I don't have breasts; I have udders.

"Oh, come on," Karen says. "You're so pretty."

"For a fat cow," I say. This, I don't mind sharing. This, everyone can see for themselves.

Laurie smiles and shakes her head at me. "Where did you ever get the idea that you're fat?"

From Ed. But I'm not going to share that either.

"You think we don't have mirrors in Northridge?" I say. Northridge is where I grew up; it's in the Valley. Our house is in a neighborhood built in an old orange grove and our yard is full of orange trees; my mom makes fresh-squeezed orange juice for Ed every morning. She doesn't even like orange juice since it gives her heartburn. I think Ed is what gives her heartburn. "Come on, let's go be charming for the Rho Delts, and if we can't be charming, we'll just have to settle for being drunk."

"I'm going for charming since I can't stand the beer either," Laurie says.

"Way to kill off your options, McCormick," I say as we walk into the fraternity house.

The Rho Delta Pi house is like all fraternity houses; it's large, sparsely furnished, and slightly dilapidated. There is no lawn. There is only dirt as hard-packed as concrete. That's one of the rules of The Row: all the sorority houses have manicured lawns and all the fraternity houses look like bomb sites.

The Rho Delts do their best to make us welcome, which mostly involves getting plastic cups full of beer into our hands as quickly as possible, which is totally fine with me. I get separated from Laurie and Karen and find myself standing next to Missy Todd.

"How's it going?" I ask, my mouth next to her ear so I can be heard above Black Sabbath. "Do you think you'll stay after the hour?"

We only have to stay at the exchange for an hour, our commitment to making Beta Pi look good accomplished after only sixty minutes. You'd be surprised how long an hour can be when you're bored to death.

Missy looks around the room critically—*openly* critically. That's the thing I've noticed about Missy. She doesn't give a damn what you think about her because she's so busy figuring out what she thinks about you. It should be as annoying as hell, but I love it. Like tonight, her brown hair is in a loose ponytail and the only makeup she's wearing is mascara. She's wearing a really casual tan skirt and an Indian gauze shirt with some tiny mirrors embroidered on it in red thread. On her feet are navy blue Dr. Scholl's. Dr. Scholl's. To a *dance*.

She looks like she threw on whatever clothes she had on the end of her bed this morning and didn't even think about changing for this exchange. It's like every bone in her body is shouting, *Screw you.*

God, I love that.

"I can't tell yet," she says. "Are you?"

"Let me swig down another beer; then I'll tell you."

Missy laughs.

"Another beer?" some guy says from behind me. "I've got you covered."

He's back in less than a minute, a beer in each hand, a smile on his face. Guys always get real cheerful when girls keep drinking. I've noticed that a lot.

"I'm Mike Dunn," he says, handing us the beers.

"And you're empty-handed," I say.

"The price of chivalry," he says, his gaze on me, practically ignoring Missy. Missy doesn't seem to mind.

"I'm Ellen. This is Missy."

He nods and smiles. He's got blue eyes and black hair and the sort of handsome bad-boy look that has always gotten on my nerves. I'm not interested in being a conquest for some bad boy.

"Would you like to dance, Ellen?" he says.

"What about my beer? I just got it," I say.

"You could drink it," he says, taking a full beer from a passing Rho Delt.

"With you crying, 'Chug, chug, chug'?" I ask.

"Would I do that to you?" he says, looking at me with a very naughty glint in his light blue eyes.

"You know you would," I say, shaking my head at him. "But I will if you will."

His eyes widen; so does his grin. "You're on."

Without any more stupid banter, we chug our beers. He wins, but just by a swallow. I let him win. What's the harm? Guys love to think they can drink girls under the table, and I'm the kind of girl who loves to watch them try.

I turn to Missy as Mike starts to lead me to the center of the room. "Go grab one of Diane Ryan's extra guys. She can't need them all."

"I don't know," Missy says, looking across the room to where Diane is standing. "She might."

Diane

Look, the reason I know so many guys is because I'm in ROTC. Sure, I knew plenty of guys before I signed on for ROTC, but that's beside the point. Then again, maybe it's the actual point. The thing is, I like guys and they like me, and that works out great. Or it should, but actually, no, it's not so great, at least not all the time.

It all started out with me having a great freshman year. In fact, it was so great that I almost flunked out. Needless to say, my dad was not pleased. Saying that my dad, a navy pilot, was not pleased is really saying something. Trust me on that.

"Diane, what in the hell were you thinking?"

That was what he said when I got home from school last summer. Naturally, Dad wasn't expecting an answer since these rhetorical questions are part of the drill. My duty as his only child is to stand there and take it, without flinching and without whining. Any lame excuse is whining, and my dad is the one who determines what a lame excuse is. Pretty much, they're all lame, and I base this on a lifetime of experience.

So here's what happened: my dad told me that he was done. He told me that if I wanted to return to ULA, then I'd have to find a way to make it happen because he sure as hell wasn't going to throw any more money down the Diane well.

I cried. I can admit it. I didn't sob, but I cried.

But Dad is not the kind of father who crumbles when faced with a few tears. Mom, having been married to him for twenty-two years, is not a crumbler either. If she'd been a crumbler, he would have chewed her up and spit her out a long time ago, like on their first date back in Meridian, the old home place. Mom and Dad met when Dad was stationed in Mississippi just before the Korean War. Mom is a true southern belle who grew up in a small-scale version of Tara, minus the slaves, the cotton, and the War Between the States, known to the rest of the world as the Civil War. It could be argued, but not by me, that Mom doesn't understand the meaning of the term *civil war.* There's no point in arguing it because while Mom didn't have slaves, she did, and does, have plenty of southern bourbon. Never argue semantics with a woman clutching a highball glass. Nobody pushes a southern belle around, not even Dad. Scarlett O'Hara taught the world that, and Dad learned the lesson up close and personal from Mom. There are no scars to prove it. Southern belles have more finesse than to leave visible scars. The movies never get that part right.

But back to me . . . No money for school and no grades to get a scholarship. Dad was very helpful about the whole thing, suggesting ROTC the way he did. He also made it clear that they didn't take just anybody, and maybe, with a good word from him thrown in, I might make the cut.

Gee, thanks, Dad.

So here I am, ROTC all the way. Go, navy. Hoo-ah.

It is a great way to meet guys—I'll say that for it—not that I have a problem meeting guys.

Hoo-ah.

Joining a sorority is supposed to be the antidote for ROTC. That's Mom's theory, not that she put it in those exact words. No, her words were more like, "Diane, certain sorts of people join the military and certain sorts join sororities. It's good to be able to mix well with all sorts." She took a healthy swallow of a bourbon and water somewhere in her declaration, though I can't remember exactly where. But she took it, believe me.

My mom was in a sorority in college and my mom, after a few drinks, likes to talk about those days. She makes it sound great. Lots of parties, fancy dresses, dates with corsages. We're talking the early 1950s here, in Mississippi, so I'm not sure how well it's going to translate to LA in the mid-1970s, but she's confident that I'll make "lovely friends" and that I'll "acquire a certain polish."

I guess I'm not all that polished right now. Plastered, sure, but not polished.

That's what I'm talking about. Mom is death on comments like that. I get the feeling sometimes that she doesn't think Dad being in the navy has been good for me, that he might be, by accident, polishing me in all the wrong ways. But, Mom being Mom, she never actually says that. She says other stuff, like how being in a sorority will be good for me and "stand me in good stead."

How're they paying for this, ULA being so expensive and Dad being your average, above-average navy pilot? I mean, he has a lot of ribbons and shit, but still, ULA sorority costs are way beyond his salary. Mom's parents are paying for it—that's how. Mom, and her mother before her . . . They really believe in the whole sorority drill. Hell, they made it sound great, one party after another, guys with corsages, a pajama party every night. What's not to love?

So here I am at a required sorority-fraternity exchange, surrounded by guys. Who says war is hell?

"Hey, do you need all these guys or can you pass a few around as hors d'oeuvres?" Missy asks me.

"I can spare a few. How many do you want?" I say.

"Two or three dozen ought to do it," Missy says.

"Take an even fifty. They're free."

Missy laughs and eyes me approvingly. I know what that look means. She was wondering if I was stuck-up, and now she's figuring out I'm not. I've been run through this same girly gauntlet since my senior year of high school, when I finally, thank God, "blossomed." That's Mom's word for it, not mine.

The guys in question, all three of them, can't hear what we're saying since Three Dog Night is blaring on the stereo and Missy has her mouth next to my ear. That, and I've got my beer cup up against my mouth.

"You don't want even one for yourself?" she asks.

"They're all yours."

Guys are great; I love them. They're adorable, fun to play with, and they hardly ever break, but I'm not interested in having some guy carry me through life, or even through a fraternity exchange. The navy is my chance at a no-holds-barred career, with no limit to how high I can go. "Diane, there's no limit to what you can do," Dad said. I believe him. I'm not going to let some guy screw that up, even the one guy who tempts me to screw that up. Midshipman Temptation is not a Rho Delt, so I can relax and let the good times roll.

"I think I'll take him. He looks good," Missy says, using her chin to point out the middle guy in the trio standing across from us. He's a fellow ROTC, so this is going to be easy.

"Rawlins! This is Missy. She'd like to dance," I say, grabbing Dean Rawlins by the arm and pulling him toward me. "You've been volunteered."

Rawlins smiles, nods at Missy, and escorts her to the dance floor—in this case, the middle of the Rho Delt living room, the couches having been pushed to the walls.

I stare at the two remaining guys. One is another ROTC and the other one isn't. I'm avoiding ROTC guys as a rule—Dad's rule—so I smile at the guy with hair that reaches his collar. "Cat got your tongue?" I say.

"You the cat? Then not my tongue," he says, a glint in his eyes. Oh, one of those. He does have that look, not that I mind. You've got to watch that type every minute, but you've got to watch them all every few minutes anyway. It's part of their charm.

"Come on, sweetie. Dazzle me with your moves."

He leads me onto the dance floor, but we all know those aren't the kinds of moves I need to worry about.

Do I look worried?

Hell, no.

Laurie

I joined a sorority so that I could make friends—I told the truth about that—but the truth I didn't tell is that I also joined a sorority, any sorority, so that I could casually bump into Pete Steinhagen during a Rho Delt exchange. The problem is that after six years of girls' boarding school, I have no skill whatsoever in casually bumping into a guy, and I certainly couldn't manage any sparkling interaction with guys on my own, but with my new sorority sisters around me, I can manage to create the illusion of ease and sophistication. I'm fairly confident of that after so many exchanges. Of course, none of the previous exchanges meant a thing to me; they were my dress rehearsal for the Rho Delt exchange.

"Why are you guys still standing around?" Ellen says, having pushed through the crowd to stand next to Karen and me. "You don't even have beers!"

"I thought we covered that on the walk over," I say.

"Yeah, yeah. I blanked that out. It was too awful. Hey, let's go over there. He's cute," Ellen says.

"The guy or the keg?" Karen says.

"Any guy standing next to a keg has a leg up on the competition," Ellen says. "Who's with me?"

"I'm in," Karen says. "Laurie?"

Karen and I have been stuck to each other, our backs against the wall, since we walked into the room. I've been looking for Pete from my corner; I haven't seen him. He, if he's here, hasn't seen me. "Sure. Why not?" I say. I need to move around, get into the crowd, and give Pete a chance to find me.

"Are you the beer man?" Ellen says to the guy. "Do you need a barmaid to help you deliver the frothy goods to the eager customers?"

He smiles. "You can be my tavern wench if you'll split your tips with me."

Ellen grins. "Tavern wenches don't get the kind of tips you can split."

"At least he thinks you'll bring in the bucks," I say.

"Is this Pimp Dialogue 101?" Karen says. "I need a syllabus."

"God, can you imagine the reading list?" Ellen says.

He shakes his head and says, "Never get into verbal warfare with one woman, let alone three. I'm toast."

"Sisters?" Karen says, starting to laugh.

"Four," he says. "And I'm the baby."

"Oh, you had it bad," Ellen says. "Okay, I forgive you the tavern-wench thing."

"So are we back to splitting your tips?" he says.

"Hey, I'm not even going to split my beer with you," Ellen says. "How's that sound to you?"

"Normal," he says, shaking his head and crossing his arms over his chest. "The baby, remember?"

"You didn't get the best of everything, all of them babying you to death?" Karen asks.

"There's a picture of me with a dozen pink and lavender barrettes clamped on my little baby head, if you want to call that the best of everything,"

"Lavender?" Karen says, looking at us. "I believe him. No normal guy knows the word *lavender.*"

"Great. Thanks," he says.

"Look, I hate to keep insulting you without knowing your name," Karen says.

"You like your insults to have the personal touch?" he asks.

"Yeah. Pretty much," Karen says.

"I like that," he says. "Shows you have standards."

"What guy doesn't appreciate the personal touch?" I say.

He actually blushes, which is kind of cute. We're giving him a fairly hard time and he's taking it well. With four older sisters, he's clearly had a lot of practice.

"I'm Laurie," I say. "I have three older sisters."

"Matt Carlson," he says. "Fellow sufferer."

"Karen. Pampered only child," Karen says.

"Ellen, oldest of two girls, official crime boss and barrette administrator," Ellen says.

"So, not a brother among you?" Matt says, handing us plastic cups full of cheap beer. "Where'd you get all your experience at torture?"

"It was my high school community service," Ellen says. "You find your quarry in the field, do the deed, get the grade. I got an A."

"She does it now as a volunteer effort," I say. "Ellen is very civic-minded."

"I am. I learned it at home," Ellen says, her voice taking on a slight edge. Ellen laughs and toasts Matt. "To the winner of the lavender barrette. Long may he reign."

"A nice take on what others might call crimes against hair," Matt says, toasting us all in return.

Matt seems like a nice guy; he's funny, easy to talk to, and not unpleasant-looking. Actually, he *is* cute. His brown hair is thick and his eyes are brilliant blue, which is not as spectacular-looking as it could be because his cheeks are lightly pockmarked and his build is relentlessly average. However, Matt's smile is truly a thing of beauty and completely disarming.

Pete's entire manner is disarming, and I have been thoroughly and permanently disarmed, though I wonder if I was ever armed to begin with. I haven't been paying that much attention to the conversation with Matt because I'm looking around the room as discreetly as possible for Pete. Unfortunately, I don't see him. I don't think he's here, not yet. He's too tall to miss, even in a crowd, and it has gotten crowded, the room filling with smoke and music, the sounds of forced male cheer hanging over the living room like heavy smog. And I do think it's forced. It has that quality to it; that pushed-out, overly loud, overtly raucous sound that boys make when they're trying to impress girls.

Pete doesn't do that. Pete is quiet when the whole world abounds in meaningless noise. Pete has to be here tonight. I joined Beta Pi so that I could be here, at Rho Delta Pi, so that I could casually find him and so that he could, so very effortlessly, find me.

Find me, Pete.

"Would you like to dance?"

When I don't hear Ellen or Karen reply, I refocus my attention and see that Matt is staring at me, his expression of kind cheerfulness fading slightly at my silence. "I'm sorry," I say. "I didn't hear you. I'd love to."

* * *

T wo fast songs later, Pete arrives. I think I noticed him the moment he walked into the room, however much that might sound like pure romance. He is wearing worn jeans and a frayed jean jacket over a faded red Lacoste shirt, the long dark waves of his hair tangling in the double collars. He is definitely dressed more casually than his fraternity brothers, and he is also the only guy in the room with hair that touches the top of his shoulders, a holdover from going to prep school in New Hampshire, I assume. My heart stops in mid-leap because, what I should have expected and what I didn't expect at all, was that Pete would have a girl on his arm. To be more precise, he has his long arm around the waist of a bleached blonde who is wearing a maroon cotton T-shirt that is too tight and a denim wrap skirt that is too faded. She is not a Beta Pi.

It doesn't matter. It really doesn't matter. It can't matter. I'm here and I'm doing my best to make it obvious that I'm having a great time. Pete will see me and he will see that, and everything will be fine. We're meeting again at an exchange, which is just as I planned. I look active and popular and busy, which is just as I planned. Pete will be drawn to that and to me, because that's the way the world works.

But I have to admit, now that the moment is actually upon me, I'm not at all confident that Pete remembers me well enough to want me.

The dance ends. No one has cut in on Matt, and Matt is giving every indication that he is going to drift away. *Not now. I can't be alone now, Matt.*

I take a step nearer to Matt, reach out, and touch his arm lightly, say, "That was great. Don't you love Chicago?"

"Yeah," Matt says loudly, nodding. "I saw them play last summer. Amazing."

The next song has started, a band I don't recognize; it's a slow song. I glance over at Pete. He and the blonde aren't dancing, not yet anyway.

I look at Matt, trying to think of something to say, something that will keep him at my side, something to spark his interest so that he will look interested in me, but I can't think of a thing; all my thoughts are of Pete.

"I saw the Supremes one summer when I was little," I eventually say. "My sister took me. All I remember are the sequins."

Matt smiles.

"No way," a girl says behind me. I turn in what I hope isn't obvious relief. It's Diane Ryan, looking as stunning as usual. It's possible Matt will stay around for Diane, if not for me. It's just that I can't be seen looking alone and lost when Pete finds me. When Pete first saw me on Mackinac Island I was alone, sitting on a rock and looking out at the water, looking poetically tragic, I'm sure. I can only look poetically tragic once; it was a moment, not a life-style. "I saw the Supremes in 'sixty-eight. White sequins, right?"

"With big white earrings," I say.

"I don't suppose you remember the music?" Matt says, looking slightly interested.

"Oh, the usual stuff," Diane says with a wave of her hand. "I knew all their songs by heart, but the outfits! I thought I was going to die of rapture."

"Because of their clothes," Matt says, crossing his arms over his chest and assuming that mildly amused arrogant male stance that boys have mastered by the age of fifteen, and that's based on my limited experience with boys.

"Diane, this is Matt," I say. "Matt, Diane Ryan."

"Matt," Diane says with a smile, "I can see you don't understand the first thing about women's clothes."

"I think I know the *first* thing," he says.

"Nope," Diane says, grinning at Matt, shaking her head. "If you did, you'd know that sequins are the holy grail, the yellow-brick road, the whole enchilada. Nothing trumps sequins, not even a song about lost love."

At the phrase *lost love*, I can't help but look at Pete. He's moved, and the blonde has moved with him. They aren't any closer to where I'm standing, and Pete now has his back to me. He has to see me. I've done too much and worked too hard for this moment. And he's not a *lost* love; he's a *found* love. I don't know why I thought that, even for a second, though the blonde probably had something to do with it.

"So does that mean you wear sequins?" Matt asks Diane. If I'm not careful, I'm going to get cut out of the conversation completely, which I wouldn't actually mind if not for Pete and the impression I'm trying to create.

I look at Diane. She looks at me. The look she gives me is inclusive; she doesn't seem to want Matt all to herself. That's not at all the impression I had of Diane Ryan, but her look is ripe with an unspoken message sent from one girl to another, and the message is: Matt is clearly an idiot, and isn't that typical? Matt, who may or may not know the first thing about women's clothes, misses the look completely.

"Do you wear the holy grail?" Diane asks.

"Do you wear the whole enchilada?" I say.

"No, I don't wear sequins," Diane says. "I adore sequins. I lust after sequins. I dream about sequins. But I don't wear sequins. Clear?"

"Got it," Matt says. "But how do you explain Cher?"

"Matt has four older sisters," I say to Diane.

I sneak a look at Pete. He hasn't moved. Walking over to him is out of the question. It's far too bold a move, even though I do know him and we do have some history. But it's not a strong, firm history, no matter how important it was to me. It was only a few days, slightly less than a week, and it was only half a dozen kisses spread out over three or four events that weren't really quite dates. Not quite dates, but almost and close enough. We were alone and we talked and touched and laughed and kissed. It was intimate; whatever else it wasn't, it was intimate.

"Oh, my God. You poor guy," Diane says. "Cher's just the tip of your iceberg, right?"

"He's got a lavender barrette story that will make you weep," I say.

"What's a lavender barrette?" a male voice says behind me. I turn, and my breath hitches in my throat for a second or two. It's not Pete, but it is a really good-looking guy. He's got blackish hair and dark brown eyes and has a Rock Hudson–crossed-with–Cary Grant sort of look going for him.

It takes only a few seconds to soak up his physical beauty; with my next exhaled breath, I've registered that he is, yes, gorgeous, but is not, unfortunately, Pete Steinhagen. I'm not the kind of person to be won over by a pretty face, and I'm certainly not the kind of person who would like anyone who tried to win me by a simple display of a pretty face. My gauntlet has been thrown down, Mr. Cary Rock.

My breathing has returned to normal. I look quickly at Diane. She doesn't give any sign that Mr. Cary Rock has done anything at all to her composure. I have to admit, I'm impressed.

"No sisters, I assume," Diane says, smiling at him.

"Not a one," Cary Rock answers, stepping closer, joining us more fully. I glance at Matt, and he doesn't seem overjoyed about

it, but now it's two girls and two guys. *Come on, Pete, find me now.*
"What did I miss?"

"All-purpose hazing," Matt says on a bark of laughter.

"I was hoping hazing was a myth," I say.

"Don't all myths have a basis in fact?" Cary Rock asks.

"The Loch Ness monster?" I ask.

"Really big fish. Really pissed off that people keep hunting it,"
Cary Rock says.

"Greek gods," Diane says over the rim of her beer.

"Messed-up family," he says. "We all know one."

"Or live in one," Diane says brightly. "How about the tall, dark
stranger? That would be you, by the way."

"Dave York," he says, clinking his plastic cup against hers. The
beer sloshes over her fingers. "And what's the myth about the tall,
dark stranger?"

"That he's to be avoided, sweetie," Diane says with a half
smile. "Any basis in fact? I'm going to warn you; I'll know if you're
lying."

"Because you've known so many tall, dark strangers?" Dave
asks, leaning toward Diane.

Diane grins. "Because I'm such a great liar myself."

It is then that Pete and the blonde join us. I'm not a great liar,
but I can fake it as well as any girl. With a shifting of my weight
and a smooth half step, I'm standing with my shoulder pressed
against Matt's arm. In this exact instant, we're a couple, at least as
far as Pete's concerned, or that's the hope.

"Pete!" I say brightly, my smile wide and surprised. "I can't
believe it! It's so great to see you again!" I don't look at the blonde
at his side, though is that a mistake? Do I look like I care too much
that there is a woman on his arm, figuratively speaking, if I don't
even glance at her? Yes, I think so.

I glance at the blonde, my smile fully in place, including her in my joy at seeing Pete. Really, I'm amazing myself; that one year I did student theater has yielded untold dividends.

I glance back at Pete, waiting for him to say something. Diane, Matt, and Dave have fallen silent, looking at Pete, and the blonde as well, I suppose. She's pretty, in an obvious sort of way. Actually, she's pretty in any sort of way.

I shift my weight again and lean my shoulder against Matt's chest for an instant. The room is crowded; that will be my defense if called upon to offer one. Thankfully, Matt doesn't seem to mind.

Girls' school has not adequately prepared me for this type of social warfare, the type involving boys.

"Laurie," Pete says. He looks surprised, perhaps even shocked, to see me here. He casts a swift glance at the blonde, not *his* blonde, just the blonde. She's smiling tentatively at me, her glance casting over all of us. Pete ignores her to stare at me. Just me. I breathe the moment down and hold it next to my heart for just a moment, the duration of a breath. "I can't believe it." He sounds like he can't believe it. He looks like he can't believe it. Unfortunately, it also looks like he might not want to believe it.

"Small world, isn't it?" I say. "How is your mom? Did she ever shake that cough?"

The blonde is smiling even more tentatively now and is looking at Pete as her smile fades into a pleasantly inquisitive expression.

"Uh, yeah. She did," Pete says, shuffling his feet slightly, shifting his weight. At my side I can feel Matt shifting his weight, in boredom I assume. Things are moving too slowly. I have to move things along, but where and how, I don't know. I only know that Pete is here, that he's not alone, and that nothing is happening the way I dreamed it would.

"Let me guess," Dave says. "Next-door neighbors?"

Pete grins in a sudden flash of humor and relief. I can sense his discomfort; I assume we all can. I had hoped for something else, something more enthusiastic and more flattering than this sense of awkward and uneasy discovery.

"Nope," Pete says.

"Same tennis team?" Diane asks, watching Pete, watching me watch Pete.

"Not even close," Pete says.

"Cousins?" the blonde asks.

She has a high voice. Not as high as Minnie Mouse, but higher than mine, a very feminine voice, very girlish. I can't do anything about that. I can't do very much about anything, it seems. I pull a cigarette from my pack, tapping it against the cellophane a few times. As I put the cigarette in my mouth, Pete gets his lighter out and lights me. He stares at me as I puff my cigarette to life. I stare at the glowing tip of my cigarette, eyes lowered, feeling his attention on me, feeling myself glow softly under it. When he lights his own cigarette, I lift my gaze to stare into his eyes as he continues to stare into mine. It takes only a few seconds, but this is the Pete I came to find. This is the intimacy I joined Beta Pi to find, but like all wonderful moments, it's over before I can fully inhale the joy of it.

"Not likely," Dave murmurs, illuminating the brief intimacy of the moment.

Pete leans back, pocketing his lighter, his cigarette dangling from his lips. I take a drag of mine and then lift it away from my mouth, staring at Pete, smiling at him.

"Not cousins," I say.

"This is like *What's My Line?*" Diane says. "I'm going to get a lousy score without some sort of help."

"Animal, vegetable, or mineral?" Dave says, grinning.

"Male or female?" Diane counters.

"Living or dead?" Matt says.

"The letter *E*," Blondie says.

Pete looks at her. "That's hangman, not *What's My Line?*, Beth."

Beth the Blonde. Beth gives Pete a quizzical look, followed by a sheepish one, followed by a comical one. Each look as it passes fleetingly over her face is adorable. She's cute in a Barbie Dream Date sort of way. I suspect that most guys prefer the Barbie Dream Date way over any other. I'm afraid my way might be poetically tragic.

"Animal," I say, smiling at Dave. "Definitely female. Definitely living." I take a short drag of my cigarette, staring at Pete through the rising smoke trail. "And the letter *E* works, Beth. You all win. Congratulations."

"This is a horrible game show," Diane says. "I don't even know what I've won, and I still don't know what I know. But as long as I won, I guess I can be content with that."

Dave chuckles and says, "Behind door number one, a brand-new refrigerator."

"What's behind door number two? I don't need a refrigerator," Diane says.

Beth giggles and leans into Pete. His arm wraps around her casually, comfortably. They've been together before. She's not tonight's pickup. I look at Matt. He's not actually my pickup; I suppose I was hoping it would look that way.

"Behind door number two is a mystery box," Dave says. "You take your chances."

"A guy standing in front of a mystery box, urging me to take my chances," Diane says, shaking her head at him playfully. "Such a cliché, Dave. I wish I could say I'm shocked."

Dave laughs, a bark of laughter that lights up his dark eyes. I gaze at Pete. Pete isn't laughing. He's looking at me. I smile at Pete. I ignore Matt.

"I met Pete last summer," I say, breaking into the laughter like a brick through a window. "In Michigan. We had fun, didn't we?" I say, looking at Pete.

"American Woman" is playing on the stereo now, the hard beat of the music pushing against me like a wave.

Beth isn't smiling anymore. Neither is Pete. As to that, neither am I. Diane shifts her weight slightly, moving closer to me, and says, "I've never been to Michigan. What do you do for fun there?"

"Sail," Pete says.

"Get hammered," Dave says.

Shut up, Dave. You're movie-star handsome, but shut up. This has nothing to do with you.

"You can do that anywhere," Diane says, waving Dave off with a flick of her fingers. "In fact, I'm sure *you* do that everywhere. So, you were in Michigan sailing?" Diane asks Pete. "What were you doing in Michigan, Laurie? Sailing or getting hammered?"

Falling in love.

"Some sailing," I say, still staring at Pete.

I can see Beth is getting more uncomfortable as she becomes more unsure of where this is going, or maybe she's uncomfortable about where this started. I don't want to hurt her. I just don't want her to exist, not for Pete and not for me.

Was I sailing with Pete? That's the question everyone wants to ask, and I almost wish someone would. I glance into Beth's eyes. She looks confused, maybe even afraid. I know the feeling and I don't wish it on anyone, not even Beth.

Look what you're doing to us, Pete.

"Where did you meet Pete, Beth?" I ask. "Sailing?"

It sounds like a slap, once the words are out, but I didn't mean it that way. Where did she meet Pete? When? Yesterday? Last year? Did she meet him after Mackinac or before? That's all I really want to know. I want it to be after. I want it to be that Pete, having lost me once I left Mackinac, stumbled into a brief, meaningless relationship with Beth. I want him to have wanted me and, upon not finding me, to have found next to nothing with Beth. *But I'm here. Find me again.*

"No," Beth says, looking at me, and then at everyone else. "Pete and I went to high school together."

I feel the floor heave beneath my feet. Melodramatic, maybe, but that's exactly what I feel. I lift my cigarette to my mouth and take a calming drag; my hand isn't shaking. That's good.

I'm okay. I'm doing okay. I'm fine.

Beth came before me. Okay . . . so what? It doesn't matter. He left her and he found me. We had something last summer, brief but wonderful. We had something and I left, but I'm here now. That's going to make all the difference. It has to.

"High school sweethearts?" Diane says, looking brightly at Beth, and then looking at me, not so brightly, moving closer to my side, edging against Matt. "That's so sweet."

Diane can't tell, can she? No one can tell that I feel sick, a cold wave of nausea rolling over me. *No one can tell.* I take another drag and push the message down into my lungs and out through my pores. *No one can tell.*

That's the important thing, to never show weakness and never show vulnerability. If no one can tell you're hurt, then you're not hurt. A blow only counts if it makes you bleed, and I'll never bleed.

I take another breath and make sure my face displays a pleas-

ant expression. I do all this like a nurse checking a pulse, a de-
tached examination of my outward signs; this is how I know I look
normal, controlled, calm, politely interested. That's all there is to
this moment; that's all I will allow this moment to be.

But his high school girlfriend? When he went to an all-boys'
school in New England?

"I thought you went to Exeter?" I ask Pete politely, just a simple
way to keep the conversation going, nothing beyond that. Certainly
nothing that could ever break my heart or crush my romantic illusions. They weren't illusions. I've never indulged in illusions.

"Oh, Pete told you about that?" Beth answers for him. She looks
a little suspicious. Pete looks like he wants to crawl into a hole. I
know what I look like. "He only went there for his last three years.
We both went to Henry James High School before that. We started
dating our freshman year. The Sadie Hawkins dance." She smiles
and presses herself against Pete's length.

She asked him out first. It's a crumb and I gobble it up like a
starving mouse.

"Wow," Diane says, her voice anchoring me to the moment,
keeping me present in the conversation. I need it, and I appreciate
it. The cold waves of nausea are still rolling over me, my skin
prickly and clammy at once, but my hands don't shake. My civilized walls are fully in place; it's only my heart that silently trem-
bles. "You guys have been dating for . . . how long?"

"Over six years," Beth says, smiling up into Pete's unsmiling
face.

Bastard. The word slips past my barriers, making a lie of my
careful civilization. I'm not civilized in this moment; I'm a barbarian queen knifing an interloper. But Beth isn't the interloper; I am.
Pete made me one, against my will and consent.

Bastard, bastard, *bastard*.

"Wow," Diane says softly, looking at me, her dark eyes soft with sympathy.

"You go to ULA?" I ask, dropping my cigarette into my beer where it floats darkly. How long before it sinks? How long before my cigarette disintegrates? My cigarette floats proudly, intact. Matt takes the cup from my hand and gets rid of it all.

"No, I go to Pepperdine," Beth says. "I don't even have a car. When Pete can get a car he picks me up and brings me to parties like this. I love it. Don't you?"

I look into her pretty blue eyes, heavy with clumped mascara, and smile. "I do," I say, shifting my gaze to Pete. "I just love it."

A touch on my arm breaks the spell and I stop counting the beats of my heart. I turn away from Pete, glad for any excuse to do so.

"There's a problem," Karen says in my ear, her breath brushing my hair. "Cindy Gabrielle. Joan Collier thinks she went upstairs with a guy. She's drunk."

I look at her; then I look at Diane. Diane catches my look and, saying something that makes Dave York laugh, presses against me, her body flush against mine.

"What's up?" Diane asks softly.

"Cindy Gabrielle is upstairs with a guy," I say, my mouth near her ear.

"If the pledge trainer finds out . . ." Karen says, her voice trailing off. It doesn't need any further explanation. "Joan's her cousin. She's worried."

"And this is not a one-man job," Diane says. "'Once more into the breach,' or whatever the hell that quote is. Shakespeare?"

"It sounds like him," Karen says.

"Where's Joan?" I ask. We're making our way across the

crowded room, trying to look casual. It's not that hard. I assume people will think we're looking for a bathroom. As to that, it's not a bad excuse to use when we find Cindy.

"Waiting at the bottom of the stairs," Karen says, and on the heels of that, I see her. Joan, also in my pledge class, looks grim and a little scared.

"Come on," I say, walking past Joan and leading the way up the stairs; I'm glad for this sudden mission, the barbarian queen with her knife drawn. It's noisy up there, the party having spread. We're not going to be alone, which isn't such a great thing when you're looking for a lost pledge.

"Hey, girls. Lost? Need a guide?" a guy says from the top of the stairs. He's barefoot and wearing faded jeans. I keep my head down and refuse to look any higher than that.

"'A three-hour tour,'" Diane singsongs.

Karen chuckles and repeats it, Diane picking up the harmony. "'A three-hour tour.'"

"Okay, so who would you be? Mary Ann or Ginger?" Diane asks, brushing past the barefoot guy, turning to him and saying, "You don't get a vote, so pipe down."

Barefoot Guy gets left behind.

"Gilligan," Karen says. "I have a thing for ugly hats."

"Ginger," I say. "It'd be my one chance to wear sequins and get away with it."

Diane smiles, and then we all look at one another, giving each other silent consent, and push open the first door on the right of a long hallway. It's empty.

Without too much hesitation, we're on to the next door.

"I don't know why I'm so nervous," Karen murmurs from behind me.

"I'm afraid of what I'll see," Joan says.

"Never seen it before, huh?" Diane says.

"Cindy just turned eighteen a month ago," Joan says.

"She's legal," I say on a sigh.

"And drunk," Karen says.

"A perfect combination for some guys," Diane says. "On three?" Her hand is on the doorknob.

I nod.

"One," Diane says slowly, and then she swings open the door. Joan gasps in surprise. The room is dark except for one of those hideous lava lamps, all oozing oil and liquid bad taste. Cindy's on the bed, her shirt off, her bra on, her pants unzipped. The guy has his shirt off and his pants unzipped. How delightful—they're a matched pair. He looks over at us and frowns. Cindy looks over at us and says, her voice sloppy with liquor, "Oh, hi, you guys. This is Glenn."

"Ben," Glenn says.

"Oops," Cindy says on a watery giggle. "Ben."

"Nice to meet you, Len," Diane says, coming into the room.

"It's Ben," he says, looking annoyed. The barbarian queen licks her metaphorical lips and strokes her metaphorical blade.

"Yeah. Whatever," Diane says. "Come on, sweetie. Time to go home."

We all cross the room together, practically pushing Glenn/ Ben/Len out of our way; he slides off the bed and falls ass-first on the floor. Cindy giggles and then says, "Are you okay?"

"He's fine," I say. "Where's your shirt?"

Cindy sits up, her hair falling forward over her face. "I don't know. Glenn? Where's my shirt?"

Glenn reaches under the bed and pulls it out; it's in a wad of pale fabric. He tosses it on the bed and stays on the floor, resting his weight on his elbows, an amazing example of heroic splendor.

Joan and Karen wrestle Cindy's shirt over her head while Diane and I look around the floor for her shoes. It's positively vile down on this floor.

"Got 'em," Diane says, lifting a pair of platform clogs in her hands. Cindy hovers just over the five-foot mark; I think she wears platforms to run track.

"Come on, Cindy," Joan says. "We need to get you out of here."

"She was having a good time," Glenn says, an extremely unattractive smirk on his unremarkable face. Added to that, he has the beginnings of a beer belly.

"That's so reassuring," I say. "Thanks so much."

"Yeah, thanks for the update," Diane says. "See you around, Ken."

"It's Ben," he says as we walk out of his bedroom.

"'A rose by any other name,'" Karen says as Joan half carries Cindy down the hall to the staircase.

"Now, that's definitely Shakespeare," Diane says. "Tell me I got it right."

"You definitely got it right," I say.

I think we all got it right, with the possible exception of Cindy.

"God, what happened? What did I miss?" Ellen says, pushing across the foyer toward us. Her blond hair is sweat-curled around her face, her cheeks flushed.

"Rescue mission. We had a man down," Diane says.

"Man down," Cindy repeats, starting to laugh.

"We need to get her home," Ellen says. "Where does Cindy live?"

"She's way over on the other side of campus," Joan says.

"Scratch that," Diane says. "I'm in an apartment right behind Beta Pi, the Stardust. Let's go there."

During this conference, we've left the Rho Delt house, having been verbally accosted by only half a dozen Rho Delts, none of them either Matt or Pete. I suppose that's for the best. Half of the houses on The Row are having exchanges tonight so our route down the block is made in front of witnesses who have no interest in us. It's a strangely comforting combination of factors.

The Stardust apartment building is across the alley and down a bit from the Beta Pi house, with not even a gate to keep out the neighborhood ruffians. Diane leads us in through a narrow passageway, though I'm not sure anymore why I'm with these girls. I've accomplished my goal of meeting Pete at the Rho Delt exchange, and I've accomplished nothing at all. I don't need to stay here. I don't need to be with these girls. I suppose it must be lethargy and a form of perpetual motion that keeps me with them, step by step, side by side. I simply don't have the energy to break away and find my way back to my own bed.

Diane's apartment is in the middle of the complex on the ground floor, which is a relief, as Cindy sounds like she's starting to feel sick and her legs are starting to drag. Joan and Ellen are wrapped around her like seaweed, urging her forward. Diane sweeps in, turns on the overhead light, walks quickly through to the bedroom, turns on that light, and does the same in the bathroom. Cindy is starting to gag.

"I've got her," Joan says, and the two of them disappear into the bathroom and close the door.

"Well, that was fun," Diane says. "Let's keep the party going. I've got rum and Coke, orange juice and vodka, and the makings for White Russians—that's if you don't mind milk instead of cream." Diane is moving around her tiny kitchen, opening cupboards, checking the fridge, an efficient whirl of motion. "Make that skim milk. And only half an ice tray of cubes."

"I'm game," Ellen says.

"Anything's better than fraternity beer," Karen says. "I wonder how Cindy's doing. Good thing Joan knew where she was."

"And the pledge trainer didn't," Ellen says. "Have a seat, Laurie. Stay awhile."

They've made themselves at home, Diane, of course, busy in the kitchen, pulling out bottles and glasses. Ellen and Karen have sunk onto Diane's nubby brown sofa, the cushions permanently dipped in the middle, the arms flattened and stained. I don't really want to stay, but I have nowhere else to go.

"Come on," Karen says, patting the cushion beside her, scooting over farther to give me room. "Stay."

"Okay," I say.

"You have to stay," Diane says. "You have no excuse. I have liquor in a variety of colors and odors. Name your poison."

"Rum and Coke?" I say.

"You don't sound sure," Diane says.

"I'm sure," Ellen says. "We'll start with rum and Coke. Do you have enough rum?"

"Do you have enough Coke?" Karen says.

"Silly rabbit. That's not the right question," Ellen says, getting up to help Diane in the kitchen.

"No stupid questions allowed until we're all buzzed," Diane says. "Whatever I run out of, I'll get more of. We will not run out of booze. That's a promise."

I sit beside Karen on the couch, shifting my weight against lumpy and compressed cushions. I'm uncomfortable, in every sense of the word. I don't know what I'm doing here, but then, I don't know what I'm doing at all anymore.

When we're each holding a glass of rum and Coke, Ellen sits down on the floor, cross-legged, and says, "So, who's going to start?"

"Start what? No brawls in my apartment. I need to get my security deposit back," Diane says.

We all chuckle at that, me included, and that catches me by surprise.

"I'll start," Ellen says. "First a swallow, and then a truth." Ellen takes a swallow of her drink. "I'm not sure the beer in my stomach is going to like this."

"Is this a truth-or-dare kind of game?" Karen says.

"All truths, no dares," Ellen says. "First truth is on me. I'm from the Valley. Northridge. ULA was the only school I applied to. Thank God I got accepted. Karen? Your turn. Same truth, your version."

"I'm from Connecticut, the Farmington River Valley, which isn't the same, but at least it's a valley. Are we getting points for consistency? I'm all about scoring points. I grew up in Avon, a small town outside of Hartford. And I applied to two schools. ULA was my top choice," Karen says. "Oops, I forgot to take a swig." She dutifully takes a small swallow of her rum and Coke, and then she grimaces.

Diane laughs. "Next time you get vodka. Laurie, would you like to go next? I am the hostess, and therefore it's my sworn duty to go last and take the smallest portion of everything served. Except for booze, of course."

"No, you go ahead," I say, rubbing my finger around the rim of the glass. I've never had rum before; I'm positive I'm not going to care for it.

"Okay. I'm a navy brat, so I'm from everywhere, Camarillo right now. That's north of LA for you out-of-towners. I applied to three schools. Top pick: ULA, naturally."

"Not naming names, huh?" Ellen asks. "I guess it doesn't matter since we're all here now. Laurie, you're up."

"I'm from San Francisco and I applied to ULA and Stanford," I say.

"Take a swallow," Ellen says. "That's part of it." And so I do, just a small swallow, and it proves me right; I don't like the taste of rum at all.

Fifty-five minutes later, Joan and Cindy are asleep on Diane's bed, Cindy's face scrubbed clean of makeup and looking all of fourteen years old, and the taste of rum is starting to make its appeal known. It does have a lovely flavor, sweet and strong and slightly tropical.

"Beach, definitely," Ellen says. "I love the beach. My parents have a place at Malibu, and if I could live there, I would. Ocean, sand, sun, surf, it's all I need to be happy. That, and a great bikini. Oh, and the body to go in a great bikini."

"Lakes," I say, leaning my head back against the crushed couch cushions, my eyes half-closed against the overhead kitchen light. "Lakes with pine trees and forests and cool nights. My family spends a few weeks every summer on Mackinac Island."

"Where's that?" Karen asks.

"In Michigan, in the Upper Peninsula," I say. "I met Pete there last summer."

"The sailing guy," Diane says, topping off our drinks with more rum. She empties the bottle into Ellen's glass. "Time to switch to vodka."

"Who's the sailing guy?" Ellen asks.

I shift my weight and check the buttons on my blouse. I didn't mean to talk about Pete. I shouldn't talk about Pete. Pete isn't mine and he can't be mine. He's Barbie's now. He was Barbie's then.

I have such a sick feeling in my stomach. I don't think rum agrees with me. I take another swallow to test the theory.

Diane looks at me, waiting for my answer. I suppose I should answer. I need to manage this somehow, control what is said and what is known. Of course, that would be far easier to do if I understood anything.

"Laurie, do you know a sailing guy?" Karen asks. Karen is lying on the sofa, her head on my lap. Ellen is lying on the floor, her head on one of Diane's bed pillows. Diane is in the kitchen, making orange juice and staring at me with compassion in her dark eyes. I never would have predicted that Diane could be compassionate. It's quite clear to me that I can't read people at all.

"He was on Mackinac with his family; his father's a doctor, a pathologist. I was sitting on a rock near the lake and he just walked"—*into my life*, is how I want to finish the sentence, but he didn't walk into my life; he walked through it—"by and we started talking."

"That's how it always starts. With talking," Ellen says. "Sneaky bastards."

"Then what happened?" Diane asks.

"Then he took me out on his parent's johnboat, and the wind kicked up and tossed water in our faces, and Pete played around in that little boat, twisting and turning through the chop, teasing me, soaking me, and—" I pause, the memory choking me, squeezing my heart.

"And he charmed the pants off you, right?" Diane says.

"No. Maybe," I say. "I've never laughed so hard in my life."

"That's step number two: laughing," Ellen says. "Rat bastards."

"Will you pipe down and let her finish?" Diane says. "Then what?"

I swallow down the rest of my rum and Coke, the sweet taste on my tongue a temporary but very lovely salve. "Then he took me out to dinner at a little place in town and I toyed with a bowl of chili while he wolfed down a cheeseburger, and afterward he kissed me under that pale Michigan moon, the scents of pine and water in every breath I took."

"Holy shit," Ellen says. "What happened?"

"For six days, I thought . . . " I say. *I thought he was mine, and that I was his.* Tonight, I found out I'm not and he's not. "I thought . . . " I try again. I shrug, the words refusing to appear.

"You don't need to spell it out. We know what you thought," Diane says. "I take it he didn't tell you about his girlfriend."

"He has a girlfriend?" Ellen says.

"He's a Rho Delt," I say. "She was at the exchange tonight."

"What a total shit! God, did you throw his lousy beer in his face?" Ellen says.

"Right. That always works," Diane says. "Karen's asleep, by the way. Don't move, Laurie. Running out of the room is no longer an option for you. Sorry, sweetie."

"What a lightweight," Ellen says. "I only wish someone would say that about me. Okay, next truth. I can't help myself, okay? Who's still a virgin?"

"Oh, nice segue. Subtle," Diane says, looking at me.

"And me without any rum," I say.

"Screwdrivers, coming up," Diane says, coming from the tiny kitchen into the tiny living room, grabbing my empty glass. "I'll start, you sadist," Diane says to Ellen. "Okay, so I'm not a virgin, but I only went all the way with one guy in high school."

"Come on. Really?" Ellen says.

"Okay, okay. Three in college, but it's not like I need to walk around with a red light over my head. I was in love in high school; it's always love in high school and it's always forever."

"No kidding," Ellen says.

"It wasn't forever, big surprise, and it wasn't even for long. And that's why they call it high school."

Ellen and I both laugh. Karen dreams on, her feet twitching against the arm of the couch.

"What happened?" I ask.

"He broke up with me over the damn phone," Diane says. "Can you believe that?"

"Yes," Ellen says.

"Shut up," Diane says, coming back from the kitchen bearing three tall screwdrivers. Ellen and I take our drinks with more enthusiasm than we took the rum and Cokes, or at least I'm more enthusiastic this time. "I got drunk at a party on the fourth floor of George's Tower—"

"You know, that's almost a pun," Ellen says.

"—and woke up at eight in some strange guy's bed, with the guy still in it, and his roommate grinning at me across a floor covered in dirty clothes and damp towels."

"Are you sure about that red light?" Ellen says.

"Yeah. It wasn't one of my better moments," Diane says. "You can see why I wanted to save Cindy from a similar fate. It's not a fate worse than death, but—"

"It's damn close," Ellen says.

"Speaking from experience?" Diane says. "Does anyone want some chips? I think I have cheese and salsa. We could have nachos."

"No, I'm good," Ellen says. I shake my head and sip my screwdriver. It's good. I must like vodka better than rum, and I think that now I like rum just fine. "And I mean that. I'm still a virgin."

"Congratulations," Diane says. "And I mean that."

"I am, too," I say.

"Congratulations!" Ellen says. "At least Pete didn't get that from you. He doesn't deserve it."

"Thanks," I say. But didn't he? I don't know what to think. I'm glad I'm still a virgin, but I'm sad that Pete is no longer *my* Pete. Except that he was never *my* Pete, and I've got to stop forgetting that.

"Hey, look, I'm not saying it was easy for me to keep my pants zipped, but I can see how you, with your face, would have been fighting them off for years. A girl gets tired," Ellen says to Diane.

"With my face," Diane repeats softly. "Let me tell you a little something about my face. I know I'm pretty now, but I didn't use to be. I used to be a very funny-looking kid with big ears and bad skin and too much hair."

"What do you mean too much hair? Like growing out of your ears?" Ellen says.

"No, like big ears sticking out from your little head and eyes too big for your face and lots of black hair covering your head, which has a tendency to embrace eczema," Diane says. "Picture it . . . picture it . . . That's right. I was a monkey baby."

"Oh, God, you were not!" Ellen says.

"I were, too," Diane says.

"How'd your mom take it?" Ellen says.

"She hid the camera," Diane says. "And when she brought it out, like for Halloween and Christmas, I was always mysteriously photographed behind a mask, or a white Santa beard. The tradition was to have our Christmas photo taken wearing Santa outfits. But you know what? Even as a kid, I knew the beard was for me."

"You clearly grew out of it," I say.

"Thank God," Diane says. "But not until I was a senior in high school, and if there's one thing I learned, and please God, let me have learned one thing up to this point, it's that the bad times drag and the good times are fleeting. So let the good times roll."

"Amen," Ellen says, draining off her screwdriver. "Karen's going to have to make up for this. We don't know if she's a virgin or not. Or if she was an ugly baby or not. Or if she threw beer in Pete's face or not. Or would like to. Or plans to. That kid's got a lot of making up to do."

Karen shifts in her sleep and, without thinking about it, I lay my hand on her head, soothing her and, somehow, soothing myself.

Diane

— Fall 1976 —

"Why do we have to move in on the hottest day of the year? This is the hottest day, right? It's not going to get hotter. It *can't* get hotter," Karen says, her arms full of sheets, a comforter, and her pillow. The pillow looks ready to tumble.

"So it's one hundred and five," Ellen says. "It's a dry heat. Everybody knows that dry heat isn't really hot."

"Tell that to a baked chicken," Laurie says.

"Now that you mention it, I *am* starving," Ellen says. "Do you want to go to the Pepper Mill after we get our stuff unloaded and into the house?"

"I'd kill for a patty melt," Karen says as we all walk up the steps into Beta Pi, the sun baking down onto our heads. I feel like I'm about to explode or melt or something equally Wicked Witch of the West–ish. I just want to move in, find my rack, get my clothes hung up, and huddle in the center of an air-conditioned house.

"I'm going to get the French dip," Ellen says. "Screw the calories. I've earned them."

"Diane? What are you in the mood for?" Karen says.

"Hired labor," I say. "Cheap."

"Remember, it's a dry heat," Ellen says on a cackle of laughter.

Now that we're in the house, it should be cooler, and it is, but the house is still hot because the damn door is open because every single girl who's living in the Beta Pi house this year is moving in. Why we all have to move in during the same two-hour window is beyond me; if they had any sense at all, they'd schedule us in shifts, but then the house front door would be open for days, not hours, and that probably would make it all worse.

Everything is worse. Just a hot, sticky mess.

We get our room assignments; I'm in the back four-way with Ellen, Missy, and Pi, a room that overlooks the roof deck, hot as hell right now, and Karen and Laurie are in a four-way with Holly and Candy. I'm dutifully lugging my clothes up from the car when I bump into Karen in a narrow part of the second-floor hall and drop half the outfits I'm carrying, and the whole mess falls onto the floor. And that's when I burst into tears.

"Diane, what is it?" Karen says to me. "What's the matter?"

Damned if I know. I can't stop crying long enough to figure it out. Before I'm required to figure it out, Karen has me in her arms and is leading me out onto the blistering roof deck, and that makes me cry harder, but she just sits me down on a chaise longue, her arms still around me, and she kind of rocks me, and all the while I'm sobbing like an idiot.

"It's okay," she says. "It's going to be okay. I'll move you in myself. I'll do all the work, and you know how I hate work, and someday you'll have to pay me back, big-time, with double-digit interest, but don't worry about that now. Don't worry about anything. It's okay. I promise. It will be okay."

"Damn loan shark," I say on a wet hiccup.

"It's a living," she says, holding me tighter, rocking me gently back and forth, her head pressed against mine. "Come on. You're okay, right? It's going to be okay."

"I'm not okay," I say, wiping my nose on the hem of my shirt. "I fucked up, Karen. I totally fucked up."

"What happened?"

"I washed out of the flight program," I say. "I wanted to be a pilot, like Dad, and I flunked math, and I can't navigate, and then I got sick in the A-4, or I almost got sick, but you can't be a pilot if you can't fly a dogfight without getting sick; never mind the fact that I can't navigate worth shit. I did the Dilbert Dunker okay, aced that, and did the swim test and deep-water survival, but I got sick in the A-4. I'm not going to be a navy pilot."

I'm not going to be able to follow in Dad's footsteps, not that Dad ever made a point of telling me he wanted me to shadow his career trajectory, but I had certain expectations that I would, and he must have had the same expectations, and now they're toast.

I flunked out.

"But you're still in the navy. There are other things you can do, right?" she asks.

"But I'm not going to be a pilot," I repeat. I've been repeating it to myself ever since flying over Arizona and trying not to blow chow all over the cockpit.

"I'm sorry," she says, running her hand over my hair, smoothing it down my back, pressing me into her side, holding me close.

Mom and Dad didn't do this. I made the story funny for Mom and Dad. I told them, "Math plus navigation multiplied by motion sickness equals not being ideal pilot material." Then I laughed. Dad didn't laugh and neither did Mom, but they didn't tell me I was overreacting either. In fact, Dad said, "It's probably for the best." They let me tell them my version, watched me pack up my car, and waved me down the street as I drove to ULA.

"I'm just not good enough," I say, talking over Karen. "I've never been good enough. I'm not pretty enough. I'm not smart enough. I'm not tough enough. And I can't do math."

"Will you shut up?" she says. "I'm trying to be nice, giving you my best mom imitation, but you're really pushing it. Not pretty enough? Are you delusional? Don't answer that. You're delusional. You're gorgeous and you know it, and I know it, and every guy on The Row knows it."

But the guy I want isn't on The Row. The guy I want is Midshipman Temptation, known to the world at large as Doug Anderson. Doug was with me at Miramar. Doug passed everything. Doug is going to be a navy pilot. And I'm not.

"Are you tough enough?" Karen says. "You made it through Rush and Initiation and countless exchanges, so I know you're tough. But what's a Dilbert Dunker?"

"It's a fake helo crash, in water, and then you have to find your way out, underwater."

"That settles it; you're tough, but what an insane way to spend summer vacation. All that leaves is math, and I can completely understand your problem with math since I have the same problem. Math is ridiculous. I don't get it either. They lost me at long division when I waved math good-bye with a hysterical little laugh. I'm sure there must be some way we can contribute to society without having to divide fractions."

I laugh, but it has a hollow sound, breathy, like I'm a hundred years old.

Karen moves off the chair and sits at my feet, looking up at me, smiling. She looks very small and cute and cheerful, ready to lead me out of any hysteria I succumb to, unwilling to judge, willing only to care. "Okay, so you didn't make it. Okay, so what? You'll be good at something else. Have you tried underwater basket weaving? People say good things about it. You've already passed the Dilbert Dunker prerequisite."

"Idiot," I say, grinning in spite of myself.

"What are you guys doing out there?" Ellen says from the doorway that leads back into the house. "I thought we were going to eat!"

"We're coming!" I yell back; then I smile down at Karen and we both get to our feet. "I just have to hang up my clothes and make my bed."

"Throw your clothes on your bed. This isn't the navy. Today, you're not a midshipman; you're a sorority girl, and sorority girls can be slobs," Ellen says. "Let's eat!"

Without any further breakdowns on my part, Karen, Ellen, Laurie, and I ditch the pandemonium of the Beta Pi house and walk down the block to the Pepper Mill, just up Figueroa from the 401 Club, the best and most frequented ULA nonofficial hangout.

"So what did you do on your summer vacation?" Ellen asks the table. "Me? I spent the summer in Malibu working on my tan and avoiding Ed. It was great."

"Did you meet anyone?" Karen asks.

"I can't be bothered to talk to anyone while I'm working on my tan. You should know that by now," Ellen says. "Next? Diane, how was your summer with the US Navy?"

"I quit the flight program," I say. We're sitting in a booth, the waitress having taken our order, and Karen is sitting next to me; she inches over slightly so that our thighs are touching. "Actually, I quit, and I also wasn't accepted into the flight program, to be perfectly honest."

"What?" Ellen says. "What happened?"

"I'm so sorry, Diane," Laurie says, her cool blue eyes filled with sympathy. "I know you really wanted that."

"I did, but when you get a D in Navigation and then almost hurl during a mock dogfight, that's the end of that," I say. Doug Anderson sat next to me in Navigation, but Doug is not the reason I got the D.

"What are you going to do now?" Laurie asks.

"Besides avoid Navigation? I'll think of something," I say.

"There's always men. You could find a nice guy to distract you," Karen says.

"Right. Just what I need," I say.

"Hey," Ellen says. "You've got that look. Who is it? You like somebody. Spill."

"You do! You do have that look," Karen says. "Tell us every-thing. We want every single detail."

"Feel free to leave out a few details," Laurie says, grabbing for her cigarettes.

"There's nothing to tell," I say.

"Ignore Laurie. Tell us," Ellen says. "And make it good."

"But no pressure or anything," Karen says with a chuckle.

"You might as well. They'll hound you to the gates of hell until you do," Laurie says.

"Are you calling me a hellhound?" Ellen says. "Because if you are, I can live with that."

"Come on," Karen says. "We're all ears."

"And no mouths, if I tell you," I say, feeling just a little bit bet-ter about the flight program flail just by thinking about Doug Anderson.

"Got it," Ellen says. "Not a word to anyone."

"Well, there is this guy that I kind of like," I say. "He's in ROTC, the flight program, and he's completely amazing."

"What's he look like?" Karen asks.

"He's blond and blue-eyed and a total hunk," I say. "Not that I'm biased or anything."

"So what's the holdup?" Ellen says. "Go get him."

The waitress brings our food over; Karen gets the patty melt, oozing with grease and cheese, Ellen gets the French dip with fries, Laurie gets a hamburger, and I get a Cobb salad.

"Way to make me feel like a heifer," Ellen says. "I shouldn't eat this, but what the hell. I was good all summer. I lost six pounds!"

"You look fantastic," Karen says.

Ellen's hair is gleaming gold, her eyes shockingly blue, and her skin is deeply tanned, her freckles almost hidden by browned skin.

"We could stop to discuss your weight, but I'd rather hear about Diane's guy," Laurie says.

"He's not my guy. He will never be my guy," I say.

"Why not?" Karen says.

"Because he's in ROTC and Dad gave me firm instructions not to shit where I eat—and that's a quote," I say.

Laurie puts down her burger. "Thanks for the info. They do say timing is everything."

"But he's in the flight program, right? And you're not," Karen says. "That makes it all right. I'd say he's fair game. What's his name, by the way?"

"Doug Anderson, and he is not fair game. He's in the navy. I'm in the navy."

"If you say *shit* or *eat* again in the same sentence, I'm going to throw this at you," Laurie says, pointing to her hamburger.

"Does he like you?" Ellen asks, dipping her sandwich into the cup of beef juice.

"I don't know. I think so. Maybe."

"I say go for it," Ellen says. "What have you got to lose?"

"How much of a hunk is he?" Karen asks.

"I've never seen anything like it in my life," I say. "And he's nice, too."

"Go for it," Karen says.

I look at Laurie and say, "Save your breath. This is not up for a vote. I can't go out with him. Besides, he hasn't asked me."

"He will," Karen says. "And when he does, say yes."

"Go ahead, Laurie, you can vote," Ellen says. "This is still a democracy."

"I'd hate to get in trouble with the navy," Laurie says, "but I say follow your heart."

"Speaking of following your heart," I say, eager to change the subject because I cannot and will not go out with Doug Dreamboat Anderson, "you went to Michigan this summer, didn't you?"

"We go every summer," Laurie says, signaling for the waitress to take her plate; she's eaten less than half of her burger.

"So, was he there?" I ask.

He is Pete Steinhagen. Laurie never talked about him after that one night last year, but I couldn't help but notice that at the spring Rho Delt exchange, where Barbie did not make an appearance, Laurie danced a few times with Pete and they talked on the front steps of the Rho Delt house when everyone else was inside dancing. I saw them walking down University Avenue once last spring and, not to get too technical about it, but there definitely seems to be something in the air between them.

"Who? Pete?" Ellen asks, grabbing a fry off Laurie's plate before the waitress snags it. "Isn't he still with Malibu Barbie?"

Karen looks out the window at the parking lot, the sunlight blazing off the windshields of the cars like search beams. Karen drops her gaze to her lap, refolding her napkin. Karen doesn't ask about Pete. Karen probably knows something I don't know, and I should, therefore, probably shut up about Pete.

"So, what did you do all summer, Mitchell?" I ask.

"No, no, no," Ellen says. "I want to hear about Laurie's summer first. Come on. What's going on with Pete? Do you still like him, even though he's a lying piece of shit?"

"He was there," Laurie says under her breath, jabbing her straw through the crushed ice. "They never go to the same place twice, according to what his mom told my mom. It was all Pete's idea," she says, lifting her gaze to me briefly, her eyes wistful. "He insisted they go back to Mackinac."

"He knew you'd be there," I say.

"So they broke up?" Ellen asks.

"I didn't ask," Laurie says. "I guess I don't really want to know."

"Oh, come on, McCormick," Ellen says. "You've got to know."

"What you don't know can't hurt you," Karen says.

"Oh, that's a great life philosophy," Ellen says.

"Hey. It works okay," Karen says. "At least you know he wanted to see you, to be with you. You know that, Laurie. That's a lot."

"It's more than I've got," I say, "and it's more than you've got, Olson, so shut up and let Karen tell us about her summer. I want details."

"Well," Karen says, "there was no Dilbert Dunker, but I had some fun."

"Who the hell is Dilbert Dunker?" Ellen says, letting Laurie off the hook. Ellen is like a rabid dog with a bone on most things, but, unlike a rabid dog, she'll allow herself to be distracted, which is more like a fluffy domesticated dog, and Ellen is nothing like that. But you get my drift.

"Crashed helicopter, deep water, lungs bursting, noise, disorientation, fight for your life. General mayhem," I say. "It's a navy thing."

"It sounds like Rush," Laurie says.

Rush. We're on the other side of it this time, our first time from behind enemy lines, not that that's really the situation, but some-

times, hearing the stories, it seems like there might be the tiniest
bit of truth to that.

W ho met her?"
            Six hands rise in the air.
    "How many want to keep her?"
    Three hands remain up. It's a tie. That usually means a discus-
sion, either lengthy and ugly or short and sweet.
    "Discussion?"
    "Her father is in insurance," Jenny says. Jenny is one of the two
who dropped her hand. She doesn't want Tracy Zimmerman, one
of the hundreds of girls rushing the twelve sororities at ULA this
year.
    "Is that a capital offense now?" Candy says.
    Jenny rolls her eyes. Candy files her nails and crosses her legs
lazily.
    Lengthy and ugly it is.
    Rush is not the nicest place on earth. It's not the most relaxing
place either. Rush lasts a week, and in that week each sorority house
hosts parties that last all day and sometimes into the night. We
put on skits while in costume, dance and sing songs in three-part
harmony, hold incisive five-minute conversations with the girls
who have been herded into the house and out again according to
a rigid schedule. You grab a girl, sit her down, talk to her, introduce
her to another chapter member with some sort of conversation-
starter opening line, and then float gracefully to the door that leads
to the town girl room where you hurriedly score the poor kid on an
index card. Why does anyone think women are the gentle sex?
After roughly an hour, the first batch troop out and the next batch
of hopeful victims troop in.

It's a Dilbert Dunker, all the way.

In the night, between rehearsing songs and choreography, we meet in the library on the third floor to review the girls, one index card at a time. It gets monotonous after the first forty or so. After the hundredth name, you don't have the strength to care much anymore. They're not people; they're names on a grimy card. That's the worst thing about Rush, the reduction of people to a one- or two-word description. *Funny! Shy! Boring! Cute!* How was I described? *ROTC! Big ears! Dad in navy!* I can just imagine the responses to that. Did the girl sitting across from me now, my sister Beta Pi, try to keep me out?

There's a happy thought.

"I liked her," Ellen says stiffly, taking out her ponytail and redoing it. It's monstrously hot in the library; the sun has been slamming into the sundeck right outside the huge windows all day before careening into the library. The air conditioner is groaning. "She's cute. We talked about our shared affliction: freckles. I thought she was funny."

"Which one was she?" Missy asks.

"Dark brown wavy hair, brown eyes, petite," Candy says.

"Freckles," Ellen adds, grinning. "She's a freshman."

"She was a little chunky," Andi Mills says. "Do we really want another chunky Beta Pi?"

"*Another* chunky Beta Pi?" Ellen says, leaning forward in her chair.

Andi shrugs and smiles.

"She was cute," Candy says. "Nice, funny, and sweet."

"We don't want to be known as the house with the funny fat girls, do we?" Andi says.

"Now she's fat? What happened to chunky?" Ellen snaps. "God, this chick is blowing up like a blimp."

"Let's vote again," the president says.

We vote, and Tracy Zimmerman can come back tomorrow, and then we're on to the next name.

"I guess this isn't the time to admit my dad works at Aetna," Karen whispers at my side.

I snort and shake my head. "Keep your dirty laundry to yourself, Mitchell. You're in now."

"Lucky me," Karen says dryly as she raises her hand to the question of "Who met her." At "Who wants to keep her," Karen's hand drops. "This is brutal. I feel like I'm in the SS, rounding up undesirables."

"Don't think about it," I say softly. "You'll go insane if you think about it." We're not supposed to be talking, but after a few hours of this, how can you stay quiet? You can't say what you're really thinking, so you say anything else, just to keep from screaming that they're all a bunch of harpies and that an old-fashioned stoning doesn't seem out of the question. But are *they* "me," and does that mean I should say *we*? God. "How long have we been up here? Ten hours? Twelve?"

"Two," Karen says. "Days," she adds on a snicker of laughter.

The president looks gloomily in our direction. "Can we all focus and just get through this, please?"

Karen and I look innocently around the room for the offenders. The next name is read.

The thing is this: every sorority wants to be *the* sorority on The Row. The way you become the top sorority is by having the best-looking girls. The reason you become a top sorority, *the* sorority, is because all the guys decide you have the best-looking girls. Don't ask me how this voting, which has to be unofficial, becomes public *and* quasi-official, but it does. What the frat guys think of you becomes what you are. It's weird, but at the same time, it makes sense. It *feels* normal, anyway. As of now, the top sorority is either the Zetas or the Xi Pis or the Sigmas, depending on the month or maybe even the semester. It's not an absolute science, this ranking stuff, but it's still accurate. The Zetas are thin and coolly sophisticated, every last one of them. The Xi Pis are all blond—okay, not actually *all*, but statistically, and we all know how great I am at math, they are more blond than not. Anyway, Xi Pis are blond and giggly. And thin. With healthy racks. Sigmas are usually blond and usually rich and always gorgeous in that rich, blond, American, you-*wish*-I-was-the-girl-next-door way. Is it any surprise that the frats rank those sororities as number one?

Beta Pis are a mixed bag. This is our curse, apparently. We suffer from too much diversity. We therefore can't be classified as a type, at least not a type a guy can easily tag and bag.

And it's all about what works for the guys, isn't it? I mean, how else to explain Presents and those damn placards floating above our heads?

Our reputations live and die by what a bunch of frat guys think of us. It sounds horrible when you say it, which explains why nobody ever says it.

How do I know all this stuff? Mom told me. She was in a sorority in Mississippi back in the early fifties, remember? She explained it all to me before I rushed last year. The fact that Beta Pi couldn't be categorized easily was a major part of its charm for me. Let's face it: since I'm still in my good-looking phase, I could have gone with any house, but the Beta Pis are a mixed bag, like I said, and I like that. I like that we're not this one thing and everything else not that one thing is tossed overboard.

Like I said, it's a real Dilbert Dunker.

Ellen

I lost six pounds over the summer, and I've kept it off. If I lie on my back and skip a meal, I can feel the sharp ridge of my hip bones. That's progress. I'm still wearing the same size pants, but they're baggier than they used to be. My bra size hasn't changed a bit. My younger sister called me Jugs once over the summer, but I called her Zits and that ended that. Thank God Ed wasn't around to hear her. We were at the beach so of course he wasn't around to hear.

Ah, summer.

"Here's your tail," Diane says, handing me a lumpy, crooked length of black fabric. "Where do you want it?"

"Not on my butt, but what choice do I have?"

"None," Diane says. "We're going as black cats. Try to be graceful about it. Think of all I've invested in this outfit: the wire hanger, the cotton balls, the scrap of fabric. I'm out a thousand bucks, easy."

"What are you, a loan shark? You can't have more than five hundred sunk into this outfit. I'm being ripped off."

"Just don't rip off your tail. Now, where do you want it?" Diane asks, holding the end of the tail over my black-leotard-covered butt.

We're in the bathroom, the big one on the second floor. There are no mirrors in our rooms, or nothing bigger than a portable makeup mirror, which isn't sufficient to the task. I look over my shoulder, standing on tiptoe, to see exactly where Diane is holding my tail.

"Too far down and I won't be able to sit," I say.

"How about here?" She holds the open end of the tail to the top of my butt. Do I know where I should have a tail sticking out of my butt? I do not.

"Go for it," I say. Diane sticks a straight pin though the fabric of my black leotard on that spot.

I start to shimmy out of my leotard. "You want me to do you?" I ask.

"I'll wing it," she says. "Watch me sew it to the front. I could wear a trench coat and go as a flasher with a super-long dick."

"I'd dare you except I know you'd do it."

"Damn straight I'd do it," Diane says with a laugh, brushing her dark hair behind her shoulders. "It would sure get the party started faster."

"So, what's the word on this guy you set me up with?" I ask.

"Great guy. Rob Thompson," Diane says. "You'll have fun."

Sure I will. A blind date is never much fun. I've been on five since I pledged the house and I'm still not a fan. It's forced spon-taneity, forced cheer, forced conviviality, forced proximity. And it *feels* forced. Until a nice alcoholic buzz sets in and then it's not so bad.

But you can say that about anything.

"What do you think of Karen not going with Greg?" I ask Diane.

"Hey, she wants to go to the party and he's at a family wedding. Why not go for it?"

"But what do you think of her not telling Greg?" I say, drawing whiskers on my face with black eyeliner.

Diane looks at me in the mirror. "What he doesn't know won't hurt him," she says.

"That's what she said."

"Yeah. I'm quoting. But it's true. And it's one date. What's the harm?"

"She's cheating on him."

"It's a date. It's one date. She's in love with Greg. This is just a—"

"Yeah, got it. It's one date," I say, working on my mascara. It's still cheating and it still bugs me. I hate to say it, but I don't think much of Karen for doing it.

"Where'd she meet him, anyway?"

"I think at the EE Tau exchange."

"Damn exchanges are going to kill us," I say, almost meaning it. "I wish Laurie were going tonight."

"How she could pick doing a paper over a party is beyond me, but that's the difference in our GPAs talking," Diane says, arranging her hair around her cat-ear headband. "She's not the party animals we are."

"You're a lot funnier when I'm drunk."

"Then let's fix that."

Two hours later, I'm in my makeshift Halloween costume with my makeshift date, in the living room of Holly Clark's parents' house in Palos Verdes. Rob Thompson is standing out on the patio by the pool, talking with some ROTC guys.

We haven't hit it off. It's probably because I wouldn't make out with him in the car on the way here. Diane and her date, some guy she met at a football game when he spilled his beer all over her, are also on the patio. Diane looks like she wants to hit Rob. Diane has my blessings.

"Uh-oh, there she is, the girl who drank me under the table last year."

I turn to my left and there's Matt Carlson, beer-meister. I held back at the fall Rho Delt exchange last year, but by the spring exchange I figured chivalry was dead and so I beat him cold. I think I left him leaning against a doorjamb, his shirt untucked and his eyes crossed. C'est la guerre.

I'm in my sixth year of French. I've learned a few phrases.

Matt looks better this year. He's lost some weight, or maybe just moved it around, and his hair looks better. Of course, all this improvement could be the lighting. It's a half a shade from being pitch-black. I don't mind a bit since it hides me wearing a black leotard, black tights, black ballet slippers, and a headband with black felt "ears" glued to it.

"Care for a rematch?" I ask.

Matt looks me up and down. I return the favor. He's wearing plaid pants and a golf shirt and carrying a golf club like it's a cane.

"You're on," he says. "But no using your tail as a hollow leg."

"You're on," I say. "As long as you don't beat me with your long, scary stick."

"Deal," he says, grinning.

I didn't remember Matt being this cute, and I'm not even buzzed yet.

Two drinks later, and I still haven't danced a single dance, Matt says, "You make a cute black cat."

"I'd say you make a cute pro golfer but we both know that's an oxymoron. Nice outfit. The only clean clothes left in your closet?"

"You calling me a moron?"

"If the golf shoes fit."

Matt grins again.

"Matt, you gonna dance with this girl or what?" a male voice says from behind me.

"Do you want to dance?" Matt asks me.

The voice slides from behind me to stand next to me. He's tall, dark, and handsome, a pure cliché, wearing a white undershirt and worn blue jeans, and he has a cigarette dangling from the corner of his mouth. The curl of gray smoke twirling up from the end of his cigarette has his eyes squinting, but even through the squint I can see that his eyes are light, light blue. Black hair and those pale blue eyes and the white T-shirt shows off a very nice build. I know this guy. I met him at an exchange once.

"Sure she does," he answers for me. "I've been watching her tail twitch for five minutes."

I hate guys like this. He's so full of himself he's overflowing. I'll bet my dad was like this in his day, minus the cigarette and the undershirt.

"I'm fine, Matt," I say with a smile; then I turn to Blue Eyes and say, "Who are you supposed to be? Marlon Brando?"

"His T-shirt was ripped. I'm James Dean," he says.

"He's dead," I say.

Blue Eyes scowls and smirks at the same time. He pulls his cigarette out of his mouth with his thumb and forefinger.

"Mike Dunn," Matt says with a slight movement of his hand. "Ellen Olson, champion beer drinker."

"Champion, huh?" Mike says, smirking some more.

"We all have our talents. What's yours?"

"Fast ball," he says, looking meaningfully down at me.

"Is that a metaphor for something?" I say.

There's a moment of stunned silence. I love it.

"Mike's a pitcher. Baseball team," Matt says.

"Not *the* pitcher?" I ask. I take a long, deep swallow of my beer. It's warm and tastes horrible. That's never stopped me before and it's not going to stop me now. "Bummer for you."

"Excuse me," Matt says. "I see Holly signaling me." Matt leaves me alone with Mike. Great.

Mike chuckles and looks me over, not even bothering to be subtle about it. "Come on. Let's dance."

"Where's your date?" I ask Mike.

"She excused herself."

I'll bet she did. Matt's date is Holly Clark, and Holly has been talking to her parents for the last half hour, and it hasn't looked like a very happy conversation. I guess the Clarks aren't loving the fact that two people have already thrown up in their junipers.

"Karen, hi," I say, hoping to distract Mike the jerk. Karen Mitchell is dressed as a flapper with cheap black fringe sewn to the hem of a cheap yellow sheath dress, her short dark hair adorned with a black velvet headache band. She's wearing a strand of very fake-looking pearls in a long column down the front of her dress; they fall in a straight, flat line, just like a good flapper's pearls should. Damn, I wish I had her body.

"Hi," she says brightly. "Have you met Gary Robertson?" A new record has just dropped down on the stereo, killing the momentary silence. "The Ballroom Blitz" blasts out of the speakers. I shake my head and put on a happy face.

Gary Robertson is tanned and dark-haired. His whole demeanor is classier than Mike Dunn's, and I don't think that's his polo outfit talking. Gary is wearing a numbered polo shirt and a beat-up polo helmet, and he's carrying a polo stick. The only thing missing is the horse. Gary is Karen's date for the night. Just a date. Some girls seem to be swimming in guys and Karen is one of them. Diane is another one of them.

Somebody has to keep score.

"Hi," I say, nodding slightly. "Karen, this is Mike Dunn."

Mike grins and pulls a cigarette out of his pack. He smokes Marlboros. He offers one to Karen, who declines by shaking her head.

"Guess who Mike is supposed to be," I ask. Maybe I can shame him into leaving me alone.

Karen studies Mike's face, her head tilted to the side. "James Dean?"

After a moment's shock, I burst out laughing. "God, you're good."

"It was the cigarette," she says. "You really need a cowboy hat, though, to get that *Giant* thing going."

"*Giant?*" I ask.

"Rock Hudson, James Dean, Elizabeth Taylor," Karen says. "Thursday night at the movies." She shrugs.

"How'd you know I wasn't James Dean from *Rebel Without a Cause?*" Mike asks.

"No jacket," Karen says.

"You assumed he wasn't just too lazy to find a jacket," I say.

"Yeah, I guess I did. Are you lazy, Mike?" Karen asks.

"I was putting all my faith in the cigarette," Mike says.

Okay, I have to admit, that was funny.

"So, Gary," I say, trying to get back on track in my evil plan to ditch Mike, "did you find your polo gear on the floor of your closet or at the Salvation Army?"

"On the floor of my dad's closet," Gary says, "which isn't too far off from the Salvation Army."

"Too bad you didn't bring the horse," I say.

"He's in my car. Wanna come pet him?" Mike says.

Jerk. But sort of funny. In a really nasty way.

I smile at the guys and motion Karen toward me with a flick of my finger; she leans in.

"Look, I'm trying to dump this guy. I just can't shake him. Don't leave me alone with him, okay?"

"I'll do my best, but I've got my hands full with Gary," she whispers.

I nod and we both straighten up.

"You girls need to go to the powder room?" Mike asks.

"Why?" I ask. "Would you give us a ride there on your horse?"

Mike looks at me, his light eyes glittering with humor and arrogance. He's such a male chauvinist. He's just oozing with it. "Sure. Right now? Let's go," he says.

Mike takes me by the elbow and walks me onto the middle of the patio where everyone is dancing. Because I have the worst luck in the world, it's a slow dance, "Stairway to Heaven," which is half a fast dance and half a slow one, but by the time you're fourteen everybody has figured out that it's best to dance the whole thing in full-body lock. So here I am, with Mike's hands wrapped around my back. You can guess where my boobs are. I put my arms around his neck, loosely, and try to make the best of it.

"It's a law," he says in my ear. "This song, must dance."

"It's not a law in my state," I say.

"I'm from Chicago. It's a law in Illinois."

"An out-of-towner," I say. "I should have guessed."

He pulls back and looks at me, smiling, his blue eyes twinkling. His arms are long and hard with muscle. His hips are narrow. His thighs are muscular. Okay, I can admit it. He's a hunk.

"You're a native. I should have guessed. Tanned, blond, blue-eyed, a real California girl."

"Tanned? I'm fish-belly white," I say.

"If you say so," he says, tightening his grip, pulling me against him again.

We dance a few turns, not talking. I can feel him against me, the hard press of him in his jeans, the soft pull of his T-shirt over the muscles in his back. James Dean. Marlon Brando. I hate that type. In theory, anyway.

"It's okay to go back to your date," I say against his neck. His hair is pure black and gleams in the floodlights aimed at the patio. "I don't want there to be a problem."

"No problem," he says, looking deeply into my eyes. He's kind of sexy. He traces a finger down my back, from my neck to my waist. I suppress a shiver. "When you need to get back to your date, let me know. Until then, I'm keeping you."

"What about your date?"

He chuckles. "I guess I forgot about her. Bad, huh?"

Bad, yes. The look in his eyes, that trace down my back . . . I feel shivery and alive: And scared.

Diane

– Fall 1976 –

Doug Anderson came to the party. Not with me, of course, but with Jenny Van Upp, who has long blond hair and the cutest profile in three states. Jenny looks a little drunk. Doug doesn't. I don't know if that means he can hold his booze better or if he's just the kind of guy to get a girl drunk, but there's no way in hell I believe that.

My date, Stan Jaworski and I are dancing. I completely gave up on Rob Thompson since Ellen seems to be doing fine with some guy in a white T-shirt. Where his date is is anyone's guess, but I'm voting for the juniper bed. It's seeing a lot of action.

Stan keeps turning our bodies to the music, so after just a few shuffling steps, my view of Doug is gone. Doug is dressed in his navy whites. Doug takes my breath away. Doug is off-limits, but Doug, not knowing that, still takes my breath away.

Stan does not take my breath away. I do not blame Stan for this; he's cute, he's nice, he's a perfectly great guy, but he's not Doug Anderson, Midshipman Temptation. I can't have Doug, but that doesn't change the fact that he's all I think about.

The music plays, we all shift with it, and my view of Doug and Jenny reappears. They're dancing, and since Jenny is a lot shorter than Doug, her head is tilted back, her blond hair spilling down to touch his hands. She's talking, smiling up at him, and Doug is smiling back. She looks very sexy, her hair cascading down that way, tickling the backs of his hands. My hair is long, but not that long, and besides, if I held my head like that, my ears would show.

Doug has seen my ears.

This is an important detail and one that I'm trying to forget. It hasn't been easy, but I'm working on it. I think there's hope I can push it out of my mind permanently. See, in ROTC no hair can touch the collar, not the top of the collar and certainly not the bottom of the collar. The guys all get really short haircuts and the girls either get really short haircuts or they wear their hair up and fastened securely, which means ugly and tight with an entire package of bobby pins holding it all in place. Naturally, my ears show. All the time. And then there's the white hat. And the ugly white man-shoes. I look hideous in my navy dress whites. You can't even imagine. I wish I couldn't even imagine, but even I'm not that good at denial.

Stan's hands are on my back, holding me close as Bread's "Make It with You" fades out, and I'm not going to comment on the perfection of that song in this moment, when I step on something behind me, twist my ankle slightly, and turn, an apology already half out of my mouth.

It's Doug. He has his hand out, holding me by the elbow, and he had to let go of Jenny to do it. It's not very nice of me, but I'm thrilled.

"Easy," Doug says. "You okay?"

"Good hands," I say, looking into his blue eyes. That was a mistake because now I can't look away, and no one with 20/20 eyesight could look away from Doug Anderson. "Nothing that a pair of crutches and a hot toddy won't fix," I say. "I'll get right on that, Mr. Anderson."

"Wait," Doug says, staring hard at me. "Ryan, Diane?"

"Affirmative, Anderson, Douglas."

That's how bad I look in my ROTC gear. He doesn't even recognize me with my ears covered and my curves on display in my thin black jersey, which is a thought I can't help but run with.

"You . . ." he says, looking startled and, dare I hope, delighted, "look great. You're a Beta Pi?"

"Affirmative," I say, grinning, looking at Jenny to see how she's taking all this. She seems to be taking it very well. She must be blitzed on her ass. "Doug Anderson, ROTC, Jenny Van Upp, Beta Pi, meet Stan Jaworski, fellow Spartan."

"Nice to meet you," Stan says with a friendly nod. "How about another drink?"

"No, thanks," Doug says, meeting Stan's eyes in that friendly, slightly dismissive guy way.

"Sure!" Jenny says on a squeak of laughter, leaving Doug's side to loop her arm through Stan's. She really must be plastered to leave Doug for any reason, including alcohol.

In a matter of seconds, not only am I alone—okay, not actually alone since there are one hundred other people around, but more alone than I've ever been with Doug before—but the song that comes through the stereo speakers is another slow one, "The Best of My Love" by the Eagles.

The lighting is dim. I'm looking sexy. The right music is playing.

Look, it's not like I planned this, but when the Great Pumpkin drops a bag of Halloween candy in your lap, what's a girl to do but take a bite?

Okay, so that might be the three vodkas talking, but after three vodkas do I really care who's talking?

Damn straight I don't.

"Are you with him?" Doug asks, nodding in the direction Stan has taken with Jenny.

"Just for tonight. How about you?" I ask.

"This is our second date."

"How's it going?"

"Better and better," Doug says with a grin.

I lick my lips and smile back. Free candy, that's what he is. A pile of chocolate, mine for the taking.

Except I can't take him, no matter how much I want to. He's the nicest guy, and the most gorgeous guy, but the nicest guy. Really. I sit three rows behind him in Seamanship class so I'm practically an expert on the guy. Of course, I don't have any hands-on experience. Not yet.

Yeah, definitely the three vodkas talking.

"I love this song," I say, universal code for *Ask me to dance.*

Doug smiles wider, offers me his hand, and says, "Would you care to dance?"

"How nice of you to ask, seeing as I've been temporarily ditched by my date. I'm trying not to sob. Please, no pity or I'll break down completely," I say, grinning as I put my hand in his.

"No pity," he says, leading me to the dark edge of the patio. "I promise." And then he takes me in his arms and from that instant on it's the best night of my life.

Laurie

"Where are we going?" I ask.

"You'll see," Pete says, wrapping his arm around my shoulders, pulling me next to him as he drives a fraternity brother's borrowed SS Monte Carlo.

To be honest, I don't actually care where we're going; I only care that we're together and that we're alone. I lied to everyone about what I was going to be doing tonight, the night of the Beta Pi Halloween party, because I didn't want to share Pete with anyone. I'm not going to include Barbie in that thought. Barbie is gone. Pete told me all about Barbie, about how his father and her father have been golfing partners for almost ten years, and about how the families belong to the same country club, and that their mothers took paddle tennis lessons together, and how all of that, all of that togetherness, resulted in Pete and Barbie being, by default, together. Barbie was a noose he had to slip. She was the girl his family wouldn't let him leave behind, but now he has because now he's with me, and I'm with him. I am most definitely with him.

Edging along Los Angeles streets, avoiding the freeways, Pete's borrowed car snakes through Vermont Canyon, climbing up toward Griffith Observatory. Pete's left arm is stretched toward the steering wheel and the other is wrapped around me, Pete's hand caressing my breast as he drives. I am breathless. I am shameless and I am breathless. I don't know when I was reduced to this, to this shaking, quivering girl sitting tucked under the arm of a Rho Delt, but that is who I am.

Pete parks the car so that we're on the edge of the view, the Los Angeles basin stretching out before us, lights fading in geometric precision into the haze.

"Nice view, huh?" Pete says, sweeping a hand through his hair, his smile moving across his mouth just before he kisses me. "But the best view is right here."

I am swept up in this, in him, and yet part of me is still onshore, watching, nervous, hesitant. When his hand slips from my breast to the button on my jeans, I put my hand over his, stopping him.

"You're killing me, Laurie. I need this. I need you," he whispers, his blue eyes staring into mine. I feel *seen* with Pete. I think I've been starving for that all my life.

"Do you?" I ask, easing the pressure of my hand, letting him stroke the inside seam of my jeans.

"I do. I want you so bad," he says, his mouth on my neck, one hand on my breast, the other between my legs.

I open my legs, releasing one more inch of control to him, laying my head back against the seat cushion, floating away on a wave of sensation.

I wasn't going to do this. I wasn't going to lose my virginity to a boy on the seat of a car. I was going to be more careful and more considered and generally more precise about everything, but Pete, with his long hair and his easy grin and his frayed jean jacket, has lured me away from the tedium of being careful.

With hands that seem to be everywhere at once, hands that push me along the hazy edge of awareness, we tumble into the backseat; Pete is on top of me, his mouth and his hands at my breasts, between my legs, on my mouth, a fury of movement and purpose, and I—I am whipped along in his wake, pulled into waves of pleasure and impatience. Somehow, I am naked from the waist up, my pants hanging from one ankle, my panties pushed down to my knees, and suddenly, it is all too real, and instead of being pulled into passion I feel pushed and shoved into something frightening and serious and not at all worthy of a backseat in a deserted parking lot.

My hands reach his, stopping him, holding him off, and his breath stops while I keep panting, trying to flick my hair out of my eyes, trying to find myself within my confusion.

"What?" he says, looking down at me. The light from a distant lamppost illuminates his eyes so that they look silver; his hair is blackest sable in the dark shadows of the backseat. He looks nothing like Pete in that instant. I'm cold. I'm uncomfortable and I'm cold. I don't want this, but I do want Pete. "Come on," he says. "Come on, Laurie. Please."

"Wait. Just wait."

He lifts his head, his throat looks so long and strong, and then he pushes his hair back with one large hand, and my heart rushes into my throat and he's Pete again and I remember that I love him and that he wants me.

"Wait?" he says. "What are you? A tease?"

"No. I'm not," I say. I don't want to be that. I want to make him happy. "Really. Don't stop."

I pull him down to me, his chest against mine, his legs bent at odd angles to fit within the car and so he can fit within me. He yanks at a condom in his pocket; I don't watch. I tilt my head back and look out the rear window. The stars have moved since we began—but that's not right; it's the earth that's moved.

He kisses me again, deeply, a wet kiss full of passion and hunger, and I fall into the heat of it. The seat is cool on the skin of my back, a fact I'm dimly aware of. Pete is covering the front of me with heat, his fingers sliding into me, wet and slick, stretching me, and then the condom edges in, the condom, not him. I feel rubber, not flesh, and that makes a difference but I can't think in what way. Pushing, stretching, and I press against him, urging him forward even though I don't feel the heat anymore, only the cold on my back.

Pete grunts, a sound of passion, and I revel in it. I groan, giving him my answering cry of passion. He kisses me, my reward.

"God, Laurie," he says, pressing into me. I feel torn, uncomfortable and too full, like a balloon about to pop or fabric about to rip. It's too much, but I smile and hold him close, willing myself to find any pleasure in this that I can.

I love him.

"You really meant it. You're a virgin," he says.

I nod. I don't want to say it out loud, now that it's no longer true.

With a thrust, he pushes in farther and I gasp in pain.

"Try to relax," he says. "Just relax."

Before I can relax he pushes in again. I feel something rip and it's me. A few more grunts and a few more thrusts into my bone-dry vagina, quite painful, and then he lets his weight fall on me. He's heavy and I'm cold and it hurts; everything hurts.

I don't know what to do with my hands. I suppose I should hug him to me; what I really want to do is press my hands against my

vulva, pressing against the raw pain throbbing with a dry heat. It
seems so silly, pondering the question of what to do with my
hands; it's such a stupid thing to wonder, but as I'm chastising
myself for that I place my hands on his shoulders and try to appear
relaxed and happy. I'm neither.

When the knock hits the side window I jump inches, almost
bucking Pete off of me.

A policeman's flashlight shines into the car; the light in the car
coming through the fogged-up windows looks gray and disjointed,
a cold light that makes everything look stark.

"Are you all right, miss?"

I nod. I think I nod.

"License and registration," he says, stepping away from the car.

Pete curses, grabbing my blouse from the floor of the car and
shoving it against my chest. I pull on my clothes with shaking
hands, thankful that the cold light has moved away from me and
left me in darkness.

Just drop me in back," I say.

Pete doesn't even look at me as he makes a sharp turn down
the alley behind Beta Pi. The Row is busy tonight and it's late
enough that most everyone will be back from the Halloween
party. I'd rather not face that.

He stops the car behind the house and reaches across the seat
for my hand. My hands are folded in my lap and I'm sitting on my
own side of the car, somewhat stunned that I'm not even wondering at the change in us. Things have changed because I changed
them. I thought it would be a change for the better, if I even
thought that far ahead, but it's not for the better. It's just change.
I didn't expect that.

"Are you okay?" Pete says, his hand lying heavily over mine. I slide my hands from beneath his and clasp the door handle.

"Of course," I say, cracking the door open. "I'll see you?"

"I'll call," he says, pulling me to him for a kiss. I slide across the seat, losing my grip on the handle, losing myself for a few moments in the heady loveliness of his kiss and his scent and the feel of his hair brushing against my cheek. But I can't stay lost. "It was great," he says. "You're great."

Am I?

I get out of the car and walk though the beam of the headlights, lit up for a few seconds, forcing Pete to see me, if force is required, and I'm not certain it's not. I don't want to slow my stride to the narrow open strip between our house and the AGs'; I want to walk with purpose and confidence. As with all things concerning Pete, I do exactly what I swore to never do: I slow my step and look at him. He's lighting a cigarette, his face lit by a dim red glow, looking mysterious and sexy and dangerous. In essence, looking like Pete.

He is not looking at me.

I walk down the dark cement corridor, my shoulder brushing against the Beta Pi house to my right, the sounds coming from the house hushed but consistent. The party is over and most of my sorority sisters are home. I hadn't planned for that. I hadn't planned to walk into a brightly lit, noisy, alive house with my virginity so freshly stripped from me, my panties wet and cold against my skin.

What did Pete do with his rubber? I can't remember. I think I should know where that is; it seems important. He might have thrown it out the window, or it might be stuck to the underside of the floor mat, or maybe he put it in his pocket.

"Laurie! Where've you been?" Ellen says.

I've wandered into the big second-floor bathroom, having

smiled and nodded my way past girls in the trophy room and girls on the stairs and girls in the hallway. They are in various stages of undress. I feel that I am in a stage of undress, some strange stage I can't define.

"I was out," I say.

"No shit, Sherlock," Ellen says. "I can see that. Were you at the library?"

"Yes. I was at the library," I say, walking into a stall and closing the door, locking it. I can see Ellen through the crack; she starts to wash her face, the whiskers disappearing in the first light touch of soap and water. I pull down my jeans and then my panties. My panties are on inside out. I slip off my shoes and my pants, sliding down my panties, putting it all on again the right way. Panties. Pants. Shoes. Everything is in order again.

When I come out of the stall, Ellen is brushing her teeth, staring at me in the mirror. "You should have come. It was great."

"How was your date?"

"Oh, okay," she says.

"Ask her about James Dean," Karen says, coming into the bathroom in her robe. Karen wears a fluffy white robe that makes her look like a cute stuffed animal.

"Shut up," Ellen says, spitting into the sink.

"Hey, are you okay?" Karen asks me, testing the water temperature in the faucet with her fingertips. Both Ellen and Karen are staring at me in the mirror. I look at their reflections, not my own. "You look worn-out."

"She needed a party and she missed it," Ellen says. "Go to bed and dream of all you missed."

Yes, I think that's exactly what I'll do.

Karen

We took Ellen's car, and Ellen drove the whole long way up I-5 from LA to San Francisco; her dad said she was the only one insured for the car, but I think that car insurance actually insures the driver, and my dad does work at Aetna so I know a little bit about insurance. Really, just a little bit because insurance, no matter what my dad says, is pretty boring. Anyway, Ellen drove, weaving in and out of traffic until we got into the San Joaquin Valley, because then, except for big trucks, the traffic really faded away. The San Joaquin Valley, which I was very excited to see since it's the big valley in *The Big Valley*—that cute western show with Lee Majors and Barbara Stanwyck (I've been a fan ever since my mom made me watch *The Lady Eve*)—is actually flat and hot and boring. It's nothing but mile after mile of crops. I fell asleep, and when I woke up an hour later, it was still crops. I wasn't actually sure we'd moved, but Laurie, sitting in the front seat, promised we had.

Eight hours. It took eight hours of pure driving to get from the sorority house in Los Angeles to Laurie's house in San Francisco.

I'm not counting the hour of potty breaks, one in Bakersfield, planned by Ellen, and one in Fresno, demanded by Diane. Diane has a small bladder and she's not afraid to use it. Then there was the time we got lost for a half hour trying to get on the I-5, Ellen swearing, Laurie calmly trying to direct her, Diane laughing, and me trying to be as inconspicuous as possible. I don't do detours well, in life or in traffic.

"Where do we park?" Ellen asks Laurie.

"Yeah, 'cause I've got to go again," Diane says.

"Again? You just went in Fresno!" Ellen snaps.

"Your point?" Diane says, crossing her legs.

"She's crossing her legs," I say. "Better hurry or you'll have a wet spot on the seat."

"There should be parking on the street," Laurie says. "There's a spot!"

This is San Francisco, the *real* San Francisco, like in *The Streets of San Francisco* and Rice-A-Roni commercials. I don't know San Francisco at all, so I have no idea where we are, but it isn't the suburbs. Laurie's house, what I can see of it from the backseat, is slapped down on a city street with wide city sidewalks like a giant blob of beige Play-Doh. It's tall, imposing, and has no windows on the street level. What it has on the street level is a black-painted door with a brass knocker. That's it.

Ellen, muttering swearwords under her breath, tries to parallel park a half a block from Laurie's house. Diane and I are silent; we don't want to distract her. Laurie is silent as well, though she looks more pensive than quiet.

The whole, long drive up, Ellen asked Laurie questions about her home, and Laurie, in the nicest way possible, changed the subject. The end result is that I feel pretty nervous about staying at Laurie's house, and that was before I saw what it looked like.

Laurie is *rich*.

Sure, I knew that about her already, mostly from all the things she doesn't say, but seeing her house makes it all very clear. The house, its size and location, practically shouts, "Money lives here!"

Maybe Laurie is pensive about what we'll think of her. My heart melts a little, thinking that.

"How close am I to the curb?" Ellen says.

Diane opens her door a few inches. "Less than a foot. We're good."

"Seriously. Can I get over any farther? Some monster truck is going to sideswipe me. I just know it," Ellen says.

"Seriously," Diane says. "You're good. Put it in park."

"You're just saying that because you have to pee," Ellen says, but she puts the car in park.

"They can both be true, Einstein," Diane says.

Laurie remains silent. I can't stop watching her. She seems so tightly and rigidly still. I'm not like this when I go home. I catapult out of the car, talking nonstop, making my dad laugh and my mom smile. I throw open the door, the smell of home as sweet as warm gingerbread. I run up the stairs to my room, the rightness of it, the pure home of it, pulling me in. Welcoming me.

Laurie looks at her home from inside the car and does none of that. In fact, we all get out of the car before she does.

"What am I? Your baggage handler?" Ellen shouts up to Laurie as she opens the trunk. Laurie drops her head a bit, takes a breath so deep that I can actually see it, and gets out of the car.

"Yeah, but don't expect a tip," Diane says, grunting as she pulls out her suitcase. We're only up for the weekend, a quick trip to watch ULA kill Stanford on the football field, but we've each packed the largest suitcase American Tourister makes. Of course, these are the suitcases we moved to college with. It's not like we have luggage options. It was either this or a paper bag, and, knowing Laurie, a paper bag wasn't really a luggage option.

"What did you pack? A set of encyclopedias?" Ellen says to me, hauling out my suitcase and dropping it on the ground.

"S through Z. I like to educate myself at all times. Even at football games," I say. "The genius in me just begs to be let loose."

"Yeah. Genius," Ellen says.

"Hey, I got you to get my luggage, didn't I?" I say.

We all laugh with nearly grim determination at that, all except Laurie, who's smiling distractedly, her gaze on the front door. No one has come out to greet us. Is that what's bothering her? My mom would have been hanging on the mailbox, counting the minutes until I came home. Ellen, Diane, and I stare at one another in confusion and concern, and then stare at Laurie, who will not stare back at us.

It's awkward, and none of us knows what to do to fix it.

"What are we doing to do—spend the weekend on the sidewalk?" Ellen says, throwing an arm around Laurie's shoulders. "You can invite us in. I promise, we won't spill anything on the carpets."

"Speak for yourself," Diane says, pressing her knees together. "My bladder and I will make our own arrangements."

"Let Diane sleep near the litter box, okay?" I say. "Give her a stuffed mouse and she'll be fine."

Laurie grins for the first time since Fresno, looking at each of us in turn. It's a moment that passes in an instant, a quiet, sunny moment of thanks. It's gone before I can even smile my response to her. Maybe we do know how to fix Laurie. Maybe we're the only ones who do know how. Or maybe we're the only ones who care enough to try.

I look at the front door of her house again, closed and silent against us.

"Do you have a key or will the butler let us in?" I say.

"The maid will," Laurie says softly.

Not her mom or her dad. The maid. And here I thought I was kidding.

The maid, a middle-aged woman with graying brown hair and a heavy bosom, lets us in. She has a warm smile for Laurie and a pleasant smile for us. I smile back, not really sure of the protocol; I'm just following Laurie and hoping for the best.

We follow the maid up the mahogany stairs to the main floor. The mahogany stairs continue up and up, winding regally into the upper reaches of the house; it's that colossal sort of staircase, the kind with heavy banisters, the kind of staircase that looks completely at home in a Tudor castle, and I base this on years of watching Hollywood movies that have given me a clear picture of old American money with European sensibilities. I was never sure if that was an accurate picture before now. Now I'm sure.

Beyond the staircase, there's a view of San Francisco Bay from huge windows along the back of the house. My gaze goes to that instantly; it's a bolt of light and air in a dark stained wood interior. We're all standing there, looking out at the view, not moving a muscle because we haven't been invited to, when Laurie says, "And these are my parents."

I turn abruptly away from the view. To my right is a stately library with a big fireplace, and in front of the fireplace are two fat chairs, and in the two fat chairs sit an older man and woman. They do not rise.

This strikes me as odd, but I don't know what to do. I stare at them. They stare back at me. They both have gray hair and blue eyes and fair skin, his skin a bit ruddy in the cheeks. They look old, very old to be parents.

"Mother. Father," Laurie says. "These are my sorority friends. Diane Ryan. Ellen Olson. Karen Mitchell."

I smile. Ellen nods hello. Diane takes a step forward and says, "It's so nice to meet you. Thank you for having us."

Mr. McCormick nods serenely. Mrs. McCormick smiles blandly. And then they look away from us, staring passively into each other's faces. Diane takes a step back.

"Yes," I say. "It's so kind of you. Thank you."

Ellen just stares at them.

They do not stare at us in return.

"Come on, you guys," Laurie says softly, and she leads us into the room with the view. The maid is gone. I didn't notice her leaving us.

The view of the bay pulls at my attention, urging me to forget Laurie's parents in the next room, to ignore the silence coming from them, to resist the lack of warmth and sound and movement. They are still. The house is still. The whitecaps in the distance on the bay, the swiftly moving clouds racing toward the famous red bridge, the boats like wood shavings being blown toward the green shore all call to me of movement and life. The house, Laurie's house, is silent.

And because it is silent, so am I.

"Amazing view," Ellen says. "Windy, though."

Laurie nods.

We continue to stare at the view, silence burying us.

"Is everything okay?" Diane asks. "It's okay that we're staying here, right?"

Laurie nods again, trying to smile. The smile dies before it's even born.

"We can get a motel," I say.

"No, we're staying here," Laurie says, still staring out at the bay. "It's fine. It will all be fine. It's just that my parents don't have overnight guests very often."

"They're shy, huh?" Ellen says.

Laurie smiles briefly and says, "Not so much shy as private. Especially with my friends. Actually, only with my friends."

"Really, is this going to be okay?" Diane says.

"Absolutely," Laurie says, turning from the window to look at us. "And if it isn't, they'll get over it."

"Shit, Laurie," Ellen says, "we don't want to get you in trouble."

"You won't. There's not going to be any trouble," Laurie says.

"You sound like a gunslinger," I say. "John Wayne in *McLintock!*"

"Do I? Good," Laurie says. "Though I liked him better in *The Searchers*."

"Except he was always looking for trouble in *The Searchers*," I say.

"He was, wasn't he?" Laurie says with a big grin. "No wonder I like it so much."

"No fair," Ellen says. "The only John Wayne movie I can remember seeing is *The Cowboys*, and he died in that one."

"Hey, the dog died in *Big Jake*. I couldn't believe it," Diane says.

"And the Indian," I say.

"The two best characters in that movie, and Big Jake's two best friends. Splat," Diane says. "What was that line? Everyone keeps thinking Jake is dead, no threat to them, and he keeps saying it when they say, 'I thought you was dead.'"

"'Not hardly,'" I say. "He says, 'Not hardly.' It's a great line. They couldn't get him, could they?"

"Who couldn't?" Ellen says.

"The bad guys," Laurie says, looking down at the highly polished floor at her feet. "Come on. Let's go upstairs and get unpacked. We're going to have a great weekend."

It crosses my mind to say *not hardly*, but I'm afraid it's true, so I don't.

Karen

The 401 Club is on Figueroa and is a complete and total dive. But they don't card, which is how the owner must be making his multimillions. The Four-O, as it's universally called, is at one end of The Row. As they say in real estate: location, location, location.

It's finals week and I've just taken my last final, Oceanography, where I discovered that there was a lab to that class that I didn't know about and never once attended.

For the first time in my life, I *need* a drink.

The outside of the Four-O looks a lot like the inside; it's dark, dirty, run-down, and disreputable. Predictably, there's the slight stench of vomit and urine, both inside and out. Am I imagining that? Maybe. But the ambience of the Four-O is pushing my imagination in that direction.

"Karen. Over here," a male voice says from the farthest corner on the left. I know that voice. It's Gary Robertson, EE Tau, senior, geology major, destined for parts unknown when he graduates, and the guy I'm cheating on Greg with.

Yeah. I know.

Of course I feel guilty. Cheating is not something I do lightly, believe me. It's just that Gary is so . . . not Greg.

I'm horrible. I'm a horrible person. But that's the truth. Gary is not Greg and, honestly, that's the main attraction.

It's the worst luck in the world that their names are so similar. I've gotten so I don't say either name, ever. I'm just too scared of mixing them up. It happened once and I had to cough like crazy to cover it up. Greg bought me a pack of lemon-flavored cough drops the next day, which is crazy because doesn't everyone like cherry flavored? Really? Lemon? Good thing I didn't really need them.

"Hi," I say, walking through the gloom toward Gary. He's not alone. I'm not worried about being seen with Gary, because Greg never comes to the Four-O since it's almost exclusively used by those who live on The Row.

Location, location, location.

Gary is sitting with Rob Thompson and Russ Bromley, both ROTC, all EE Taus, and this gorgeous guy with dark blond hair and blue eyes who looks like an angel, if angels looked like well-built, physically flawless men, which I think they might in certain religions.

Gary makes a motion like he wants me to sit on his lap. That is definitely not happening. Gary doesn't exactly know about Greg, but he knows by now that I don't do any public displays of affection. I don't think he understands why, but he doesn't need to know why. No PDA. No exceptions. I smile and walk over to a chair at another table, all set to drag it over.

Angel hops up and says, "Take my chair. I'll get this one."

"Thanks," I say. I'm a little breathless, and not from moving the chair two inches. Up close, he's even more devastating. "I feel pretty honored to be sitting at the EE Tau table."

"Oh, I'm not in EE Tau," he says.

"He's in ROTC," Rob says.

"Hi," he says. "I'm Doug Anderson. Am I still welcome at the EE Tau table?" he asks me with a shy grin.

Doug Anderson. Diane's Doug. No wonder she's crazy about him. My heart flutters the tiniest bit and I say, "I hate to break it to you, but I'm not in EE Tau either. I guess my disguise fooled you."

"I thought you were sporting a ROTC disguise," he counters, sitting down next to me, his knee pressed against mine under the table, his blue eyes gleaming brightly. At my puzzled look, he runs his hands over his hair and says, "I think your hair's even shorter than mine."

"Doug," I say, running a hand over the nape of my neck, "if you can't say something nice about a girl's hair, not only should you not say anything at all; you should start running before she beats you to death with her shoe."

Gary snorts with laughter. Rob and Russ hoot and stomp their feet on the sticky floor. Doug smiles sweetly and says, "I didn't say I didn't like it. I do like it. It looks great."

"Nice save," I say. "I'll keep my shoe on. For now."

"Karen! Hi!" I turn to the blast of sunlight coming through the curtain that shields the open door of the Four-O, the sharp line between darkness and daylight quickly narrowing as the curtain falls back into place behind Diane. "What are you doing with the scum of ROTC?"

"Slumming for a free drink," I say. "No luck yet."

"I got it," Gary says, signaling for the waitress.

"Thank you," I say politely, distantly.

I haven't told anyone about seeing Gary. Greg is my boyfriend. Gary is my secret.

How does Gary feel about this?

I haven't asked him.

Three hours later and the bar is full of people I know well, know slightly, and know not at all. There's something about finals week, some desperate joy mixed with exhaustion. What's done is done. Either you passed or you failed, got the grade or got the boot. Either way, it's over. For a few days, anyway, and then it starts all over again.

I'm cheating on my boyfriend, the man I plan to marry. I always do this, and I don't understand why it always feels so inevitable that I do this.

"You okay?" Laurie asks me, leaning her shoulder next to mine. "How'd your final go?"

"I skipped the lab," I say, laughing weakly.

"How many times?" she says, draping her arm over my shoulder.

"Every time," I say. "I don't know how I missed that. I didn't know. I honestly didn't know."

"If you were going to flunk, they'd have told you before now," Laurie reasons. "Nobody flunks without a warning shot over the bow."

"Or a flare fired from the deck," I say. "Okay. Yeah. You're right. But, Laurie, Diane is having a horrible influence on us, all those naval metaphors!"

We both burst out laughing.

"There is no such thing as too many naval metaphors," Diane says from behind us. I tip my head back. Diane is standing behind us, holding two drinks, tequila shots by the look of it. "Watch your step or I'll report you."

"Aye, aye, sir," I say, still laughing.

Laurie and I are roommates; we're in the two-way in the middle of the second floor, near the back stairs leading down to the kitchen and the dining room. The kitchen, the domain of Melba, the day cook, is mostly off-limits to us. There's an ice machine and a fridge in what I guess is supposed to be a butler's pantry, and Melba keeps a big pitcher of orange juice for us in the fridge. I've always hated orange juice. I don't anymore. I've discovered that if you pour anything over ice, it's drinkable. Hence the appeal of alcohol.

I really am drunk.

I push my empty glass across the table and cross my arms over my chest. I'm done.

"Where's Greg?" Diane asks from somewhere over the top of my head.

"Spanish final at three," I say.

"Well, hell, it's six now. Isn't he ready to party?" Diane asks.

Diane is always ready to party, and it's one of the things I love about her. Greg, on the other hand, is never in the mood to party, especially not with anyone in a sorority or fraternity—people, it has become very clear to me, he holds in contempt. "Born with a silver spoon in their mouth," is something he says often, like every time he walks me home down The Row. Like I'm living with silver spoons.

"He's got an English final tomorrow morning," I say instead. "I'm sure he's hitting the books hard."

"Admirable," Diane says. "From a distance. Too much studying up close . . ." She shudders. "I don't want to catch anything."

I smile and slink down lower in my chair. It's a hard-backed, hard-seated chair, but when you're a little bit drunk, it doesn't really matter about the chair.

Diane brings her tequilas to Doug Anderson, angel come to Earth, and with much noise and cheers, they lick salt off their hands, shoot the shots, and suck a lemon wedge. Diane holds her shot glass aloft and dances a little dance around Doug, who watches her with a big smile on his perfectly gorgeous face.

She can have him if she wants him, and who wouldn't want him?

"She's got it bad," Laurie says at my shoulder, her voice low, a thrum against my ear.

"And that ain't good?" I say, quoting some song I can't remember. "It sure looks good to me."

Laurie looks at me. "How's it going with Greg? You two okay?"

"Fine," I say, staring down at the tabletop. It's dark, scarred, and stained, like my soul.

More symbols, more metaphors, more similes; and there are only more English courses in my future. I may not survive intact, my brain forever after trained to think in symbols, my sentences burbling out in either iambic pentameter or haiku. Wouldn't Greg love that? The thought makes me laugh, sourly. Like a tequila lemon.

See? Another simile. I'm drowning in them.

"Are you going home for break?" I ask Laurie. I'm not. It's too far. ULA's schedule is unlike any other college schedule; we get a two-week break at Christmas, come back to school for a week or so of classes, then a week of finals. At the end of all that, in mid-January, we get a few days off before spring semester starts. Only those students who live within driving distance of LA go home for semester break. I'll be stuck on a campus that's mostly empty, sitting in my room reading English novels and watching *Colombo* and *Kojak*.

Laurie looks across the room, her gaze scanning the dark corners of the Four-O. Her eyes stop briefly on a group of guys hugging the bar, and then move on. "Missy and I are catching a ride with Joan. We're leaving Saturday morning, trying to miss the Friday San Francisco traffic."

Laurie lights a cigarette, her gaze going back to that group of guys at the bar. I think they're Rho Delts.

I just keep watching Gary, wondering if anyone can tell that I'm with him, you know, in the biblical sense.

Okay, so I've had sex with Gary. I admit it. I also admitted that I'm a horrible person. That covers all the bases, doesn't it? I'm all about covering my bases.

Greg.

Gary.

Horrible person.

Yeah, bases covered.

Laurie doesn't answer me; she's looking again at the far corner of the bar, smoking her cigarette slowly and casually. But her eyes aren't casual. I look over at the guys she's looking at: three of them, one of them really tall with longish hair. Pete.

"What's going on with Pete?" I ask, tilting my chin in their direction.

Laurie shifts her gaze away from them and reaches across the table to flick her cigarette ash into the ashtray.

"Nothing much," she says, her hair sliding forward to hide part of her face from me.

"Did you guys have a fight?" I say, looking him over.

"No. We're okay," she says. "We're just not serious."

"Oh," I say. What else is there to say? I'm always serious. I don't date if it's not serious. I don't understand nonserious dating. What's the point if it's not serious?

Laurie shrugs and takes another drag off her cigarette. She's switched from Winstons to Virginia Slims recently, though I don't know why. Living with a smoker when I don't smoke doesn't bother me; my parents both smoke. I'm used to living life in a haze.

I think that was another metaphor.

"He's a nice guy, but we're taking it slowly," she says. "You want a beer? I'm buying."

I shake my head as she stands up and walks to the bar, about five feet from where Pete Steinhagen is standing. He hasn't taken his eyes off her since she started moving. She hasn't looked at him once since she started moving.

I know what that means. When a girl is too careful around a guy, it can only mean she really needs to be careful around him.

I don't think that sounds as profound as it actually is.

"Karen," Gary says. I look up. He's standing next to me, his crotch at my eye level. I tilt my head back and look up at his face. He's got a very nice face. "Do you want to get some air?"

I look around the Four-O for a few seconds, watching to see who, if anyone, is watching me. No one seems to be. Look how careful I'm being. I'm always so careful. I always have so much to be careful about.

"Why not?" I answer, scraping back my chair.

Gary and I leave by the front door, passing Missy and Cindy Gabrielle as they're coming in. We nod and say hello, but Gary is pressing me through, his hand on my back, and so I keep moving. It's dark outside, except for all the streetlights and headlights and taillights streaming up and down Figueroa, and the light over the door of the Four-O, but still, it's pretty dark. And it's cold.

Gary is wearing dark blue cords and a light beige cotton crew-neck sweater. He doesn't look cold. I'm wearing a skintight pair of JAG Jeans and a red V-neck sweater. I'm freezing.

"It's freezing out here," I say.

"How do you ever make it in Connecticut?" he says

"I wear a coat. And gloves. And earmuffs."

Gary smiles, drags me over to a parked car in front of the Four-O, leans his butt against the fender, and nestles me against him, his thighs bracketing mine. I'm not cold anymore.

"You're a great coat."

My head is tucked under his chin so I can feel the smile disappearing from his face. I tuck my arms up in front of me and press against his chest, nuzzling my face into his neck.

"I need to tell you something," he says.

"Don't hold back," I say, kissing his neck.

"I, uh, graduated."

I lift my mouth from his skin and look up into his eyes. "Are you sure? You don't sound sure."

"I'm sure. I graduated. Early. This month. I won't be coming back for spring semester."

He's looking down at me, his hands on my waist, almost like he's holding me tight so that I won't fly into some sort of girly, screaming rage. I mean, why would I do that? He flirted with me, slept with me, and ditched me. It's not like he didn't know he was graduating a semester early three months ago. It's not like he didn't know it two months ago, when I first slept with him. Or three days ago, when I had sex with him in the carrels at Darvey.

I feel a little sick, to be honest.

Sure, I feel my heart crack right down the middle. Sure, I want to cry and hit him a few times. Sure, I have to bury the daydreams I'd nourished of him proposing before he graduated in June and of the life we might have had in one of those little Texas oil towns. It won't be hard, once I get used to this dream being dead. I've had other dreams die, dreams that looked just like this.

I thought I was going to marry my eighth-grade boyfriend; I didn't bother to think about what he'd do for a living, but we'd live in Connecticut and have two kids and spend every Christmas Eve with my parents. I felt so mature, willing to give up Christmas Day to his parents.

I thought I was going to marry my tenth-grade boyfriend, that we would go off to college together and live a pretty life in a pretty town somewhere in New England. He cheated on me and then I cheated on him, and a year after doing that to each other over and over again, we finally broke up for good.

I thought I was going to marry my senior-year boyfriend, but he went to college in Ohio and I didn't.

I know what this particular chain of pain feels like, every link of it.

I think I'm going to cry.

But I won't. I just won't. I can't, because that would make it all worse, you know? It would make it all true, like I really am a slut and he really never cared about me at all, and no one wants me forever because I'm not pretty enough.

Gary doesn't want me.

No. No, it's not that. It's that it didn't work out because the timing was off, and I don't really want him anyway. Not really.

I'm pretty sure I wouldn't have liked living in Texas anyway.

"Congratulations," I say, stepping away from him, crossing my arms over my chest. "I wish you'd told me sooner. I could have gotten you a nice gift."

Gary takes a deep breath. His shoulders relax. He takes another deep, loud breath. Feeling better, are we? All the potential drama averted?

What a coldhearted bastard. I can't believe I ever thought I cared about this guy.

"It just worked out, a last-minute kind of thing."

"Really. Congratulations."

I take another step away from him. What was I thinking? Snuggling against a guy, a guy who is not my boyfriend, in front of the Four-O. Like everyone in the world couldn't see me?

In the biggest jinx of all time, the jinx of all jinxes, as if just thinking that thought made it happen, Greg drives by. He's in the passenger seat of his roommate's car, a white Ford, which I happen to know on sight because the paint job is so bad that even I can spot the car a mile off. I see Greg's face, a flash of white in the neon darkness of LA. I see his scowl; I see the car slow, swerve slightly, and then keep going. There's no slowing down here, not on Figueroa, not in front of the Four-O. But they can always go around the block and drive by again, or find a parking spot, or something. Something bad. Something that forces me to have a confrontation with my boyfriend about why I'm standing outside a bar talking to a guy who is really just giving me the most coldhearted brush-off of all brush-offs.

"You know that guy?" Gary says, looking after the Ford.

"Yeah. I do," I say, watching to see if the Ford tries to make a U-turn. It doesn't. Gone for good, or coming back?

That was another metaphor, wasn't it? I can't take any more metaphors right now.

I'm not going to tell Gary how I know Greg or who Greg is. What he doesn't know won't hurt him, will it?

"Look, have a nice life," I say to Gary. "Good luck in the desert."

"Thanks," Gary says, stepping close to me, looking like he wants to hug me or kiss me or something. "You're great, Karen. You've been great."

How? Like in bed? Like I was a good lay, thanks a bunch, gotta run?

I'm not going to cry. I'm not.

"Thanks," I say. I'm trying not to be sarcastic, but it's an uphill battle. "So, I'll see you around. Or I guess I won't." I laugh, keeping my distance, but Gary keeps closing the gap. What does he expect? One for the road?

What is not going to happen, besides one last quickie, is that I let Gary see that this hurts. He's not getting one more thing from me. There's always another guy out there, right there, close by and ready to scoop up. When one drifts off, another steps up to home plate, ready to go all the way, hit all the bases.

That was a rotten metaphor. I can't believe I even thought that.

I'm not alone. I'm never alone. Guys can smell when a girl is alone and desperate, hunting for some guy, *any* guy to want her. I'm never hunting. I'm never desperate. I've always got one guy, at least one guy. There's always another guy, right? Always some guy who . . . who what?

Wants a piece of tail.

No. I'm not going to think that.

Gary's history, and Greg, my lovely boyfriend, Greg, just reclaimed home base.

It's true. I'd preferred Gary to Greg, just a little bit, just the very beginning of a brand-new love to take the place of a tired old one. But Greg is great, really great, and I love him. I love him completely. I just got distracted for a little bit.

I don't know what's wrong with me. Why can't I just be happy with the guy who loves me?

I will be. From now on, I will be. Just don't let Greg find out. Please, God, don't let Greg stop loving me.

"It's been real," I say, half turning away from Gary. "Are you going back in?"

Gary studies me, trying to figure out . . . what? That I'm not going to cry? That I never cared all that much? That I'm putting a good face on a broken heart?

Let him wonder.

"No, I've got my last final tomorrow. I need to get going," he says.

"Good luck. Hope you ace it," I say, smiling freely and easily. No broken heart here, Gary; keep moving. Nothing to see.

"Okay," he says. "Well, bye, Karen. It's been great."

I don't bother to answer. I've said good-bye, wished him well, played it cool ten times in the last two minutes. The performance is over.

Gary jaywalks across Figueroa and disappears slowly into the city-bright darkness, walking hurriedly toward The Row.

It hits me then like a club: the crawl of pain banging at my heart, that upswell of nausea, the tears pressing against the back of my throat and behind my eyes.

"Hey! Are you coming or going?" Ellen shouts from across the street. She's about to jaywalk her way over. She just has to wait for a few cars to get out of her way, one of them an ugly white Ford.

I clear my throat and say, "Going. I think." I shrug and point to the car that's double-parked for a fraction of a second while Greg hops out.

Greg came back. Okay. Here we go. The performance isn't over yet. God, I'm so tired. I just want to rest for a minute, to let down my guard and weep for a few hours.

"Where is he?" Greg says softly, but his look isn't soft. It's hard and angry. "Who was that?" He's not making a huge scene because of Ellen, because if there's anything Greg hates, it's making a scene and looking like a fool.

Join the club.

"Just some guy I met at an exchange once," I say, which is nothing but the truth. It's just not the whole truth. This isn't a court of law; I'm not under oath. There is no penalty for perjury.

"He was hugging you."

"I was hugging him. He told me that he just graduated. Congratulations, you know?" I say. Again, the truth. Sort of.

"Hi, Greg!" Ellen says, breathless from running across the street. "Are you all finished?"

She means is he all finished taking tests, but the words have a different meaning for me. Are we all finished? Is Greg finished with me?

He can't be. I love him. I can't imagine life without him. Or not easily imagine it.

"No. One to go," Greg says, all smiles for Ellen. He's like that. Greg really hates to not look good, to not look perfectly composed and charming and on top of things. I'd say that's perfectly normal. "How about you?"

Ellen raises her hands in the air and does a little dance. "Finished! The end! Let the party begin!"

Greg laughs easily, but I can feel the chill buried in his eyes, hiding behind the happy twinkle he's displaying for Ellen's benefit.

"Karen? You done?" Ellen asks. "Are you ready to party with me? Greg can't, poor slob. He has to crack the books."

"I'm done, but I'm exhausted," I say. "I'll see you later at the house, Ellen."

"Okay," she says joyously. "See you later."

Greg smiles until Ellen swings past the curtain into the Four-O, the sounds of talking and laughter, the smells of smoke and beer, slithering out into the street.

Greg and I stand on the sidewalk silently. I'm looking at him. He's looking out at the street.

"I'll walk you home," he says after a few tense moments.

"Thanks," I say. I slip my hand into his and we wait for a break in the traffic. "I'm really going to miss you. I wish we could spend semester break together, don't you?"

"Yeah, I do," he says as we rush across the street.

I mean it. I make myself mean the words because I actually do, even if I don't feel the words. Say what you mean and mean what you say, and I do. I really do. I just don't say what I feel, or even feel what I say. Not this minute, anyway. But I will feel it. I will. I'll love Greg again because he'll love me. He *does* love me, and that's the only thing that matters.

"Do you still need to study for your English final?"

"Yeah. I guess you want to go home."

We're in front of the Beta Pi house, our steps faltering. The brick walk calls to me, but I can't give in. I have to make sure everything is fine with Greg.

"No, not at all," I say. "Why don't we go to your place?"

He smiles slightly and, holding hands, we walk down The Row. His apartment is just off Adams, a long walk down The Row and across Vermont. Greg is talking about his roommate and his Spanish final and how his mother's uncle taught him how to ride one summer; Greg likes to talk and he mostly likes to talk about himself. I don't mind. He's an interesting guy. At the moment, because of trying so hard to get my Gary reaction under control, I'm not actually paying much attention to Greg. It's foolish of me, I know, but I feel kind of loose and weepy at the moment. I'm definitely not at full strength.

Why I should need to be at any strength just to be with my boyfriend is a question I'm in no mood to wrestle with.

We climb the concrete stairs to his second-floor apartment and walk in as his roommate, Bruce, is walking out.

"Hi. I'm going to see a movie. I'll be out late," Bruce says, taking the steps two at a time, slowing long enough to give me a leer and Greg a grin. I don't enjoy being leered at, but what can I do about it?

Greg ushers me in to his apartment, an almost identical layout to my apartment last year. The carpet is rust-colored shag that hasn't seen a vacuum in months, and the kitchen is a single sliver of linoleum and Formica dotted with dirty dishes, a dingy washrag, a quarter of a bottle of Joy, and a stained dish towel hanging on the oven handle. Beyond the kitchen is the sole bedroom with two twin beds sitting on the floor. The curtains only have two-thirds of their hooks. It is, overall and in particular, a dingy, unhappy, unloved-looking apartment. Of course I give in to the urge to love it and take care of it whenever I'm here. I can't help myself. Who could?

The kitchen table is piled high with textbooks and spiral notebooks and a dirty coffee cup. Greg doesn't seem to notice the mess, or even his books. Greg puts his arms around me from behind and presses himself against my back, murmuring against my hair, "You look so good."

The drapes are open and the picture window is black and shiny, reflecting us. I don't know who's out there in the courtyard watching us, but anyone could be. Greg doesn't seem to care. I guess it doesn't matter who sees us. We're in love and we're only hugging.

"I just look good in red," I say.

"You look better out of it," he says.

Still behind me, his hands come up to cup my breasts. I can see this in the reflection. I can feel it, too, but it's seeing it that has me sort of frozen deep inside. *I have to do this.* . . . What a stupid thing to think. I want to do this. I love him. He loves me. We've been together for more than two years, so I know that this is the real thing and that this is the guy I'm going to marry. Greg is real. Gary was a distraction. I've got to stop letting myself get distracted.

Greg, his arms wrapped around me from behind, walks me to the bedroom, kissing my neck as we go. The bedroom is dark, the light from the alley streetlamp dim behind the dingy curtains. I can feel his hard-on at my back, an insistent, heavy weight, pressing against me. Greg turns me in his arms and I wrap my arms around his neck, standing on tiptoe to kiss his mouth. Two kisses later and I'm naked and on my back, Greg lying between my legs, his hands on my breasts.

I'm trying so hard. I'm trying to lose myself in this, to feel something, to want Greg and to want this. And I do. Kind of. I almost do, if he'd just give me a few more minutes, just a few more kisses and a few more caresses and just one whispered *I love you.* But instead I get a hard shove into me that goes nowhere. And I get Greg shoving a pillow under my butt so that I'm angled up toward the ceiling.

"Here we go," he says. "That works."

And then he's pushing into me, and I can feel that I'm not wet enough, but I guess he can't feel that because he grunts his way to orgasm and then lies down on me with a smile of pure bliss, and I hold him to me, tight. Holding him to me, pressing him against me, molding our bodies together. That's what I do, whispering, "I love you," against his neck, running my fingers through the hair on his nape, embracing him with my whole heart and my entire body.

"Me, too," he whispers, sliding out of me.

He goes to the bathroom and gets a washcloth and hands it to me; I wipe the wetness from my crotch, trying to look pretty and sexy while I do it, and then he says, "I've got to study. That exam is going to be a bear and I still need to analyze three poems I haven't read yet."

In a minute or two, we're back in the living room, Greg at the kitchen table, dark head bent over his books, a contented air about him. The light in the living room and kitchen is so bright, so painfully bright. I put my arms around Greg from behind, hugging him, kissing his neck as he sits at his studies.

"I've got to study, Karen. Can you keep yourself busy for a while? Then I'll walk you back to the house," he says.

"Sure. Take your time," I say.

I look around and pick up some newspapers that were on the floor, straighten them into an orderly square, no ragged edges, and put them on the coffee table. I plump the cushions on the couch and close the drapes. I go into the kitchen and wash a frying pan, three plates with melted cheese stuck on them, five glasses, a butter knife, and three forks. I put the dishes away, humming a little tune that has no true melody, just something I'm making up as I go.

"Karen, could you keep it down? I'm trying to study."

"Sorry."

I straighten the dish towel on the oven handle and scrub the sink. I make sure the Joy bottle is perfectly straight and lined up with the faucets. I walk into the bathroom and go, fixing the toilet paper so that it unwinds the right way, then wiping down the sink and countertop so that they're spotless and dry. I fold and straighten the towels.

Greg is still at his books, seemingly oblivious to my presence. That's okay. He's got to study.

I wander into the bedroom and make his bed so that no one can tell what we did. Even me. And then I wander back out to the living room, things looking much better, much tidier and more organized and as pretty as things can look in a college apartment shared by two guys. There's not a single picture hanging on the walls, but there is that Farrah Fawcett poster, the one of her in the red bathing suit. I don't look anything like Farrah Fawcett, nothing at all. She's so beautiful.

"I need to get going," I say to Greg.

"Can you wait awhile? I'm having trouble understanding this one poem."

"Which poem is it?"

"'In Distrust of Merits,' by Marianne Moore."

"I know that poem," I say. "'Hate-hardened heart, O heart of iron / iron is iron till it is rust. / There never was a war that was / not inward . . .'"

I've remembered those lines; I don't want to think why. Also, the last line: *Beauty is everlasting / and dust is for a time.*

"That's it. It's nuts."

"What don't you understand?" I say. "Maybe I can help."

And so I do. An hour later, Greg, feeling less nervous about his final in American Literature, walks me home. We hold hands and he tells me about a summer camping trip with his parents at Yosemite when he was eleven and of a prank he played on his high school girlfriend that wound up in the yearbook. I listen and laugh at the right moments. At the steps of the Beta Pi house, Greg kisses me good night and then I wave good-bye.

I let my eyes wander over to the front of the EE Tau house twice during Greg's monologue. Okay, maybe three times, but overall, I think I did pretty well.

Actually, I think I deserve an Academy Award.

Ellen

– Spring 1977 –

"I thought this class was supposed to be a Mick," I say.

Mick is short for Mickey Mouse, shorthand for an easy way to get course credits in required fields. It's a ULA thing.

"That's the word," Karen says.

"I needed one more class to max out my biological sciences," Diane says. "Hello, Human Sexuality."

"Have you read any of the book?" Karen says. "It's five hundred pages."

"And cost forty bucks, used," Diane says.

"You're the one who talked us into taking it," I say, looking at Diane down the row. We're sitting in the dark of Bowman, the room nearly full, the professor talking, everyone sitting quietly, taking notes. Everyone but us. We're sitting side by side, whispering.

"Hey, I heard it was a Mick, too!" Diane says. "No one said the first midterm was twenty-six pages long."

"Selective memory," I say.

"They said it was a Mick," Karen says. "*Everybody* says it."

"*Everybody* is a liar," I say. The first test was brutal. Does it really matter that I know how many sperm are in a single ejaculation when it takes only one to do the job?

"At least today we're seeing a movie," Karen says, balancing her purse on top of her books, on top of her lap, snuggling down in her seat. Karen loves movies like nobody else I know. She's seen them all, not just the famous ones.

"Yeah," I say, already wondering what kind of movie they're going to show us in Human Sexuality. It can't be X-rated. It has to be illegal to show a bunch of minors an X-rated movie. Still, the midterm was twenty-six pages long. All bets are off in this class.

The professor says from the stage, "And so our perception of male and female sexuality is formed and controlled by cultural norms that become fossilized over time. Today we're going to see two films on masturbation—"

"What?!" I say.

"Oh, God, no," Diane moans.

"—and I want you to notice the differences in the artistic quality of the films and how those differences, subtle or not, influence your reaction and therefore define your perception. I'll leave it at that for now, but be ready to discuss this once these two short films are finished."

The lights go out. The professor gets off the stage and sits in the front row. Karen hunches down in her seat, looking like she wants to crawl under the seat in front of her. Diane has her hands over her mouth. I'm too shocked to move. There are more than a hundred people in this room and I'm being forced to watch somebody masturbate.

I can't believe I just thought that.

The film starts. A nice-looking girl with a trim figure and long dark hair walks into a bedroom. She's in her underwear. It's a nice room. It's clean, her bed's made, there's a cute little lamp on her desk, and the lamp is on. She lights a candle and the flame looks kind of cozy. She puts a record on the stereo in her room, all her movements calm and deliberate, like she knows what she's going to do next and she's cool with that. Soft music begins to play, not hard rock, but something upbeat. She takes off her bra and lets it fall to the floor. She lies back on her bed and starts touching her breasts, rubbing her hands over them, playing with her nipples.

Some guy four rows down and off to the side makes a chortling noise. The professor turns around and looks at the students in his class. We all sit perfectly still, eyes front, like students are supposed to do.

The girl slides her panties off. One hand stays on a nipple and the other winds its way down to her crotch. The camera stays steady, not moving, and the shot is from the side so we don't actually see the goods, just her hand going like crazy between her legs. Then her legs twitch, her breath gets short, she dips her head forward, and she makes a *here I come* noise.

The audience is silent, watching her.

The shot fades out, the music still playing, until that dies out, too.

The next film starts right away; I barely have a chance to look over at Diane and Karen. Karen is wide-eyed and so low in her seat that I don't know how she can see over the chair in front of her. Diane has her hands over her eyes and she's shaking her head.

All I know is that I feel assaulted and shocked. I don't have anything in my head but pure horror.

In the next film, there's no music and the lighting is really dim, almost murky. There's a sloppy-looking guy with messed-up hair and dirty jeans in a pigsty of a room. His bed is unmade and the sheets are gross. There is crap all over the floor: record albums, an overflowing ashtray, piles of clothes. He looks at a *Playboy* centerfold, drops his pants, grabs his dick, and jerks off as fast as he can. The whole thing takes less than five minutes, and I'm talking about the film. The guy jerking off, maybe three minutes. The minute he's finished catching the goo—oh, excuse me, three hundred million sperm—in a dirty rag he picks up off the floor, he wipes himself, yanks his jeans on, and that's the end of it.

I've never seen a guy naked before, never seen a dick, and this is my first look. Fucking fantastic.

The lights come up in the auditorium.

The professor walks up to the stage and looks at us expectantly.

There's not a sound in the room. Even the guys aren't chuckling. In fact, the guys in the room look embarrassed. Damn straight.

"So, what are your thoughts? How would you describe your reactions to these two very different portrayals of masturbation?"

"I think I'm going to puke," Diane whispers, her head buried in her lap.

"I think I'm going to tell Ed just what his twelve thousand a year is paying for," I say.

"I think I'm going to try to forget I ever saw this," Karen says.

"Like that's going to happen," Diane says, and then she gets up and leaves the auditorium.

Karen looks at Diane's retreating back, then at me; then we do what we have to do. We get up and follow Diane out of the auditorium and into the chilly spring sunshine. Our bikes are all parked next to each other, crammed in with the others, foot pedals tangled. Diane has her head down and is twirling her lock dial like a safe cracker.

"Okay," I say. "I'm up for ditching class today."

"Where to?" Karen says, yanking her bike free of a rogue pedal. The offending bike falls down. "Time to make our escape. Pronto. Before I get yelled at for the dead bike in the road."

"Serves 'em right for crowding you," I say. "Diane?"

Diane has unchained her bike and lifts her head to look at me. She looks green around the gills.

"Come on, Diane," Karen says, rolling her bike out of the pack to the street. "Let's blow this pop stand."

"Don't say *blow*," I say.

Diane snorts a laugh and then shakes her head. "You have no shame."

"At least I don't masturbate on camera," I say.

"Your standards are impressive," Karen says.

"Haven't I always said so?" I say.

"That was just vile," Diane says, getting on her bike, her books dumped in the basket in the front. "My dad would kill someone if he knew they showed us that."

"Really? Let's tell him. I'd like to see that professor bite the dust," I say.

Karen laughs. "Come on. If we're going to ditch, let's do something fun."

"Let's hit the Dust," Diane says. The Stardust Apartments is where Missy lives; she calls it the Dust, so we call it the Dust. Why not? It's dusty. "But let's get some food on the way."

"We just had lunch an hour ago," Karen says.

"What is your problem, Mitchell?" I say. "It's never too soon to have . . . ?" I look at Diane.

"Boston cream pie," Diane says, a light in her eyes.

"That'll settle your stomach," Karen says.

"Damn skippy, it will," Diane says. "Let's roll."

We climb on our bikes and head down University Avenue, dodging bikes until we're in the stream of students heading off campus and merging in with them.

"What if Missy's in class?" Karen says.

"She leaves the door unlocked, for casual strangers, like us," I say.

"Safety first," Karen says.

"Yeah, we're talking about Missy," I say.

We ride for a while, comfortable in the throng of bikes and students, making our way to The Row. The crowd thins slowly the farther we get from campus until it's just the three of us riding side by side down The Row.

I cast a glance at Karen; she's looking at Diane. I look at Diane.

"Will you guys stop staring at me?" Diane says. "What are you expecting? My head to turn around on my neck like that girl in *The Exorcist*?"

"I was kind of expecting the green vomit," I say.

Diane chuckles and Karen says, "Are you okay?"

"Jim-dandy."

Karen and I look at each other again.

"Let's park at the house and then walk to the Dust," Karen says.

"Jim-dandy," I say.

Diane shakes her head, her black hair blowing back behind her shoulders. "Find your own catchphrase."

"Eat shit and die," I say.

"Sorry. I think Missy already grabbed that one," Karen says.

It's as we're in front of the Zeta house, just a few down from ours, when Laurie comes out of the house and starts unlocking her bike.

"Hey! McCormick!" I yell. "Ditch class with us! We're going to hang at Missy's and eat Boston cream pie."

We're in front of Beta Pi by the time I get it all out, and Laurie is looking typically Laurie, slightly interested and ready to blow us off. She's been ready to blow us off for months now. I can't figure out what's wrong with her or what we did.

"Who's got the pie?" Laurie asks.

"You. Once you buy it and truck it over to the Dust," I say.

"Slick, I have to admit," Laurie says.

"I'll go with you," Karen says. "I don't want to be with Ryan, anyway. She's going to pull an *Exorcist* any minute now."

"That sounds pretty," Laurie says, "but why?"

"A simple case of masturbation overload," I say.

"I've heard that can happen," Laurie says, staring at Diane.

"Olson, shut the hell up," Diane says. "I need pie. I need it now. McCormick, are you going to be in my rescue party or what?"

We're all staring at Laurie, so she finally says, "Okay. Boston cream pie it is. I'll just skip Spanish. It's not like I have to pass it or anything."

"Adios, chica," I say. "*Donde esta la* Boston cream pie?"

"*Dejeme en paz!*" Laurie says.

"Well, that sounded rude," I say.

"Diane, throw up. Break the tension," Karen says. "Come on, Laurie, let's go. Save a Coke for me."

"Got it," I say. "Let's go, Ryan. We can't have you puking on the Beta Pi lawn. It's a Standards offense for sure."

Less than one hour later, Karen and Laurie are in the Dust, Diane is laughing, Missy is swearing, and I'm cutting the pie into very healthy chunks.

"Okay, so I want the full scoop on Greg," I say to Karen. "Are you guys getting married?"

"Yes," she says. "We plan to, once we graduate."

"He's cute," I say. "Kind of quiet, but cute."

"It's called discretion," Laurie says, taking a plate of pie. "Some people have it."

"And some people don't," Diane says. "And them that's got it, spread it around. Or maybe if they have discretion, they don't spread it around. Line judge! We need a ruling over here."

"Whatever the ruling, spreading it around sounds sleazy," Karen says, waving off the pie, sipping her Coke out of the can. She probably doesn't trust Missy's glasses, and I can't say I blame her.

"Eye of the beholder," I say. "So, Greg actually asked you?"

Karen looks down at her soda and rubs her finger around the hole. "Yeah. Of course."

"What about you, McCormick? You've been with Pete for how long now? Is it serious?" I ask.

Laurie shrugs and looks down at the carpet. The Dust put in new carpet over the summer. It still looks like shit.

"What are you doing, taking a survey?" Diane asks me.

"Yeah. You got a problem with that?"

"Since you asked, yeah. I do. Unless you want to share what's going on with you and Mike. When are you going to fish or cut bait with that guy?" Diane says.

"I'm not following," I say. But I am. Kind of. Mike Dunn is a jerk. I know he's a jerk, but he's a fascinating jerk who every now and then seems so sexy that I can barely breathe. We're not exactly dating. It's more like he's Jaws and I'm the girl swimming in the dark. Everybody knows what happened to her.

"Are you dating him or what?" Diane says.

"Or what," I say. "He's cute, but what's the rush? I'm busy anyway."

I am busy. I'm the president of Beta Pi this year. It was my idea to run, and then it was my idea to convince Karen to run for pledge trainer and Laurie to run for Panhellenic delegate and Diane to run for Rush chair. Diane refused to run; she's too busy being the editor of the *Seahorse*, the Navy ROTC yearbook. Karen and Laurie fell in with it. It only took me ten minutes to get to Karen. Laurie was a harder sell. But when isn't she?

"We're all busy," Diane says, "but when has that ever been an excuse for giving up guys?"

"I'm not giving up guys," I say. "I'm just taking it slow."

"Same here," Laurie says.

"Not me," Karen says. "I say damn the torpedoes and full speed ahead."

"It's been said before," Missy says.

"Yeah, and I think the guy who first said it died," Laurie says.

"Admiral Farragut," Diane says. "We all die anyway."

"Might as well get a cool quote out of it," Karen says, getting up from the floor to gather our plates and take them to the kitchen.

"Jim-dandy," Diane says. "I'm going to have to come up with a new one. I don't want that on my tombstone."

"Eat shit and die is taken," I say. "Missy grabbed it, didn't you?"

"I can live with that," Missy says. "Gotta pee. Don't say anything fun until I get back."

Missy walks to the bedroom in the back and closes the door to the bathroom.

"Are you still resisting Midshipman Temptation?" Karen asks. Before Diane can answer, Karen says, "You've got more willpower than I'd have."

"Glad you think so," Diane says.

Laurie raises an eyebrow. "Maybe taking him to the last party was a mistake."

"Only if you think willpower is a good thing," Diane says. "Which I'm sure you do. How's Pete feel about that?"

"Hey, come on," Karen says, everything about her screaming *Settle down.* "Doug is the most gorgeous guy I've ever seen, so who can blame Diane? And Pete is obviously in love with Laurie, and what could be wrong with that? Okay, so Mike is kind of a thug, but I think we can all agree that Ellen can take him."

We all laugh at that, even me. Because even though I'm not sure I can take Mike, I like the idea that I can.

"So, everyone's dating? Everyone has the man of her choice by the scruff of his neck? Nice. Nice and tidy. I love it," I say.

Mike isn't my boyfriend, even though I am sort of dating him, but I want him to be my boyfriend, mostly when I'm drunk, and then I sober up and know that that's the dumbest decision in the world. And then I get plastered and he looks so good again. It's exhausting, but I'm young. I can take it. I'd just like to get the feeling that I'm not alone in my romantic struggles. I feel alone.

"I just dumped Brian. You can have him if you want him," Missy says, coming back into the room.

"No kidding! What happened?" Karen asks from the kitchen, the water running into the sink.

"Things went south after I met his mother."

"Bummer," I say. "I'll pass."

"Better now than later," Diane says.

Karen finishes the dishes while we lie around, feeling full and sleepy.

"What the hell was that professor thinking?" I say after a few minutes. "That was so gross. What do I know now that I didn't before? I could have told you that watching a guy jerk off is never going to be a Hollywood moneymaker."

"I saw a guy jerk off once," Karen says. "Well, he kind of jerked off."

"Isn't it an either-or thing?" I say.

"Like I'm an expert?" Karen says. "He was retarded or had water on the brain—I'm not sure—but he was in my high school and sat right in front of me in American History, and one day he put his hand down his pants—he wore really loose pants—and he started going at it."

"Oh, my God!" I say, starting to laugh. "Nobody did anything?"

"Like what?" Karen says. "Even the teacher didn't know what to do."

"So what happened?" Diane says.

"I watched. I couldn't look away, and I tried."

Karen starts laughing and then we're all laughing.

"Guys are kind of gross," I say.

"Now, now," Karen says, coming out of the kitchen. "That's just your cultural prejudices speaking."

"I can live with that."

Diane

— Spring 1977 —

Doug is lying on his bed, in his apartment off of Adams, naked and beautiful, and I am lying next to him, naked and exposed, feeling nervous about the sex, nervous about my ears, nervous about my less-than-perfect butt.

I just had sex with Doug Anderson. I just had sex with the guy I've been fantasizing about for two years. It was amazing. It was amazing because I love him; I want everything about him to become every single part of my life. I want to absorb him into me, which I have just sort of done, and I want to be locked to him for the rest of my life.

I love him.

Everything is so extremely and unbelievably perfect.

I run a hand over his chest, the hard, perfect hairlessness of it, the pale gold perfection of it. He lays his hand over mine, stilling me. I smile and we lie there, being still together, the intimacy of his bed, his sheets, the scent of sex binding us.

I love him. I love everything about him.

"You should get back to the house," he says. "You'll get in trouble."

"I can handle a little trouble," I say, teasing him, reaching down to touch his penis.

He shifts his body, moving away from my touch, a polite smile on his face.

"Really. It's okay," I say. "No one will know if I come in a few hours from now."

He sits up, his bare feet on the floor, his muscular back to me. He's so beautiful I want to sob just looking at him. I can't believe such an incredible guy wants me. All the years of being Monkey Baby fall away. I'm beautiful, really beautiful, because he thinks so.

"I don't want you to get in trouble," he says.

"Me neither," I say on a chuckle.

He's so cute, being so protective of my reputation. Dad is going to love him. Mom is going to fuss over him, buy his favorite booze, and we'll sit around and tell navy stories over the dinner table. It will all be so completely perfect.

"So, what time do you think I should head back?" I ask, sitting up and pulling the sheet around me. My boobs look better from this angle; plus my ears are covered by my hair.

"Now," he says, reaching over for his jeans, slipping them on one foot at a time, standing up to zip them.

"Now?"

"Diane," he says, looking down at me, naked in his bed. "I don't want you to get the wrong idea."

"Okay," I say, staring at him. His eyes still look so blue, even at night, even in the dark.

"I mean, this was great. You're great," he says.

"Thanks," I say, interrupting him, feeling this nasty thing building up inside of me, this weird vibe that it's all going wrong, that this isn't where I want the conversation to go and I'll do anything to head it off, to stop it cold, to freeze time and make it go back just sixty seconds. Just to the moment where we're lying side by side, barely touching, peaceful and content.

"I just feel like I need to be honest," he says.

"Good plan," I say.

Stop. Stop talking. Stop whatever it is that's in your head and that you're about to say to me. Go back sixty minutes to where you're kissing me and seducing me, urging me out of my clothes, pleading with me to let you in, to love you. Because I do love you.

I love you.

"Diane, this has been great, but I want you to know, I feel like I have to tell you, to be honest with you. I feel no love for you."

I feel no love for you.

I feel no love for you?

What the *hell*?

"What?" I say softly, my throat closing, suddenly feeling very, very naked. I'm afraid to move, afraid to show more of myself, to reveal myself to him. He's seen it all, but now I feel naked.

His blue eyes melt into mine. "I'm just being honest."

I exhale sharply and hear the heaviness of tears in my throat. No. *Hell*, no.

"Okay," I say, looking around the room for my clothes. They're all on the floor, scattered. I think my top is on the couch in the living room. "Yeah. What?"

"Diane," he says. He looks embarrassed, uncomfortable, like I've messed this up somehow and he's too much of a gentleman to lay it all out for me, that explaining it to death would just humiliate us both. "Come on. It's just not going to work out."

It's not going to work out. How does he know it's not going to work out? Because he saw me naked? Because I'm frigid or something? I'm not frigid. At least, I don't think I'm frigid.

"Yeah. Really. Okay," I say, because I don't know what to say. I don't understand a single thing that's happening; all I know is that I've got to find my clothes and get the hell out of Dodge. "Could you give me a minute?" I say.

Doug looks a bit startled, but then he nods and leaves the bedroom. I jump out of bed and start rooting around the floor for my panties. I slide them on, backward, and I don't give a damn right now. I need to get out of here before I really embarrass myself by sobbing and clinging to him and begging him to love me, goddammit, please, why can't you love me? What is so wrong with me? I grab my jeans and pull them on, rooting around with my toes for my wedges. Doug comes back in with me half-dressed, naked from the waist up, running a quick hand through my hair. He's got my blouse.

"Just leave it," I say, grabbing it off the bed when he tosses it there. I half want to run out the door, putting my shirt on as I walk, but I'm trying so hard to keep the tiniest bit of dignity. And then I think, *Little late for dignity, Ryan,* and so I walk out of the bedroom, thrusting one arm through a sleeve, see my bra smashed down in between the cushions of the couch, grab that, and walk out the door.

Doug is murmuring something, but it's not an apology and it's not words of love or regret, so I keep moving; once I'm out, down the concrete stairs and out the gate and onto the street, I shove my bra into my purse and finish buttoning my blouse.

I made it. I got out without making a scene.

That's when I start to cry.

I'm still crying when I get to The Row, and it's quiet, it's almost dead, and so I'm alone on the street. Bastard didn't even walk me home. I could have been raped, or mugged.

"Hey, baby, what's crawling out of your purse?" says some guy sitting on a lawn chair with a beer in the middle of what should be a lawn but what is, in fact, a dry patch of dirt. "I think you forgot something!" He laughs, swigs his beer, and I shove my bra deeper into my purse.

"Up yours."

It's past midnight, about one, I guess, and I just want to get into the house and crawl into bed, but then I look at the house, that big light over the door, and I can't face it. I can't face anybody yet. They'll be up—someone will be up—and they'll see my face and they'll know I was out with Doug, and . . . Shit, I just can't face it. It's as I'm veering away from the house, digging around in my purse for my keys, when Karen comes out the front door. She's wearing wide-legged jeans and her old navy blue high school sweatshirt.

"Diane?" she says, holding the door open behind her.

Shit. I don't want anyone to see me now. I try to hide in the shadows, but I can't; there are too many damned lights on The Row.

"Diane? Are you okay?" she says.

"Yeah. I'm fine, sweetie. You go back to bed."

She comes out, the big door closing behind her. She's barefoot, and the hem of her jeans is dragging three inches on the ground.

"I was playing backgammon with Ellen and saw you through the window. What happened?"

Then I start to cry again and she comes down onto the sidewalk and puts her arms around me and starts rocking me, like she's my mom or something, only my mom's not much of a hugger.

"What happened?" she says, rubbing my back, stroking my hair.

"I've got to get out of here," I say, my breath hitching in my lungs, my nose running like a faucet. I wipe my nose on my sleeve, trying to suck it up and pull myself together, but I can't. I'm in a million, billion pieces and I can't get it together.

"Okay," she says. "Let's go." I pull back to stare at her and she grins at me, pushing my hair back behind my shoulders. "You're the one with the car, so I hope you have your keys."

"I have them," I say.

"Where should we go?"

"Sweetie, it's after midnight. I can't just drag you off——"

"If I had the car, I'd drag you off. How much gas do you have?"

"Enough . . ." I say, sniffing hard, smiling a little bit. "Enough to get us to the beach and back."

"Great. I've always wanted to see the sun come up over the ocean."

"Wrong ocean," I say.

"Close enough," she says.

And so on the long, dark drive to Santa Monica, I tell Karen everything and she listens and swears at all the right parts and we do watch the sun come up, and it is close enough.

I'm sure by now everyone knows what happened. I fell into a dead sleep when Karen and I got home from the beach, skipped all my classes, but I told Karen she could tell the crew what happened. Actually, I wanted her to tell. Better her than me. I didn't want to relive the whole thing again and again with each telling. When you live in a sorority house, there's one true thing: no secrets.

I take a deep breath, feel it catch in the bottom of my lungs as a huge sob, choke it down, and walk into the front five-way, the house party room. When we switch up rooms every semester, everyone wants this room.

The conversation stops instantly and four pairs of eyes hone in on my face like 'sniper rifles. Of course they do.

Missy is lighting up, the sound of her lighter clicking the noisiest thing in the room in that instant. She looks at me on a stiff inhale, her eyes squinting against the smoke.

Karen and Pi, who room in the five-way this semester, are scattered and sprawled on sloppily made beds around the room.

Ellen is over at the window.

It's a shocked tableau, like the last supper or something. All of them caught in mid-gossip, and here I appear, like Christ on the mountaintop.

Or something.

"Diane," Pi says, "what the hell happened? What did that stupid shit Doug Anderson think he was doing?"

Pi is ten sticks of dynamite. She's Hawaiian and her real name is Linda, but no one has called her Linda in years. Because she's Hawaiian, someone started calling her *the Pineapple*, and before a week was out, she was Pi to everyone on The Row. As the phrase *stupid shit* slams out of her mouth, she enfolds me in a quick, hard hug.

I love Pi.

"I think I'm the stupid shit in this case," I say, walking across the room to plop down next to Karen.

Karen leans her shoulder against mine and puts her hand on my thigh. "You don't have to talk about it," she says.

"What's there to talk about?" Ellen snaps. "I say we kill him."

We all laugh a little at that, and it lightens the pain more than the crying did; plus, I don't feel so alone in all this self-inflicted agony. I knew better; Dad told me what to do, or not do, and I didn't listen, and now I'm so completely messed up. I did this. I'm responsible.

Laurie walks into the room just then, stops cold, and says, "Oh, my God. Who died?"

"Doug Anderson. In about twenty-four hours, give or take," Ellen says.

My heart wants to laugh, even if my face doesn't have the strength for it.

"What happened?" Laurie asks, dropping down on the floor to lean against a bed.

They all look at me. Of course they all look at me. It's no secret that I've had it bad for Doug Anderson since forever. It's also no secret that we've been going out for a few months, if by *going out* you mean hanging at the Four-O and taking him to Beta Pi parties, which I do. "I did the deed with Anderson last night," I say as casually as possible. "Anybody got a Coke?"

Laurie gets up, slings her purse over the back of her desk chair, and reaches up for a Tab from her stash on the shelves above her desk. She holds the Tab out toward me, a questioning look on her face.

"I can't drink that shit, McCormick," I say. "Forget it. Anyway, back to the sordid tale of my unruly love life." Karen squeezes my leg and puts an arm around my shoulder. "He took me to a movie in Westwood, then back to his apartment, and so we did it, and then about a half a second later he gets all weird and turns to me and says, 'Diane, I like you, and this was great, but I have to tell you something. I feel no love for you.'"

Of course, now I'm crying again, and not even a Coke to drown my sorrows in.

I'm not going to mention the little detail that I told Doug I loved him while we were doing it. Some things you just don't share with anyone. I'm really sorry that I shared it with Anderson. Just look where it got me.

"'I feel no love for you'? Who the hell says that?" Ellen snarls.

"Doug Anderson," Missy says.

"Did he tell you he loved you before?" Pi asks, pacing around the room.

"Yeah. Sort of. He said that he really *thought* he was falling in love with me," I say. Because I don't just sleep around, okay? And I really love him. Or I did.

No. I still do.

The tears start up again, burning a hole in my chest.

He was everything I ever wanted. Everything. I just couldn't believe he was actually paying attention to me, wanting me, falling in love with me.

I guess I should have remained skeptical.

He said he was falling in love with me, or that he could see himself falling in love with me, things like that. Circling around it, like a shark around a baby seal, and I'm the seal, with big monkey ears. But when he was saying this stuff, when those beautiful words were coming out of his beautiful mouth, I believed every word. I wanted to believe. Who wouldn't?

I still want to. How could he have said all that, looked at me like that, and not meant any of it? He meant it; he had to have meant it. I must have screwed it up somehow, messed it all up, been boring or ugly or something equally unforgivable and sloppy and stupid. I had him, and then I blew it.

I just wish I could figure out what I did wrong.

"But once he sampled the goods, then he figured out he didn't?" Ellen says. "What a dick. Oops. Sorry, Diane. I didn't mean to hit so close to home."

"God, you are so sick," I say, laughing weakly. It feels great. For a few seconds, and then the sledgehammer hits me in my chest all over again. I start to cry mid-laugh. "I really loved him," I sob. "Stupid prick. Oops," I say, giggling through the tears.

"He's a total jerk," Laurie says. "I never understood what you saw in him."

"He's kind of boring, isn't he?" Karen says. "All he does is stand around and wallow in his good looks. Did he ever say anything interesting? Ever?"

Karen has her arm around my shoulder, brushing my hair back from my face. It's a very motherly gesture and I really appreciate it at the moment. I've never been big on motherly gestures from people, including my mother, but I think I could get talked out of that.

"'I feel no love for you,'" Missy repeats, working her jaw to make smoke rings that drift toward the ceiling. "It's not exactly Shakespeare, but it does linger."

"Like a fart?" Ellen asks.

Missy laughs and kicks off her shoes.

"How in the hell does it work that he figured out that he didn't love you once he got into your pants?" Pi snaps. "What did you do—tie his dick in a knot?"

"There's a thought, but I think I missed my big chance," I say, smiling through my tears.

"He's got a way with words," Laurie says. "Doug *I feel no love for you* Anderson."

"Hell of a middle name," Missy says, stubbing out her cigarette.

"And yet, it works," Ellen says. "I never liked him. He was too perfect. Fake to the core. I hate that kind of guy."

"You acted like you liked him at the last party," I say, slumping down farther on the bed, my shoulders braced against the wall, my soul braced against despair. I feel like I'm sinking into the darkest, coldest, blackest depths of the sea, the weight crushing me so that I can't breathe, and my heart is beating sideways and lopsided, but my mind is still cruelly intact. I can still see his face and I can still hear him say, "I feel no love for you," and I can still feel the sharp pain of that moment. I'll always feel it. I know I will. I'll remember those words, and that moment, forever.

"I was faking it for your sake," Ellen says. "It's a hell of a relief that I can tell you what I really think about that guy. Finally."

"Yeah? Don't hold back," I say. I mean it. Someone, please, blast Doug so hard and so far away that I don't feel the pain of this anymore. I'm that ugly girl again, the monkey baby with the Halloween mask, the girl not pretty enough to take out in public.

My tears burn in my throat, begging to be let out.

"Finally?" Pi says on a bark of laughter. "She's been badmouthing Anderson for the whole semester."

"Yeah?" I say. I can hear the thready hope in my voice; I'm both embarrassed and too exhausted to be embarrassed. "What? Tell me."

Pi and Ellen exchange a look and my heart begins a downward spiral into the murky depths again. I can't breathe. I'm collapsing in on myself. It's all a lie; they never said a bad word about Doug. He *is* perfect. I'm the one who's not perfect. He didn't want me. No, that's not quite it. I failed the taste test.

"In case I didn't say it well the first time," Karen says, shifting her weight to sit cross-legged on the bed. "I thought he was boring. *Boring.* Come on, did he ever make you laugh? Come *on.* Be honest. Laughing because you're falling-down drunk doesn't count."

"Him or me?" I ask.

"Either," Pi says. "Come on. He was a stone-cold snore, right?

I mean, once you close your eyes and can't get assaulted by all that Ken-doll prettiness."

"Ken doll . . . That about fits," Missy says. "Was he, you know, missing his man parts like a true Ken doll? It's okay —you can tell us; we won't breathe a word."

"Speak for yourself," Ellen says. "I'm stealing a megaphone and riding up and down The Row with it."

"He's not in a fraternity," I say.

"Yeah, but he hunts here," Ellen counters.

That's probably true, isn't it? I feel like I've been hunted, gutted, and tied up on a car hood, Idaho-style. I have an uncle who lives in Idaho. I've seen the snapshots.

I should have kept my mask on. I shouldn't have let him see me, the real me, the me who is scared she won't make it in the navy and the me who is only occasionally secure about her looks and the me who struggles in Navigation. I should have been the me he expected. I should have stayed slightly drunk and completely cool and very sure of myself. I should have shown him I was perfect, and then he would have loved me. But I didn't do that. No. I let him see *me*, and he bolted, kicking me out of bed.

"He's a total bastard," Missy says, lighting another cigarette and popping a Tab. "You wasted enough time on him, Ryan. Life's short. Move on and move up."

Move up? That doesn't even make sense. There is no moving up from Doug Anderson. Doug Anderson is everything I've ever wanted, even before I knew I wanted it.

"Hell, yes," Pi says. "McCormick, give me a Tab."

Laurie tosses Pi a Tab across the six feet that separate them. Pi backs up and puts her hands over her face. "Dammit, Laurie! What am I? Some sweaty AG jock? I'm supposed to catch the damn thing?"

By this time we're all laughing, my giggles turning into hic-cups and then back into giggles. "I know it's a damn AG who's knocking over our bikes," Ellen says. "She does it every damn day. I'm going to catch her at it."

"That explains the window watch," Karen says. Since the AG house is right next to ours, it's not difficult to see what's going on over there.

"I thought you were impersonating a lighthouse keeper," says Laurie. "All that's missing is the thick fisherman's sweater. I've got one, if you want to borrow it."

"I think I could fit maybe one boob in one of your sweaters, Laurie, but thanks for the fashion tip," Ellen says.

"God, not you and your boobs again," Pi says. "You need a damn theme song for them."

I laugh, even though I feel like I shouldn't, and not because my heart's breaking for Doug, though it is, but because Ellen really has this pure hate relationship going with her boobs, among other things. It's not like she has monkey ears or anything like that, something truly hideous.

"There goes one," Ellen says, staring out the window. Laurie moves to stand next to her. Missy and Pi join them after a minute. I'm too wrung out to move; Karen stays at my side, her body pressed against mine, a warm core of comfort that silently promises to be as strong as steel cable. I lean against that promise and it holds, taking the weight of my pain and need without a quiver.

"Did she knock over the bikes?" Karen asks. "I was expecting a play-by-play."

"No," Ellen says.

"But she was joined by her fellow delinquents," Missy says.

"How many?" I ask.

"Four," Pi says. "No, five. One more just crossed the street. Damn AGs, standing right in front of our house."

"I think the sidewalk is public domain," Laurie says.

"Don't tell me you're taking their side in this!" Ellen says, not taking her eyes off the street.

"Absolutely not!" Laurie says. "I just wanted to be clear about the legality of everything. For the lawsuit. Later."

I find myself laughing. I'm not sure why, but I love it, and I'm grateful.

"Here comes the one who's a cheerleader," Pi says. "She's dating a fraternity brother of Jared's."

Jared is Pi's brother, a total fox, and a great source of blind-date material for half the house.

"She looks like a slut," Ellen says.

"You think so?" Pi asks.

"Totally," Ellen says. "Look at her panty line. I can see it from here."

"At least she's wearing panties," Karen says. "Did you see Cindy Gabrielle yesterday? She wasn't wearing anything at all, and you could see her pubes through her white pants!"

"God, no! Where did you see her?" Pi asks.

"We have Geography together," Karen says. "I couldn't take my eyes off her. The professor did an admirable job, though. He looked once, and then didn't look at her again for the whole class."

"I really like Cindy. What the hell happened to her?" I ask.

"She fell in with Andi Mills. She's been turned," Ellen says. "I'll be so glad when Andi graduates and gets out of here. Maybe we can turn Cindy back once she's gone."

"Did you ever see *The Omega Man*? With Charlton Heston?" Karen asks, standing up to look out the window with the rest of them. I get up, too. I might as well take a look at the AG mob hanging around on our part of the sidewalk.

Various murmurings are all Karen gets as reply.

"Yeah. So?" I prompt.

The AGs *are* looking pretty aggressive, standing near our bikes like that. Six slender, pretty girls with dark hair of various lengths and textures wearing adorable, if sporty, outfits, talking pleasantly outside the Beta Pi house. Definitely a mob. Definitely up to no good.

"So everybody gets this virus and gets turned into a zombie or a vampire or something equally gross," Karen says, "and that's it. Once you get turned, you're turned. There's no going back."

"Oh, my God," Ellen says, glancing away from the window to look at the rest of us. "Cindy's gone Omega."

"She can't be turned," Karen says.

"I guess we'll have to kill her," Laurie says. When we all look at her, she says, "Hey, I saw the movie. That's all that's left to do once they turn Omega."

"Maybe all we have to do is kill Andi. She's the one who turned her," I say.

"If only it were that simple," Karen says. "And I mean that."

Nobody has forgiven Andi and her clique for how they were during Rush, dinging girls because they weren't pretty enough or thin enough. It was disgusting. And now she gets this whole group of previously nice girls to act just like her. Add in that she's a complete slut, and that's all she wrote. Like I have room to talk.

"Let's go to the Four-O," Ellen says. "I can't look at these AGs for another minute."

The Four-O. Doug might be there. I don't think it's such a great idea, which has to be a first for me when someone mentions the Four-O.

"I've got psych in twenty minutes," Laurie says.

"Stop whining, McCormick. You need to get drunk. We all need to get drunk," Ellen says. "Come on, Diane. The first shot is on me."

"I don't know," I say. "I look like hell, my eyes are puffy and bloodshot—"

"Missy, blow some smoke in her face. Blame it on that," Ellen says. "Come on. We're going. Don't let Doug *I feel no love for you* Anderson take the Four-O away from you."

"Damn straight," Missy says, smiling at me.

I want to hide. I want to flaunt myself and drive Doug insane with desire and regret. I want to turn back the clock and do it all differently, finding my way into a place where Doug loves me. But none of that is going to happen so I might as well get drunk.

"Damn skippy," I say, retucking my shirt into my pants and then fluffing my hair. We all do a little fluff and puff on our hair, all except Missy. "Laurie, screw psych. We all need a good drunk right about now, right?"

Laurie looks at me, grins, grabs her cigarettes, and says, "I was probably flunking that class anyway."

Laurie

An hour later and we were all well on our way to being drunk. I don't get drunk as a rule, but this was a special occasion, an act of friendship and support for Diane because Doug broke her heart while his feet were still tangled in the sheets. Pete might be doing the same thing to me.

Yes, I'm still with Pete, though I'm not sure what the phrase *being with Pete* actually means. We're dating and we're a couple, but I can't forget Barbie, and I sometimes think that I'm his ULA girlfriend and that Barbie, on that high cliff above Malibu, still thinks Pete is hers. I want to believe that Pete loves me and that he truly broke it off with Malibu Barbie. I want to believe that he'll propose to me before he graduates in a few weeks. I can seduce myself into believing so many things. I can create defensive lines of belief and refuse entrance to all errant thoughts, barring the door to doubt and dismay and disbelief. My defenses are so very firm and so long established now.

Defenses. I need defenses with Pete.

"No! I can't eat my burger listening to 'Heart of Gold'!"

I look over and see Matt Carlson, aka Lavender Barrette, his fists full of hamburger raised to his mouth, and his expression shocked, outraged, and purely comical.

"What's wrong, sweetie?" Diane says from the back of our booth. "You don't like doper music? That's un-American, son."

"Take pity on me," Matt says. "Cover my ears so I can eat. I'm starving."

"When did you last eat?" Missy asks, slumped next to Diane, toying with her cigarette against the ashtray.

"Lunchtime," Matt says with a silly, sweet expression on his face. I've never paid very much attention to Matt before and I can't understand why I am now. I might be well and truly drunk, for the first time in my life. As it's for a good cause, I'm not going to regret the hangover I'll surely have tomorrow. Like all drunken declarations, this is so easy to say now.

Karen bursts out laughing. "Poor baby. What is it now? Five?"

"What music do you like to eat to, Matt?" Diane asks, her arms draped across the back of the red vinyl booth, looking at Matt like he's a mouse and she's a cobra.

What I'm going to remember about this moment is that Diane does not look like a brokenhearted woman. She looks confident and happy and ready for anything. She looks like she never heard the name Doug Anderson and wouldn't care if he walked in and danced naked on the bar. She looks like a woman in control of herself and of every guy within the sound of her voice.

I adore this woman and this moment. In this one small way I want to live in it forever.

"With a hamburger?" Matt responds with a grin, putting down his burger. "Rock and roll. What else?"

"How about a Sammy's burger?" Diane asks. Sammy's is a wild burger dive a few miles from campus. The burgers are juicy, thick, and sloppy with secret-ingredient chili piled on top. I've found it to be an acquired taste.

"Pink Floyd. Or Cheech and Chong. Depending on how hammered you are," Matt says.

Diane nods. Missy laughs. Karen smiles and asks, "And with a hot dog?"

"A polka," Matt answers promptly. "Don't tell me you didn't know all this."

"Food and music for one hundred, Art," Diane says. "Is played whenever tuna salad is served. Please remember to give your answer in the form of a question."

"What is . . . the Starkist jingle?" Matt answers, picking up his burger again and taking a healthy bite. "I'm guessing, though. Being a guy, I never eat tuna salad. That's chick food," he says, his mouth full of hamburger, a gob of ketchup stuck to one corner of his mouth. He licks it off a second later.

"Come over here so I can slap you," Diane says. "I'm too lazy to get up."

"By the way," Matt says, apropos of nothing, "it's not five. It's seven. How long have you guys been in here?"

"Oh, crap. I think I have class tonight," Karen says. "What day is it? Thursday?"

"Thursday," Diane confirms.

We all slide out so Karen can escape. Missy slides out at the same time. Ellen is at the bar, laughing with some guy I've never seen before.

The door to the Four-O opens and we all—all of us who are here to comfort Diane in her hour of Doug crisis—swing our heads to look. We've been doing that since we got here. If Doug comes in, and he easily could—we don't own the Four-O, after all—it's going to get ugly. I'm not sure how it's going to get ugly, but it will. We're in a very ugly mood.

Sleeping with a girl just to throw her out of bed after she gave you everything she had to give, every last bit of herself.

ROTC jerk.

But it's not Doug Anderson coming in the Four-O. It's Pi, with her brother Jared in tow. I forgot that Pi left about half an hour ago. I think it was half an hour ago. Things are getting very fuzzy. I think being fuzzy might have a certain appeal, under the right circumstances, and this is clearly one of them.

Pi has more than just Jared with her. Following them in is a really cute guy with chlorine blond hair. He's tall. His hair is wet. I look at Pi and Jared again. Their hair isn't wet, so it's not raining.

I look at Wet Head again. Yes, it's definitely wet.

"Look who's been playing in the fire hydrant," Diane says.

"Maybe he was in a wet T-shirt contest," I say.

"I'd vote for him," Diane says.

Pi drags Jared over; Wet Head follows.

"Guys? You've met my brother Jared, right?" Pi asks, pushing Jared in front of her like he's a treat she's offering. "This is Jared's friend from the water polo team, Craig McAllister. Jared, Craig, meet Diane, Laurie, and this is Missy."

"Water polo team? You didn't say your brother was on the water polo team. Talk about holding out," Diane says.

"He quit," Pi says as Jared is opening his mouth to answer. Jared smiles, grabs Pi's arms by the elbows, and gently shoves her into the next booth, where she lands on the arm of a guy who doesn't seem to mind at all that a pretty girl was just shoved nearly into his lap.

"I decided it was time to explore other options," Jared says diplomatically.

"Like drinking," Craig says, running a hand through his damp hair.

"You don't drink, Craig?" Diane asks.

"I'm really sure I didn't say that. I like anything wet," Craig says, grinning at her.

"Oh, man, I think we're in for trouble tonight," Diane says on a laugh.

"Define *trouble*," Missy says, coming up to stand next to Craig. Missy looks like a cat on the prowl. Craig doesn't look like he minds being hunted. Let the games begin. "You don't look like trouble to me. Do I look like trouble to you?"

"Define *trouble*," Craig says, staring first at Missy, then at the rest of us.

Pi disengages herself from the guy she landed on, the guys at the other table laughing. "Poor Craig doesn't get out much. All that water, you know."

"What year are you, Craig?" Missy asks.

"Junior. You?" Craig says.

"Sophomore, but I'm very mature for my age," Missy answers.

"And very shy," Diane says.

Pi has drifted off to join Ellen at the bar. Missy is working hard to drift off with Craig, who looks happy enough about it. Jared sits down on the edge of the booth next to Diane, and we all scoot over to make room for him. I'm on the other end of the booth, my back to the door, but Diane is still in the middle, protected from . . . whatever might come through the Four-O door.

"Are you interviewing yet, Jared?" I ask.

"Some," he says. "I'm thinking about law school, though."

Jared starts talking to a guy in the booth behind him, leaving Diane and me alone, in theory at least.

Diane isn't looking at Jared and doesn't seem to be paying much attention to the conversation at our table. Her eyes are half-closed, her head is resting against the high-backed seat, and she's spinning a ring on her finger methodically.

"Are you okay?" I ask softly.

"I'm okay," Diane answers briskly. She sits up and fiddles with the gold chain around her neck. "Enough about me. How are things with you and Pete? How come you're not on a date with him tonight?"

"Besides the fact that it's a Thursday and I've been holed up in here for most of the day?" I ask on a laugh.

"Yeah. Besides all that," she says. "I haven't seen him lately. Are things okay with you guys?"

"Fantastic," I say, and then I pause. Do I have to lie about this? Do I need defenses against this topic, with this girl? I'm not sure anymore. I only know that this wall feels comfortable and familiar; I can hide here indefinitely. Things aren't truly fantastic with Pete, but they're not disastrous either. We occupy a middle ground that is often murky, but again, familiar. I'm not unhappy. I'm simply unsure, and even that feels familiar. He always seems just out of reach, like he's about to float away from me unless I hang on tight.

"I was expecting you two to be engaged by now," Diane says.

I jerk my gaze to hers, shrug, and say, "He wants to find a job first."

Pete hasn't actually said that, but I've inferred it. It is the most logical reason, as well as being the most practical.

"What's his major?"

"Business," I say. "I think he's hoping for IBM."

"That would be cool," Diane says lazily, leaning her head back against the red vinyl again.

"Is it going to be okay for you, seeing Doug at all that ROTC stuff?" I ask.

"It's going to have to be, isn't it?" she says, her eyes closed.

I have no answer to that. I live in the same world, the world of deciding that everything is okay when a rebellious corner of your heart cries that it's not okay.

We sit silently for a few minutes, the jukebox switching from "Heart of Gold" to "Good-bye Yellow Brick Road" to "Money."

"Finally! A song worthy of my burger!" Matt crows. Of course, the problem is that he's finished his burger already. Matt throws down his paper napkin, stands up, and runs his hands over his belly. He doesn't actually have a belly. Actually, Matt looks better and better, just flat-out better-looking, every time I see him.

"Are you okay?" Holly asks. I look up from my hands, my cigarette burning down dangerously low to my fingers, the orange glow teasing my skin. I crush out my cigarette and glance over at Diane, certain that the question is for her. "I just heard about it from Bill. I didn't even know you guys had broken up."

Holly is staring at me. Why is she staring at me?

"What are you talking about?" Diane asks.

The entire bar seems to have fallen silent. Funny, but I can hear my heart beating in my ears, even over Pink Floyd.

"About Pete," Holly says, crouching down next to me, her weight balanced on the balls of her feet. "About Pete getting engaged to some girl at Pepperdine. When did you guys break up?"

Diane grabs my thigh under the table and squeezes it. I know she's squeezing me—I can see her hand, clearly. It's only that I can't feel it. I can't seem to feel anything. All I can feel is my heart beating, the sound of it in my ears like a rock-band drum.

But I don't feel anything.

I don't feel anything.

That's the beat. That's the song. That's what I keep repeating.

It's true.

It's going to be true and it's going to stay true. I'll make it true. Everything is numb and is going to stay numb.

He doesn't want me.

Numb. Let me be numb. I'm building walls as fast as I can, building up my defenses against this, forcing back the pain, denying the rejection, ignoring everything I feel and everything he doesn't feel. I won't think about how alone I am.

I've always been alone.

I look down at Diane's hand on my leg. She's got a death grip, holding on to me.

"A while ago," I say, punching my pack of cigarettes until another slides out. "I didn't want to bother you guys about it."

"Okay, Laurie," Diane says softly, gripping my thigh just above the knee where no one can see. "Okay."

She keeps saying *okay*. I don't know why because I am okay. I don't feel a thing. Or I won't. In a minute. Just give me a few minutes, God, to pull myself together. I've got to keep it together. There's no one to keep me in one piece except for me.

Just me.

Ellen

— Spring 1977 —

"Look who Missy snagged," Pi says. "It took her all of fifteen seconds."

I look down the bar and see Missy talking to a cute pool-blond guy with slightly damp hair. "He's a hunk," I say. Mike Dunn enters the Four-O just then. He looks good, and bad, kind of tough and very sexy. I remember when I hated the guy. I don't hate him anymore. I almost wish I did.

Life was a lot easier when I had everything figured out.

"Way to go, Missy," Pi says, snorting laughter.

I make myself keep looking at Missy, her brown hair as mussed as usual, her jeans tight and blouse unbuttoned a single button too low, leaning into the guy from her waist up, smiling, talking into his ear. He looks happy about the whole deal. What guy wouldn't?

"She likes to have a good time," I say. "She's very *take no prisoners*."

"What's she going to do? Kill him?" Pi says, waving the bartender over so she can order another beer. Pi drinks, but not a lot. She's purely a social drinker. I'm not sure what that means anymore.

"If she did, he'd die with a smile on his face," I say.

"I heard Missy got called in front of the Standards Committee again," Pi says.

A sorority is sort of a mini-government, with committees all over the place and elected positions like president, vice president, chaplain . . . Yes, chaplain. We all need a taste of a high moral tone every now and then, don't we? That's the rumor, anyway. If the Standards Committee thinks you're doing anything that could reflect badly on Beta Pi, you get called in and called out. That the Standards chairman last year was Andi Mills is hysterical since Andi never met a bra she liked and never met a button she could manage to button. This year, the year measured from January to December, the Standards chairman is Dana Woodcock. Missy getting called to answer to Dana Woodcock is a joke. Missy could eat Dana for breakfast, and probably did. What happens in Standards is supposed to be entirely secret, which means only five or six people know about Missy getting called in. Today. Give it a week and we'll be into double digits.

There are no secrets in a sorority house. This is Lesson Number One, and if you don't learn Lesson Number One on Day One, you're going to get what you deserve.

"Huh," I say. Since I'm the president of Beta Pi, I know Missy was called in and I know why she was called in. As the president, I'm not going to be the one to spill my guts in the Four-O. Or anywhere else.

Mike is working his way deeper into the Four-O. I know he's seen me, but he's taking his time. He does that a lot and I hate it.

"I heard she got home from a date at eight in the morning wearing the clothes she was wearing the night before," Pi says.

"That never looks good," I say.

I love Missy. I do, but that really doesn't look good. As the president of Beta Pi, I have to care about stuff like that, about the reputation of the house and shit. Missy doesn't care about how things look. It's one of the things I love about her and one of the things that scares the crap out of me. You just never know what she's going to do. She has no brakes.

"She's just having fun," Pi says, looking at me meaningfully. We know something about Missy that no one else knows, and since Missy didn't spill it to us in the Four-O, we're not going to talk about it in the Four-O.

I guess there are some secrets in a sorority house.

Missy has juvenile diabetes. According to Missy, she can't expect to live very long. I got the idea that her mom spoiled her rotten and treated her like a fairy princess come to Earth and that she's gotten very used to doing what she wants. I can vouch for that. She also can't be bothered to put up with anyone else's shit. You've got to love a girl like that.

The other side of it is that she abuses her body like hell, does whatever she damn well pleases and doesn't do anything she doesn't damn well please, and is on a fast downhill ride. The longer I know her, the more I know I don't want to be around to watch when she bottoms out.

"Since you're a wash on spilling Missy scoop, I need to get out of here. I have a paper due Monday. Are you staying?" Pi asks.

"No, I'm going, but let me go check on Ryan, say good-bye to Missy," I say to Pi.

It'll get me moving and show Mike I'm not waiting for him like a bug pinned to a board.

Missy and her mystery date are head-to-head. They aren't actually touching, but they're close enough to be sharing the same air.

"Hey," I say, touching her on the arm. She turns, her blue eyes friendly and curious. She doesn't look drunk, or at least not *too* drunk. "I'm leaving. Just wanted you to know. How's Diane doing?"

"Okay, I think," she says in my ear. "Paranoid" by Black Sabbath has just started on the jukebox; it's not music made with conversation in mind. "Are you staying?"

"Sure," Missy says, looking over her shoulder at her guy of the moment.

"Who is he?" I ask.

"Water polo," she answers. "I'll be checking him for webbed toes later."

"How much later?"

"Not that much later," she says, and then laughs.

What can you do? I laugh right along with her.

"You'll stick here? Make sure Diane's not alone?" I ask.

"No problemo," Missy says.

With a nod and a grin, I leave her to it. I don't blame her. I don't even think less of her. If I had only a few years to live, what would I do?

Diane is sitting in a booth with Laurie, both looking a little weird.

Holly and her boyfriend, Bill Staniszeski, a Rho Delt, are standing in front of the booth, talking to them. Holly and Bill have been together for most of this school year; I can't remember where they met. Maybe I never knew. They make a cute couple.

"Hi, guys," I say, coming up to stand next to Holly and Bill. It doesn't take more than an instant to feel that something is very off. "What's going on?" I stare at Diane. Diane looks at me for an instant and then looks at Laurie.

I look at Laurie. She looks like she swallowed an ice sculpture. She looks frozen.

"What's going on?" I repeat, staring at Diane.

"Pete's engaged," Holly says. I can barely hear her, the music is so loud, but the words are clear on her lips.

Pete's engaged. But Laurie's not engaged.

Shit.

"We broke up," Laurie says, her lips barely moving. "A while ago."

"She didn't tell us," Holly says. Holly clearly doesn't believe a word of it. Who would? It's a lie. We all know it's a lie, but damn, if all Laurie needs is a lie to save face, I'm up for that.

"She didn't tell *you*," I say to Holly, sitting down on the edge of the booth, squeezing next to Laurie, practically sitting in her lap. "She told me—oh, when was it?" I say, looking at Laurie. Laurie stares back at me. She's frozen.

"A week ago Tuesday?" Diane says. Diane's not frozen. Diane is as hot as bubbling lava. "Maybe Wednesday. All I know is that Pete is some kind of schizo to lose one girl and propose to another a week later. No wonder you told him to flake off. Good move, Laurie."

"Way to dodge the bullet," I say, nodding.

"It's like the Grand Canyon of all rebounds," Holly says. "I wonder how long it will last?"

"The marriage or the engagement?" I ask.

"The engagement," Diane says. "He's obviously just doing this to get back at Laurie for dumping him."

Laurie is silent, staring down at her hands on the table, twirling her cigarette lighter between her fingers like a little baton. Her eyes are bright, but she's not crying. Way to go, Laurie. Never let the bastards make you cry.

"No way is he going to marry her," Diane says.

"And if he does, that just shows he's an even bigger douche bag," I say.

Laurie doesn't so much as blink, but I can feel the tremor that runs through her bones, like a mini-earthquake. Pete marrying that girl is going to kill her.

"Why did you break up with him?" Holly asks.

I look at Holly, still kneeling, still holding on to the edge of the table for balance. Nice girl, sweet girl, but not too bright. Why won't she let this drop? Even Bill looks like he wants to run into traffic.

"I got bored," Laurie says. God, she's good. I half believe her.

"Let that be a lesson to you, Bill," I say. "Don't be boring."

"Got it," Bill says with a nod, reaching down to put his hand on Holly's shoulder. "Let's go. I've got a test tomorrow."

Holly rises to her feet in one smooth move, smiles at us, and leaves, Bill's arm draped over her shoulder.

"You want a drink?" I ask Laurie.

"Sure. Why not?" Laurie says, tapping out a cigarette and putting it between her lips.

"I'll buy."

Mike.

I wish I could say he appeared out of nowhere, but I watched him work his way over here. He watched me watch him. He came close enough to read the mood, offered to buy, and then made himself scarce. I really want to hate this guy, but he's making it tough.

Diane, Laurie, and I are left alone in the booth. We each take a deep breath and slump down, our spines curved against the cushion.

"I'm sorry, Laurie. What happened?" Diane asks.

Laurie takes a long drag of her cigarette and blows it out before answering.

"I wish I knew," she says. "I probably bored him."

"You're being too easy on him," I say, leaning forward. "And too hard on yourself."

"You think so?" Laurie says. "I don't know about that. He's

the one who left me. I must have done something . . . or not done something. . . . I guess I'll never know." She tries to laugh. The sound that comes out of her doesn't sound much like laughter.

"Did you have any idea?" Diane asks.

"No," Laurie says softly, her breath hitching. "Maybe. Not enough of one, I guess. I'm such an idiot."

Laurie takes another deep drag on her cigarette, closing her eyes as she inhales, closing her eyes as she exhales.

If you close your eyes, you can make it all go away, or that's the theory.

"I'd say let's start a club, but we're already in one," Diane says.

Laurie laughs and so do I. The mood eases slightly, and briefly. By the next breath, both Diane and Laurie have slumped down farther against the red vinyl.

"It's Barbie, right?" I ask.

"Yeah, I think so," Laurie says softly. "I thought we were going to get married. How stupid do I look?"

Lynyrd Skynyrd starts singing "Sweet Home Alabama." Matt Carlson shouts something unintelligible and throws a wadded-up napkin at the jukebox. It lands in some girl's beer at one of the center tables. Diane smiles for a second, but not Laurie.

"You love him," Diane says. "That's not stupid. Or it's not supposed to be."

We're all silent after that, the painful truth of their mutual situations too tender to discuss. God, let me never fall for a cold-hearted bastard.

Naturally, at the thought, my eyes go directly to Mike Dunn, who I'm nearly positive is a coldhearted bastard. It's not like they wear a sign announcing themselves, but he sure acts like one. Sometimes. Other times he's very . . . not exactly sweet, but engaging. Charming. Like the wolf dressed in granny's clothes, he's engaging.

Shit. I'm in nearly the same boat as Laurie and Diane. The only difference is that I haven't gone all the way with Mike. I think Laurie slept with Pete, though I'm not completely sure about that. Either way, she was in too deep and now she's buried.

Mike comes back with our drinks, four beers, sets them down in front of us, takes one look at our faces, and says, "I'll go feed the jukebox. Any requests?"

"'Heart of Gold,'" Diane says instantly. "A little gift for Matt."

"'Here Come Those Tears Again,'" Laurie says. "Just because."

Diane and I look at Laurie. She smiles and puffs on her cigarette. It's a very sad smile.

"'Saturday Night's Alright for Fighting,'" I say. "Because when I find that AG who's knocking our bikes down, she's going down."

Mike just nods and smiles, mentally writing it down.

"Let me give you a dollar for that, Mike," Diane says.

"No way. My treat," he says, retreating from us across the dark room. It's so nice, all of this. Maybe he's not a bastard.

"I wondered if he was cheating on me," Laurie says after a few moments. "Now I know he was, with her." Laurie barks out a weak laugh. "He cheated the whole time. First on her and then on me."

"Did you know?" I ask. I can't help myself.

"No, not at first," Laurie says, staring down at her cigarette, the dim orange ember trailing a thin wisp of smoke. "Later, I wondered. But I didn't know. Because I'm an idiot."

"You're not an idiot," Diane says. "He's the idiot. I really will think you're an idiot if you can't keep that straight. I've had a tough day. Don't make me work so hard, McCormick."

That induces a chuckle out of all of us. It's been a helluva day—that's for sure.

"What are you going to do when you see him again?" I ask.

"Am I going to see him again?" Laurie says.

Mike is lingering by the jukebox. He might be a nice guy or just a complete genius at self-preservation.

"Because life is so full of generally shitty moments, my vote is probably," I say.

"Preferably through the scope of a rifle," Diane says just before she slugs down her beer.

Laurie shakes her head, a half smile on her face fighting to stay alive. I slug down my beer, just to be sociable.

"What are you going to do when you see Doug again?" Laurie asks, not unkindly.

Diane sets her nearly empty beer glass down. "Scope. Rifle. Try to keep up, Laurie."

This time Laurie does laugh, a genuine laugh of pure, lovely, malicious pleasure. It's a great sound; it's a far better sound than sobbing into beer, which is another very real option.

"What about your guy?" Diane asks. I play dumb for a few seconds, but they both stare me down. I abandon my *what are you talking about* look. "Is he in or is he out?"

"God, that sounded dirty," Laurie says on a half choke, half laugh.

"Neither," I say.

"That sounds really uncomfortable," Diane says, wriggling her dark eyebrows. She's half-looped. I couldn't be happier for her.

"Mind. Gutter," I say just before taking another drink.

"No, really, what's going on with you guys?" Diane asks.

"Nothing," I say. "He's just some guy I met at the EE Tau exchange last year. We've gone out a few times. I see him around some. Nothing to report. Over and out."

"God, I'm really rubbing off on you, aren't I?" Diane asks.

"Roger that," Laurie says.

That gets a good laugh. It's while we're laughing when Mike rejoins us. I guess he figured that the coast was clear.

"Black Dog" by Led Zeppelin comes out over the speakers. Mike raises his glass again, lifting it toward the jukebox. "Here they come. That's song number one of my five. I figured something a little upbeat."

"Upbeat? They didn't have 'Climb Every Mountain'?" Diane asks on a bark of laughter.

Mike doesn't even look confused. "No show tunes. I think it's a law that you can't listen to show tunes in bars."

"Come on," I say. "You know that song? How many times did you see *The Sound of Music*? I promise your dirty secret won't leave this table."

Laurie laughs. It's a nice sound coming from her, a real laugh that seems to cleanse her soul, if only for a minute. Hey, a minute here, a minute there . . . they might eventually add up to something. Even a minute-by-minute recovery is better than nothing.

"I have a mother, in case you wondered," Mike says, grinning.

"Which means?" Diane asks.

"That I know you're lying. There's nothing a girl likes better than a dirty secret," he says.

"Guilty," I say. "Now, enough stalling. How many times?"

"Three," he says, hanging his head in mock shame. "In the theater. My mom saw it four times. The last time I faked being sick so I wouldn't have to go."

"Wow, three times," I say. "Do your fraternity brothers know?"

Mike laughs and leans back against the booth, his arm stretched out behind Diane. "Don't know. Don't care."

"I think it should go on your job application," Diane says. "It makes you look so . . ."

"Sensitive," Laurie says.

"Dorky," I say.

"Musical," Diane says. "I bet you cried when the Nazi boyfriend blows the whistle. Come on, admit it."

"This is what I get for giving you 'Black Dog'?" he says, smiling and shaking his head.

"No, *this* is what you get for 'Black Dog' and the beers and whatever else you can think of," Diane says, leaning over and giving Mike a quick kiss on the cheek.

My heart squeezes shut in a hard, cold clasp, and then pounds to life again. It's a moment that I know I will never forget. Gorgeous Diane kissing dangerous Mike. They look like the perfect couple in that frozen instant. Something rips into my heart in that moment, and even though my heart keeps beating, the rip is still there.

It takes my breath away.

Three hours later and Laurie is gone, Pi is gone, Diane is gone, Karen is gone, Missy and Wet Head are gone, but I'm still here and so is Mike and things are getting out of control. I'm out of control. I don't even mind; that's how I know I'm out of control.

I'm the president of the Brain Trust when I'm drunk.

"What's so funny?" Mike asks me, his arm around me. We're in a booth in the back and I'm pressed against him, and it's taking all the control I don't have to keep from throwing my leg over his. I feel like I want to slide all over this guy. I've never felt that way before. I hate it. I also love it.

I'm a chocolate mess.

I look at him. Just a quick look into those icy blue eyes and those black brows, and the dark shadow of his beard looks rugged and tough, and I just feel like I need to kiss that. Kiss all of that. But, hell, no way am I going to do that.

"I'm checking out the guys in the room," I say. "Making a list, checking it twice. I'll let you know how you ranked later."

"I'm number one and you know it."

"Don't be ridiculous," I say on a snort of laughter.

"Want to know where you fall on my list?"

"Hell, no."

But I lean my head against his shoulder and rub my leg against his under the table. I can't help myself.

"You're right on top," he says.

My heart does a little squeeze so tight it hurts.

"Did you not hear me say hell no?" I say, breaking the moment. I have to break it. I'm drunk and so is he and we're in a bar. Nothing real ever happens in a bar. That's why I love bars.

"Yeah. I heard you," he says on a growl, his eyes boring into mine. He leans down and kisses me and I feel like I'm going to melt. In fact, I do melt a little around the edges. He lifts my legs and lays them over his thighs. I'm practically sitting in his lap and I love it.

I'm in such deep shit.

I'm drunk and I'm a virgin and I'm with a guy who melts me. This is a really bad combination. Even drunk, I know that. I want to stay a virgin and I want to stay drunk and I want to stay on Mike's lap, Mike's hands on my hips and Mike's mouth on my face and . . . hell. Where was I going with this thought?

"Watch it," I say, leaning back.

"I'm watching it," he says, grinning at me, his eyes going to my bust.

"Cool your jets," I say. Diane came home from her summer cruise saying that, and I've been saying it ever since. It seems to fit this situation perfectly.

"You got a mouth on you," he says, his finger tracing along my lips. I feel tingles down my spine and across my thighs. I squirm on his lap, but I don't get off. That's right. I'm plastered and I'm melting.

"And I know how to use it," I say. What the hell did I just say?

"Yeah, you do," he says, and then he kisses me, right on the edge of my mouth. My breasts feel full and heavy, my nipples tingling and hot. I lift my breasts toward him, aching for him to touch me.

He grins and leans back, eyeing me from eyes half-shut. With one finger he traces the edge of my scoop-neck T. Back and forth. Back and forth.

"I went to Lake Forest to visit my aunt Irene every July for nine years."

I want to make some sarcastic remark, something snide and angry and hostile. All I can do is watch his mouth. All I can do is feel his finger on my skin, wishing he'd dip his fingers in and touch my nipple, wishing he'd pull me to his chest and kiss me.

This is war. Don't think I don't know that. I'm not going to do anything. I'm not going to make any kind of move at all. He wants me to. I can tell by his eyes, by everything he's doing with that damned finger, that he wants me to.

"There's a sailing school on the lake. Lake Michigan. I learned how to sail there. Just a Sunfish at first, but after a couple of lessons, bigger boats. I'll never forget my first solo. It was great."

"A sailor, huh? I'd never have guessed," I say. My voice sounds breathy, like a Marilyn Monroe impersonator.

"I know. You don't know me very well."

That damn finger keeps teasing against my skin, slower and slower, like he's thinking about grabbing me. I want him to.

I'm in such trouble.

"When are you going to say, 'Shiver me timbers'? That's what I'm waiting for. You know you want to," I say.

He smiles—no, he smirks—at me, his finger tracing up my throat. "Just one timber. You can feel it, can't you?"

"I don't speak sailor," I say, leaning toward his mouth.

This is how girls become sluts. From this. From feeling this. From being toyed with like this.

"Surfer girl," he says. "Little surfer girl."

"You like the Beach Boys? Know all the words to 'Little Deuce Coupe'?"

"'Catch a wave and you're sitting on top of the world,'" he says, quoting "California Girls." "'Midwest farmer's daughter . . . She makes you feel all right.'"

"God, what are you—a Beach Boys groupie?" I say. But I know all these songs, too. I've sung every one. I love the Beach Boys.

"'I wish they all could be California girls,'" he sings, his mouth hovering just above mine.

"You know all about farmers' daughters, don't you?" I say. I know he does. He's that kind. He's the kind who gets around and only goes with girls who get around.

Just before he kisses me, just as his mouth is touching mine, he pulls back, grins, and says, "I've gotta go. I'll walk you home."

He lifts me off his lap; my legs will barely hold me up and I lean against the side of the table as he gets out of the booth. With a knowing smile, he starts walking away from me.

"Are you coming? Let's go," he says.

I walk toward him, dizzy with lust, unsteady, pissed off, and hating him for doing this to me on purpose and for some sick joke. But I follow him, and when he drapes his arm over my shoulder, I lean into him.

Deep shit, shit up to my chin.

Laurie

Pete is marrying Barbie in two days. I know this because, some-how, through stealth and debasing desperation, I managed to sneak the information out of Lavender Barrette, who is going to be one of Pete's groomsmen. I even found out that he has to wear a pale peach cummerbund; she really is Malibu Barbie.

I can't sit in my parents' San Francisco home, staring out the wide window at the bay, listening to the downstairs maid dust and the two cooks murmur over the sounds of the countertop kitchen TV, a concession my mother allowed only because the muted noise of the television was more pleasant to her than actual human voices talking in actual living, breathing conversation. I can't sit still in that house, watching nothing, hearing nothing, waiting for the day when it's time to pack for Michigan, knowing Pete won't be there and that every rock and tree and sandy path will remind me that Pete is not there and that he won't ever be there again.

I had to leave. I had to go somewhere, and so I invited myself to Karen's for three days. On the fourth day, I'll leave for Michigan. On the fifth day, I'll walk the streets of Mackinac and pretend that

I'm having a wonderful time, just in case my family is watching, which I don't expect they will be.

Karen sounded a little surprised for half a minute when I called her and asked if I could come for a short visit, but she rallied quickly and was warmly excited once she'd asked her parents about having a houseguest and they'd said, according to her, an enthusiastic *yes*.

Karen is picking me up at the airport, Bradley International, an airport I'm very familiar with since my days at Miss Porter's. I'm making my way to the baggage area when she arrives, trotting, out of breath, and laughing.

I feel my heart lift instantly.

"I got lost! I know, I've been here a million times and should know my way, but my mom always drives and you know, if I'm not driving, I'm not really, you know, paying *that* much attention." She gives me a hug, her tanned and bare arms wrapping around my neck, giggling softly into my hair. I feel like I've come home. "Breathe a word of this to anyone and I'll leave you on the side of the road for the skunks."

"You drive a hard bargain," I say, pulling back to look at her. "I accept. As long as you can promise you know the way home."

"I promise. Just don't time me. We may make a few unscheduled detours, but I *will* get you there!" She laughs, her whole face smiling at me, her entire body vibrating with joy and pleasure.

Home. This is what coming home must feel like.

Connecticut in the summer is an explosion of lush green that tumbles over everything, from the weeds thriving next to the asphalt roads to the trees splashing against the bright blue sky. Frame houses painted white, brown, or barn red sit calmly and politely in the midst of emerald green lawns. It is nature buttoned down and managed in that taciturn, decorous way that is distinctly

New England. I didn't love Miss Porter's. I didn't even love living here, not consciously, but I liked it. I appreciated it, and I still do.

Karen drives a blue Malibu, the front seat pulled as far forward as it will go, and she still leans forward to reach the wheel. Karen looks smaller than I remember her.

"Have you lost weight?" I ask, looking at her thighs flattened against the vinyl seat. She is wearing very short white shorts, white sandals, and a red T-shirt, tucked in. Plastic red earrings, tiny balls, adorn her ears. She's tanned and slim, her cheeks and nose lightly sunburned. She looks like summer.

"I knew I liked you," Karen says, laughing. "Now, don't say another word. I think I need to turn around here. Somewhere."

"I see skunks in my future," I say on a sigh. "I could have taken a cab."

"Like they have cabs in Connecticut."

We turn left at what must be a major crossroad, judging by the multitude of wooden signs stuck at odd angles next to the road. It's still a two-lane road with wide gravel borders. No sidewalks, no signal lights, no proper metal road signs.

"Yeah, this looks right," Karen says, fifty yards past her turn. "This is the right way home."

The right way home. I'm feeling nostalgic for something that isn't even mine.

"So, what do you want to do?" Karen asks me. "Change, first thing, right?"

I'm wearing white pants and a pale pink short-sleeved blouse. The blouse is sticking to the back of my seat. Karen has the air-conditioning on full blast; I adjust the vents to aim directly at my face. The humidity of a Connecticut summer is something I've only heard stories about. I need to get into a pair of shorts immediately.

"How's my mascara holding up?" I ask.

"Running quite nicely, if you want to know."

I rub my fingertips under my eyes and sigh. "I really want to look like a raccoon when I meet your parents."

"My mom will think it's some weird San Francisco fashion statement. I'd run with that."

"If I knew where we were, I'd demand to be let out of this car right now. It's only because I'm lost, confused, and dripping that I'm staying right where I am and letting you insult me."

"I knew there had to be a good reason," she says, making another turn, this time without hesitation. We must be close to home.

The road, two lanes and winding, passes old homes from previous eras, some of them made of stone, some of wood, all of them looking distinguished and reserved. After another turn or two, the road becomes something less than a two-lane, a lane and a half, countrified even more than before, but the houses are newer as we climb up a hill.

"It's so pretty here. I'd forgotten," I say.

"It is, isn't it? If only it weren't for the mosquitoes. You'll be covered in bumps and scabs in twenty-four hours, and that's a promise."

"First skunks and now mosquitoes. Are you sure you want me here?"

Karen brakes and looks over at me as we pull into her driveway. "Definitely. I'm so glad you're here, and here we are."

The house is colonial and painted a mid-tone gold with dark gold shutters. The driveway is gravel and the trees hovering over it all are tall and old. There's a walkway to the front door composed of flagstones set in pea gravel. The garage connects to the house, and there's a long open porch from the garage to the front door. On the porch is an iron ring half-full of firewood. It looks like something out of a Currier and Ives postcard, a picture-perfect colonial home set in an original-thirteen-colonies state. It looks like the most ideal example of an American home that Norman Rockwell ever dreamed of, and it's Karen's home.

For just an instant, I'm awash with waves of envy and longing.

"Okay?" Karen asks me. "It's not as nice as your house, but we do have a guest room, and you'll have your own bath."

"It's beautiful," I say, looking into her eyes. She looks nervous. Why, I have no idea. "Thank you so much for having me."

"Beautiful, huh?" Karen looks at the house through the glare coming through the windshield. "It looks pretty yellow to me."

"You know, some people actually like the color yellow," I say.

"Yeah, you're about to meet the president of that fan club."

The car crunches on the gravel, announcing our arrival to Karen's mom, who has stepped out on the porch to wave at us. I wave back, smiling. Karen's mom, Mrs. Mitchell, is taller than Karen and has brown hair in loose waves just past her chin, and a trim figure. From here, she doesn't look old enough to have a college-aged daughter. Karen will probably age just like her. Slowly.

"Your mom is lovely," I say.

"Really? Thanks," Karen says. "She's very excited about your visit. You're her first Beta Pi sighting. No pressure or anything."

"Oh, great," I say on a moan as Karen puts the car in park and turns off the engine. "I hope I don't blow it."

"Yeah. Me, too," she says, looking at me with a glint in her eyes. Karen's eyes look almost green in this light. I'm struck by how pretty she looks in this instant with her tanned skin and silvery green eyes, her dark hair in wisps around her forehead and neck. She looks like a woodland sprite or an elf or something equally fairy tale—ish. Then she laughs at me and the image breaks; she's just Karen again. Sweet, funny, cute Karen. The girl who'll share her home with me simply because I asked her to. "Come on. Let's get going or my mom will think you don't want to come in or something."

"Perish the thought," I say, opening the car door and getting out. My feet have to struggle to find purchase on the uneven gravel, sinking in loudly; I reach behind me as casually as I can to pull my sweat-damp shirt off my back.

"Hi, Mom!" Karen calls out as she shuts her car door. "This is Laurie. Laurie, this is my mom."

"Hello, Laurie. Welcome!" Mrs. Mitchell calls to us, her smile wide. "Did you have a nice flight?"

"Yes. Thank you. It's so nice of you to have me," I say.

"We're happy to have you. Can you girls manage the luggage?" Mrs. Mitchell says.

The house is on a small hill, and the driveway is set below it; the walkway is stepped and steep and it's not going to be fun dragging my suitcase across gravel and up stone steps, which even from this angle don't look precisely even. Rustic Connecticut; they take a certain pride in that, I think. Nothing too fancy or too polished. It's almost the exact opposite of San Francisco, but that's a big part of its charm, especially in June. In January, it's far less charming.

"I've got it," Karen says to her mom. To me she whispers, "If you make me carry this thing all by myself, I'll put skunk cabbage between your sheets."

"What is it with you and skunks?" I say, chuckling, grabbing my suitcase out of her hands, and saying loudly for Mrs. Mitchell's benefit, "No, I've got it!"

"We'll split it. You carry it to the stairs; I'll carry it up the stairs and on the walk; and once we get inside, you take over," Karen says.

"You think they plan military assaults with this much precision?" I say, laughing. I'm so happy. I'm so delighted to be here. I feel like I could float into the treetops and sit looking down on the world, a tiny white cloud of pure joy.

"You're asking the wrong girl," Karen says, grunting as she lifts my suitcase up the first high stone step. I probably did pack too much, but I wanted to be prepared for anything. The only thing I left behind was my black formal. "But I do know how to manage these steps. Carefully."

"How do you do it in winter?"

"I don't. I go through the garage. Don't ask why I'm not taking the garage now. There's no way my mom would let me bring you in through the garage. Tawdry, to say the least."

"To say the least," I echo, beaming with suppressed pleasure. They want to make a good impression on me; they've thought of everything to make a good impression, to please me and make me feel welcome and wanted. And I do. It's exhilarating.

We enter the house through the front door, the proper door, and Mrs. Mitchell is standing in the foyer, waiting for us with a big smile on her face. At this distance, she looks more her age; there are lines from her nose to the corners of her mouth, lines around her eyes, a sharp line just above her nose, a scowl line. Still, she's a good-looking woman and must have been stunning in her day. She's very slender, still trim through the waist, though her belly pouches out a little. She looks so different from my mom, so lively and present, not distant at all. She's wearing navy, pink, and burgundy plaid Bermuda shorts and a pink Lacoste shirt, her feet in navy espadrilles. I thought she'd be wearing yellow. I look askance at Karen for an instant, the thought in my eyes, and Karen looks back, repressed laughter shimmering all over her face.

"Come in! Come in!" Mrs. Mitchell says. "Karen, why don't you put Laurie's suitcase in her room while I get you both something to drink. Would you like lemonade? Soda? We have Pepsi."

"A lemonade sounds perfect," I say. "Thank you so much." I keep thanking her because I can't stop feeling thankful. It's that simple.

Karen starts to drag my suitcase out of the foyer and through the living room, throwing me a hard glance over her shoulder.

"Oh, let me take that," I say, on cue. Karen smiles and releases her hold on the suitcase.

Mrs. Mitchell seems to catch our hidden conversation and says, "Karen, don't let Laurie carry her own suitcase. Laurie, you just relax. You've had a long day. What time did your flight leave?"

Karen grabs hold of the suitcase again and carries it through the living room, her mom and I following while I try to take in the look of the house and carry on polite conversation with Mrs. Mitchell. The foyer and the stairs to the second floor divide the house in two; the living room is to the left and the dining room to the right. All the floors are dark polished wood. The overall décor of the house is restrained colonial; there aren't any spinning wheels or cobbler's benches artfully arranged in useless abandon around the rooms, but there is a general sense of American colonial style in its most timeless forms: mahogany candlestick tables, camelback sofas, wing-back chairs upholstered in flame-stitch fabric, barley-twist legs on the dining chairs, braided rugs. The biggest break from New England colonial expectation is the color; Karen's mom has done it all in shades of yellow and gold and russet. It looks surprisingly modern, in an old-fashioned way. It's homey and charming and comforting—all the things a home should be.

I follow my suitcase, and Karen, not sure where else to go, telling Mrs. Mitchell my flight time, how long I've been traveling, how my parents feel about my trip to Connecticut. It's difficult not to give one-word answers, but these questions don't require more than a one-word answer. My flight time was five hours. My traveling time was six and a half hours. My parents felt "fine" about my trip to Connecticut. I asked if I could go. My mother said, "Fine." If I'd *told* her I was going, she would also have said, "Fine."

There is a short hallway that connects a first-floor bedroom to the kitchen: a maid's room, by my definition, but it is a nice room with a full bath attached. The room has two windows that face impenetrable woods, as far as I can tell. There isn't a neighboring house in sight.

Karen puts my suitcase on the floor next to the bed. The headboard is tiger maple, the bedspread is butter yellow, and there's a russet and tan braided rug. Karen looks at me in both accusation and humor. "Well. That was fun."

"Karen," her mom says disapprovingly. "Do you have everything you need, Laurie? There are fresh towels in the bathroom, and toothpaste. There's also a new toothbrush, in case you forgot to pack yours."

"Yeah, because you're not using mine," Karen says.

"I think I remembered mine," I say, trying not to laugh at Karen, trying to keep the joy of this inside, where no one will see it and it won't embarrass me. I'm a weekend guest here. I'm not a long-lost cousin.

"I'll leave you girls, then. The lemonade is ready whenever you want it," Mrs. Mitchell says, smiling at me before she leaves the bedroom.

I look around the room and peek into the bathroom. The bathroom has a yellow tile floor and yellow tile wainscoting; above the tile the walls are painted ivory. There is a big window next to the toilet and wooden shutters on the window. The towels are white and thick. It's a very happy-looking bathroom, very playful in a spare sort of style. My bathroom at home looks nothing like it.

"What do you think?" Karen asks me.

"It's great. I love it," I say, saying far less than I could say, and far less than I want to say. *I want this*, is what I want to say. *I wish this could all be mine.* I can't say that. I don't think Karen would understand, even if I could make myself say it.

"Once you get changed, I thought I'd drive you around town, show you my high school, just for the pure thrill of it, and then I could drive you by Miss Porter's if you want. Tomorrow I thought we could go swimming at Barkhamsted. Then tomorrow night, would you like to go to the Chart House for drinks? I could call some of my high school friends if you want, or we could go alone. Whatever you want. We could drive into West Hartford to shop or see a movie, or both. Really, it's up to you. What sounds good?" Karen asks.

Every bit of it. Small-town life in the trees, a family home with an actual family in it, lemonade in the kitchen, and swimming in the local lake. I feel like I'm in an Andy Hardy movie.

"It all sounds wonderful," I say. "Can we do it all?"

Karen laughs. "Sure! Get changed and we'll get going. But first, lemonade with my mom."

"Of course," I say.

Karen leaves me alone to change, which feels odd to me. We live in each other's pockets at ULA, four or five girls in a room the size of this one, sharing a bathroom with eight to ten girls; privacy is not possible and it becomes a thing barely remembered by October. But this is June and we've been apart, so the old rules, the pre–Beta Pi rules, have reemerged.

I miss her. She didn't need to give me my privacy. I keep my shirt and change into white shorts, following Karen's lead. I slip on white sandals and fluff my hair. My lemonade awaits. I feel almost giddy.

I follow the sounds of female voices down the short hallway from the bedroom to the kitchen. The room has a large mullioned window looking out over the wooded backyard; there is a flagstone patio next to the house, a huge oak tree on the edge of the lawn, and a tire swing twirling gently in a negligible breeze. The kitchen table is a huge oak circle with a thick pedestal base and it's next to the big window. The working part of the kitchen is U-shaped, with the sink at the base of the U and facing another window into the backyard. There is also a window box with red geraniums gleaming in the summer sun. The room is large, open, and wall-papered in a lemon yellow and white plaid, Blue Willow serving dishes hanging on plate hooks on the walls. On the long wall that leads into the dining room and, I think, the family room, there is a series of family photographs. I walk to that first. It's irresistible. Family photos in the family kitchen. Of course. How right that is.

Mrs. Mitchell and Karen stop talking when I enter the room, their faces open and smiling as I walk to the picture wall. The black-and-white photos are mostly of Karen: Karen's first Christmas; Karen's first day of school; Karen in her Brownie uniform and missing one-third of her teeth but still smiling enthusiastically; Karen going to the prom.

I stop at that picture, struck by it, studying it, shocked and struggling not to be.

Karen as a teenager in her prom dress, a pale halter dress that does her figure justice, her dark hair long and softly curled and tied back with a small ribbon near her face . . . Karen with a different nose from the one she has now.

"Here's your lemonade," Karen says, getting to her feet, bringing the lemonade to me, trying to pull my attention away from the photo.

I turn, smile, and take it. I take a sip and smile its goodness and my thanks. I walk to the table and try to think what I should say, or whether I should say anything at all.

"I don't suppose Karen told you," Mrs. Mitchell says, "but she had her nose done right after she graduated from high school."

Karen flinches slightly, a tightening of her spine and her mouth, but then she smiles and shrugs, looking at her mom as her mom keeps talking.

"Doesn't she look better? She's always been an attractive girl, in an unusual way, but her nose was rather enormous, and really, it's such a simple thing to have taken care of. She looks so much better now, don't you think?"

I have no idea what to say. I stare at Karen, lost for a response. Karen saves me.

"I couldn't wait to have it done," she says. "I hated my nose." Mrs. Mitchell nods vigorously. "It didn't even hurt, though I couldn't go swimming for a few months afterward."

"A few months of nuisance and then, poof, you're done with it and you look so much better as a result," Mrs. Mitchell says. "Of course, it's not something we talk about, but it's not really a secret either. There's nothing shameful about cosmetic surgery. It's changed so many lives for the better."

I nod and sip my lemonade.

"I look at it the same way I do orthodontia," Mrs. Mitchell says, getting up and walking to the sink. "If you have crooked teeth, you get them straightened and no one thinks a thing about it. Karen had braces, too, and there's no shame in that."

Karen grins a huge grin, showcasing her teeth.

"You never went to an orthodontist, Laurie?" Mrs. Mitchell asks me. "Some people don't need it—lucky them—but if you do need it, it's so nice that it's so readily available."

"I didn't, no," I say, pressing my lips together. My teeth are slightly crooked, both top and bottom, but I don't have an overbite or an underbite.

"You're one of the lucky ones, then," she says, washing tomatoes in the sink, water droplets spraying around her arms, the geraniums glowing in the sun. "Though I think nearly everyone could do with a little improvement. You might think about having a consultation with one, just to be sure that everything is as it should be."

"I suppose so," I say, looking at Karen. Karen knows I didn't get my teeth straightened because my parents didn't arrange for it and I was never home long enough for them to do so. I was away at school, and my teeth were away with me.

"Mom, we've got to go," Karen says, saving me again. "I want to drive Laurie around before dinner, see if we can find any cute guys at Lums." Karen laughs and gets to her feet, pulling me with her. "Bye, Mom! We'll be home by six."

"Bye, girls. Have a good time. And run a comb through your hair! You never know who you'll run into, and you want to look your best," Mrs. Mitchell says, still at the sink with the tomatoes.

As we walk back down the flagstone steps to Karen's car, I'm fumbling for the appropriate thing to say, not sure there is one, yet certain that I should say *something*.

"I didn't know," I say.

Karen chuckles, a nervous sound, and says, "That's okay. Actually, that's good. I don't want it to be obvious, and it *is* kind of a secret."

"Okay. I won't tell anyone," I say as we both get in the car. After Karen has backed out of the driveway and started down her street, I say, "Do you mind my asking . . . did it hurt?"

"Nope. Not a bit. My mom told me it wouldn't and she was right, as usual."

"That's good. Did you always want to change your nose? You've got a cute nose now, by the way."

"Thanks," Karen says, winding through her neighborhood, the sunlight skimming her arms and neck, throwing her profile into sunny relief. "I did. I always hated my nose. If I could have lived life like Bazooka Joe, my sweater pulled up over half my face, I would have."

"Always? That must have been miserable."

"Well, maybe not always. It just seems like always when you're waiting for the surgery. I thought I'd never be old enough. You have to be eighteen," she says, looking at me. "You have to have stopped growing. Where do you want to go? We could cruise for cute guys."

"That sounds good," I say.

"I spent half of high school cruising for guys," she says with a grin.

"You dated a lot in high school, didn't you? You always had a boyfriend."

Karen shrugs. "Yeah."

"Why did you think you needed a new nose? I mean, it's not as if the guys thought there was anything wrong with the way you looked." Karen shakes her head, a twisted smile on her face. "I'm sorry," I say. "This is none of my business."

"No. It's okay. I don't mind telling you." She brakes for a stop-light and looks over at me. "I think I was about eight years old; I might even have been seven. Some kid at school—I can't even remember if it was a boy or a girl—said I had a big nose. I still remember how confused I was by that, how I couldn't even see where that came from. So when I got home I asked my mom if I had a big nose. You know what she said?"

I shake my head, staring at her. The light changes and Karen slowly accelerates, the trees a blur of green as we pass them on the winding road.

"My mom said, 'Well, it *is* rather enormous.' I'll never forget that moment. Never. I remember everything about it. I looked at my face in the mirror after that and I hated what I saw. I hated my nose. I hated . . . everything."

I can't think of what to say to that. I can't even grasp what I should think.

"I think you're pretty," I say. "I like your nose."

"Yeah, the new one's okay. The old one was a disaster," she says, grinning at me, humor and gaiety and warmth shining out of her eyes just like always.

But it's not just like always.

"I can't believe your mom said that to you," I say, angry on her behalf.

"Oh, no, she was right," Karen says. "It was too big. I look bet-ter now. I'm glad she was honest about it. It would have been worse to have her lie and tell me my nose was fine."

I was right. I don't even know what I should think.

Karen

— Fall 1977 —

Monday nights in a sorority are unlike Monday nights anywhere else. I haven't done the research on this, so it's technically a guess, but still, I know it has to be true.

Sorority house Monday nights are full of requirements. One: you have to be there. If you can't make it, you're going to need a doctor's note, which is just barely an exaggeration. Two: you have to wear a dress and just generally look nicer than you normally would for eating a normal meal. Three: you have to use your best, most polished manners. To do otherwise will result in public humiliation of the most ritualized sort, and that's no exaggeration. Four: you have to attend the chapter meeting after dinner, which is truly an exercise in endurance and self-control. I mean, come on, I don't think the Bataan Death March was much worse than the Monday Night Dinner and Chapter Meeting package.

That might be a slight exaggeration, but only a slight one.

"I don't think I have a clean dress left," Laurie says, running into the room, dumping her books on her desk.

Laurie and I are in a second-floor two-way this semester. Diane is rooming with Lee in a two-way next door to us, and Ellen has a room to herself since she's the president.

"I've got a skirt you can borrow," I say, tying my belt around my waist. I'm wearing my striped cotton dress with the wrap-tie waist. It wrinkles if you look at it, but it will look good enough to walk into the dining room. After that, all bets are off.

"Thanks, but I think this will work," Laurie says. She shakes out a pair of dark gray gauchos a few times and yanks them on. It goes okay with her white cap-sleeved T-shirt. She sits on her bed to pull on a pair of Frye boots.

"You're going to die of the heat in those boots," Diane says. "It's got to be eighty degrees today, which puts it at one-twenty in the chapter room."

"I'll try to snag a seat next to Jenny Van Upp in the chapter meeting and sweat all over her," Laurie says.

"Good plan," Diane says. "Mitchell, we're going to plant ourselves downwind."

"Roger that," I say. "We've got five minutes. We need to get down there."

They keep roll and you get dinged if you're late. Monday Night Dinner is just one thrill after another.

"Hey, wait a minute," I say. "Are those new? When did you get diamond studs?"

I rush across the room, careful not to trip on the popcorn machine cord, and take a close look at Laurie's ears.

"Saturday," Laurie says, smiling slightly, brushing out her hair. "I figured I wasn't going to let Joan Collier one-up me."

"They're gorgeous," I say. They are, and they're bigger than Joan's. If you're going to one-up someone, you really have to, you know, do it. "How big are they?"

"Half a carat," Laurie says. "I went to the diamond district downtown."

"I'm going to kill you in your sleep—you know that, right? You've had fair warning," I say.

"I'll be sure to mention that at your trial," Diane says.

"I'll split them with you," I say to Diane.

Diane grins. "I'll be a very uncooperative witness. They won't get a thing out of me."

"Deal," I say.

Laurie just smiles and keeps brushing her hair, her eyes closed.

Laurie has never been what you'd call raucous, but since Pete married Barbie last summer, she's been more reserved than ever. She's just sort of still, inside and out. It's not a bad way to be, if it happens naturally or from the womb or something. But this isn't natural. This is heartbreak and lost hope and dashed dreams and all that other stuff the best poems are about.

Naturally, we don't talk about it. Laurie is a very private person, and besides, what is there to say? The guy she was crazy about married someone else; plus he strung her along before he did it.

No, there's nothing to talk about. In fact, since I think I might be in the same position, I *really* don't want to talk about it.

I haven't cheated on Greg again, not since I was home for the summer, though I've been tempted a few times. Oh, I've flirted a few times this semester, but nothing came of it. I didn't want anything to come of it either, just to get that straight. I love Greg. I'm not going to mess this up. Still, it seems like it's getting messed up all on its own.

Greg has not proposed, not formally. It's getting to be kind of a thing, actually. I mean, I've been dating him since before I became a Beta Pi, and all the Beta Pis know him, and we've been to nearly every party and now we're seniors and . nothing.

"You look really nice tonight, Karen," Laurie says. "Any special reason?"

See? That's what I'm talking about.

It's at the Monday Night Dinners that girls get pinned and engaged. Nearly every Monday night, especially in the spring, there's this heightened tension, wondering if it's going to happen, and to whom.

"Yeah, the reason is that this is my last clean dress," I say. "You know I'd tell you guys."

"You'd better," Diane says, buckling her cream high-heeled sandals as she sits on the edge of my bed. Diane is wearing a dark green wrap dress with a pale beige geometric design on it. She looks as gorgeous as usual. I've gotten used to it.

Diane hasn't dated since the debacle with Doug Anderson. She's gone on dates, but she hasn't dated. That jerk really blew her up. We all hate him—deservedly so, right?

Definitely.

What is it with guys that sleep with you and then . . . nothing?

Greg again. He says he wants to marry me, that he's going to marry me, but he hasn't actually formally proposed. Don't think I haven't asked him about it because I have. I want the ring ceremony at Monday Night Dinner. I want the date set. I want to start planning things with my mom.

My mom doesn't say a word. Well, she tries not to, but a few choice words slip out. Greg has met my parents a few times; the most recent was last year when they came to the West Coast for a week's vacation during spring break. They met Greg before we all went on a driving trip up to Monterey to visit a friend of my mom's from college. It wasn't just the few words about Greg my mom tossed out, but my dad's total silence on the subject. That combination was chilling, and there doesn't seem to be anything I can do to fix it. I've sung Greg's praises; they're deaf to it.

Some days it feels like I'm the only one out of all of us who wants us to get married.

I know he loves me. He tells me he loves me, though not very often. I tell him I love him a few times a day, but he says he doesn't like to "wear it out." Like telling a girl you love her ever gets old and worn-out. I don't even know what he's talking about. I always tell him I love him, like shaking salt on French fries, the more the better, and he'll occasionally tell me he loves me, like he's sprinkling diamond dust every time he has to say, "I love you."

I can't understand what's going on. He says he loves me. He tells me he wants to marry me.

Okay, then, marry me.

I actually thought being a senior was going to be less stressful than this. All it would take is a little diamond ring to make everything all sparkly and bright. And safe. I want to feel safe. Being married will make me feel safe. I don't know why that's true, but it is. I want to get married. I've always wanted to get married.

That may not sound very modern, but I don't know anyone, any girl, who doesn't want to get married. I guess we're supposed to blame that on Cinderella and Doris Day movies, but I don't believe that. Being married, sharing your whole life with someone, someone who loves you, who promises to love you forever and then actually does it, that's in the bone. That's not a dream you can blame on Walt Disney. As to blame, why blame anyone? Being married, being loved, those are good things. Wonderful things.

Greg sees that. He wants what I want. He says so, but not as much as he used to.

"I'm ready," Laurie says, grabbing her cigarettes. "Let's go."

We go down the back stairs, the stairs closest to the kitchen, and there's the usual Monday night mob. We stand around on the stairs, waiting for it to clear once the dining room doors open and we can go in and get seated. From my perch eight steps up, I can see Mrs. Williams, our house mother, coming out of her room on the first floor, making her way down the hall. Mrs. Williams, at a guess, is about ninety-two years old, and I'm basing that entirely on the way she wears her hair. She wears it in a 1930s kind of style, gray, of course, but how old are you when you were in your prime in 1936? She's nice, quiet, soft-spoken, and unobtrusive. A watchdog, guarding our sterling moral fiber, she's not. Naturally, part of Monday Night Dinner is being lovely and gracious to Mrs. Williams, taking turns sitting at her table—no one really wants to sit at her table for obvious reasons. It's a real conversation killer, even if she is only seventy-five. My grandmother, who's eighty, has more zip than Mrs. Williams.

How does a woman end up being a house mother? Because she never got married and has nowhere else to go in her golden years?

Not being engaged is ruining my senior year and warping my psyche; I think that's pretty obvious.

We start down the stairs, one slow step at a time, like a wedding procession, and squeeze into the dining room. Ellen is already in and is standing next to Missy and Lee at one of the tables in the middle of the room. She lifts her head in hello and invites us over with her eyes. Laurie, Diane, and I dutifully obey her silent summons, slinking through the crowd until we get to their table.

We stand behind our chairs, sing the song that starts dinner— yes, a song—and then, once Mrs. Williams has taken her seat, we all sit and start the first course: salad and a roll. The dining room, a large room full of circular tables and long windows on one side, curtained since the only view is to the side of the AG house, is done in shades of white and blue and yellow. The whole house got redecorated in the summer of 'seventy-six, turning it from a scrambled-egg blend of dingy white and golden yellow into a crisp, smart, new space of white and navy with accents in lemon yellow. It looks amazing now; I really love it. Very fresh and clean-looking. I'm just not a fan of white and yellow; that's been well established.

"I heard the Zetas got a new hasher," Ellen says, shoving her roll away from her. Ellen never eats her roll, or her butter. The butter is sliced and sitting in an artful array of ice chips. Yellow and white again. It's everywhere. "He's supposed to be gorgeous."

Our hasher comes into the dining room at that exact moment, looking sweaty and overworked. His brown hair hangs in oily clumps against his shiny forehead. His white coat is covered in old stains and new. I have no idea what his name is. Hashers serve and clear and clean. They don't speak, or I've never heard ours speak. Being a hasher is the lowest job on earth. It's hard manual labor and, to the girls in the sorority, you're invisible. Is there anything worse than being invisible to the opposite sex?

No. There is not. No amount of money is worth that.

"Why can't we ever get a gorgeous hasher?" Diane says.

"Like you'd be able to do anything with him if we did," Lee says.

The hasher arrives at our table and we all lean back in our seats so he has clear passage to take away the dirty dishes.

What must it be like to be the only guy in a house full of women? He is, literally, the only guy. Of course, he has to come through the back door, stay in the kitchen, and is only allowed in the dining room to clean up. He's not here for very long either. A sorority is a female-only domain, unlike anything else I've ever experienced. It's actually sort of relaxing, in an emotionally charged kind of way.

The hasher rushes through the rest of the room while we all talk, the noise level in the room rising, and then the main course is served: chicken and rice and peas. Monday Night Dinner is the best meal we get all week. The door to the kitchen, a big, sunny room, opens off of the butler's pantry, but it's strictly off-limits to us. I mean that.

Anyway, during the rest of the week, we eat a lot of tuna salad. I mean, a *lot* of tuna salad. Sometimes Melba, the day cook, will mix it up and we'll get taco salad. The thing is, with all the bike riding to class and my unpaid job cleaning Greg's apartment and then all that salad, I've lost quite a few pounds. Ellen practically wants to hit me when I complain about the starvation diet they have us on, so after saying something in a chapter meeting about how we could, once in a while, have lasagna, I haven't said another word about it. But I'm down to a size five, and when I joined Beta Pi I was a size seven. Pretty soon I'll be shopping in the toddler department.

Greg hasn't said a word about me dropping a size. I don't think he notices that kind of thing. He, on the other hand, has gained more than a few pounds since we started dating. And I'm the kind of person who notices. I'm not sure what that says about me. Maybe just that I'm more observant about the person I love.

"How's Craig doing, Missy?" Diane asks.

"He's fine. He's thinking of quitting the water polo team," Missy answers.

"No kidding! How come?" I ask.

Missy shrugs. "He's sick of all the traveling, all the workouts. I think he's seen three football games since he got here."

"Bummer," Diane says. "What do you think? Do you think he should quit?"

Missy shrugs, leaning back in her chair. She's eaten half her chicken, all her rice, and none of her peas. "I don't have an opinion. He can do what he wants."

"How's it going with you guys?" Ellen asks.

Missy and Craig have a volatile relationship; they started hot and heavy, had a fight, broke up, got back together a week later, were hot and heavy for a couple of months, had a fight, broke up, got back together the next day. I think their last breakup and makeup was over the summer; it's been quiet since then. Still, with them, you never know.

"No complaints," Missy says, picking apart her roll.

We all eye Missy cautiously. She and Craig have been dating since they met in the Four-O last spring. I don't think Missy meant it to get serious, and I'm really not sure it *is* serious, but it's sure starting to look serious. Missy's a junior and Craig's a senior; they're old enough for it to get serious.

Aren't we all?

Suddenly, in the middle of our hasher starting to take away our plates, the lights are flipped off, the hasher makes a discreet exit, and one of the girls brings in a bouquet with a lit candle sticking up out of the middle of it.

Sighs and moans of excitement float through the room. At least twenty people turn to stare at me, their faces smiling. My stomach plunges down a few inches. I start to shake, my hands trembling and my knees knocking together a little. Until now, I thought knocking knees was a literary device. But, that literary observation aside, I feel sick. Sick at heart and sick soul-deep and horribly, physically sick.

It's not me.

It's not *me*.

The thing is this: when a Beta Pi gets pinned or engaged, a candle bouquet makes its way around the Monday Night Dinner dining room, girl by girl. Each girl takes the bouquet, the candle illuminating her face for a moment before she passes it on. Or blows out the candle. The one who blows out the candle is *the one*, the girl getting pinned or engaged. If engaged, the ring is slipped over the candle so everyone can admire it. If pinned, the guys from the fraternity are waiting on the front lawn to serenade her in front of us, watching her get pinned by her guy in front of all of us. It's the most romantic thing in the world. It's like something out of *Romeo and Juliet*, if their families hadn't been feuding and they hadn't, you know, died.

The candle passes from girl to girl, from one table to another, each girl's face lit by that warm yellow glow. Some girls laugh and get rid of the bouquet as fast as they can, passing it on like a baton in a relay; others linger over the bouquet, teasing us, dragging it out before passing it on. You get a feeling for these candle ceremonies. You get to know which girl is ready to get pinned or engaged. You date a guy for long enough, the relationship calm enough and happy enough that it's just the next logical step, then the candle ceremony feels nearly inevitable, like falling out of a tree. The yum-yum tree.

I'm the logical choice. We're so completely and perfectly the logical choice. Greg and I have been together for three years. He loves me and I love him. We're stable. We're happy. We're graduating in a few months.

And it's not me.

The bouquet is passed to our table, to Ellen first, who laughs and passes it on to Diane, who smiles at me, a smile that is a question, and then passes it on to Lee. Lee looks at the ring, makes a face that shows she's impressed, and then she passes it to Missy. Missy, her blue eyes sparkling in the light of that single white candle, looks at Ellen and grins, looks at me and stops grinning, and then she blows out the candle.

Missy. It's Missy.

There's a stunned silence that lasts for a few seconds, a few eternal seconds when I can feel every wondering and confused eye on me, and then applause and shouts of joy for Missy and Craig. Craig, who met Missy six or seven months ago in a bar. Craig, who *knows* he wants to marry Missy. Craig, who bought the ring and is ready to set the date.

"I thought it was going to be you," Diane whispers to me.

I smile, a wobbly smile that won't hold its happy shape. My eyes are teary. I can't talk.

"You okay?" Laurie mouths to me silently.

I nod and smile harder, forcing my features to make a happy face.

"When are you guys getting married?" Ellen asks Missy, but I'm asking myself the same question. When are we getting married? I know the answer. I've known the answer for a long, long time. Maybe I've known for years.

When are we getting married?

We're not.

"We're thinking June of next year," Missy answers. "His parents and my parents are negotiating now."

Craig nailed her down, staked his claim, made it official, and is going to make it permanent.

In that instant, I hate Greg.

The ceremony over, the hasher gets back to business and brings out dessert: yellow cake with white frosting, kind of like a wedding cake.

I can't swallow a bite.

I still love you," Greg says. "But I don't want to marry you. Not now, anyway. Maybe later. After I get a job."

I start to cry. I can't help it.

"Shit. Do you have to do that?" Greg says. He looks around in grim embarrassment. We're on University Avenue and it's two o'clock and it's Tuesday and we are not even close to being alone. A girl with chin-length brown hair and a red skirt rides by on her bike; she gives me a sympathetic look and then gives Greg an accusing one. I appreciate it.

I sit down on the curb and bury my face in my arms.

"I said I still love you," he says.

Big deal.

I look up at him, wiping my nose with the back of my hand. "I love you, too. I thought we were going to get married. You told me you wanted to marry me a month after we started dating. Didn't you mean it?"

"I did. I just don't . . . I think we should wait."

"For what?" I wipe my nose again and then wipe my hand on the back of my pants.

"I'm not ready. It just doesn't feel right. You can feel it, too. I know you can."

If I can, I don't want to admit it now. I haven't wanted to admit it for months, maybe years. But I love him. I love Greg. Even now, as he's breaking up with me, he still loves me. That has to count. That has to mean something.

Why doesn't it mean that we're going to get married?

"Come on," he says, holding a hand out to me. I sniff and take it. He pulls me into his arms and I sob against his chest. "I'll walk you back to the house."

I'm not sure what to do now. I've had a boyfriend"—and a second on the side every now and then—"since I was twelve. I don't like being without someone to love and without someone to love me; I feel amputated," I say.

"You'll be fine. It's only been a few days," Ellen says. Laurie doesn't say it. Diane doesn't say it. Of course not. Ellen doesn't know what it feels like to be cut into chunks. I hope she never does.

"I guess," I say, sitting on the floor of my room, shaking the dice for our backgammon game, the smell of popcorn strong in the air.

"You just need a date," Ellen says. "Want me to set you up?"

"No!" Laurie says before I can open my mouth. I let the dice fall out of the cup. "No offense, Ellen, but that guy you set me up with was either on parole or on his way to do a bank job. What did you ever think we'd have in common?"

Ellen winks at me. "I told him you were loaded. He sure liked you."

I move my backgammon pieces, not really thinking about the game. Ellen shakes, rolls, moves, and kills me. Game over.

"Let me set you up with one of my guys," Diane says. "At least they've passed a background check."

"Which one?" Ellen says before I can open my mouth. I keep shaking the dice in my cup, the sound hopeful somehow, as if things can still roll out okay, that you can win if you just keep shaking the dice.

"Rob Thompson," Diane says immediately.

"Isn't he the guy you set me up with last year?" Ellen says. "The one who ignored me all night at the Halloween party?"

"He's matured," Diane says. "He's a junior now."

"I'm too old for him," I say.

"Does he have a crush on her?" Laurie asks, scooting me over so she can take my place at the backgammon board, facing off against Ellen. Ellen is the queen of backgammon. She could hustle backgammon and live like royalty. I lift myself onto my bed, looking out the window at the side of the AG house. There's nothing going on. I'm not used to having so much time on my hands. Without typing Greg's papers and doing his dishes, the hours crawl by.

"I don't know," Diane says. "A date's a date. He can crush on her later."

"Too young," I say, still staring out the window, my shoulders resting against the wall.

"Russ Bromley," Diane says. "He's such a doll. And he's a senior, so you won't be cradle robbing."

"I had a class with him last spring," Laurie says. "He's cute, Karen. You should go out with him."

"Why don't *you* go out with him?" I say, looking at Laurie. It's a rotten thing to say, and I regret it instantly.

"If he asked, I would," Laurie says quietly.

"Well, he hasn't asked me either, so we're in the same leaky boat," I say.

"You could thumb wrestle for him," Ellen says, moving the backgammon pieces into the starting position. "Best two out of three."

We all laugh and the mood in the room lightens.

"It's only been a couple of weeks," I say. "I'm just not in the mood to date yet."

"Okay," Diane says, "but after Christmas break for sure."

"Triple date?" I say. "Fix up Laurie, too, and then I'll go. We'll all go. Someplace ritzy. Like Sammy's."

Laurie snorts.

"Laurie?" Diane asks.

"You're sure about the background check, right? I don't want to end up as the getaway driver in a jewelry heist," Laurie says.

Ellen throws a piece of popcorn at her. It hits Laurie on the forehead and then drops into the hole of her crossed legs.

"Two points! And a rim shot, too," Ellen says.

"You don't need any extra points," Diane says. "You're the only one of us with a steady guy. How's it going with Mike?"

"Okay," Ellen says. "Grad school's going fine."

"When's he going to graduate?" Laurie says.

"He's not sure," Ellen says. "It depends on if he can get the classes he needs or not."

I exchange a look with Diane, who's sitting on the floor against the bed opposite mine. Mike Dunn was an undergrad for five years and now he's in grad school. Just when is this guy going to get out and get a job? Of course, it's one of Mike's friends who is the bank job guy, so I'm not actually disposed to trust him. Ellen is. I still can't figure that out. She didn't even like the guy that much, and suddenly, mostly because he worked at it so hard, she's in love with him and it's serious. Or it looks and sounds serious. Looks can be deceiving, can't they?

"Okay, hold on," Diane says. "I'm setting you two up, but who's setting me up? I'm not asking one of the ROTC guys, you know. So where does that leave me?"

"Walk down The Row in a pair of shorts and a halter top," Ellen says. "That should take care of it. I'll bet you have half a dozen offers within fifteen minutes."

"I'm not arguing that I'd get offers," Diane says. "It's what kind of offers that I'm wondering about."

"Really? You're wondering?" Ellen says. "What's your GPA again? Two point stupid?"

"About that," Diane says. "Why? You only hang out with smart people?"

"Obviously not," Laurie says dryly.

I look back out the window again. It's a little after four o'clock. Dinner is in two hours. I fly home to Connecticut in nineteen days. I'll spend two weeks with my parents in the snow, the yellow house looking like a broken egg on a thick white dinner plate; once I'm home I'll tell my mom Greg and I broke up. She'll try not to jump for joy and recount all the reasons she was right about how wrong he was. My mom will take me out to lunch, shopping, and a movie, or some combination of all three for most of the two weeks I'm home. I'll see a few old high school friends and we won't have much to say to one another. They have new friends; I have new friends.

I take a shallow breath that I fully intended to be a deep breath. I started shaking when Missy blew out the candle at Monday Night Dinner, and I haven't really stopped since then. I feel shaky all the time, my own private little earthquake that won't stop. All the foundations are cracked and broken; college didn't turn out the way I wanted it to. I have an education, but I don't have anyone. I wasted three years on the wrong guy; it's the worst mistake I've ever made. I'm graduating in a few months and I don't *have* anyone.

Empty, hopeless time runs in front of me, mocking me.

"It'll work out," Diane says to me. "It takes time; that's all."

Dinner is in two hours. I fly home to Connecticut a handful of days from now.

Little bites. I just have to look at my life in little bites, one thing at a time. Graduation is months away. I don't have to think about that now.

I don't have to think about Greg anymore.

I'm just going to have to be happy about that. I'm going to just flat-out be thankful that I didn't end up married to a guy who was happy to use me as his personal whore, maid, and tutor. I thought I'd meet my husband in college. I didn't go to college just to find a husband; I'm not some "getting her MRS degree" joke, but I did just sort of basically expect to meet him here. Where will I meet him now?

Of course, college isn't over yet. I could still meet someone. Or maybe even get back with Greg.

I loved him.

I still do, I think.

I turn away from the window. There's nothing out there. It's not like Greg is going to come over and beg for me back, is it? I might have thought it was a possibility at first, but if he came right now, I wouldn't take him back. I'd talk to him, sure, but he'd have to say just the right things. I'm not even sure what the right things are anymore. He told me he loved me, and that's always been the only right thing a guy had to say. That, and he thought I was pretty.

"How did your parents meet?" I ask.

"Who, mine?" Ellen says, staring down at the backgammon board. It's a close game. Laurie has a good head for backgammon.

"Yeah," I say. "Mine met in college. My dad was in school on the GI bill and my mom was a sophomore. On their first date they went to a Yankees game. My mom's a complete baseball nut and my dad thought that was so cool. He proposed during the seventh-inning stretch two months later."

"I knew baseball was slow, but a two-month-long game?" Diane says.

"Shut up," I say, smiling. I can still smile. That means something, doesn't it? "You know what I mean." I sit down on the desk chair next to the window, my back to The Row and all the possibilities that didn't happen there. "She said yes and they eloped to Niagara Falls a week later."

"Really?" Diane says, shuffling over on her hands and knees to shove the popcorn popper against the wall, the cord still dripping dangerously into the middle of the room. "That's so romantic! Why didn't they wait and have a real wedding?"

"They never said, not really," I say, "but I got the feeling that they *couldn't* wait."

"Nope," Ellen says sharply. "We are not going to talk about— we are not going to *think* about—our parents having sex. That's completely gross."

"You think they waited? For real?" Diane says.

"Gross!" Ellen shouts, throwing her dice cup down on the gold shag carpet. The cup doesn't even bounce. Shag is like that. I dropped an earring into it once and never saw that earring again.

"I thought everybody waited back then," Laurie says. "It was the forties."

"Yeah, like Betty Grable didn't have sex," Ellen says.

"Rita Hayworth," I say.

"Doris Day," Diane says. "Doris Day was not having sex!"

"Not on-screen anyway," I say, shrugging. If I can keep my sex life secret, and I do, then so can Doris Day. You can't tell by looking, I know that for sure. Can guys tell by looking? I'm not as sure about that. "I think my parents waited. I can't think they didn't wait; that's for sure."

"No shit," Ellen says on a bark of laughter, leaning back against the bed, splaying her legs out in front of her.

"Come on," I say. "Your turn."

"This is like some sick version of *The Newlywed Game.* I don't want to think about how my parents met."

"Come on," I repeat. I need to hear this. I need to hear stories of love, marriage, and a baby carriage. I guess that shows on my face because Ellen sighs and starts talking.

"My parents met while my dad was in dental school," Ellen says. "In fact, he went to ULA dental school. My mom was working as a receptionist for a dentist who taught at the school. They met over dental stuff—"

"Like the spit sink," Diane cuts in.

"Very funny," Ellen says, throwing a piece of popcorn at her. It misses her and bounces off the bed. "They met because my dad was in the office a few times, and he thought she was cute, I guess." Ellen stops for a minute, looking down at the shag carpeting.

"And?" I prompt.

"And after hanging around for a few months he finally got the nerve to ask her out. They were married six months later."

"Once he got going, your dad didn't waste any time," I say.

"He wanted to stop hanging around the spit sink," Diane says.

Ellen throws another piece of popcorn at Diane. Diane catches it and pops it in her mouth with a grin.

"Your turn, Diane," I say. "A few more details would be nice."

"What? Are you writing a thesis?" Ellen asks.

I shrug. "Maybe. You will not be acknowledged in the credits or the footnotes. Your story lacks heart, warmth, and all those details that make the best stories."

"Only because the participants lack those qualities," Ellen

says, throwing a piece of popcorn at me with a grin. It misses me and lands in the gold shag. It blends in nicely.

"*My* parents met while my dad was stationed in Mississippi," Diane says. "My poor grandparents were so upset that my mom fell in love with my dad, all that moving all the time. I don't think my mom wanted to fall in love with a naval pilot, but . . ." Diane's voice trails off. This is hitting too close to Doug *I feel no love for you* Anderson territory. That scar is still flaming red even after all this time. Will I still be scarred from my breakup with Greg a year from now? Two years from now?

Am I scarred from Guy or Craig or Billy or Jack? Have any of the guys I've loved and lost left their scars on me? Maybe, but the scars are so tiny and so old that they're just a part of me now, just nearly invisible lines that are part of who I am. That's not bad, is it? I can live with that. I *will* live with that. I'll live with it and move on, just like I always do.

"But we all know how pushy your dad is," Ellen says to Diane, filling in the gap and coming to the rescue. "The one time I met him he kept pushing and pushing me to take a drink. I finally gave in. Just to be polite."

"Yeah. Big sacrifice," I say. "You poor thing. How did you ever bear up under the strain?"

"I'm plucky," Ellen says.

"Is that how you pronounce it?" I say, grinning. I feel better, much better. I'll meet someone. I will. Everyone meets someone eventually. Hearts don't stay forever broken. I know that. Dreams do come true. I believe that. I have to believe that.

I think Tinker Bell said that first, or maybe it was Cinderella. Life according to Disney.

"How did your parents meet, Laurie?" Diane says, popping open a Coke. "Your turn."

Laurie keeps her gaze down at the backgammon board, her cigarette sending up a trail of smoke from the ashtray near her right knee. "The usual way."

"Way to fill in the details," I say. "You flunked freshman English, right? Had to take it—what?—five times?"

"I don't know. They never told me," she says softly, moving her pieces on the board.

"What?" I say, stunned, embarrassed, and ashamed of myself for teasing her.

"What do you mean, they never told you?" Ellen says. "How could they not tell you?"

Laurie shrugs, her eyes on the backgammon board. "It just never came up."

"You never asked?" Ellen says.

"They never offered," Laurie says. "You just don't ask my parents something that . . . personal. You met them. You know what they're like."

We're all staring at Laurie, feeling horrible, feeling horrified, but still staring. Everything shifts, the picture I've had of Laurie changing right in front of me. I always thought she was so coolly sophisticated. Now I see that she's just so alone.

"I know that the upstairs maid met her husband at a bowling alley. They've been married for over twenty years. They're still bowling, too, on a husband-and-wife league. That's devotion," Laurie says, her eyes still on the backgammon board.

I'm just staring at her, not sure what to say. I look around the room and Diane and Ellen have the same response as I do: dumb, shocked silence.

"Devotion to bowling or each other?" Ellen finally says, her voice rich with sarcasm. Her normal voice. A normal thing for her to say.

"Both?" Laurie says, laughing a little. There are tears in her eyes. She won't look at us. She's staring at that backgammon board like it's a Ouija board, able to unlock secrets for her, like the secret of how her parents met and married.

"Jesus, Laurie," Diane whispers, staring at her. Diane is starting to cry. Ellen makes a noise and Diane looks at her. Ellen shakes her head and frowns. Diane lifts her head back and her tears evaporate.

Laurie wouldn't want us to cry for her. Laurie wouldn't want to feel that exposed. I get that. I really do.

Laurie ignores Diane, ignores us all. She picks up her cigarette and takes a drag, closing her eyes and lifting her face to the ceiling. "I really loved the upstairs maid, Meg. She'd play Monopoly with me sometimes. She'd tell me such funny stories about her husband and her kids. She has two kids, both boys. The oldest is probably in high school by now. I really missed her at first when I went away to school. She quit and I lost touch with her."

The silence rises unbroken, a wall of velvety, dark silence that shrouds pain and unimaginable isolation. This time even Ellen can't find the words to break it down, to enter the place where Laurie lives, to carry her out on the back of our laughter and our love.

"Your roll, Olson," Laurie says, flicking the ash off her cigarette.

The sound of the dice banging against the cup is Ellen's answer. It's the loneliest sound I've ever heard.

Winter 1978 —

It's raining and my last final before semester break is over. It was for my Middle English Literature class, which should have qualified as a foreign language since it wasn't actually English, but does anyone care about that in administration? They do not. So, here I am, walking from the philosophy building back to The Row as fast as I can, my jeans soaked to my skin, my hands like icicles, my hair plastered to my head underneath my yellow slicker hood, when this blue Mustang pulls up next to me as I reach The Row. I keep walking, but I look.

Staring up at me from the Mustang with a big, friendly smile is Doug Anderson.

He's just as handsome as ever. His eyes are as blue, his hair is as golden, and his features are as Ken-doll perfect as they were when Diane was going out with him.

"Hey, Karen," he says. "How are you doing?"

"Hi, Doug. Fine," I say.

I'm not sure what to do. Keep walking and try to talk to him? Stand in the rain and talk to him? Keep walking and not talk to him?

"Are you on your way to the house?" he asks.

"Yeah," I say. "I just took my last final."

"That's great!" he says, smiling like he won a cash prize. "Hey, you look miserable. Let me give you a ride."

I stop walking again to stare at him. Every instinct that I've picked up from years of being . . . well, picked up . . . is shouting that something very weird is going on here and that I should not be seen talking to this guy. Believe me when I tell you that I don't ever remember having that instinct before. I'm pretty sure this is its maiden run. Doug Anderson is the enemy. All the Beta Pis hate him, those who haven't gone Omega, because we love Diane and he didn't.

But he's the most gorgeous guy I've ever seen. And he's paying attention to me.

"No, it's okay," I say. "I'm almost there."

I'm about a block away, but that really is *almost there* considering how far I've already walked. Can I admit at this point that I'm sort of wishing that Greg will somehow see me talking to Doug? I'm petty that way.

"Really," he says. "Hop in. I can't bear to see you looking so miserable."

"Thanks, but it's okay," I say, smiling at him. He smiles back. My heart skips a beat. It really does.

"You're sure?" he says, his car still keeping pace with me, his smile tender and encouraging. Tender and encouraging? How does he even know who I am?

He looks at me like he thinks I'm pretty, and desirable, and irresistible. I'm soaked. I'm sure I have mascara stains under my eyes. I'm not pretty in the best of circumstances, and this is probably the worst of circumstances. Why is he acting like he's trying to pick me up?

"I'm sure," I say, my heart thudding under my yellow slicker. "See you around."

"You, too," he says, slowly accelerating.

I keep a pleasant expression on my face and a little spring in my step as he drives off, just in case he's still watching me in his rearview mirror.

Spring 1978 —

"Karen!" a female voice shouts up the stairs. "Karen Mitchell!"

I get up from my typewriter, leaving my paper about Keats to cool, which is not a good thing since I was on a roll and it's due tomorrow at nine, and walk down the hall to the top of the stairs. I look down and see Missy staring up at me, looking ominous.

"Yeah?"

"There's someone here to see you," she says, coming up a step.

"Okay. Who?" I say, coming down a step.

"A guy," she says.

Naturally, I think it's Greg, coming to beg me to come back to him. My heart does a little leap, and then it flops around in a very lackluster way. Do I really want Greg back? No, not really. It's just I've never gone so long without a boyfriend before. In fact, I can't even get a date. That date with Diane's ROTC guy never happened. Both Laurie and I sort of chickened out and kept making excuses about how the timing wasn't right and how she had a big accounting exam and I had a paper on symbols in Victorian poetry. You know, the normal dodge to avoid a date. It's not that I don't want to meet another guy—I do—but I've never been set up before in my life. I never needed help finding a guy. What's wrong with me now?

I know exactly what's wrong with me now. I'm reeking of desperation. My mom told me that guys can sniff desperation from a hundred miles out. I'm oozing desperation so naturally there's not a guy in sight. I'm graduating in a few months, leaving the land of abundant, available guys, and I don't have a boyfriend, never mind a fiancé.

Every day I wake up and have one, blinding, overwhelming thought: crawl in a hole and die.

That's attractive, isn't it?

"Yeah?" I say. "Who is it?"

Missy comes up another step, and then another. When she's only two steps down from me, she whispers, "Doug Anderson."

My stomach drops and flips, and there's nothing halfhearted about it. Missy looks at me in a combination of curiosity and accusation. We all hate Doug. No exceptions, no exemptions, and no excuses.

"Oh," I say.

We stare at each other for a moment, I blink a few times as innocently as possible, and then I move around her and walk down the stairs as casually as I can. I can be pretty casual when I want to be.

Doug is waiting for me in the living room. He's the only person in there, which is not unusual since the television is in the trophy room. All the living room has in the way of interest is a fireplace. Who cares about a fireplace and a few long sofas when you can watch reruns of *Starsky and Hutch* crammed on a love seat in the trophy room?

Doug is standing, facing the wide doorway to the foyer as I enter. He's smiling. It's a shy, sweet kind of smile that doesn't match at all the image I have of him from watching him with Diane. He never looked like this with her. I don't know what to think anymore about Doug. I'm holding my *I feel no love for you* ground with one toe, and it's slipping. After his aborted pickup in the rain, he's been gently hounding me, in the sweetest, most innocent, most ardent kind of way. Not in a creepy way at all. Being creepy would have helped.

A sweet pursuit is the hardest to resist, and I don't have any practice at all at resisting pursuit, not even the clumsy kind. Doug is the furthest thing from clumsy. But that's part of the problem; he's too good at this, too perfect, and that has my guard up. Plus, I can't and won't forget Diane. He destroyed something in her and she hasn't been the same since.

I really can't believe he's here, in enemy territory. And he is the enemy. We, as a house, have made his life as miserable as possible without breaking the law or inconveniencing ourselves. Things like crank calls. Things like shouting his name at the top of our lungs whenever we see him. I know that doesn't sound too bad, but walking down The Row and having a girl's high-pitched voice shouting, "Anderson! Doug Anderson!" is more than a little disconcerting, based on Doug's reaction, you understand. He tucks his head down into his shoulders, turns a little red around the neck and ears, and picks up his pace. As torture, it seems to work.

Since that day in the rain, he's caught me riding my bike on the wide path that connects The Row to campus and kept me talking for a few minutes. Everyone, absolutely everyone, uses this path to get from The Row to campus; there's no other way to get there, not to mention the eight or ten apartment houses along the same route. Talk about being obvious. Anyone could, and probably did, see us.

Why's he so interested in me all of a sudden? I'm not gorgeous like Diane, and if he could throw Diane out of bed, what could he want with me?

Then there was the time he saw me on campus and stopped me to chat. At Sammy Spartan. Sammy Spartan is a huge bronze statue of a Spartan warrior nicknamed Sammy for some mysterious reason, and it's located just outside Bowman Auditorium and at the main crossroads on campus. It's kind of hard to be on campus and not walk by Sammy Spartan. So of course I was living in fear that someone would see us talking pleasantly together, Doug flirting, me trying not to flirt back, which accounted for my curt responses and lack of a smile. At least I don't think I was smiling. I tend to smile a lot, even when I don't mean to. I heard somewhere that people respond favorably to a smiling face; I think that's why I got in the habit of smiling so much. It's certainly not because I'm so damned happy all the time, Sammy Spartan and Doug Anderson being a case in point.

Why is this happening to me? Has Doug made me some kind of test case? Because that's what it feels like; like he's doing this, paying attention to me, flirting with me, for some weird reason that clearly has nothing to do with my beauty or personality. Beauty? That's obvious. Personality? He doesn't know me well enough, especially since every time I see him I'm ready to run in the opposite direction.

That's all the bad stuff. The good part is that I'm so secretly flattered that I think I'm going to burst. *This* guy thinks I'm worth pursuing? Maybe I'm prettier than I thought.

And it's with those two reactions storming around inside of me that I smile, big surprise, and greet Doug.

"Hi," I say.

"Hi, Karen," Doug says. "I hope it was okay for me to just drop by?"

"Sure," I say, because, really, what else can I say? "Would you like to sit down?" I gesture toward the two or three sofas in the room. Doug picks the one with its back to the foyer wall; the one that no casual passersby will see. Smart move, Doug.

I didn't gesture toward the eight or ten chairs in the room. Smart move, Karen. We'll be sitting side by side. Hey, he came to me, remember?

We stare at each other for a few awkward seconds, or it's awkward for me. I'm not sure Doug knows how to feel awkward. He's just so ridiculously handsome. I can barely take a full breath. I don't think I've ever been this close to someone so handsome. In fact, I know I haven't.

"I heard you and Greg broke up," Doug says.

I'm not sure how he could have heard this, or where, but whatever.

"We did," I say, maintaining eye contact. Just admitting it, the words rolling around inside my mouth, is painful. Greg didn't want me. What is *wrong* with me? Someone opens the door to the house and runs up the stairs, a voice calling out to her as she passes the trophy room, and I look down at my fidgety hands.

"I'm sorry," Doug says. "You went out for a really long time, didn't you?"

"We did," I repeat. What an awkward conversation. Why is he dragging me into it? It seems cruel.

I look deeply into his eyes and see blue eyes shining with concern and genuine interest and not a grain of cruel intent. He looks as innocent and as lovely as sunshine. As usual.

"What happened?" he asks, and though his eyes don't change, I feel something shift. I feel it like I feel an aftershock, even though nothing falls off a wall or splits cement. I *felt* something.

My guard goes up, like closing a gate or pulling up the drawbridge, something physical like that, something seen.

I smile and say, "Nothing major. Not everything lasts forever." Maybe nothing lasts forever. Maybe that's my problem. I believe in happily ever after.

"I'm sorry," he says again.

I can't believe it, but Doug might actually be boring. You really can only get so far on a pretty face, not that I wouldn't like to give it a try.

"Look, I'm going to be really honest and just say what I came to say," he says. "I'd like to take you out."

He's looking at me earnestly, sweetly, you know, the look he reserves for me. I never saw him look that way at Diane. Diane got *devil-may-care sexy.* I get *sweet.* Why?

I've been dating a long time now—that's obvious at this point—and when you factor in all the boyfriends and all the guys on the side and all the pickups, and I mean that in the most innocent way possible, well, that's a lot of guy experience under my belt, figuratively speaking. So, having said all that, there is something so seriously off about this guy. He's too smooth and his approach is too practiced. I don't feel pursued. I feel targeted. And that's not the same thing at all.

What it means is that this isn't about me at all; this is all about him. If there's one thing I know, it's that when a guy is falling for me, it's actually supposed to be all about me.

I nod slowly, still smiling. I've really got to work on that. "You do?"

He smiles, and my breath catches in my lungs. Honestly, I feel a little dazzled.

"I really like you, Karen. I want to go out with you."

Is this how it started with Diane? Did he dazzle her? Did he *I've only got eyes for you* her?

Diane. I'll never forget what he did to her. He broke her heart. He mangled her spirit. He *used* her. She'll never forget it, and neither will I. She deserved better. And so do I.

Again, the seismic shift . . . The earth I've been standing on my whole life shifts under my feet, and everything looks different. I *feel* different. Doug is still staring dreamily into my eyes; he hasn't changed. But I have. Everything feels different, even though nothing has changed.

"I don't think so," I say.

His smile fades and his earnest expression ramps up. It hits me that I'm watching a virtuoso performance by a master performer. He's not experienced at rejection. For just a second, I almost feel like laughing.

"I've wanted to go out with you for a long time, but you were with Greg. When you guys broke up, well . . ." He smiles shyly, his blue eyes so beautifully earnest. "I thought that, you know, we could spend some time together, get to know each other. Go on a date."

Every word he speaks is killing something inside me, and building something inside me, something new, something that wasn't there before. I don't *want* him, no matter how he looks or what he says. For once, for the first time, what I want matters to me. Not what he thinks about me or whether he, the universal *he*, wants me or not. Just me. What I want. What I think.

I have the right to say no, no thanks, not you, not now, not ever.

And I'm not going to do anything that might hurt Diane. I know this would hurt Diane. I also know she would deny that it would hurt, but that only makes me want to protect her more.

"I'm not going to go out with you," I say. I'm not smiling, and because everything is different now, it's easy.

"Is it because of Diane?" he says. He doesn't look earnest or sweet anymore; he looks frustrated and a little angry. "Because if it is," he says, without waiting for my answer, "you only know her side, not mine. All you Beta Pis have got the wrong idea. I don't know what Diane told you, but she has her version and I have mine."

I'll bet he does. I don't care about his version; I know Diane and I know what happened.

"Did you have sex with Diane?" I say. And without waiting for his answer, because the look on his face confirms it, I say, "That's all I need to know. I'll never go out with you, Doug."

He looks really angry now. He acts like he's never been turned down before, which actually may be true. Why did I ever think this guy was good-looking?

I stand up. He stands up. I'm not giving him much choice.

"You don't know anything about me. You don't know what happened," he says.

"I know what I need to know," I say.

"Do you think you'll change your mind?"

I look at him, at the blond perfection of him, and a small part of me can't believe I'm saying this, let alone thinking it, but I say, "No. I won't."

It's true. It will stay true as long as I live. I will never care that this guy wanted me and I will never regret turning him down. I don't want *him*.

I feel like I could fly.

Ellen

There are the Omegas, and then there are the rest of us, the nice people of the world. Yes, I'm one of the nice people. Don't act so surprised. Since I had this figured out after a year in the house, getting called to the president's room was a bit of a shock. What could she have to say to me? I wear underwear every day, don't I?

Colleen, the current president, isn't alone in her room. Kim, the vice president, is with her. Kim and Colleen are both juniors and were both in my pledge class. We've never been close, but we've never been enemies either, even though Colleen and I were usually at odds during Rush voting. I don't remember how Kim voted.

"You wanted to talk to me?" I ask.

Colleen nods and motions for me to sit on her bed. She's sitting on a chair near the window; Kim is sitting on a chair pulled up to the desk, ready to take notes.

Shit. Notes? What the hell?

I sit on the bed and say, "What's going on?"

"Ellen, I wanted to talk to you about . . . well, about what it means to be in a sorority," Colleen says. She looks uncomfortable, like she has a stick up her butt.

"No kidding," I say.

"If you could just sit and listen to what I have to say, without interrupting me," Colleen says, giving me a hard look. "This is important."

"Sorry," I say. I didn't interrupt her, but things probably look a little funky when you've got a stick up your butt.

"People join a sorority to make friends," Colleen says, looking at me in stern superiority. "The girls who pledge this house want to feel like they belong to something bigger, like they could be something greater than they could be on their own. We all have to remember that, to work together and individually to make sure that everyone gets what she wants out of Beta Pi. We're all sisters here."

"Uh-huh," I say, nodding fractionally to show her that I'm listening and not interrupting.

Colleen glances at Kim. Kim blushes a little bit, shifts her gaze to me for an instant, then drops her gaze to the pad on the desk, clicking her pink Bic pen. Colleen looks back at me.

"Do you agree?" she asks me. "You agree that that's what we're doing here? Trying to include everyone? Make sure everyone has a chance to be a part, a real part of Beta Pi?"

"Sure," I say, shifting my weight on the bed.

"I'm glad to hear you say that," she says. Whenever anyone says that particular phrase, you can bet that you've been led into some kind of verbal trap. Ed's been pulling it on me since I could talk. "There's been some talk about you and your friends—"

"Like what?" I say, interrupting her, breaking free of the trap. "Who do you mean?"

Colleen squirms on her chair and sits forward, looking a little aggressive. "You know who I mean. You and Karen and Laurie. Diane Ryan. Missy and Lee. Holly. Candy Chase. You're so exclusive. You've become an exclusive group of friends, and that makes everyone else feel cut off and left out. It's not what a sorority is all about."

"Exclusive? An exclusive group of friends?" I say sharply. "Really, Colleen? *I'm* the snob?" Now I'm leaning forward, my elbows on my knees, my eyes staring her down. She holds my stare, looking almost as angry as I am. It's a fake. No one is as angry as I am right now. "Who was it who fought for Debbie Brown? She was a little chunkier than Jenny Van Upp liked. She got dinged. I had an accounting class with Debbie; she's a great girl and would have made a great Beta Pi." I stand up. I'm so mad I can't sit still anymore. Colleen and Kim stay where they are. "*I'm* exclusive? Because the way I remember it, Missy and Laurie and I, and all the rest of the *exclusives*, were the ones who liked the girls no one else seemed to like. Exclusive? Hell, you want to be friends, let's be friends. That's about as exclusive as we get. How the hell is that exclusive?"

"You all sit together at lunch every day," Colleen snaps.

"Anyone who wants to sit with me at lunch, can. Come on over," I say, cutting her off. "I had lunch with Kim just yesterday. Right, Kim?" Kim doesn't say anything. Kim is keeping her head down. "There aren't any rules and there aren't any barriers with us. If you want to call somebody out for being exclusive and driving a wedge into the house, call out the Omegas."

"That's what I'm talking about," Colleen says, looking at Kim for backup. Kim's keeping busy by looking busy, her pen flying across the paper. "You've created this division, calling another group of girls *Omegas*. What does that even mean?"

"Remember Cindy Gabrielle? Remember how she was on Bid

Day?" I say. "See what she turned into? She started staying out all night, sleeping with anything that moved, was drunk half the time, forgot how to wear underwear, and would barely talk to anyone who didn't do the same. So we call it going Omega. I can't even remember when that got started, but that's all it means."

"And your group of friends is any different?" Colleen says. Kim looks like she wants to run out of the room, crying.

"Colleen, you don't know what the hell you're talking about. Karen barely drinks. Laurie barely leaves the house. Diane is so busy with ROTC shit that she barely has time to sleep. Yeah, we hit the Four-O when we can. But we're all different, and we're all good with that."

"According to your description of what it means to be an Omega, Missy Todd should be one. Why isn't she?" Colleen says. She really does have a stick up her butt. It's hard not to do her a big favor and pull it out and beat her with it.

"That's my whole point," I say hotly. "We're not exclusive. You want to hang with us, you're in. It's that uncomplicated. Yeah, Missy could have gone Omega, but she's not excluding anyone and neither are we. We hang together because we want to be together, with anyone who wants to be with us. Hell, there is no *us*. It's just . . . us." I walk to the door, my hand on the brass knob. "Kim, are you sure you got all that down? 'Cause if that's it, I've got nothing left to say. Is that it, Colleen?"

When Colleen just stares at me, her mouth open, I say, "Great. Thanks. Have a nice day. See you at lunch, huh?"

And then I walk out. Verbal trap, my ass.

"You'll never guess what just happened," I say, coming into my room, one of the second-floor two-ways I share with Missy.

"You finally picked a dress for the wedding," Missy says, her arm buried in her closet, shoving hangers out of the way.

Oh, yeah. Mike and I are getting married. The candle ceremony was last week. I wasn't sure I wanted the candle ceremony,
but Mike was for it, and it was great. I must have a secret romantic side hidden under all my ruthless common sense.

I'm marrying Mike Dunn.

I'm still trying to figure out how that happened. He was
always *there*, and I got used to him being there. And when he
wasn't there, it bugged me.

He makes me laugh. He turns me on. He knows he turns me
on, and that makes him laugh, and that bugs me and turns me on
at the same time. He drives me nuts half the time. It's crazy, but
I love it.

Mike drives Ed nuts most of the time, and I *really* love that. Ed
and Mike, two bulls in a tight pen and Mike's the young bull. Of
course Ed hates him. I really love that.

I can't believe I'm getting married; half the time, it seems so
unreal. The wedding is in late June. I'll be a June bride. I'm working hard to get a tan for the wedding. No way am I going to be a
pasty bride.

"Nope," I say, flopping down on my twin bed. Our beds, both
barely made, are covered in yellow rip-cord bedspreads. The drapes
are white and held back with yellow-and-white plaid ribbon. The
windows face the AG house. It's not a pretty view, but Missy and
I get a lot of pleasure out of staring at the AGs and saying stupid
stuff we know they can hear. Usually, they glare and shut their
drapes. It's the little pleasures in life that mean the most. "I just
got a private talking-to by Madam President."

"What could Colleen Larson have to say to you that she
couldn't shout out at lunch?" Missy asks, pulling out a white shirt
from the closet, looking it over, and then crumpling it up and tossing it in her laundry bag. She continues the hunt.

"Funny you should mention lunch. She was all over me about how we're an 'exclusive group of friends,' " I say.

Missy stops rummaging in her closet and stares at me. "What?"

"About how we—meaning you, me, Diane, Karen, Laurie, fill-in-the-blank—are making some of the girls in the house feel excluded."

"Excluded from what?" Missy says, throwing her butt on the bed and reaching for her cigarettes on the desk. She lights one up and leans against the wall, crossing her legs underneath her as she takes her first drag.

"From . . . us," I say. "Supposedly, we're too exclusive. We're an 'exclusive group of friends' and we make other people feel excluded."

"Well, hell, if they want to be included, join the party!" Missy snaps, her blue eyes sharp against her skin. Missy is very pretty, in a *get the hell out of my way* way.

She was that girl in high school who every other girl was sort of afraid of and in awe of, and the girl all the guys followed with their eyes, even if their feet were too afraid to do anything. Honestly, I'm not sure what Craig and Missy see in each other; they're so different. Craig seems so . . . sweet.

You know what I mean.

"That's exactly what I said. I don't think I convinced her. I also don't think I care."

"And what's she going to do? You're graduating in three months. I'd love to know what she thinks she's going to do," Missy says, puffing angrily on her cigarette. "Does she think she can assign us seats?"

"What's going on?" Cindy Gabrielle says, coming into the room. Against all odds and the Hollywood code regarding zombies in movies, we're turning Cindy back. She's no longer an Omega, not to the bone. I don't know how we did it, but we did. Score one for the Exclusives. "Can I bum a cigarette off you, Missy?"

"You don't smoke," I say as Cindy plops down on the bed next to Missy.

"I'm thinking of starting. It'll make me look older and I won't have to worry about getting carded," Cindy says. Missy does not give her a cigarette.

"Cut it out," I say. "You've never in your life had trouble finding booze. Don't start smoking. It ruins your teeth. Missy, show her your lousy teeth."

Missy grimaces, showing Cindy her teeth on command. Missy's teeth are perfect, so as an object lesson, she's a dismal failure.

"Yeah, I can see how grungy they are. Give me a cigarette?" Cindy says with a grin.

"You are such a mooch," Missy says. "First booze and now cigarettes. Here's one. The rest are on you. Welcome to the chain gang." She hands Cindy a Newport and lights her. Cindy takes a tentative puff. Predictably, she coughs.

"It's like living in an opium den," I say, opening the window wider. I see an AG across the way, changing her shirt. I move the window so that it catches the sun, reflected sunlight flashing her like a mirror. She turns, scowls at me, shouts something, and pulls the blind. "You don't have to actually smoke it. Just hold it and look tough."

Cindy couldn't look tough if she was riding the back of a Harley. She's got a face like Tinker Bell with freckles.

"What'd she say?" Cindy says, staring at the AG.

"I missed it," I say. "You know, she's the one I saw knocking down some of our bikes last week. Just bumped a few on her way down the sidewalk and kept going, just turned around and yelled, 'Sorry!' Like that fixed anything."

"Guillotine! Guillotine!" Missy whines theatrically.

"Or Sammy's! Sammy's!" I say, starting to smile.

Missy looks over at me, a smile spreading crookedly across her face. "You want to?"

"I could eat," I say. "And then, you know, we could toss what's left at the side of the AG house."

We've done this before. It's gotten to be something of a tradition.

"Are we going to Sammy's?" Cindy says. "I could really go for a Sammy's burger."

"Missy! Missy Todd," a voice calls down the hall.

"You're being paged," I say.

Missy gets up and stands in the doorway. "Yeah?"

"Colleen wants to see you," Joan Collier says.

"Your turn," I say to Missy. "Try not to leave bloodstains on the carpet."

"What the hell do I care? It's not my room," Missy says, walking back into the room to grab her ashtray.

"Hi, Joan," I say as Joan comes into view. Joan is a hard one to figure. I like her. She seems nice, but she's very, very reserved. Her cousin, Cindy Gabrielle, is being de-Omega-fied, and even though Joan never followed her into the Land of the Omegas, she stayed close to Cindy. I've always felt kind of sorry for her. I'd hate to lose a relative to the Omegas. "How's it going?"

"Okay," Joan says. "What are you guys doing?"

"We thought we'd make a Sammy's run. Do you want to come?" I say.

Missy, on her way down the hall, sticks her head back in and says, "Don't leave without me, okay? This won't take long. If you hear screams, give me a few minutes to hide the evidence."

"Roger that," I say. "Want to come, Joan?"

Joan looks at me cautiously. Joan looks at everyone in the house cautiously. I've never been able to figure it out. What does she think she joined? Charles Manson's splinter group?

"Sure," she says. "I guess so."

"Great. Who's driving?" Cindy asks.

"I'll drive," Joan says.

"Shotgun!" I yell just before Cindy does.

"You got me while I was trying to inhale," Cindy says. "Unfair."

"That's what you get for smoking," I respond with a shrug. "Life lessons, Cindy. Pay attention."

Cindy throws Missy's pillow at me. I duck and it lands at Joan's feet. Joan smiles, an unguarded smile, and picks up the pillow, tossing it back on Missy's bed.

"Let's see who else wants to go," I say, running a brush through my hair. I'm wearing JAG Jeans that have been hemmed to perfection, that little silver emblem shining on my butt, and a light green sweater. And my diamond studs. I got them for Christmas from my parents, but I know my mom is the real Santa on this one. Diamond studs are the latest must-have, and a total of eleven girls in the house got a pair for Christmas, Karen and Diane included. Missy didn't bother.

"You go make the rounds. I'm not wearing white pants to Sammy's," Cindy says, running out the door and down the hall to her room in the back five-way.

Joan clearly doesn't know whether to stay or go, so I say, "Do you need a wardrobe change?"

Joan looks down at her gray slacks and cream blouse. She's also wearing diamond studs, but she had hers before the Great Christmas Diamond Shower. In fact, Joan is the one who started the whole diamond stud craze.

"I wouldn't wear white," I say, slipping on a pair of navy espadrilles.

"I'll meet you at the bottom of the back stairs?" Joan says. She acts like we're going to ditch her.

"Roger that," I say. "You're driving, so don't leave without us. How many can you seat?"

"I have a Mercedes, two-door," Joan says, walking down the hall to her room, a two-way three doors down from mine.

"Okay, we're good for five or six," I say.

"You're only saying that because you called shotgun!" Cindy yells out from her room.

"Damn straight!" I yell back.

Joan laughs, a small, quiet sound. It's a good sound. Joan needs to lighten up. I laugh all the time and I've got Ed for a father. If I can laugh, anyone can.

Sammy's isn't too crowded, the line only five or six people long. Sammy's is an institution, as much a part of ULA as Sammy Spartan, even if it isn't on campus. Sammy's is on the corner of Beverly and Rampart, kind of a dive, but it's open twenty-four hours and is strictly take-out, though mostly we eat in our cars and not at the filthy tables crammed between the line and the parking lot. Will Joan's car survive? Yes, but not in its present pristine state. It is impossible to eat one of Sammy's burgers and not get it all over your hands, if not your shirt.

I'm thinking this as I'm standing in line, listening to Cindy talk about the guy she likes in her biology class; then I see Laurie leaning her butt against a car hood, trying to delicately eat a Sammy's burger. There's no way, but she's giving it her best shot.

"Laurie!" I call out, waving. Laurie jerks a bit in surprise, I guess, and straightens up. It's then that I see the car she's leaning against is Doug Anderson's car, Doug at the wheel, digging around in his glove compartment. Doug drives a blue Mustang in need of a wax job.

Shit.

This has to be an accident, right? Some kind of weird *I ran into him and we did not come here in the same car* Bermuda Triangle of bad coincidence. There is no way Laurie is seeing Doug. Laurie is so damn polite that she wouldn't know how to tell Doug to get lost if he was asking for directions to the Land of the Lost.

That has to be it.

"Hi," she says, walking over, tossing her burger into the nearest fly-swarmed trash can. "Did Colleen talk to you?"

"Uh-huh," I say, trying not to stare at Doug, who is watching Laurie and watching me and smiling that *I am so gorgeous* Doug smile.

"I had the idea she was going to hit everyone," Laurie says. "I thought I'd get a Sammy's to cleanse my palate."

"Doug Anderson's your chaser?" I say.

"Not intentionally," Laurie says, pulling on that ice queen coat she wears so well.

I'm shuffling forward in line, Joan and Cindy and Missy listening in on every word.

"Uh-huh," I say. I don't want to think what I'm thinking, but I'm thinking it anyway.

"You drove?" I don't see her car. Laurie bought a car when she turned twenty-one.

"Yeah," she says. "I'm over there." And she points to a spot behind a white van. I guess I'll have to take her word for it.

"All by yourself?"

"Have you ever been to Sammy's all by yourself?" she asks, looking a little more reserved with every word.

Laurie has levels of reserve, from full tank down to what you think has to be an empty one, but Laurie is never running on empty with reserve. You think she's out and then, wham, another few whiffs still left that the gauge doesn't quite register. But you do. Laurie can do cool reserve like no one I've ever met. I don't actually mind it. No one does. In a lot of ways it makes her very easy to be around, all that reserve at her disposal, able to calm things down nearly effortlessly.

"No, never," I say. "So what's up with Doug? Did you manage to dump half your burger on his car?"

Laurie smiles and says, "I was working my way closer, but I think he was getting suspicious."

I laugh. It's an effort.

Doug is off-limits. Doug is Diane's bad news and that makes him *our* bad news. Doug is a total shit and he deserves to be pushed off a high cliff. We all know this. This doesn't require discussion. Since it doesn't require discussion, it's impossible to find a way to discuss it. Especially at Sammy's. Especially with Doug sitting right there, looking at us.

"I'd better go," Laurie says. "I have a midterm this week."

"Yeah. See you later," I say.

We sound stiff with each other. I hate that, but there's nothing I can seem to do about it.

God, Laurie, not Doug Anderson. Please, not Doug.

Laurie

— Spring 1978 —

In the most innocent way imaginable, I'm spending time with Doug Anderson. How it started, I can't quite remember, possibly because it's such an innocuous relationship that it can't have an official, memorable starting point. Somehow, I just found myself talking to him and then seeing him more often, and he's kissed me. It was an innocent kiss, nearly European, and completely spontaneous. I was devastated instantly, but after thinking about it, I've decided there is nothing to feel guilty about. Diane and Doug were long ago. We're all graduating in a few weeks. Everything that happened in college, all these bonds, these fragile and ephemeral relationships, will disappear like smoke the second after we receive our diplomas.

There will be no Doug and Diane in July, no solid memory held firmly in place by a houseful of Beta Pis. It will all be as smoke, too inconsequential to last.

I'm sitting on the floor of my room this semester, the three-way that I'm sharing with Karen and Diane, smoking a cigarette and looking out the window, thinking all this through for the ump-teenth time, when I see them coming.

"Rho Delts!" I say, starting to laugh. This is the end of all this, the bittersweet, wonderful end.

"What?" Karen says from her desk. She's typing a paper for one of her classes. I think it's her twenty-ninth paper this semester, literally. "What about them?"

"Can't you hear them?" I say.

In the next moment she can. The Rho Delts are doing a panty raid on us. They charge the door, which is locked, hollering like the average American male eager to get his hands on feminine underwear, and they start grabbing girls on the sidewalk in sort of a hostage-style takeover, trying to get someone to key them in.

It's silly and scary all at the same time.

The girls in the house start screaming and running around, filling water balloons to drop out of windows on male heads, and since my room has the big window right over the front door, it doesn't take more than a minute before my room is filled with girls and dripping water balloons. It's complete pandemonium and I love every minute of it. The only problem is that someone—I think it was Joan—knocked my ashtray out the window while she was leaning over to drop a balloon.

"Sorry!" I yell.

"Sorry!" she yells.

They're not taking *sorry* in the heartfelt way in which it was rendered. Men are such barbarians.

"Here, get out of the way," Missy says, elbowing her way to the front of the pack by the window, throwing three or four pairs of bikini underwear out the window to the guys. There's a general sound of male appreciation at that.

"Way to make them work for it," Ellen says just before she heaves a massive water balloon over the windowsill, only to have it split and break in her hands before she can launch it.

"I don't mind giving it away," Missy says.

"No, really?" Cindy says. "Hi, Tim!" she shouts to the guys below.

"Tim? Tim's out there?" Diane says, pushing her way to the front. "Tim! Get the hell out of here! You've got enough pairs of Cindy's underwear!"

"Oh, my God! I can't believe you said that!" Cindy squeals. "That's not true!" she shouts out the window.

I'm not sure if she can't be heard over the uproar below or if the guys just don't want to hear that kind of disclaimer. I'm inclined to think it's the latter.

Matt Carlson is standing on the front lawn with his fraternity brothers, smiling at the general mayhem. Matt catches my eye and we smile at each other. I might actually miss him. I know him well enough to be glad to see him every time I see him. I think I'll ask him to the last party; he'd be a fun date. It would be too awkward to ask Doug.

I look around, down to The Row and the snarl of foot traffic our panty raid is causing, at the girls in the house screaming and laughing, at my friends pressed around me, these girls who were strangers three years ago and who are now my closest friends.

I'm going to miss this. I'm going to miss all of this.

One of the guys gets a fire extinguisher and starts blasting it through our mail slot. Some of the guys yell at him to stop, but not too many. Most of the girls start yelling at the guys to stop, opening the front door to do so.

They rush in, shoving past the girls in the foyer, rushing up the stairs, girls screaming more shrilly now, the pounding of heavy male feet, the slamming of doors up and down the hallway as girls try to barricade their rooms shut.

Cindy laughs and rushes out into the hallway.

Joan leaves the room, walking calmly into the melee.

Ellen rushes out, yelling at the Rho Delts to get the hell out.

Karen smiles and keeps typing.

Missy folds herself next to me on the floor and we light up together, looking out at The Row, the lovely smell of cigarette smoke coiling around us.

"I didn't expect all this when I joined Beta Pi," I say. Missy blows smoke rings and looks at me, brows raised. "I never expected to feel so at home."

"It's been great, hasn't it," Missy says, "but I was hoping for great. What are you going to do now?"

All I know for sure is that I can't go home.

"I've applied to law school," I say. It's not because I've always dreamed of the law; it's because I have the grades and it will take three years and that's another three years taken out of my hands.

"Cool. When will you know?"

"I heard. Yesterday, in fact."

"Is it a secret or something?" Missy asks with a smirk.

"No, I just . . . I don't know. I guess I don't want to think about it until I have to. I have a lot to do. I'm putting it off."

"Good plan."

"Do you really think so?" I ask. Because it doesn't sound like it to me; it feels like a fall back to the trenches, a *cover my ears and hide under the covers* move.

I have a trust fund. I have nowhere I need to be, nowhere I need to go, no one who needs me to be with them or to go where they go. I'm just making it all up as I go along.

"Sure. That's what I do," Missy says, stabbing out her cigarette. "What else can you do?"

"No life plan? No great strategy?" I ask.

"Life laughs at plans, McCormick. Haven't you figured that out yet?"

I guess I haven't.

Diane

The theme of this party, the last party for the seniors, is to dress as what you're going to be doing five years from now. I'm wearing fatigues. I look *so* pretty. I can't wait to see the photographs.

For this party, I brought Dave York for two reasons: he's adorable and he's funny. I can relax with him. We've spent a lot of shared hours in the Four-O together, swapping drinks and stories. Oh, and another plus for Dave: he's not ROTC.

I guess it goes without saying that all the ROTC guys know about Doug and me, and what happened, and then what didn't happen—namely, us becoming a couple. It was awkward for a really long time, which was hardly surprising, but the guys were cool about it for the most part. I got through it, but I don't want to go through it again. Ever. Navy guys and my love life have *got* to stay separate, just like they've stayed separate since Doug kicked me out of bed.

Yes, that's how I think of it. And, yes, it still hurts like hell.

Something's going on between Laurie and Doug, something that she wants to keep a secret but isn't quite a secret. They've probably gone out already, knowing Doug. I should tell her she should avoid Doug like the plague, but she won't listen to me because Doug has that effect on girls. They just don't want to say no. Trust me, I'm an expert.

The party, the final Beta Pi party for me, is at Stephanie Haynes' house. Her house is in the hilly part of Beverly Hills, so parking is a bear, but the house is gorgeous. It doesn't look that big from the street, big enough, but not huge, but when you go inside, the house just opens up and there's a big pool overlooking what looks like an endless forest, which we all know is impossible in LA. Stephanie's dad is a big name at one of the studios and her mom was an actress in the forties. They probably bought this house for forty thousand dollars in 1950.

"They're running low on vodka," Dave says, bringing me my drink as I sit on the diving board. "If you want more, you'd better hurry."

"Is this some sort of male thing? How to get a girl drunk in twelve easy lessons?" I say.

"Are you telling me you'd need twelve lessons to learn how to get drunk?" Dave says.

"Dave, that is not even close to what I said. I think I just got you drunk in one easy lesson."

"I didn't pay tuition for this class."

"You can take it pass/fail."

"You are not making any sense at all."

"That must mean it's time to switch to scotch."

"Diane, that part I understood," Dave says, chuckling.

He's a fun guy. Why couldn't I have fallen in love with him?

Okay, no. No. No. No. I'm not going to think that, not anymore. And especially not here, with Laurie just across the pool from me, sitting on the edge of the pool, her feet on the steps in the shallow end, Matt Carlson at her side. You can do that when you're wearing shorts and a cute Hawaiian shirt and Jap flaps. Me, I'm wearing combat boots. They're black. I look like a mushy G.I. Joe doll.

"You're a brave man, coming out with me looking like this," I say to Dave.

"You're nuts," he says, shaking his head and looking around at the crowd.

"What? You had a thing for G.I. Joe when you were a kid?" I say.

"Nah," Dave says, looking down at me. "I was all about Barbie. Taking her clothes off . . . watching her stiff-leg it around, naked . . ."

"God, you are one sick puppy," I say, laughing.

"Hey, a guy's got to get experience somewhere."

"Poor Barbie, so defenseless."

"Yeah. That's what made her so perfect."

"I am officially throwing up now," I say, standing up to shove him away from me. I'm laughing, so it kind of spoils my harsh and highly justified rejection of his Barbie mangling.

"You're throwing up? Already?" Karen says, walking toward the diving board across the pool deck.

"It's not what you think," I say. "It's Dave and his sick Barbie fascination. It literally made me sick. Well, almost. Give me a minute and I'll make it literal."

"Anything I can do to help?" Dave says. "Barbie had this red velvet cape and I—"

"It was velveteen, you moron," I say. "God, why am I helping him? Stop. Just stop with the Barbie debauchery."

"Wait," Drew, Karen's date, says. "A red cape. I'm seeing it. What else?"

"Okay, that's it," I say. "We are officially entering Barf City."

"What is it with you? Did you get a job at Mattel or something?" Karen asks Drew.

Drew is a senior, not in a fraternity, and is nice-looking in a scruffy, Italian sort of way. "No, but as the home of Barbie . . ." Drew says, his voice trailing off suggestively.

"Why don't you two get a room so you can have privacy to play with your Barbies," I say.

"You make it sound so dirty," Dave said with an offended look.

"What sounds dirty?" Cindy Gabrielle says, joining us at the diving board. Cindy, since she's not a senior, can wear whatever she wants. She apparently wanted to wear white pants, a pale gold silk shirt tucked in, and a gold braided belt. She looks great, I have to say. She got a Dorothy Hamill cut a year or so ago and it really suits her. Her eyes look enormous and her neck is about as thick as a number two pencil.

Cindy is working her way back from being an Omega. It's a beautiful thing to see. Joan Collier has been working on her, and since Joan is hanging with us more, the Exclusives, we've been working on her, too. Oh, yeah. We've taken that set-down about being an *exclusive group of friends* and run with it. We're now calling ourselves the Exclusives. It's pretty funny. Not what Colleen expected, I'm sure.

"Barbie," Karen says.

"Barbie's not dirty. I played Barbies all the time and there's nothing dirty about it," Cindy says, a puzzled look on her face.

"Play it with Dave," I say. "You'll be scarred for life."

"You played Barbies?" Cindy's date asks Dave.

Cindy's date has longish, blondish hair and a nice tan. That's all I know about him.

"This is Rob Gottschalk," Cindy says, introducing him. "We're in the same accounting class."

We all nod or say mumbled hellos, eager not to get in the way of Dave's response to Rob. This should be good.

"I played *with* Barbie, if you get what I mean," Dave says, grinning.

We all look at Rob to see if he'll get it.

Rob grins and nods. He gets it.

"I vote for an official change of topic. Before I hurl. Who's with me?" I say.

I raise my hand. Karen raises her hand. Cindy hesitates, looking at Rob, then at Dave.

"Cindy, you're with us," I say. "Raise your hand."

She raises her hand, laughing.

"Okay, that passed. No more Barbie talk," I say.

"It was three to three!" Dave says.

"Beta Pi party, Beta Pi home-court advantage. You lose. Try not to be a baby about it," I say, grinning at Dave. He's such a fun guy to party with.

"Fine," he says, shaking his head. "I need a refill to buoy my incredible grace in losing. Anyone else?"

"I have always heard that Rho Delts were great at losing. All that practice, I guess," I say, deadpan.

It goes on as parties do, mixing and mingling, talking and teasing, drinking and laughing. Stephanie's parents had greeted us all at the door, but they've made themselves scarce since. Her mom looks like an aging movie star, still pretty and casting a glamorous shadow.

Everyone is here tonight, every Beta Pi, and I find I can't stop looking at them all, memorizing faces, remembering moments between us. It's over. This is the last party, the last Beta Pi event.

The music changes.

"Oh, my God!" I say. "They're playing 'Brick House'! Let's go!"

"Brick House" is one of the best dance songs of all time. It's way better than "Stairway to Heaven," with all those weird tempo changes. If the Beta Pis have a theme song, and we actually do but it's too sweet to be our *real* theme song, it's "Brick House." Whenever it's played, we go nuts and dance like we're on *American Bandstand* mixed with *Soul Train.*

Every Beta Pi is already dancing, arms up, hips moving to the beat, laughing and dancing with one another, *for* one another. I jump right in, howling my happiness, pulling Karen along with me. We're laughing and dancing to the most chauvinistic song ever recorded, but who cares? You hear it and you've got to dance.

The guys are dancing with us, sort of. But really, it's just us, just the Beta Pis, dancing to our favorite song at the last sorority party we'll ever attend.

"Photog! Photog! Take our picture!" I yell. The photographer dutifully obeys and the flash lights us up for a second, the moment captured.

The only thing left to do, to end the night perfectly, is to hit Sammy's and throw Sammy's burgers at the side of the AG house. We'll take Joan's car.

Laurie

"So, what do you think? I know it's just a card table, but with the tablecloth on it, you barely tell, right?" Karen says, standing across the room, her hands on her hips, her expression both critical and hopeful.

"It's wonderful," I say. "I don't know how you did it, but the whole apartment looks charming."

"Well, we were starting out with standard Hollywood 1950s style. It's hard to go wrong from there," Karen says.

I could have gone wrong from that start, but I leave it at that. Karen and I rented an apartment on Riverside Drive in North Hollywood. It's a two-story apartment building with all the apartment doors on one side of the building, the second-floor balcony walkway providing an overhang for the first-floor apartments below. We got a first-floor apartment, which is a good thing since I'm positive we couldn't have carried our mattresses up a flight of stairs, let alone a couch.

"I can't understand how you made maroon-and-peach tile look cute," I say. There is peach tile with maroon trim tiles in the kitchen and the bathroom. The walls in the apartment are painted cream and the only air conditioner is a unit hanging out the bedroom window. The carpet is brown shag with the shag so tired at this point that not a single strand is sitting up at attention. The apartment was old, tired, a little grim, and small, but it was the right price at $245 a month, and it's a half a mile from the 101.

"I just didn't fight it," she says, straightening the tablecloth that was perfectly straight to begin with. "Go with the flow, you know?"

"If you say so," I say.

"With that attitude, I think this is the beginning of a beautiful friendship," Karen says.

"*Casablanca*," I say. "See? I'm learning."

"I'm so glad we're still rooming together; aren't you? It makes it seem almost like we haven't graduated. I still can't get used to not living in the house. It's so quiet with just the two of us!"

It is, and I'm not sure how long it's going to take me to get used to that, or if I ever will. I've lived for so many years in the midst of a throng of women, hiding in plain sight, able to become a part of something bigger than I am, even if it's only for a year or so. Now it's just the two of us in a one-bedroom apartment on the edge of the Valley. It is very quiet.

"I'll try to talk more loudly. Will that help?" I say.

"Give it a try. We'll see how it goes," she says. "So, really, you like what I'm doing with the apartment? You didn't have much say in it."

"I had no say in it, but that's fine with me. I think it looks great. I don't know how you did so much with a card table and two twin beds, but I'm impressed."

"Don't forget the white Naugahyde couch," she says, grinning. She got it at a consignment shop on Sunset, and it was vile, but after scrubbing it with cleanser and piling it with pillows from Nepal, it looks almost chic.

"You got a couch? I'll take it for a test flight."

We'd left the door open because of the heat, and there, crossing the threshold and walking into my apartment, is Doug Anderson. My heart shivers as he enfolds me in his arms for a quick hug.

"You found it!" I say. "Isn't this the cutest apartment? Karen gets all the credit."

"Hi, Karen," Doug says.

"Hi," she says. "I need to get the closet in order. You guys don't mind me."

With that, she walks into the bedroom and closes the door.

Doug walks over to the couch and sits down, spreading his arms across the back, grinning at me. One of the pillows slips to the floor. "It's a nice apartment. I'm glad you and Karen are living together again. She's always been your closest sorority friend—am I right?"

"Yes. I guess so," I say. "Can I get you something to drink? We have sodas and milk. We still need to buy a coffeemaker. Sorry."

The sound of the cars on Riverside can be heard inside the apartment. From the bedroom, I can hear the faint clink of hangers being pushed together. Above us, someone walks across his apartment and turns on a faucet.

"It's a little noisy, isn't it?" Doug says with a smile. "I'm sure you'll get used to it."

"I can't get you anything?"

"Nothing from the fridge," he says, patting the spot next to him.

I settle down next to him, leaning into his shoulder, smiling from my heart. I don't know how I ended up with Doug, with Diane's Doug, but I did. It all happened very fast, and it's still happening, in a way; we're still getting to know each other, finding our way into a relationship that was born as the college years were dying. Diane is gone now, stationed in Virginia, a continent between us, and Doug, at least for now, is here with me. It won't last. He's only going to be here for another week, leaving just before Ellen's wedding, which is probably ideal timing. I wouldn't want to face Ellen with Doug at my side, not at her wedding when she's supposed to be a blissful bride, though I can't imagine Ellen ever being blissful about anything, at least not for very long. It's easier with Karen. Karen has the knack for making everything easier, even my dating Doug.

"I thought I'd take you both out to dinner," Doug says, his hand stroking the back of my neck, kissing my temple. "I'd like to make up for not helping you move in."

"You couldn't help that, though we would have loved some muscle for the heavy lifting."

"How'd you manage it?"

"Karen ran into a guy getting out of his car in the parking lot, had him laughing in about a minute, and, presto chango, he held one end of the couch while we held the other."

Doug smiles. "Strategic strike. Well-done, Karen."

"I'll ask her if she's up for dinner," I say, kissing him quickly on the mouth before I get up. He pulls me back down and kisses me harder, a passionate kiss that makes my knees weak. "Or not," I say on a breath of air.

"No, go ahead," he says. "I'll behave myself. That's a promise."

"Hey," I say, opening the bedroom door to see Karen with a pile of clothes on her twin bed about two feet tall. "Doug would like to take us to dinner."

"Oh, no, you go ahead. I've got to get this organized before I can relax and even think about eating. By the time you get home we should be able to sleep in these beds."

"Really?" I say, looking around the room. It's a complete disaster, and half of the disaster is mine, but Doug is here and I want to go. It's as cold-blooded as that.

"Well, don't ask me to sign in blood, but yeah, it's possible you might actually be able to sleep in your bed tonight."

"I can't wait."

"Hey, would you mind if I hung some pictures without you? I just want to get everything set up the way I want it. Unless you wanted to do it?"

"No, go ahead. Whatever you want to do, I'm fine with it."

"Okay, thanks. And have fun."

She's back to tossing clothes around her bed before I can close the door behind me, grabbing some up by their hangers, moving others to the foot of the bed, making sense of it, obviously, though I can't see her method. I'm not even sure why I'm bothering to close the door to the living room, but she did it first, and so I do it.

Doug is standing right behind me, just barely on the living room side of the doorway, and I almost step on his foot as I turn around and face the living room. He catches me with a grin.

"Sorry. I just wanted to see how big the bedroom was," he says.

"Just big enough for two twin beds and a dresser," I say. "Would you like to see the bathroom?"

"No, I'm good," he says. "I take it it's just the two of us?" When I nod, he smiles and says, "Perfect. Let's get Mexican. I heard of a good place in Sherman Oaks. When do you need to be back?"

"Anytime. The night is ours."

"Just what I wanted to hear," Doug says as he escorts me out of the apartment.

Ellen

"So, we all want to know," Pi says, "are you still a virgin?"

I look around the room, the tiny living room in Laurie and Karen's new apartment. Half of us are sitting on the floor, but I've got the best seat in the house since I'm the guest of honor; I'm on the right side of a white couch that squeaks every time I shift my weight. It feels like the hot seat.

"You all want to know? Who wants to know?" I say.

Missy, Pi, Cindy, Joan, Candy, Holly, and Lee raise their hands. Laurie doesn't. Karen calls, "Don't tell us," from the kitchen. Diane abstains since she's in Virginia doing her navy thing. It's a toss-up whether Diane would raise her hand or not.

Pi looks around the room. "The *want to knows* win by a landslide. So. Are you?"

I grin. "To the bitter end. Hey, I made it this long. I'm going the distance."

"But you're not going all the way," Missy says.

"Not for another thirteen days," I say. "Somebody tell me the wait is worth it."

"Ask Mike," Pi says. "He'll tell you."

We all laugh at that. Mike hasn't been nice about waiting. I haven't been nice about being pushed. But then, there's never been anything nice about our relationship.

"I think it's good you're waiting," Karen says, coming around the corner from the kitchen with a tray of drinks. We're drinking mimosas because it's the only thing Karen knows how to make, besides screwdrivers, and Karen says *mimosa* sounds prettier than *screwdriver*, and who can argue with that? We're all dressed up, most of us in dresses, except Missy, who's wearing white pants and a blue silk shirt, slugging down mimosas at my bridal shower. I can't believe I'm getting married. I'm finally going to go all the way.

"So, come on. What can I expect?"

"You'll like it," Cindy says. "Just don't expect it to last very long."

"You need to go out with a better class of guy," Missy says. "It can last all night, if you want it to."

"No wonder Craig quit water polo. You wore him out," Pi says.

Missy smiles and lights a cigarette. "Have you heard him complain?"

"No guy is ever going to complain about that," Candy says.

"Can you open the door? It's getting hot in here," Holly says.

Laurie opens the apartment door. Laurie is not in this conversation. Laurie doesn't dare be in this conversation. We all know she's going out with Doug—Karen told us that—and none of us is cool with that. There's nothing to be done about it, but we sure as hell don't need to hear about it from Laurie. I can't understand what's wrong with her that she'd go over to the enemy like that. It makes me wonder if I ever knew Laurie at all.

"And it's not the conversation because you haven't told her anything," Joan says.

"Joan, okay, I'm actually asking this, but are you a virgin?" I say. "I can't tell."

"I guess that's good," Karen says, laughing. "Look, when do you want the cake? It won't fit in the fridge and the icing is looking drippy."

"Let them eat cake!" I say. Karen disappears around the corner to do her cake thing, Laurie right behind her.

We all look at Joan. Joan looks down at her drink and says, "I haven't been a virgin since I was sixteen. I lost it to Benedict."

"And you guys are still together. Wow. That's cool," I say.

"I wish I'd waited," she says.

"You mean, like, till now?" Pi says.

Joan shrugs. "Probably not. But I still wish I'd waited. I was so young."

"And felt so old. God, I thought I knew everything at sixteen," I say.

"You still think that," Missy says.

"No, now I know I know everything."

"Are you glad you waited?" Cindy asks.

"Yeah. I just hope it was worth it."

"It will be," Karen says, coming back in with the cake. It's a cake with white frosting and the words *This is it!* in red icing on top. "See how well I know you?"

We all laugh. I cut the cake; we eat it and slug mimosas until there's no more champagne and we're stuck with plain orange juice, but that's okay. It's time to start sobering up for the drive back to Northridge, back to Ed and my childhood bedroom, back to the pool where I played Marco Polo with my Girl Scout troop, back to the yellow kitchen where I ate Oreos and drank milk every day after school. Back to childhood.

Only thirteen more days. I'll be Mrs. Ellen Dunn in thirteen more days. I'll finally be able to scratch that itch that Mike starts in me every time he looks in my direction. He'll sure as hell be happy about that. Me, too.

Karen

I got promoted in March and could finally quit that drive downtown every day. It was brutal, not seeing the apartment in daylight except on the weekends. I'd leave in the dark and get home in the dark. I felt like a mole. It didn't help that my office didn't have a window, and that some idiot had painted it deep forest green. I was starting to feel like a character in a Grimms' fairy tale. Laurie dating Doug also added to the generally Grimm feeling.

Anyway, I got promoted to department manager at the store in Century City, literally on the border of Beverly Hills, and now the drive is through Coldwater Canyon, in daylight. I feel like a new girl. Plus, Doug isn't in California anymore and doesn't get leave much. It may not be very nice to think that, but I think it anyway.

I don't have time to date since I work too many hours. I also am not meeting anyone to date. Just a tiny detail, right? Every guy I meet is married, because they all married their college sweethearts, naturally. I knew this would happen. I couldn't seem to do anything about that and so it happened to me. I'm alone. The girl who was never without a guy, is without a guy. There's not a guy in sight.

You know what? I'm not happy about it, but I thought it would feel worse than this. I'm actually doing okay.

"I just got a call from the buyer and she's concerned that Heller isn't moving as quickly as it did last year at this time," I say to my assistant manager. "I want to come up with a new display and get it set up by Saturday morning. Any ideas?"

My assistant manager, Kent, says, "We did the rainbow theme last year."

"So we're not doing that again. I'll just look around and try to think of something. Would you check the stockroom and see how much Heller we have back there? I may want to pull it all out."

Kent leaves the floor and I start wandering around, looking at all the displays, wondering where to move things, imagining what things will look like. I'm the manager of five departments, one of them being pictures/mirrors. I wonder if I could do something with mirrors and the Heller plates? All of my departments are spread in a semicircle around the top of the escalator; it's a great place for grabbing a customer's attention. In theory, anyway.

No, my English degree has nothing to do with this job, but this is the job I got right out of school. It's an old, familiar story, isn't it?

"Excuse me. I'm looking for Helen?"

I turn and say, "Helen? Sorry. My name's Karen."

And then I look, and he's cute and tall and lean and has dark brown hair and dark brown eyes and he's smiling at me in that confused way guys smile when they're lost in the big, scary mall.

"Hi," he says, obviously looking me over. My hair is still short, but not as short, and I've gotten a perm, which I regretted instantly, and I'm wearing work clothes, which means a really nice outfit that I'm also not averse to getting dirty in the stockroom. "So you don't know a Helen? My mom wants Helen, plates or cups or something. For Mother's Day."

"She gave you an assignment, huh? And sent you to the mall and now you're lost and confused and can't find Helen."

"That about covers it," he says, looking sheepish and funny and just plain adorable. "Help?"

"I think what your mom wants is Heller plates. They're really high-quality plastic and they come in every color you can imagine and, since I can tell that your mom is a discerning shopper with exquisite taste, she's going to love having Heller dinner plates. Heller mugs. Heller salad plates. And anything else Heller makes that I carry. If I sell you everything we carry in Heller, believe me, I'll be fine with that."

I laugh. He laughs.

I tingle. I'm not sure if he tingles, but he's sparkling. He buys four Heller dinner plates in purple and walks over to the escalator without looking back. Until he's on the escalator; then he looks back.

The next day, while I'm on a ladder at the top of the escalator landing, hanging bright yellow plastic watering cans by clear fishing line from the ceiling panels, the escalator deposits him almost at my feet.

"Hey, that looks dangerous," he says.

"Imagine how it feels," I say. "I give everything to my art."

"Don't you need someone to hold the ladder for you?"

"I'd prefer it if someone would climb the ladder for me."

He laughs. I laugh.

I climb down from the ladder with only three out of nine watering cans hung.

"I thought I'd get my mom more Heller. I mean, four plates. She might need some cups, right?"

"Four purple plates," I say. "Would you like four purple mugs or would you like to spice it up and get hot pink? Or maybe yellow?"

I walk over to the Heller display—the old Heller display. The new one, with yellow watering cans, will be finished by tonight. He follows me. I can feel him behind me, and I like the feeling.

"I'm never against spicing things up," he says.

"Does your mother know that about you?" I say, looking at him.

"I think she suspects."

"Then she won't be surprised if you don't match purple with purple. I mean, your mom must be pretty adventurous herself if she wants purple plates."

"Well, she didn't ask for purple plates, but I think she'll like them."

"She has to like them. It's your Mother's Day gift to her; it's, like, a law."

He smiles. I smile. We ignore the Heller display.

"I'm Jim."

"I'm Karen."

"I remember. Karen . . . ?"

"Karen Mitchell, department manager and ladder climber."

"Jim Nelson, pharmaceutical rep and Heller expert."

"You're a Heller expert?"

"I plan to be," he says.

I grin. He grins.

Summer 1979 —

I walk into the apartment and Doug is there. I halt at the entrance, my key still in the lock, feeling like I just walked into a brick wall.

"Hi, Karen," he says with a smile.

"Hi," I say, pulling out my key and tossing it into the pewter dish on the desk next to the door. "Where's Laurie? I thought she had class."

"She does. She said I could hang out here until she gets back, sleep on the couch. I'm only here for two days. You don't mind, do you?"

"No, that's fine," I say, walking past him and into the bedroom. I normally change my clothes the minute I get home from work, but now I don't want to. I walk down the three-foot hall to the bathroom and do my thing in there, and when I open the door, Doug is standing right in front of me. "Hey. It's all yours."

"No, I'm good," he says, backing up just enough for me to get out.

I walk through the doorway into the kitchen and open the fridge. "Can I get you anything? We have sun tea."

"Thanks."

I pour two glasses and hand him his. He doesn't move. I do. I walk out of the kitchen and into the living room. It's a small apartment and there's no place to go where he isn't going to be five steps away from me. The fact that he seems determined to be in whatever room I'm in only makes it worse.

I don't like Doug. I haven't liked Doug since he reacted so badly to my refusing to go out with him. I don't like that Doug asked me out and that he asked Laurie out. He should have left all of us alone once he did what he did to Diane. I don't let myself think about what Laurie should or shouldn't have done. I love Laurie and I want to keep loving Laurie, but Doug makes it all very complicated and it's pretty obvious that he doesn't care that he makes it complicated. I don't like that either.

I sit at the desk chair in the living room. He can have the couch or the armchair. I'm past caring if he thinks that looks rude because, okay, it is a little rude, but he makes me uncomfortable. Doug comes into the living room, sees me at the desk chair, smirks, and sits back down on the couch.

"Hard day at the office?" he says.

"About average," I say. "I'm sorry not to be better company, but I need to get some bills paid. Can you entertain yourself? The TV's all yours." I turn to face the desk and pull out my checkbook. I only need to pay two bills, but if I dawdle, I might be able to make it last for twenty minutes. I don't know what I'll do after that. Clean out my purse?

Doug gets up off the couch—I can hear the squeak—and walks across the room toward me. I turn, moving the chair so that it's facing out, and stare at him.

"What's wrong, Karen? Don't you like me?"

"I like you just fine."

"You don't act like it."

"I lied. It was a hard day at the office. I'm just exhausted."

"Sit on the couch. Relax," he says, hovering over me.

I bolt up from the chair and say, "Oh, my God, I forgot. I need to return a library book. It was due yesterday."

Doug smiles and it's not beautiful. He's not beautiful. Oh, he's still gorgeous—I'm not blind—but he makes my skin crawl.

"I'll go with you."

"No. You stay. Laurie will be home any minute."

"Laurie doesn't get out of class until six, and then she'll be stuck in traffic, so I'm thinking, seven? Seven thirty? What should we do with ourselves until then?"

"I'm going to the library. You do whatever you want to do."

I grab my keys and my purse; the door is only a few inches from where I'm standing, but I can't seem to get to it. Doug steps around me and in front of me and suddenly I'm backing up toward the TV and the bedroom door.

"I just feel like there's this thing between us," Doug says. "I want us to be friends."

"The thing between us is Laurie," I say.

"I thought it was Diane," he says.

"Either. Or," I say. "Take your pick. Oh, yeah. You did."

"I tried to pick you. I wanted to pick you," he says, looking down at me in what I'm sure he thinks is confused compassion or something equally false. "I've always liked you, Karen."

"Yeah. You told me."

His shirt is unbuttoned to his nipple line, and then he unbuttons another few buttons, opening his shirt all the way. His chest is nearly hairless and dark gold in color. He's the golden boy, and he knows it. He's always known it.

"How about a hug? Between friends?" he says.

"Doug! I'm back! They canceled my last class," Laurie says from the doorway.

Doug turns around calmly and smiles at her, opening his arms for her. She drops her purse on the floor and is swiftly enfolded in his arms.

"I'll leave you guys alone. I need to run some errands anyway," I say, sliding around them.

"Thanks, Karen," Laurie says, turning in Doug's arms to look at me.

"Yeah. Thanks," Doug says with a sweet smile.

I shut the door behind me. It slammed a bit, but I'm blaming that on the wind.

Laurie

– Spring 1981 –

Today, Karen got married, just a half hour ago. I was not one of her bridesmaids, a fact that jolted me at first, but which I have come to accept with a sort of muffled heaviness.

Today, Doug Anderson and I have been dating for three years. I don't want to believe these two facts, not being a bridesmaid and dating Doug, are related in any way.

Even if they are, I love Doug.

He takes care of me, something I appreciate more than I thought I would since Karen and I shared our apartment for only a year. Karen said she needed to move to be closer to her job; she moved to a one-bedroom apartment in Santa Monica. I bought a condo in Marina del Rey, which is also closer to ULA than North Hollywood.

I know she said she needed to move, that it was all about the commute, but I think my dating Doug had something, maybe a lot, to do with our separating. The memory of him being Diane's Doug still hung between us then, between all of us. He hadn't become my Doug yet, I suppose.

Three years of dating, and Doug still hasn't asked me to marry him. I have to admit to being surprised, and a little hurt, by that. I try not to think about it; being at Karen's wedding has lowered my mental resistance and now I find myself thinking unwelcome thoughts.

I've been sleeping with Doug almost from the first date, not at all like me, and I don't know how it happened except to say that Doug is irresistible. I love him. What I felt for Pete Steinhagen is like a dream compared to what I feel for Doug.

I talked about it with Karen in North Hollywood, telling her I was in love with Doug, that he was *the one*. Karen kept a neutral expression on her face and let me talk and talk and talk. She's such a good friend.

Doug asked Karen out on a date once, back in college. He told me that. It was very sensitive of him, and very adorable, how afraid he looked when he told me, hoping I wouldn't think the worst. The worst? That he asked out a cute Beta Pi? I was extremely moved by his consideration; in fact, that moment on the white couch in our tiny living room, Karen not yet home from work, was when I first knew I was falling in love with Doug. That confession, so unnecessary and so disarming, was so completely and so remotely different from Pete, who never told me anything and who kept everything from me, two very different things. That confession, yes, that moment, his eyes so blue and so hopeful and so vulnerable—that was the moment I knew I loved him. It was September 1978, the sun was setting behind the trees, the light scattering across the shag carpeting of the apartment, and his golden hair was sparkling in the light. He laid his heart out to me, and I picked it up.

But from that day to this, little has changed in our relationship. I don't see him that often because of his navy duty stations, but when I do see him, it's blissful. If only we were married, then I wouldn't be alone so much, and neither would he.

I really need to stop coming to weddings.

Pete and Beth live in Chicago now. I just happened to hear that from one of Pete's old fraternity brothers, Matt Carlson (also known as Lavender Barrette), when I saw him at Bill Staniszeski and Holly Clark's wedding. I didn't ask Matt about Pete. I think that's important. I don't even remember how or why Matt brought it up, but he did. Maybe he thought I still might care, and I know I showed him that I didn't. But it was good to see him again; he's a fun guy, a nice guy, and he always can find a way to make me laugh about the craziest things.

I never talked to Pete after he and Barbie got engaged, except for that one time in my senior year when, just to hear his voice again and in a moment of pathetic weakness on my part, I called him; he answered the phone, the phone in the house he shares with Barbie, and I listened with my heart in my throat. Then I hung up without saying a word.

I have to admit that I don't understand why Doug hasn't proposed. We talk about getting married all the time. We say things like, "After we're married we ought to get a place in Palos Verdes." Things like that. I want to marry him. I feel like I've always wanted to marry him. Sometimes, most pointedly at other people's weddings, I wonder why he doesn't seem to want the same thing.

Pete used to say that I thought too much. Maybe he was right about that.

I don't drink at weddings, which is not the non sequitur it might seem; I don't drink because I don't want to get sentimental, demanding, weepy, or any combination of the above. I have only lately come to admit to myself that I do this so that I can keep everything calm and cool for Doug. No tearful questions about getting married. No questions of any sort. No demands.

Karen and Jim had a whirlwind courtship that lasted six months before he proposed. The wedding is twenty-two months to the day of his first receipt for the Heller plates. Yes, he kept it.

I spent a lot of days thinking about that after Karen called to tell me about Jim and about her wedding; when she first told me she was engaged after only a few months of dating him, I was worried about her and told her she should wait. I think even as the words were coming out of my mouth I knew it was the wrong thing to say, that it sprang from jealousy that Jim could fall in love with her so utterly and so desperately that he would be in such a hurry to marry her.

The comparisons are inescapable.

Karen was sweet about it, even though I was raining on her parade. She kept telling me that she knew what she was doing, that she and Jim were sure, and that she appreciated me being worried about her.

So Karen Mitchell married Jim Nelson in the gardens of the Bel-Air Country Club.

Jim is from La Jolla, but he works in Century City, and since Karen and her parents are all here in Los Angeles now, the wedding is in Bel Air. I think everyone was excited that there was an open date at the Bel-Air Country Club. It's a beautiful, serene place.

It actually has a very countrified feeling to it, a very upscale, *every blade of grass accounted for* country feeling. Karen and Jim are having a garden wedding. The trees are huge and overarching, the flowers lush and colorful, the air soft and warm. I've never considered a garden wedding before now, but this is quite lovely. I think this might be a good idea. I wonder what Doug would think of a wedding at the Bel-Air Country Club, though I also wonder if Karen would feel as if I "stole" her wedding.

"Laurie," Karen says, coming over to me and giving me a hug.

She looks radiant. She's grown out her hair so that it just brushes her shoulders. I've never seen her with hair that covers her ears, let alone touches her shoulders. She looks feminine and young, completely bridal.

"It was beautiful," I say. "You are beautiful. It was a beautiful ceremony. I'm so happy for you."

"Let me grab Jim," she says. Turning her head this way and that, she spots Jim across the lawn, rushes over to him, and slips her arm through his, apologizing to the elderly couple he was talking to, dragging him over to me. Jim is smiling the whole time, laughing at her, putting his arm around her waist and holding her next to him as they walk over to me.

"Laurie, hi. Thank you for coming," Jim says.

"You couldn't keep me away," I say brightly, pulling him in for a hug. Where is Doug? He should be at my side for this informal couples moment.

"As if we'd want to," Jim says.

"As if I'd let him," Karen says, her words tripping on the back of his. "All the Beta Pis are here—well, most of them. Have you seen Ellen? She looks exhausted. Make sure you talk to her, okay? I just wish Diane had been able to make it. I miss her so much; don't you?"

Yes, I do. But not as much as I probably should because, as much as I fantasize otherwise, being with Doug does make things slightly uncomfortable, particularly with Diane. In fact, Diane, Karen, Ellen, and I haven't been together, in the same room, since college. I think we all know, without having to dissect it, that it's better that way. Or perhaps it's not better, only easier.

"I do, and I'll track down Ellen the first chance I get. I think work is very hard right now, and with Mike still being in school . . ."

I let the thought trail off, and Karen and I exchange a look ripe with unspoken frustration and confusion about Ellen and Mike. She works and he goes to school. He never seems to graduate; he just stays in school. He could be Peter Pan's older brother.

Diane is in DC now, and very lonely. I need to get out and see her, before I start my job at Higgins, Stafford, and Lee, a law firm in Pasadena. I graduated from law school a week ago.

"Congratulations on the job. I hear they're a good firm. Good people," Jim says, reading my mind.

I nod and smile. They are a good firm. I had good grades. I also had good connections: my father was in the same Rho Delta Pi pledge class as Roy Stafford. I did not mention that in my application, but my father mentioned it to Mr. Stafford on the phone; I know this because Mr. Stafford told me about that phone conversation the day I was formally hired. It was on my lips to say, "Thank you," but I didn't. It didn't seem the appropriate response somehow.

"Speaking of good people, have you met Jim's cousin Jeff?" Karen says on a shudder. "I've been trying to figure out how to get him deported. No luck yet."

"I aced that test. I think I can help you out. Pro bono," I say.

"You two are lethal as a pair," Jim says, laughing. "I'm overmatched."

"We'll go easy on you since it's your wedding day," I say.

"Laurie, would you excuse us for a minute?" Jim says with a huge smile of regret. "I need to introduce Karen to my aunt. She came from Virginia and is only staying one night."

"Sure," I say. "Again, congratulations."

Jim leans forward and gives me a quick hug. Karen does the same, her hug lingering and fierce.

"I'll be back in a few minutes, okay?" she says. "Don't go anywhere."

I nod and watch them walk across the lawn, saying hello to everyone they pass, arm in arm, easy in each other's company, at ease in their effortless couple-ness.

The sense of isolation and longing rises in me so hard that it hurts. While the pain creeps along my spine, I look for Doug. He left for the restroom thirty minutes ago. How long could the line be?

At the thought, Doug appears at one of the French doors to the ballroom where the reception will be formally taking place; we've been lingering in the garden, the sunlight and roses enticing everyone to stay outside. Everyone except Doug. Doug has been to the bathroom.

I find that more annoying than I probably should.

Doug, his dark blond hair glimmering, his skin glowing, his eyes gleaming as blue as the sky—in short, looking as magnificent as any man has ever looked since men started bathing and shaving—beckons me and motions toward the wide French doors. The wedding reception is about to begin. I move through the crowd to join him, my heart wobbling just a bit, my smile a bit loose and happy. I swing between so many emotions, between annoyance and delight, confusion and joy. I'm a swirling top of emotions. This must be love, to quote an old song, although Karen and Jim do not seem to be enjoying the same brand of love that I am.

"Where were you?" I ask Doug once I have fought my way to his side. He has remained by the door, waiting for me. Annoyance makes an appearance. I look into his smiling blue eyes and try to find delight. Annoyance whispers, *Why didn't he come for you?* Delight answers, *He waited for you.*

"The line was a mile long," he says, taking my elbow and leading me into the room. The room is large and high-ceilinged, airy and sunlit. It's just the sort of room you'd expect to see overlooking such an exalted garden. There are circular tables covered in white tablecloths with pale pink linen napkins folded on top of the white china plates. In the center of each table is a floral arrangement of light pink tulips and dark pink tea roses and white calla lilies. The whole room looks like hope and joy and love, like springtime promise and eternal youth. "Where are we sitting?" Doug mumbles, looking at the table. There are no place cards on the circular tables. The only "assigned" seating is at the head table, a long rectangle where Karen and Jim and their bridal party sit. Jim's parents and Karen's parents are making the rounds of the room now, saying hello to everyone, stopping at each table. It's informal, nicely so. It's friendly and social and warmly inviting. My sisters did not have wedding receptions like this.

"I can't understand why you're not in the bridal party. You two are best friends," Doug says. "Where are we going to sit?"

I wouldn't be sitting with him if I was in the bridal party, but I don't bother to say that. There's no point in saying that.

There are tables of Beta Pis: Ellen and Mike; Cindy and her husband, Bob, married for only seven months; Lee Deming and Tom Foster, a guy she's been dating for about a year; Pi and Dan Coble, their fifth date; Missy and Craig. These couples take up the better part of three tables, scattered throughout the room, not clustered together, grouping into a tight unit. That's not our way. I think all those years of Rush have seeped into our bloodstream; we mingle. We are bonded, always aware of one another, yet we mingle. Because I know that, I don't feel excluded that no one has saved two seats for Doug and me.

Doug and I find a place at a table with Jim's aunt and uncle from Rhode Island, not to be confused with his aunt from Virginia, a widow. At our table are also friends of Mrs. Mitchell's from her college days, a college friend of Jim's and his wife, and two female friends of Karen's from the Broadway. We are ten to a table and we are a lively group. Doug is smiling and friendly; the girls from Broadway are shy and giggling in his presence. He smiles away their nervousness, comforting them, comforting the whole table with his confident manner and his beautiful bearing. I have seen him do this before. In fact, he does it all the time. It is just part of who he is.

My family has not met Doug yet, but they will like him very much. He is the kind of man that people are drawn to, that they admire, that they seek out. I wish Doug's schedule were such that he could be around more; the only reason he's here today is that he's stationed in Lemoore, just south of Fresno, but he wasn't always stationed there. It's been difficult having a relationship with a navy pilot, but I know I'm not the first woman to say that.

After dinner Karen and Jim circulate through the room, chatting with everyone. I watch them together, so easy in their awareness of each other, so effortlessly in tune. They look *good* together.

I look at Doug. Doug is bent over, retying his shoe, his shoulder bumping the table and setting the flowers to trembling against the confines of the clear vase. I look away from the vase and the flowers and Doug to watch Karen and Jim. In their circuit of the room they've saved our table for last, on purpose, I think, because Karen collapses into the chair left vacant by one of her work friends, motioning for Jim to do the same, which he does with a grin of delighted compliance. Karen slips off her white pumps and lifts her stockinged feet onto Jim's lap. She sighs in high exaggeration. Jim chuckles as she wriggles her toes.

"Laurie tells me you've bought a house," Doug says to Karen. Jim is rubbing Karen's feet, one at a time, his large hands dwarfing her foot. Jim's affection for Karen is so casual, so ordinary, that I catch my breath.

"We did," Karen says, smiling. "It's not a big house, but it's on a quiet street, so we're happy. We can add on later."

Jim groans and starts rubbing Karen's other foot.

"Are you still in Santa Monica?" Doug asks. The other couples, the older ones, have left the table with quiet excuses, leaving the four of us to ourselves.

"La Crescenta," Karen answers. "It feels like the country with big trees all around the house and a beamed ceiling in the family room, and the house is tucked against a hill. It's just so cozy and cute," she says, her voice getting more and more animated.

"Laurie didn't tell me you'd left Santa Monica," Doug says, looking at me.

Didn't I? I mentally shrug. Was it important that he know that?

"It's a shorter drive to Santa Anita, where my parents are, so that was appealing," Karen says. "And Jim's parents gave us the money for the down payment as a wedding gift—wasn't that sweet of them? So Jim's moved in already and is painting old woodwork and stripping wallpaper, and I moved out of my apartment and back in with my parents until the wedding, but I've been over to the La Crescenta house so much, doing this and that, that I feel like I live there already."

"Funny. It didn't feel that way to me," Jim says.

"Jim's got wallpaper elbow," Karen says.

"Is that what it's called these days?" Jim says, grinning.

"Manners, manners," Karen says, giggling.

Giggling. When was the last time I giggled?

"It's so nice that your parents live here now. That must be great," I say.

"Well . . ." Jim says on a drawl. Karen kicks him in the ribs, still giggling.

When it was obvious that Karen was staying in Los Angeles, and it became blindingly obvious once she met Jim, her dad retired and Mr. and Mrs. Mitchell moved to a two-bedroom house in Santa Anita, where I hear they've become regulars at the track and have made a whole new group of friends. I think I had a harder time than Karen did, thinking of that lovely home in Avon belonging to another family.

"Speaking of moving," I say, "did you know that Cindy and Bob live in San Diego now?"

Karen nods. "I heard that. Didn't he get a job with the Padres, something about baseball?" Jim laughs and shakes his head at her. "I'm a newlywed," she says, grinning at him. "Don't mess with me."

"Roger that," he says. Karen and I look at each other, our eyes wide in mirrored delight, and then we burst out laughing.

It's Diane. We caught the navy bug from Diane and it hasn't let us go. Doug doesn't laugh, and it occurs to me for the first time that I didn't catch the navy bug from him. "Candy and Steve are still in Hawaii, aren't they?" Karen asks. She's been busy planning her wedding and working long hours and most weekends; it's fallen to me—how, I'm not sure—to keep up with everyone. I nod my response. "I thought that was temporary," she says.

I shrug. "I think it's going well. She loves it there and he just got promoted, again. They bought a condo right on the beach. It's older, just one real bedroom and then an open loft bedroom, but it's right on the beach."

"We should go and visit her," Jim says briskly. "I'm sure she'd love to see you. And me."

Karen laughs and pokes Jim with her foot. Jim grabs her feet with both hands and holds her still. She grins in delight to be so fully captured.

"She says the door's open. Anytime," I say.

"Have you been?" Karen asks, looking at me.

"Laurie and I went to Kauai for a week last October," Doug says. Karen's gaze skims to Doug, registers his remark, and then looks back at me.

I nod. "It was wonderful. We had the best time, and Candy was amazing. She's such a great hostess she might even be in the running with Diane. We didn't lift a finger if she could help it, and she has a little girl who is just adorable."

"I'd love to see her," Karen says, looking at Jim, lowering her feet to the floor, her toes searching blindly for her shoes.

"We just bought a house, remember?" Jim looks at me. "Have you got any sorority sisters who can swing a hammer, work a chop saw? They don't even have to be nice. We're not fussy."

Karen laughs and shoves her palm against his shoulder, knocking him backward about an eighth of an inch. Jim just grins. I feel my heart melt a little and look at Doug, wanting to share the moment, make our own moment of melting hearts.

Doug is looking at Karen with a small, fixed smile on his face.

My heart stops melting.

"You should really try and go," Doug says to Karen. "There's only one bathroom, but being on the beach like that . . ."

"The view is amazing," I add, looking at Doug.

Karen is shaking her head, grinning at her husband, when Doug says, "There's a great restaurant about a mile from their house. You can walk down the beach to get there. We did. It was fantastic; wasn't it, Laurie?"

"It was," I say, watching Doug. Watching Doug watch Karen.

"It sounds amazing," Karen says, "but, aside from the house—and what *is* a chop saw?—I don't want to leave my parents."

"How are they?" I ask, looking discreetly around the room for them. Mr. and Mrs. Mitchell are sitting at a table near the high table, their backs to the wall, their faces tired and relaxed. Mr. Mitchell looks a little gray and completely exhausted.

"Dad's getting old," Karen says. "He's looking old, you know? But Mom's great, full of energy and ideas."

"*Lots* of ideas," Jim says.

"Oh, shut up," Karen says with a grin. "Your mom has ideas."

"My mom lives in La Jolla," Jim says. "Her ideas have farther to travel."

It all sounds truly wonderful. I don't have any of it. My family is scattered across the world; my sisters are all married with children and husbands and in-laws of their own. I have a niece who was just sent away to boarding school, falling in line with family tradition.

"Well, back to mingling," Karen says, standing up, reaching a hand out to Jim and mock-pulling him to his feet. He towers over her, his height looking protective and sheltering. "Don't skip out, okay? I want to talk to you some more before we leave," she says, staring at me, her eyes seeing things in me I don't want her to see.

Living with Karen for that year, the two of us in that apartment, changed things. They changed things in me and in her; I'm not sure why or how, but they did.

"No skipping," I say. "I promise."

But I'm not sure if I mean that or not. *Just be happy, Karen. Be happy today!* My eyes tell her that even if my mouth doesn't, and I know she can see that in me, because she smiles her biggest smile, her eyes beaming down into mine, and links her arm through

Jim's and says, "Come on and show me a good time, cowpoke," and off they go, Jim laughing under his breath.

Doug and I are alone at the table, deserted in some sense, and I *feel* alone and deserted. I don't understand why. The feeling hangs over me until all I can think of is how to escape it.

"I'm going to say hello to Mr. and Mrs. Mitchell. I'd like to introduce you," I say to Doug. I don't know why I'm being so formal. Why can't I sling my arm through his and say, "Follow me for a good time, sailor," or some such silliness? Why can't we *play* together?

"You go ahead," Doug says. "I'm going to get something from the bar. Would you like anything?"

So formal. Have we always been like this? I can't remember anymore.

"No. I'm fine. I'll find you at the bar; this won't take a minute."

I make my way to the front of the room and Mr. Mitchell smiles to see me approach. He was a middle-aged, slim man with a fringe of grayish hair when I met him that summer in Connecticut; now he's a skinny old man with a rim of silver hair. He's aged two decades in four years. He looks frail and brittle, as if he'd crack into shards if he fell to the floor. But his smile is still wide and welcoming, just as it was then. He welcomes me as if I'm precious, because he believes I am precious to his daughter. Perhaps I am. I hope so.

Mrs. Mitchell looks just the same. She gazes at me warmly, her smile brilliant, but I still approach her somewhat hesitantly, and I feel guilty about my hesitation, but that doesn't change anything. Mrs. Mitchell intimidates me, just a little bit.

"Congratulations!" I say, leaning in to give them both a hug. They've risen to their feet to hug me in return. "It's a beautiful wedding and a beautiful day, and doesn't Karen look amazing?"

"Oh, do you like her hair?" Mrs. Mitchell asks, sitting back down and offering me a seat with a wave of her hand. "I prefer it shorter," she says, without waiting for a reply from me, "but I suppose you girls like long hair for a wedding."

"It's traditional, I suppose," I say.

Mr. Mitchell just smiles at the two of us; I'm not certain he understands the undercurrents of the conversation. I'm not sure I understand them either.

"Well, hair is hair. It can always be changed," she says. "Now, what are you up to, Laurie? Karen tells me congratulations are in order. Congratulations on finishing law school and being hired right off the bat! Your parents must be so pleased."

"Thank you. Yes. They are," I say. I think it might even be true.

"Are you excited?" Mr. Mitchell asks, smiling at me. He's the most genial, pleasant man.

"I am. A little scared, but mostly excited," I say. "But how about you? Are you two enjoying retirement?"

They laugh together, at the same time, and fully in harmony, looking at each other askance. It's just the way Karen and Jim are: the same harmony, the same bone-deep humor.

"We're staying out of trouble," Mr. Mitchell says, a gleam in his pale gray eyes.

"At the racetrack?" Mrs. Mitchell responds, laughing at him and at themselves.

Mr. Mitchell shrugs and laughs in mock innocence, his hands raised.

"Now, Laurie, when is it going to be your turn?" Mrs. Mitchell says, turning the conversation back upon me like a ricocheting bullet. "Any marriage plans?"

Marriage plans? I have nothing but marriage plans. The problem is that I don't have a marriage proposal. But I don't say this out loud, even though the words crowd against the roof of my mouth, pounding against my teeth.

No, I don't say anything, but Mrs. Mitchell must see something of it in my face because she loses her smile and leans toward me and says, "Laurie, it's none of my business and your own mother should be saying this to you, if she hasn't already, but if he hasn't proposed by now, after all this time and at your age, he's not going to. I wouldn't say anything, but I hate to see you hurt, and I hate to see you waste any more time on a man who isn't going to marry you. You're a sweet girl. I just want you to know what you're getting into."

Or not getting into.

The words hang in the air, between us, before slicing into my hopes.

I smile woodenly and get to my feet. "Thank you. I'll keep that in mind. It was so good to see you again. Congratulations!"

I walk away before the words have reached their ears, but I've said them; I've said all the right things in just the right order. I haven't said anything that I'll regret later. I haven't said anything of importance either, but that's the price of civility and decorum and the appropriate level of personal privacy. It's a perfectly reasonable price and I'm more than happy to pay it.

Ellen waves me over to where she's sitting, giving me a destination. The band has started and Karen and Jim are dancing their first dance, grinning at each other as newlyweds do, so aware of each other, so aware of everyone witnessing this moment in their lives, this joining. It's a moment both so private and so public, I can't think of any other moment like it. I sit in the empty chair next to Ellen. Mike is nowhere to be seen, and for this I am thankful; I tolerate Mike—even more, I work to not actively dislike him. I wish I had the precise word to describe what it is about him that I don't care for, but I blame him for that. He's a very difficult man to describe. He can be charming, in a dangerous way, and that eternal bad-boy type appeals to a lot of women, but not to me. It's that he knows he's a bad boy, which makes it all so false, so premeditated. Does a true bad boy know he's bad? Isn't he just being himself? I think that's the heart of it; Mike is too self-aware, and that seems very calculated, and that I don't like. I also don't like that he can't seem to find his way out of the schoolhouse. There's something very calculated about that, too.

"They're beautiful together, aren't they?" I say to Ellen, looking at Karen and Jim. The band is playing "It Only Takes a Moment" from *Hello, Dolly.* It's an unapologetically romantic song, and it seems exactly like Karen to choose it.

"She looks amazing," Ellen says, swirling the melting ice in her water glass, her legs crossed, one leg swinging under the table. "I like her hair like that; don't you? I like it short, too, but this is nice."

"I do," I say, thinking again of Mrs. Mitchell, and then refusing to think about Mrs. Mitchell. "Are you going to stay much longer?"

Ellen looks at me sideways. "I'm staying until they run out of booze. What's the matter with you, McCormick? Do you have the flu or something?"

I laugh and shake my head, looking around the room. Doug is standing in a nearly empty corner of the room, talking to one of the Broadway girls, the one with the blond Farrah Fawcett hair, like twin sausages rolled next to her cheeks. It's not that I hate the hairdo; it's that, if you're going to do it, do it right. Mike Dunn is standing with a couple of guys I don't recognize at a table three over from us. He's drinking a beer out of the bottle.

It's tacky. This is a wedding, after all, with tablecloths and centerpieces, not a backyard barbecue or a fire pit at the beach.

"I'm just tired," I say.

"All that book learning will do that to you," Ellen says sharply, setting down her glass and crossing her arms. I know this isn't about me. The last few times I've been with Ellen, she's been like this; as cutting as a knife, honed down to razor sharpness. She's like this with everyone lately, and I know that because we've all been comparing notes, sharing our impressions of Ellen and discussing possible causes and corrections. We've all come to the same conclusion: Mike.

"How's it going with Mike?"

"Same old, same old," she says, picking at her cuticles, her modest wedding ring winking dully.

I reach over and put my hand over hers, stilling her fingers. "Are you okay?" I say softly.

"He's still in school, Laurie," she says on a rasp of congealed fury. "He can't seem to find a way to get a job. I never planned to work for the rest of my life; that was his job. He works. I stop work to have a baby. Then I stay home and play mommy. How the hell did I wind up the breadwinner?"

I shake my head, afraid to speak, afraid my dislike of Mike will show no matter how carefully I choose my words. A woman can rant and rail about her husband all day long, but let another woman join the chorus and that friendship is over. Mrs. Mitchell told me that, via Karen. I have a few issues with Mrs. Mitchell, but on the whole, I think her motherly advice is sound.

"Are you trying to have a baby?" I ask.

Ellen snorts. "On my salary? Sorry," she says, the result of my unintentional cringe.

"No, go ahead. What?" I say.

Ellen shakes her head and licks her lips, hesitating. "I want a baby. I want to get pregnant, but I can't. Not when it's like this. What if he never gets a job? What if nothing ever changes?"

"He will get a job eventually. You just have to hang on," I say, wanting it to be true.

"Oh, believe me, I'm hanging on," she says, looking across the room to where Mike is standing. He seems to feel her gaze because he looks at her then, his gaze both smoldering and arrogant, as if he's daring her to do something—what, I can't imagine. Then he drinks another swig from his beer, staring at Ellen the whole time. "But, hey, don't worry about it. I'm just tired and in need of some fun. Which is why I'm not leaving this party until they lock the doors. Are you leaving soon?"

She doesn't ask about Doug. No one asks about Doug, nothing beyond the barest polite question, quickly dismissed once I answer. Is this the same tactic as the one I use when talking to Ellen about Mike?

The dancing continues, Karen dancing with her father, Jim's father, Jim again. Other couples find their way to the small dance floor next to the long wall of French doors. Doug finds his way back to me and Mike finds his way to Ellen's side, and there we sit, Ellen and I listening to Doug and Mike talk about the traffic and the price of gas and the state of ULA football. Listening to the sounds of male bonding when no bond actually exists. Ellen and I, we have a bond. Our bond is so firm that we don't need to talk our way to it, finding it, reaffirming it through words. I feel her lingering depression, the aura of hopelessness that she is fighting off with both hands, and I sit beside her so that she will know that I am there with her, willing to fight if she will only tell me how.

What she feels in me, I don't want to know.

In a sudden burst of energy, Ellen pushes back from the table, saying, "Enough of this!" She slides around the side of the dance floor as I watch her; the men stopped their conversation for only a few seconds at her outburst and are now back to whatever they were saying before, which was the cost of fuel for an F-14. I don't care about that. I don't need to know about that.

Ellen says something to the bandleader, he grins and nods, and then she's coming back toward me, flashing the ULA victory sign, two fingers in a V. Yes, the same two fingers held in the same position make the peace sign, a staple of our childhoods, but the ULA victory sign is aggressive; the arm is extended, the fingers pointing toward the "enemy," the wrist making a well-timed nodding motion. Victory. Victory for us, it mutely shouts. We will be victorious. There will be no peace. There will be only victory.

When the song finishes, the opening chords of "Brick House" waft over the room and Ellen starts laughing, pulling me by the hand up out of my seat, toward the dance floor.

"Not 'Brick House'! Not at my wedding!" Karen wails, a smile splitting her face.

"Stop whining, Mitchell!" Ellen yells, moving her hips to the beat, dragging me with her. "Come on, Laurie. Let's go," she says, dancing in front of me.

I look around the room. Jim has taken a seat, his arms crossed behind his head. He is grinning from ear to ear. Mr. Mitchell is laughing. Mrs. Mitchell is shaking her head and smiling. Pi and Cindy and the other Beta Pis get up, laughing, running to the dance floor, their hair a wild tumble, their arms raised as the singer wails, "She's mighty mighty at letting it all hang out." Karen's wedding dress is lifted into a ball in her hands, holding the white silk in front of her like a wadded-up towel, dancing wildly to our song at her wedding to Jim Nelson.

Some of the other Beta Pi husbands sit around Jim at his table, watching us, laughing, urging us on. Doug sits where I left him. As I dance, he gets up and leaves the room.

It is on the drive home when things that I didn't even know were connected, connect. Maybe it was the wedding or the fact that I have a shiny new law degree. I don't know, but suddenly, certain things, unwelcome things, drop into place.

We're on the 405 going south toward my place in Marina del Rey, when Doug says, "You know I asked Karen out, right? I told you that."

"Uh-huh," I say, staring out the front window at the traffic in front of us.

"Why wouldn't she go out with me?" Doug asks. I can see him out of the corner of my eye, glancing at me as he brakes.

"I don't know."

Right after Doug and I started dating, Karen told me that Doug had asked her out. I suppose it was an effort at full disclosure on her part, but there was also the thread of warning in what she said so long ago. She told me that Doug had asked her out, and that he'd kept asking. She told me that she'd never gone out with him and that she'd never even been tempted to go out with him. I heard that as a clear sign that he was mine for the taking, not that she could have had him and didn't want him.

How many times do I hear what I want to hear? See what I want to see?

I didn't hear that he wasn't worth taking.

Right now, at this moment, stuck in traffic, I'm starting to realize that Doug doesn't want to believe that someone rejected him. Worse, he doesn't seem to understand how someone *could* reject him.

Does he love Karen? Does he suffer from unrequited love for Karen?

My mind swirls back to all the images I have of Doug and Karen, all the strange, focused looks he gave her, and her reactions to him. The time I came home early to our apartment in North Hollywood and Doug was there with Karen, and Karen looked harried. I thought she'd had a hard day at work, and I said as much, and she didn't deny it. But what had they been doing? Back then, I couldn't have suspected Doug of anything remotely suspicious. In the years since, my imagination has given birth to various, typical suspicions that I have ruthlessly killed in embryo.

"She never talked to you about it?" Doug asks. His voice is urgent. This is not a casual question. Why isn't it a casual question?

"No, not really," I say, staring at the lights, willing my brain to stop. My brain disobeys me flagrantly; I will my thoughts elsewhere. The traffic is moving fairly well, not in fits and starts, but at a steady forty or forty-five miles per hour. It's not very fast for a freeway, but you take what you can get on the 405.

You take what you can get.

"She never told you why she wouldn't go out with me?" Doug says. "She never gave you a reason?"

The same question, though put in a slightly different form. Badgering the witness.

"Didn't she give you a reason?" I ask, still staring at the lights. I close my eyes and shift in my seat.

Closing my eyes so I won't be hurt—how long have I been doing that?

"Yeah," he says, changing lanes in one sharp swerve of the

wheel so that we're now behind an eighteen-wheeler, the view to the front completely blocked by diesel-streaked metal and tattered mud flaps with a silver metallic girl showing off her large metal breasts and flowing silver hair. "She said she didn't want to go out with me. But there has to be a reason. She never told you why? You never talked about it?"

Asked and answered, my new legal mind says dispassionately.

I can't see in front of me anymore; all I can see is the truck and the image of huge metal bosoms.

"Laurie?" Doug asks, prompting me.

"No, we never talked about it," I say. "I don't know why she wouldn't go out with you. The next time you see her, you should ask."

But he won't see her again.

All the little pieces, falling into place. A thousand conversations, a hundred things unsaid, every expression analyzed, every event of my life since Doug waltzed into it peered at with new eyes, with Mrs. Mitchell's unwelcome counsel and Karen's stiff wordlessness covering it all like cheap, waxy frosting.

Doug doesn't love me. He doesn't want me. I'm convenient, at best. I ask no questions and I apply no pressure. I don't need him financially, and I have been too carefully reared to push for what I want.

The girl with the metal bosom flashes reflected light into my eyes, agreeing with me.

Diane

— Fall 1981 —

Mom's dead.

I say it, but it doesn't mean anything; it doesn't seem real. It came out of nowhere, just nowhere. We just didn't see it coming. Dad is a shell, just a washed-out, messy shell of himself. He can hardly dress himself, and I have to call every day and ask him if he's bathed, eaten, taken the trash out, I'm stationed in San Diego now, as of September, so that helps—at least I'm closer—but Camarillo is a long drive from San Diego. Still, I drive up every weekend. He talks about her all the time. "Diane, Mom wouldn't want her dish towels hung like that." "Diane, Mom wanted the photo albums arranged *this* way." "Diane, no, we have to keep that; Mom and I bought that in Tijuana in 1955."

She's been gone five weeks.

I don't know what we're going to do without her. I don't know how I'm going to take care of Dad and do the navy shit. I don't know what to do now. Mom's gone.

"Dad? I'm home! Where are you?" I say, opening the door and walking into the foyer of my house, the house I grew up in, the house my mom made brownies in, the house where Mom and I decorated the Christmas tree, Bing Crosby always singing "White Christmas" when we hung the ornaments, Dean Martin singing "Baby, It's Cold Outside" when Dad strung the lights (it muffled the sound of his swearing). My house. This is my house. This is my dad's house. Even though my mom is gone, it has to still be our house. If it's not, then where are we supposed to go? This has to be home, and I have to make sure Dad knows it's home. But who's going to remind me?

I need this to be home. I don't have anyplace else to call home.

"In here," Dad says from the living room.

I walk up the short flight of stairs and see him sitting on one end of the beige couch, his end, the TV turned on low to some football game. He's got a drink sitting on the end table, on a coaster. Mom was fanatical about coasters. I don't think Dad leaves this spot. He's here every time I see him, whether I'm coming or going. I think he sleeps here.

"You'd better be watching UCLA," I say. "And we'd better be winning."

He smiles briefly and says, "UCLA versus Cal. UCLA is getting their ass handed to them in a bucket."

"Couldn't happen to a more deserving ass," I say. "Though I feel for the bucket."

It crosses my mind that, in some families, the daughter would give her grieving dad a hug or a kiss in greeting, but we're not a Hallmark kind of family—never have been—and it's too late or too weird to start that kind of thing now. It would only make us both feel uncomfortable, our grief exposed for all to see, even if it's just the two of us.

Just the two of us. God, what are we going to do without Mom here to hold us together?

"What do we got?" I say as I walk into the kitchen.

"Pabst, Coors, Johnny Walker, some cheap vodka Irene Inhulsen brought over."

I look in the fridge and see the bread I bought last weekend, half-gone, the cheese I bought last weekend, one-quarter gone, a jar of strawberry jam, almost full, an unopened half gallon of milk, and the container of orange juice I made him just before I left last Sunday. Oh, and a rotten head of lettuce.

"Dad? What are you living on? Peanut butter? I'm going to run to the store, get some eggs, make us an omelet." I throw out the lettuce. The garbage is overflowing. "Dad? Empty the trash, will ya? We'll get roaches."

"I haven't been hungry. I'm fine."

Yeah, you're fine. We're both fine. I feel like I'm going to cry. Worse, I feel like I might as well sit and cry and just give in to all of it, the hopelessness, the exhaustion, because why the hell not? It doesn't make any difference what I do. Mom will still be dead. Dad will still be grieving. And I'll still have to drive back down to San Diego tomorrow and have to get up for work at oh-dark-thirty. What's going to change? So the trash overflows? So what?

I grab a Coors, pop it, and walk back into the living room. I don't sit on the other end of the couch—that's Mom's spot—but I sit in the green chair closest to the window. That's my spot. We're each in our spots, everything in place, except it's all blown to hell.

"What quarter is it?" I ask.

Before he can answer, a car toots its horn out front. I ignore it. Another toot. I lift myself up by my elbows and look out the front window. A car is in our driveway. Then another. Another pulls up on the street.

It's them, the Exclusives. Karen, Ellen, Laurie, Pi, Missy: the local Beta Pis. Candy's in Hawaii and Cindy's in San Diego, pregnant and hovering over a toilet fifteen hours a day, to hear her tell it. I saw her two weeks ago; I believe every word. She looked like death—happy, but like death.

Karen sees me peering out the window at them, waves, big grin on her face.

I crank open the window. "What are you guys doing here?"

Ellen looks up and shouts, "Open the door! We come bearing gifts!"

"You know what they say about Greeks bearing gifts," Laurie says, waving a hand at me while she opens her trunk and lifts out bags of groceries.

"The Spartans were the crazy Greeks," Missy says, "so be careful, but open the damned door."

"What's going on, Diane?" Dad says, barely bothering to glance over his shoulder, hypnotized by the TV and the grief that is holding us both in its slimy grasp.

"It's the Exclusives, Dad. I think we're hosting a party."

I run down the stairs, let them in, and they surge in like freshwater into a stagnant pool, sweeping the grim reaper out of the house, pushing silence away from them, gathering me in on a tide of laughter and bitching.

"Get out of my way, Ryan; the ice cream's melting all over my hands," Pi says, pushing past me and rushing up the stairs into the kitchen. "Hi, Diane's dad!" she says to Dad as he sits, dumbfounded, on the couch. The sound is hitting him, I think, all these female voices, washing over him. He's missed this. Mom and I must have sounded like this, on a smaller scale, of course.

"They had this fantastic sale on bread," Karen says, holding four bags at once. "So, I bought a few loaves. You can freeze it."

"She bought every loaf they had," Missy says. "It was embarrassing."

"Hey, they want to sell bread, two for a dollar, I'm going to buy bread," Karen says. "It's all wheat. I hope your dad likes wheat."

"After ten loaves, he'll develop a taste for it," Ellen says. "I was in charge of fruit. I got your dad bananas and apples. If he doesn't eat them, the fruit flies will hound him from room to room, so he'd better eat them. Hi, Mr. Ryan! How about a banana?" Ellen says as she rushes through the living room to the kitchen.

Laurie comes in last, carrying three bags that look heavy. I reach out through my shocked delight and take one. "I was in charge of drinks," she says. We both stare into each other's eyes and burst out laughing at the same moment.

It's been weird with Laurie ever since the Doug thing. I mean, she went out with him for three years, and then she broke up with him right after Karen's wedding. I haven't seen her much since we graduated, mostly just heard from everyone else what she'd been up to, and I know she's gotten the word on me through the grapevine, but it's been weird. Awkward. I guess there was no way it couldn't have been, but I appreciate this moment so much, this quick slide into the relationship I used to have with her. I've missed her.

"I bought the stuff I didn't think he'd have, like milk and cranberry juice and V8. Cranberry juice is supposed to be really good for the urinary tract, you know," she says.

"Geez, no, Doctor, I had no idea," I say as we climb the stairs together and head to the kitchen. Dad has turned off the TV. He's starting to get up off the couch; I almost expect to hear creaking, like a bridge being raised.

"She's been talking about the urinary tract for an hour," Ellen says. "I tried to shove a loaf of wheat bread in her mouth, but Karen wouldn't let me waste it."

"Two for a dollar!" Karen says over her shoulder.

The kitchen is jammed with girls, cupboards being opened and slammed shut, the fridge being reorganized. They're talking over one another, reaching over one another, arguing and laughing and *living*. Bringing life. Bringing food and life.

"What were you in charge of, Missy?" I ask.

Missy turns to look at me, leaning her butt against the sink, getting shoved aside by Karen, who is looking under the sink for something. Karen comes up with a can of Comet and a new sponge and starts attacking the kitchen sink.

"Paper goods," Missy says. "I bought a lot of toilet paper. I figure we can TP somebody on your street later. Who deserves it?"

"Irene Inhulsen," Dad says, standing just outside the kitchen, taking it all in, a smile just starting to life on his face. "She gave me cheap vodka."

"God, what a whore," Pi says. "Does she have no shame?"

"Clearly, we have to get rid of it," Ellen says. "Oh, you have orange juice! Already made!"

"I insist we wait until five before we start drinking," Karen says over the sound of the tap.

"Prude," Ellen says under her breath. Pi laughs.

Laurie looks at me, then at Dad. Dad looks so weak, so weary, so fuzzy around the edges, and on the face. When was the last time he shaved? Laurie looks back at me and says, "Got any laundry? I bought some new detergent that I'd love to try. On someone else's clothes first. You know, test run."

"I thought you were in charge of drinks?" I say, looking at Dad's clothes. He has stains on his pants and his shirt looks greasy.

"It only took a minute to do drinks, and I got bored, so I broadened my base to include all liquids," Laurie says, a wry smile on her face. "So, clothes?"

"Roger that," I say, tears starting to fill my eyes. I turn to Dad and say, "Come on, Dad. Let them do their worst. We're having a party. Go grab a shower and make yourself pretty for the ruffians."

"Go on, Diane's dad," Pi yells. "Doll yourself up for the TP party at the Inhulsens' later tonight!"

"After we can drink and get in the proper frame of mind," Ellen says, looking daggers at Karen. Karen squirts Ellen with dry Comet as a reply and, with a grin, starts on the stovetop.

I love these girls.

It is at twenty-three hundred, after Dad is in bed, in clean sheets that smelled April fresh, and the kitchen cleaned (again), and the toilet paper put away in the linen cupboard, only one roll having been tossed over Irene Inhulsen's massive juniper next to her mailbox . . . Reformed? Us? Come on. Yes, I'm an officer in the navy, but I still know how to toss a roll. Anyway, at twenty-three hundred, sitting around the coffee table in the living room, Missy tells us she's getting a divorce.

"What happened?" I ask.

"Who's doing it? Are you divorcing him or is he divorcing you?" Laurie asks, running over my question.

"Yeah," Ellen says. "Who started it?"

"It's not a playground fight," Karen says.

"It might be," Laurie says.

Laurie is a lawyer fresh out of law school; I keep forgetting that.

Missy takes a drag of her cigarette, blowing smoke rings at the ceiling. When she lowers her gaze back to us again, her eyes look shiny. She blinks a couple of times, looking down as she taps ash off her cigarette, and then looks at us. Her eyes look fine now, but I know the drill. I know all the ways to hide that you're crying when you're really and truly crying inside, and that one little bit leaks out and you have to kill that leak so you don't humiliate yourself.

"He did," Missy says, "but he's right. It's over. Time to move on."

We all look at Missy, at the tough, hard chick that Missy is and always has been. I've loved it about her. We all have. But now I wonder how much of tough-chick Missy is from necessity and not nature.

"What happened?" Karen asks.

Karen is the only one who can ask, who has the clean romantic history that allows her to ask. Laurie had Doug, and that ended badly. I can say that because I had Doug and it ended badly. Experience is the mother of all teachers. Ellen has Mike, but something is going wrong there; you can hear it in everything she doesn't say. Pi dated a guy for about two years, her senior year of college and then the year after college, but it didn't go anywhere. He just drifted off . . . and married the next girl he dated eight months after he took her out. Pi hasn't had a real boyfriend since. I should talk. I've had dates because, come on, I can always find a date, but I haven't been in love. I can't seem to fall in love. Sometimes I wonder if Doug burned me up and left me in ashes. Mostly, I try not to think about it.

"He wants kids," Missy says. "I can't do kids, not with the diabetes. Too risky."

"He knew that going in," Ellen says.

"Yeah, but it means more now," Missy says, crushing out her cigarette.

"What are you going to do?" Karen says.

Missy gets up from the floor, collecting our dirty glasses from the table, walking toward the kitchen. "I'm going to get divorced."

Karen

I stare at her profile for a moment, the sunset fading to purple and gold, casting her face in a soft warm glow. I haven't been alone with Laurie since we shared that North Hollywood apartment; that seems important now. I feel like I've lost something with Laurie, that our connection, through benign neglect, is frayed and thread-thin.

I let the silence in the car build, convincing myself it's not an uncomfortable silence. I tell myself that Laurie is concentrating on her driving. I tell myself that it will all be fine once we get to Diane's apartment in San Diego, once all the other Exclusives surround us, buffering us against the awkwardness of secluded intimacy.

I used to have the knack for lying to myself. I'm out of practice.

"He used to ask about you all the time," Laurie says, staring at the road. "Doug, I mean."

I look at her. "No kidding," I say.

I don't know what else to say. Pursue it? Let it drop? Doug broke her heart, which is bad enough, but he also broke into us,

the Exclusives, and broke something we had between us. He did
it through Laurie, and I don't think I've ever really let myself
think about how angry that made me at Laurie. She should have
shut him out. She should have put us first. If I could, the girl who
couldn't say no, she should have, too.

"He always asked me why you wouldn't go out with him. He
couldn't let it go. He always wanted to know what your *real* reason was."

Is this why my connection to Laurie got so thin? Did Doug
drag me into the middle of them?

"My real reason? Like I had a fake one? What did you tell him?"

"I told him I didn't know. I told him to ask you. I told him that
whatever you'd told him was the reason, *was* the reason."

"That's true," I say.

The silence stretches out again. It's my turn to offer something
up. I know what I want to say, but I don't know how to say it. Old
scars and old wounds, sloppily healed, thick and ugly. It was a long
time ago, and yet it's still so fresh, and still so important. How
does everything, every hurt and every memory, stay so fresh and
real and important when it's so very old?

Bodies age; memories don't. My mother told me that.

"What was the reason?" Laurie asks me, her eyes lit up by the
headlights of the car behind us as the light bounces against her
rearview mirror.

"The biggest reason? I couldn't do it to Diane," I say, still star-
ing at her. If I'm going to strike a blow, I'm going to face her when
I do it. I'm not going to thrash around with my eyes closed. "He
hurt her so much. Diane seemed torn up about it for a long time,"
I say. "I still worry about her." *And about you.* But I don't say that.
I can't quite make myself say that.

"He does that," Laurie says softly. "He tears you up. What were the other reasons?"

I sigh, not wanting to say it, knowing there's no nice way to say it. "He just seemed too good to be true, you know? Like a fake ruby, too red, too sparkly, exactly what you think a ruby is supposed to look like, except they don't. How could he seem so perfect for Diane, and then do his snake-charmer thing and seem so perfect for me, then so perfect for you? He just keeps reinventing himself."

"You didn't trust him."

"That's the short version, yeah."

"I think he cheated on me," Laurie says.

"I'm so sorry," I say. "He seems like the type." I pause, trying to hold my tongue. I can't. The lid has been pried open. "How could you go out with him, Laurie?" I ask. "I didn't understand it then and I still don't understand it. He was so brutal to Diane."

Laurie stares straight ahead, her face expressionless, the sunlight sliding down to deepest mauve, the headlights slicing into the growing darkness.

"He asked me. He was . . . nice to me," she says. "He was just so nice, so attentive. I thought he was charming. I guess I still do, looking back."

"And he was so damned handsome," I say, looking at her. "His not-so-secret weapon."

"Yes. That didn't hurt."

"Except that it did hurt," I say. "Right?"

"Old wounds," Laurie says, adjusting her rearview mirror. "Old history."

He was nice to her. That was all it took? Sadly, I believe it. Laurie, all alone in the world, falls for the first guy who bothers to pay attention to her for more than five minutes at a stretch. I

suddenly feel like crying. Why was I mad at Laurie? Laurie is
defenseless.

Laurie keeps her eyes on the road. After a few seconds, she says,
"Do you think Diane has . . . I mean, it's been a long time now . . .
Do you think she was upset about it?"

"I don't know. You might want to talk to her about it," I say.

Laurie glances over at me and smiles briefly. "Yeah. I probably
should."

We drive on in silence after that, Doug Anderson hovering in
the air between us.

The restaurant is nice. It's dark and atmospheric, and the service is good. I'm not sure where it is since I don't know San
Diego at all, but it's on the beach.

There are eight of us, but the table isn't long enough to make
conversation difficult. We sit three on one side and three on the
other with one on each end, a rough plaster wall separating
the restaurant from the bar at my back. The restaurant is Friday-
night full and noisy. But we're noisier, as usual.

I'm sitting across from Laurie with a nice view of the ocean.
Ellen and Holly are next to me, and Missy and Cindy are surrounding Laurie. Diane and Pi are at each end of the table. We've
eaten, taste-testing off one another's plates, something I don't do
with just anyone, and while we're waiting for the dishes to be
cleared, and not impatient that it be done, somehow the conversation aims directly at Laurie's love life.

I swear it wasn't me.

"You've been dating him—what?—how long?" Ellen asks. "Is
it even dating? It sounds like whenever Rick feels like giving you

a call, he does, having you drop everything so that it's all on his time, his schedule. Otherwise, he can't be bothered."

"It's not like that," Laurie says stiffly, looking across the table at Ellen. "He's a father. He's a *good* father. He has to put his kids first. He wants to be there for them."

"So what? He's a saint now? So he's a dad," Ellen says, her voice rising. "Can't he be a dad without treating you like a piece of shit?"

"Please, can we not do this?" Diane says from her end of the table.

"You don't even know him," Laurie says. "Besides, we're not even dating anymore."

"That's my point! You were *never* dating him. You were just there for him, whenever, or not, if he didn't feel like it. God, Laurie, when are you going to go out with a guy who doesn't treat you like shit stuck to his shoe?"

"Guys, come on," Diane says, looking around the restaurant.

People are starting to look at us. I'd feel more uncomfortable if I didn't think Laurie needed to hear this, even if Ellen's timing and choice of words aren't the best. At least someone is saying it. Holly is toying with some noodles on her plate, mashing them back into soggy flour. Cindy is looking at Laurie, her gaze sympathetic, her jaw locked tight.

"He's a nice guy. You don't even know him," Laurie says with quiet dignity. "I know him. I know the choices he's made. They're the right choices for his kids. He's just thinking of his kids."

"But he never thinks of *you*, Laurie; that's the problem," Ellen snaps. "Why do you keep zeroing in on guys who can barely stop to give you the time of day? First Pete, and then Doug, and now Rick—"

"Oh, God," Diane moans, resting her elbows on the table and putting her hands over her eyes.

"You keep falling for the wrong guy, the guy who just wants to screw you over until something better comes along. Find someone who actually cares about you—"

"Stop it!" Laurie says sharply. We all snap our gazes to her. Laurie never speaks sharply, about anything. Calm. Cool. Composed. Classically restrained. That's Laurie. "You think this is what I want? You think I have guys falling all over me? You think I don't know what you all think of me?"

Her eyes are full of tears, her hands clutching her napkin. She casts a gaze around the table, looking at Diane the longest.

"Laurie, it's okay," I say softly, remembering our conversation in the car, wanting to shoot myself.

"You think I planned that I'd be alone? Maybe I deserve it. That's what you think. Maybe there's just nothing in me to love. You think that, don't you? You all think that," Laurie says, her voice high and strained, her tear-filled eyes finding mine. Accusing me silently.

That big, silent, empty house she grew up in until she was twelve, until she was sent away. Those silent parents who don't come to anything important to her, like her graduations from prep school and college and law school. Parents who were never there except to pay a bill. Parents who taught her without saying a word that she was on her own. Parents who didn't show her she was loved simply by paying attention to her.

Doug was *nice* to her. So she fell in love with him.

I shake my head, my eyes filling with tears, and reach across the table toward her. "We don't think that. Why would we think that? We love you, Laurie. We just want you to be happy."

Laurie snorts and twists her napkin on her lap, shaking her head nervously.

"I don't think so," she murmurs.

"I love you, Laurie," Ellen says, her voice lowered. "We all do."

"Really. We do love you, Laurie," Diane says. "We do. I do."

Laurie looks at Diane, her eyes full of tears. Diane nods at her, smiling.

"We just want to see you with a guy who appreciates you, who treats you right, the way you deserve," Ellen says. "Hell, the way we all deserve."

"Yeah, well, so do I," Laurie says, her voice a sliver of sound.

"And that settles that," Diane says. "We all agree that Laurie is wonderful, and guys, in general, are pond scum. Let's get the check and get out of here."

The check does not come on command, and so we sit, staring at our laps, at the tabletop, at our dirty dishes, trying not to look at Laurie or at one another. But I do catch Diane's eye. Diane looks at me, tears in her eyes, and shakes her head once, briefly.

In that simple moment, I know that Diane forgave Laurie about Doug, if forgiveness was even required, long ago.

"God. I'm sorry," Ellen says.

We all look at Ellen.

"Hell has officially frozen over," Pi says. "What are you apologizing for? I want to get this down in my diary."

"I'm being a bitch," Ellen says.

"Yeah, not worth writing that down," Missy says, smiling at Ellen.

"Look. Shit. I've got good news and bad news," Ellen says, looking around the table at us. "I'm pregnant."

"Congratulations!" Holly says. Holly and Bill had a baby last

September, a blond-haired, blue-eyed boy who looks almost exactly like Bill. Holly told us that she finds that extremely annoying since she's the one who did all the work. "When are you due?"

"Is that the good news or the bad news?" Pi asks.

"Oh, nice," I say. "Congratulations, Ellen! I'm so happy for you!"

"What's the bad news?" Diane asks, trying to signal the waiter for our check.

"I've left Mike," Ellen says.

We're all quiet for a moment, the air sucked out of us. But only for a moment.

"I'm still waiting for the bad news," Missy says.

Ellen, who has been holding herself very still, suddenly bursts out with a laugh. The old Ellen laugh. It strikes me that I haven't heard her laugh like that, like herself, in years.

"You're right. It's all good news," Ellen says.

"What happened?" I ask.

"Besides him still being in school," Laurie says.

"Yeah, that's been fun, huh?" Ellen says.

The waiter arrives at our table, looking harried, and Diane says, "Bring us a cheesecake. The whole thing. Thanks." She waves him away with an apologetic smile.

"I thought we were leaving," Cindy says.

"You thought wrong. For this kind of conversation, we need cake," Diane says. "It's tradition. Go on, Ellen. What was the final nail in his coffin?"

"He cheated on me. With a coed. Okay, so she was older than your average coed, but still—" Ellen says.

"So's he," Pi interrupts.

"If he did it once, he probably did it ten times," Ellen says.

"How'd you find out?" Laurie asks.

"The regular way," Ellen says.

"You did a Sam Spade on him?" I ask.

"Enter the eighties, will you, Mitchell? I'm exhausted trying to keep up with your old movie references," Pi says.

"Okay, substitute Magnum for Spade," I say.

"Uh, this is about me right now," Ellen says. "Try to stay focused, people."

"Go ahead," Laurie says. "What happened?"

"I walked in on him. That's what happened," Ellen says. "He was with her at Paradise Cove. Can you believe that? Doing it on the couch where I used to sleep with my sister when I was ten. Doing it with her in my favorite place on earth."

"Oh, my God," Diane says. "That's disgusting. What a jerk."

"Tell me about it," Ellen says. "So I open the door and there they are; his pants were down and her skirt was up and her blouse was off and they looked like a couple of teenagers, going at it in Daddy's house. Which, now that I think about it, is basically the gist of the whole situation."

"Asshole," Missy says.

"What'd he do when you caught him?" I say.

"He swore," Ellen says. "Honest to God, I think he was swearing at me. He didn't look the least bit guilty. He just looked mad."

"Oh, Ellen," I say. "I'm so sorry."

"Well, I'm not," Pi says. "I always thought you were slumming with him. Good riddance."

"You know something?" Ellen says. She pauses as the cheesecake appears, waits while the waiter serves eight plates with eight dessert forks, waits while the waiter asks us if we need anything else. Diane thanks him and waves him off. "Want to know what my first thought was? *I'm not going to let him ruin this place for me.* That's what I thought. That. Not, *I'm having a baby and what am I going to do?* No, I thought about Malibu. That's when I knew it was already over. Because my first thought was about the beach and that house and how I wasn't going to let him screw that up for me. So, really, it was over before he took off his pants."

"Amen," Missy says.

"What did your parents say?" Holly asks.

"That's the weirdest thing," Ellen says. "Ed is completely for it. I told them the whole deal and Ed looked me in the eye and said, 'You're better off without him.'"

"Go, Ed!" Diane says.

"What are you going to do about the baby?" Cindy asks, picking at her cheesecake.

"Have it," Ellen says. "Should I be scared? I'm not. I'm just glad Mike is out of it."

"You hope he's out of it," Laurie says. "Do you have an attorney yet?"

"Well," Ellen says, looking at her, playing with the crust on her cheesecake. "I was kind of hoping you'd be available. I need a shark. You're it."

Laurie looks at Ellen, and the look they share is so full and so—I don't know—deep and connected. Forgiving, that's what it is. No matter what's said or what's happened, or what will happen, they're there for each other. We all are.

My eyes fill with tears and I wipe my nose with my napkin.

"I'd be delighted," Laurie says. "When can we get together?"

"What's wrong with right now?" Cindy says.

"As hard as it is for you to grasp, some things are confidential," Ellen says.

"But not much," Missy says, lighting a cigarette. "How many people know the pants-down-in-Malibu story?"

"As many as you want to tell," Ellen says, laughing.

That laugh again. Ellen is that laugh. Mike stole that from her. I'm glad she stole it back.

I start to cry, tears of joy, I'm pretty sure.

"What are you crying about? Haven't we agreed this is all good news?" Ellen says.

"Delayed reaction," Diane says. "She's having a bad reaction to the cheesecake."

"No," I say. "Well, maybe." Sniffing, I add, "I have some news, too."

"Oh, God," Pi says. "They're going to throw us out of here in a minute."

"Not until we pay, they won't," Diane says. "What is it, sweetie?"

I smile, sniff, and say, "I'm pregnant."

"I've got to get the hell out of here," Pi says. "It's obviously catching."

"Congratulations, Karen!" Diane says. "That's fantastic!"

"I'm so happy for you," Laurie says.

"How far along are you?" Ellen says. "I'm six weeks."

"I'm at thirteen weeks," I say.

"Thirteen? God, you still look like a straw," Ellen says. "I'm already having trouble buttoning my pants."

"Back away from the cheesecake," Diane says.

"Shut up," Ellen says, grinning.

"Can we pay the bill and blow this pop stand?" Pi says. "We have stuff to discuss and we need privacy to do it."

"We discussed divorces and pregnancies here," Ellen says. "What else is there?"

"How we're going to RF Mike," Missy says.

"RF?" I laugh. "I haven't heard that since college." RF is short for *rat fuck*, and if anyone deserves to get RF'd, it's Mike.

"In honor of Mike Dunn, we're bringing it back," Missy says.

"I knew I loved you guys, but it's always great to have proof," Ellen says, eyes gleaming.

It is at Sunday brunch, before we all have to head back to our real lives and our home addresses, that the subject of Missy and her diabetes comes up. Why this stuff always has to happen in restaurants, in the public eye, mystifies me. It's probably because it can't get too ugly or too personal in public. I'm not sure that's actually true, but it feels like it should be true.

"How's it hanging, Missy?" Diane asks.

Diane hasn't seen Missy in months, not like those of us who live in LA. The change in her must have been startling. Missy doesn't look good. She's in a war with her diabetes, and the diabetes is winning.

"Low and floppy," Missy answers, pushing a sausage around on her plate. It leaves a grease trail. "But at least it's still hanging."

There's a silence at the table while we all look at Missy, each thinking our own scary thoughts. The prognosis doesn't look good, though Missy stopped talking about her medical issues just over a year ago. Missy isn't one who could ever be pushed to do anything she didn't want to do, and we don't want to push her anyway. We just want to be there for her, to be whatever she needs us to be, whenever she needs it.

"Do you want to talk about it?" Diane asks. We all stare at Diane. Diane isn't playing the game the way Missy has taught us to play it.

Missy just stares at her.

Diane says, "Look, when my mom died, I wish I could have talked about it with her. She had to have known something was wrong, but she wouldn't talk about it, and then she died and there was no talking about it ever again. It left a big hole."

"Maybe that's the way she wanted it," Missy says. Missy's hair has gotten very thin; the light from the parking lot outside the window shines across her scalp and gives her face a death-mask quality. But the Missy fire is still in her eyes and she still looks like the kind of woman who could take down a serial killer.

"It was hard on the rest of us," Diane says, holding Missy's glare.

"Yeah, well, dying is hard on the person doing it. Maybe they should get to call it," Missy snaps.

We all take a breath, looking back and forth between Missy and Diane. Even Ellen is holding her tongue.

"So go ahead. Call it," Diane says. "What's going on? What do you want? What can we do for you?"

"Come on, Diane," Holly says.

Diane ignores her. So does Missy. Missy is staring Diane down, but it's not working since Diane is just staring back. Missy shakes her head and smiles at Diane. "Okay. I want a blowout, drunken brawl of a funeral. That's what you can do for me. None of this sad-sack shit. I'm going out and I want you guys to party, and I want you to act like I'm there with you. And if Craig shows up, I want somebody to kick his ass."

"I'm in," Ellen says.

"I knew the ass-kicking would get you," Missy says.

"You're sure? That's it?" Diane asks. "Nothing else, like, between now and then?"

"Do you need anything now?" I ask.

"Hell, no. I'm fine," Missy says. "Where'd you learn that stare-down, Ryan? I used to be able to have my way with you."

Diane barks out a laugh. "I'm a naval officer. I do stare-downs every damn day."

"I knew having a ROTC sorority girl was a bad idea," Missy says.

"At least I didn't carry a backpack," Diane says, throwing her napkin at Missy.

The waiter comes over to refill our water glasses, which is the only thing that prevents brunch from turning into a napkin war.

Ellen

— Spring 1983 —

So, I'm pregnant. I'm divorced. I'm a new broker with Dean Witter and making ends meet. I'm in labor.

That is my life.

I should probably be panicking. I'll get to it later, when I have more time.

"Shit," I say, rubbing my back.

"Four minutes apart," Karen says, looking at her watch. "Your back hurts?"

"Like hell," I say.

"Might be a back labor. They're gruesome, from what I've heard," Karen says. "Mine was normal."

"Normally painful?" Diane says, holding up a hand as Karen opens her mouth. "Shut up. I don't want to hear about it. It's *all* gruesome details."

"Your mom should be here soon. I called her from the restaurant," Laurie says.

We'd been out to dinner in West Hollywood. Diane is still in San Diego, but she got a promotion and a transfer, and because of my due date being two weeks ago, we were out celebrating Diane's promotion and Karen's first girls' night out after her delivery in LA territory. Figures I'd go into labor before my Alaskan king crab was delivered. Laurie paid the tab, when all we'd had was drinks and half a basket of bread. That figures, too. Laurie likes to pay when no one is looking, and then we shove folded bills into her purse when she's not looking. Tonight, everyone is looking at me.

"At least your water didn't break," Karen says. "Mine did with Ben, and I had the whole thing planned in case it happened in the grocery store, like they say. I was all set to run to the pickle aisle and chuck a bottle on the floor and call it pickle juice."

"Who the hell says that?" Diane says.

Karen shrugs. "Everybody. It's what you're supposed to do, to hide it."

Diane starts laughing. "Where'd your water break?"

"In a Hallmark store," Karen says, starting to laugh. "Not a pickle in sight! I could have thrown down a bunch of cards, maybe sop it up, but . . ." She shrugs, still laughing.

"They'd probably have made you pay for the cards," I say, feeling another backache coming on.

We're in Laurie's car, a nice four-door Mercedes, leather seats. I really don't want my water to break in Laurie's car. I'm sure she feels the same way about it.

"We're almost there," Laurie says. "I'll park the car and you guys go in."

"No, I'll park the car," Karen says. "You go in with her. You're the one who's good with legal forms and stuff."

"Thanks, Mitchell," Diane says. "What are we, pickle juice?"

"Basically," I say, the pain subsiding. "What? You didn't know?" I say to Diane, her profile lit up by a streetlight. I can see her smile, but it's a nervous smile. She hadn't planned on this. I'd planned on it two weeks ago.

"You can follow us in," Laurie says. "Follow the paper trail."

"If that's what you want," Karen says to me. "Believe me, it's not a spectator sport. You might not want an audience."

Karen had Ben nine weeks ago; she's the resident expert on kids and pregnancy, and I don't know how I would have managed this whole pregnancy deal without her. She and Jim have been there for me every step of the way. She even found a crib for me, and then Jim set it up. I call that sacrifice above and beyond the call of duty.

Blame the phrasing on Diane.

Another pain hits me. It starts in the back and wraps around my hips, pulling and tugging, aiming low.

"Just under four minutes," Karen says. "Good thing we're here. I'll park. You go. Diane, stay with me. We'll walk through the scary parking lot together."

"Roger that," Diane says.

Laurie stops the car, we do something very closely resembling a Chinese fire drill, and then Laurie has me by the hand and we walk into the brightly lit hospital together.

And here I thought I was having a kid by myself.

Six hours later, and not only am I not by myself; I do have an audience. My mom is not part of the crew; turns out she can't stand to hear her daughter scream. Diane is with my mom in the hall trying to convince her that it's completely normal not to want to hear screaming. Diane's holding her hand. I can tell, even from where I'm screaming.

"Seven centimeters," the nurse says just before she leaves the room. "Not much longer now."

"She's been saying that for three hours!" I . . . yeah, I scream it.

"Try to relax," Karen says. "It goes faster when you don't tense up."

"If I could move, I'd kill you," I say, laying my sweaty head back on the pillow. Every single thing annoys the shit out of me. My skin hurts. My eyes hurt. My throat hurts.

Karen rubs a cold washcloth on my forehead. "If I had a mirror, you'd kill yourself."

"Bitch."

"Play nice. I'm the one with the working body, the washcloth, and the checkbook," she says.

"Checkbook?" I say, feeling another pain building up steam, getting set to launch itself down my exhausted body.

"I figure, since these are desperate times, I could try bribing someone for drugs."

"God. Do it!" I say as the pain grips me, stomping across my abdomen and knifing between my legs. "Damn kid. Killing me."

"I talked to the nurse," Laurie says from the other side of my bed, her hand lying over mine as I grip the side rails. "About drugs. She said you're too far along and by the time they took effect the baby would be born."

"You believed that shit?" I say. "Bitch-slap her. Get me some drugs!"

"I tried," Laurie says.

"Get tough, McCormick. You're too soft to be a drug mule. God, where's Missy when I need her." The contraction fades out, slowly and reluctantly.

Karen chuckles and says, "Take it easy between contractions. Try to relax."

"You're insane."

"Yeah. Do it anyway."

"I'll go get the nurse," Laurie says. "Someone needs to stay in here and monitor you."

"Coward," I say, holding Karen's hand with the washcloth in it over my eyes. She brushes my hair back from my face and straightens the light blanket around my waist. "Am I going to be able to do this, Karen?" I say softly over my sore throat.

"Piece of cake," she says.

"No. Really. This whole motherhood thing. I'm scared. Too late to do anything about it, but I am."

I really am. I've been careening between joy and terror for the whole nine months. I'm exhausted and confused and flat-out terrified. I don't know if I can do this. I don't know if I have a maternal bone in my body. In fact, I don't think I do. What if I'm like Ed?

That's the terror at the core of my nightmares.

Karen takes the washcloth away from my eyes and looks down at me. She's smiling. "You're a natural. You're going to be the best mom any kid ever had."

"You're just saying that because it's too late to say anything else," I whisper. I can feel another contraction coming.

"Caught in the act," she says, smiling down at me.

"Bitch," I say on a tired laugh.

"Exactly," Karen says forcefully. "That's what motherhood does to you; it turns you into a snarling bitch, and all that bitchiness is aimed at protecting your kid from all the bad stuff out there. Are you the kind of woman to sit back and let your kid take it on the chin? Hell, no."

"Hell, no," I repeat, just as I start to scream through another contraction. When it fades out, I say, "So, you're saying I'm a total bitch, and because I'm a bitch I'll be a good mom. Kind of a downer of a pep talk, Mitchell."

"Of course you'd put it like that," Karen says, placing another washcloth on my face. "In my version you're a fighter. You've never been afraid of a fight. That's what a good mom does; she fights for her kid. Like I said, you're a natural."

I smile up at Karen and she smiles down at me, and I feel the terror lift, fading away like a birth pang. This whole motherhood thing might just work out. I just might be a better parent to my kid than my parents were to me. What would my life have been like if my mom had been more of a fighter?

Hell, what would Ed's life have been like?

That's a vision that's good for a laugh. Until the next contraction starts.

Laurie and that worthless nurse come back in as I'm in the middle of it, the nurse lifting the blanket covering my bottom half like, hell, let the whole hospital look down there and explore around. "You're doing fine. You're at eight centimeters. I'll go get the doctor," the nurse says.

"Thank God," Laurie says under her breath.

Diane pokes her head in and says, "Could you pipe down? Your mom is having a serious panic attack out here. Plus, you're disturbing the other pregnant women with all your screaming."

"Somebody throw something at her," I say.

Diane comes in and stands next to Karen. They look down at me, these three friends of mine, these unexpected sisters. My own sister moved to Kentucky three years ago; I've seen her twice since then.

"Hang in there, Olson," Diane says. "Show that kid who's boss."

"You are so full of shit," I say.

"I'd say your tail's in a knot, but I was just down there and no tail, no knot," Diane says.

They look tired. They all look tired. It's fourteen minutes past one in the morning and it's showing on them. Their eyes are bloodshot, their lipstick gone, their hair a wreck. They're not going anywhere; I know that.

"You guys look like hell," I say.

"She hasn't looked in a mirror, right?" Diane says to Laurie.

Another contraction, and then the doctor comes in and mumbles his name. I have no idea who this guy is; he's not my OB, but at this point, I don't give a rip. Just get the kid out of me.

He lifts the sheet, peering in between my legs, feeling around down there, the nurse at his side, everyone on the damn floor free to take a peek, and says, "Looking good."

Diane snorts. Karen elbows her in the ribs.

"You're almost there. Here comes another contraction, and I'm just going to press . . ." Doctor Mysterious sticks his fingers into my throbbing, aching hole and presses against my walls as they're contracting. I do what comes naturally, without even thinking about it. I kick him in the chest. Not actually on purpose, but just to get him the hell away from there and stop making the pain worse with his damn fingers.

The doctor falls back on his rolling stool, almost on his ass; the nurse gives me a horrified look and snaps, "You can't *do* that!" And my friends all look at the doctor with bland, unsurprised expressions.

"That wasn't a good idea," Diane says.

"She can't *do* that!" the doctor says.

Karen shrugs. "That's Ellen."

Laurie nods.

The doctor gets back to business, nothing with the fingers this time. I suffer through another three contractions. I hear, finally, "Push! Push now."

I push. It feels fantastic—well, as good as it can, just like scratching an itch. I'm pushing; Karen has her arm around my back; Diane rushes out to tell my mom to get in the room before she misses it; Laurie is standing at my feet, watching the show, a stunned smile on her face. Me, I'm still pushing when my mom and Diane come back. I'm still pushing for what seems like an hour, but is only fifteen minutes, and when I think I'm never going to get this kid out of me, out she slips like a little seal, smooth and slippery.

"It's a girl!" the doctor says, triumphant.

I hurt like hell all over. My eyes hurt. My throat hurts.

But there she is. My girl. I have a daughter.

Karen and my mom are crying. Diane has her back against a wall, shaking her head like she doesn't believe it. Laurie is watching the nurse wash the kid off, wrap her up, bring her to me. Laurie watches it all, that little smile on her face. Me? I'm having trouble staying awake.

Labor? Yeah. I've never worked so hard in my life. If this is the first fight I fight for my kid and it's a taste of things to come, then I'm going to spend the rest of my life being exhausted.

I can do that.

"Here she is," Nurse Ratched says, handing my daughter to me. "Eight pounds, five ounces."

"Hi, Megan," I breathe, looking down at her sheltered in my arms. "I'm so glad to see you. I'm your mom."

The doctor is talking down at my feet, looking between my legs again, the pervert, talking about the afterbirth. So I deliver that as well. It's nothing compared to the kid. I just keep staring at my girl. My perfect daughter. My kid.

Diane

– Winter 1988 –

Missy killed herself on January 22. She was driving out in the desert just east of Palmdale and crashed. She was going over 100 mph and it was 2:14 a.m. when she lost control of the car and it left the pavement. It rolled six times, landing on its roof. She was not wearing a seat belt.

The accident was declared just that: an accident. She was not drunk and she had not been drinking. They think that she was speeding and one of her tires blew.

She killed herself. We all know she killed herself. Missy was the one who did what she damn well pleased, every time, and she was not going to let diabetes eat her up piece by piece, swallow by swallow.

Laurie is paying for a big party at the Beverly Hills Hotel. She rented the space and organized the food. Ellen, Karen, and I are paying for the liquor. Pi did the invitations; there were five hundred of them. Pi contacted everyone Missy had ever known, from kindergarten to the job she'd had the day before she killed herself.

We don't talk about how she killed herself. We just know that she did. We can see it in one another's eyes, the horror of it, the shame we feel that we couldn't fix it, couldn't make it all go away, couldn't find a way to fight for her in a way that would have any fucking meaning.

We're throwing a damn party for her because that's what she asked for, but dammit, it's not enough. It's not even close to being enough.

I feel like shit, like I want to cry all the time, but I can't and I'm holding it down and it's going to drown me. I can't get any time off—that's a given—so I sent a check to Karen, and I'm here for the weekend to play at being blitzed and happy at a party that Missy said was the only thing she wanted of me. So, okay. I'm here. Let's get the fucking party started.

"You can't cry," Laurie says. "We promised Missy we wouldn't."

"She's not here to see me," I say, the tears leaking out of my face. I'm not crying. I've never cried like this before. I'm absolutely silent, no hitched breathing, no sobs. God, I think I'm *weeping*, old-fashioned weeping, like in a Victorian novel. "And I'm not crying. I'm *weeping*," I say. "Get off my case, McCormick."

We drive to the hotel on Sunset, avoiding the freeway since it's always a mess, not saying a word. Sunset curves and winds beneath tall, waving eucalyptus trees, multimillion-dollar stucco homes on lush green lawns, office buildings, recording studios, restaurants, eighty-thousand-dollar cars cruising past homeless people hanging around bus stop benches. LA. La-la land. I soak it all up soundlessly. I miss it.

I miss Missy.

How the hell did a girl like that ever end up with the name Missy? She should have been named Delilah or Lefty or something.

We're the first ones here, because we left early and didn't take

the freeway, and I stand like a wounded buffalo while Laurie talks
to the chick from the hotel.

"Let's go see where the bathroom is from the reception room,"
she says.

"Okay," I say, walking at her side like some freak-show reject.
I can't seem to pull it together. It's like Mom all over again, only
different, because I didn't see it coming with Mom and I saw it
coming with Missy for about a decade, all in slow motion. It was
like a dream that you couldn't wake up from no matter how hard
you try, and then when you do wake up, thinking it's finally over,
the reason it's over is because Missy is dead.

I can feel the tears running down my face. I think I've been
crying nonstop for a week.

"You're not the only one, you know," Laurie says stiffly.

"The only what?"

"I miss her, too. I'm grieving, too."

"I know that," I say, stunned.

I'm blowing it, and I don't know how. Am I not grieving in the
proper way? Is there a rule book for this, too? Of course there is.
Don't be an idiot, Ryan; get your mask back on and look at the
camera like a good little girl. Don't let anyone see the ugly stuff.
People can't stand looking at the ugly stuff, like naked grief, like
shaking insecurity, like raw fear.

But this is Laurie. Can't I let the mask slip with Laurie?

I look at Laurie in the bathroom mirror. She looks slightly stiff
and very composed, even more pulled together than usual. She's
wearing a dark blue suit with a champagne-colored silk blouse,
her dark blond hair pulled back into a low ponytail. She could be
going to a deposition or a bank meeting, but she's going to a funeral masquerading as a party.

"Thanks for driving," I say, watching for her reaction.

She snorts a little bit, lifts an eyebrow, and turns on one of the faucets.

"Hey, are you okay?" I say.

"No. I'm not. Thanks for asking," she says, looking at me in the mirror.

"Well, go on. Spill it. If you think I'm a first-class bitch, go ahead and say so."

She wipes her hands on a towel and reaches in her purse for her lipstick, but she doesn't use it; she just pulls the cap off and on, off and on. Considering that this is Laurie, it's like watching a first-class nervous breakdown.

"I loved her, too," she says.

"I know that."

She doesn't say anything more, but I can feel that she wants to, that there's this tidal wave of words just begging to be let loose.

"Just say it, Laurie. Whatever it is, just say it," I tell her. "If we can't be honest with each other by now, what the hell's been the point?"

Laurie looks at me, her eyes sad, her mouth tipped up in a reluctant smile that lasts a millisecond.

"Sometimes I feel like you get there first, that there's . . . no room for anyone else."

This isn't about Missy; this is about Doug. We've never talked about Doug, never said a word to each other to tie off the dripping vein of pain and humiliation he opened up ten years ago. I didn't think we needed to talk about it; haven't we shown each other that there's nothing to say, that he did his thing and we made it and hooray for us? I guess that's not enough, at least not for Laurie, and maybe even not for me. Maybe I need to tell her what I've wanted to say and she might have needed to hear. I've got to make myself say something, face it down and shut it off, once and for all.

I've got to be brave enough to talk this out and bury it.

I'm really, really horrible at confrontation. I guess when all's said and done, I like life behind the mask, which is so damn pathetic that I'm suddenly disgusted with myself and with life in general.

"I'm sorry," I say, turning to face her, my hip resting against the counter. "I don't mean to do that. I don't want to get there first. Most times I don't want to get wherever the hell I'm going at all."

Laurie looks at me, a brief glance, and then she looks at the pattern the lights are making on the ceiling. "Yes, you do. I'd want that. I'd want to be first, to have the first claim."

"Laurie, look, let's not do subtle. We're talking about Doug, aren't we? Well, okay, I was in love with him and you were in love with him and he screwed us both over."

Laurie turns to look at me, her brows raised, looking a bit shocked.

"Hey, I could have said *fucked*. I'm trying to be sophisticated because we're in the Beverly Hills Hotel." She smiles a little bit, but it fades almost before it begins. I smile back and try to make it stick. "I'm just trying to say that I wanted him to love me, and when he didn't, and when I could see straight again, I wanted him to love you, and when he didn't, when he blew it, then I wanted him to get thrown from a fast-moving train. That's all. If I could have avoided being first for that Mexican hat dance, then I would have. But not," I say, grabbing her hand, "if my being first sent up a warning flare that he was a total shit and you should run for your life. But it didn't. And I was first. There's nothing I can do about that except to say I'm sorry that you feel like you're second to me in anything. You're not. We both know you're not."

I stop talking because I don't think I'm making sense anymore, if I ever did.

"You're not mad?" she says. "That I went out with him after he . . ."

"Kicked me out of bed? No, I'm not mad. I was never mad; I just didn't want him to hurt me, and then I didn't want him to hurt you."

Laurie smiles, and it holds. Then we're hugging each other, messing up each other's hair, and pushing our mascara to the edge, but it's okay. It's all okay. Missy's gone, but Laurie is here and I've got her and she's got me and we both know that. That's all that matters, in the end. Hell, that's all that matters in the beginning and the middle.

"As long as he didn't hurt *us*, then it's okay," she says. "Well, not *okay*, but . . . okay. I didn't want to lose us, Diane. Especially after Missy . . . It just all overwhelmed me, all these thoughts and regrets. I don't want to lose us, any of us," she says.

I smile. I know exactly what she means, and I think, really, for the first time, I understand what Missy had in mind when she commanded us to have this party when she died. She wanted us to remember that we are an *us*, and that we can't lose us or we'll lose everything.

"Let's go party. Let's go be us. For Missy," I say.

And that's exactly what we do.

Four hours into the party celebrating Missy, when most of the non-Exclusives have left and it's only Missy's extended family and us still taking up space at the Beverly Hill Hotel, Ellen sits down next to Laurie and grabs her hand.

"I need to ask you something," Ellen says. "I need to do something."

"How drunk are you?" Karen asks. "You sound drunk, not that

Missy wouldn't approve, but you can't drive home like that. I'll drive you. Is Megan with your parents? Are they okay with keeping her overnight? I'll take you to my house and you can stay with me."

"God, will you shut up? I am not drunk," Ellen says. "I have something to ask Laurie, and you are not invited into this conversation."

"Well. Thanks a lot," Karen says, starting to laugh.

"She's more fun when she's drunk. Have you noticed?" I say.

"After a decade? Yeah. I've noticed," Karen says.

"Laurie, ignore them," Ellen says. "I really need to ask you something. Something huge."

"I can do huge," Laurie says.

"Is this the beginning of a fat joke? 'Cause I'm out of here if it's a fat joke," I say. I went up a size. I'm feeling kind of hysterical about it.

"Laurie," Ellen says, ignoring me, "I really want to thank you again for buying Mike off."

"Is that what we're calling it?" I say.

"What else is it when you tell a guy that all he has to do is disappear forever, and that if he does, he'll never have to pay a dime?" Karen says.

"A payoff," I say. "Without any money changing hands. Very tidy, Laurie. You sound really good at what you do. If I ever get married and divorced, you'll be my first call."

"And," Ellen continues, throwing me a dirty look, "Missy dying so young has made me think about Megan, about how, if I go before she's of age, then she'll have no one."

Karen and I share a look and keep our traps shut.

"We've talked about this before," Laurie says. "I'm glad you're finally taking it seriously."

"It's a serious day," Ellen says. "In a drunken-brawl kind of way."

We all smile a bit at that. It's exactly the kind of day Missy wanted and, though she's not here, I feel her in every conversation and every corner of the room. It was a party, a good old-fashioned wake.

"We need to meet at my office because you need to talk to a lawyer who specializes in this kind of thing," Laurie says, pulling out her pocket organizer. "Give me a call on Monday and I'll see what Milt's calendar looks like."

"Yeah, fine," Ellen says, "but that's not exactly it. It's more than that. I'm about to ask you the biggest favor I've ever asked anyone. Are you ready?"

Laurie

Am I ready?

I know what she's going to say before she says it. I can see it in her eyes, all the memories we share, all the small moments that become large memories, memories that fill a life and make it warm.

"Remember the strawberry jam?" I say, leaning forward and taking Ellen's hands in mine.

"I wish I could forget it," Ellen says with a grin.

"What's the deal with strawberry jam?" Diane asks.

"Be glad you were gone," Karen says with a shudder.

"Okay, now I have to know. Just because I'm off serving my country—" Diane says.

"God, okay. I'll tell you the strawberry jam story," Ellen says. "Megan was two, not even, and Laurie was over at my place; we were going to Paradise Cove to see my mom. So when Laurie got to my house, I jumped in the shower—"

"Which sounds innocent enough, doesn't it?" I say. "But Megan got into the pantry while I was washing the dishes, and she dropped a jar of strawberry jam, one of those huge jars——"

"I don't think the size of the jar was the problem," Ellen says. "So I hear Laurie screaming for me to get out of the shower, and so I do, and there's Megan, covered in red——blood, jam, who can tell?"

"I thought she was bleeding to death, right in front of me," I say. "The kitchen floor was covered, and then she was crying hysterically and waving her hands around, and blood is flying all over the white cupboards."

"I threw on a beach cover-up and flip-flops, my hair soaking wet, and we ran out the door, Laurie holding Megan while Megan is screaming like a banshee," Ellen says.

"Who can blame her?" Karen says.

"So I'm driving like a bat out of hell," Ellen says, "while Laurie's in the backseat with Megan, holding her thumb with a dish towel——"

"I didn't know if she'd severed it completely or not," I say. "There was so much blood, and her fingers were so tiny." I can feel the tears building in my eyes, just like they were when it happened. "I kept telling her how sorry I was."

"Yeah, I'm driving, hitting every light, because, you know, that's my karma, and all I can hear is Laurie whispering, 'I'm sorry. I'm sorry. I'm sorry.'"

"I'll bet," Diane says.

"So I get to the pediatrician's office, because it's closer than any hospital, run her in there, Megan still crying her heart out, and the blood hasn't even slowed down, and then they put her in one of those boards where the kid is tied down. That was fun. I just kept stroking her head, telling her that she was going to be all right," Ellen says.

"Four sutures in that tiny little thumb," I say. "I stayed in the waiting room and filled out the paperwork."

"You could get a real nice career going, doing that," Diane says.

"I don't know how I held the pen; I was just crushed with guilt. After about thirty minutes, Ellen came out holding Megan, who was still whimpering, her little beach outfit stiff with blood, Ellen's hair still damp, and she said . . . she said . . ." I hesitate, my eyes overflowing and my throat tight.

"I said, 'Well, that's it for me and strawberry jam. I assume that's unanimous?' Which seemed the only logical conclusion," Ellen says. "That was three years ago. We're still a grape-exclusive jelly household."

"Me, too," I say.

"Damn," Diane says. "After that, me three."

"So, the strawberry jam story," Karen says. "Is this going where I think it's going?" Karen has tears in her eyes, but she's smiling.

I can't smile. It's too much and it's too important, and though I'm the one who's been urging Ellen to get the paperwork on this done, to get her legal house in order, I didn't see this coming.

"Laurie," Ellen says to me, her blue eyes full of hope and trust.

"Of course," I say, smiling at her, cutting her off, not forcing her to say the words, words no mother should have to say. *Will you be my child's mother? Will you love my girl if for some reason I can't?* "You don't even need to ask."

Diane

"Is it my imagination, or do we always move on the hottest day of the year?" Karen says.

"It's not your imagination," I say. "God. Please tell me you have a pool."

"I have a pool," Laurie says. "Hey. I have a pool!"

"Yeah, heard you the first time," Ellen says.

"Is it anywhere near where I'm going to dump this box of pots and pans?" I say. "Because that would be *muy necesito.*"

"Way to break out the Spanish lingo," Ellen says, carrying in a huge bag of new bedding. "Which bedroom do you want this in?"

"I've numbered the doors," Laurie says.

"Of course you have," Ellen says on a sigh.

"That's . . . door number two."

"It's so gorgeous, Laurie," Karen says. "It's like something out of a fairy tale. Hey! Did you guys ever see *The Enchanted Cottage*? It's with Robert Young and Dorothy McGuire and it's about—"

"You mean Dr. Welby and the mom from *Swiss Family Robinson*?" Ellen says as she walks down the hall. "What the hell, Mitchell, those two don't go together."

"Will you shut up and let me tell you this story? It's so romantic, about how he's disfigured in the war and she's really ugly——"

"Oh, my *God*!" I say. "What is wrong with you? That's what you call romantic?"

"Well, they do fall in love," Karen says, "and this house reminds me of that. It's dreamy, like that."

"I just want to know if Laurie's the disfigured one or the ugly one," I say. "That's all I really want to know. Maybe we should vote on it."

"Like Rush," Ellen says, coming back into the foyer.

"Oh, shut up. That is not at all what I meant," Karen says, laughing. "Laurie, I love your house."

I drop the box of kitchen stuff on the kitchen counter. The kitchen looks like it came straight from 1962 without stopping for gas, but it does have a great view of the front yard, which is crowded with old sycamore trees giving abundant shade, and the lot is gigantic. In Los Angeles, it really doesn't get much better than that. And La Cañada is only a short ride from downtown LA, and it really doesn't get any better than that.

"Laurie, the movers are right behind me. Where do you want all the rest of your stuff?" I say.

Laurie takes over directing the movers; Karen takes over unpacking and putting things away. Ellen and I look at each other, exhaustion seeping from our pores.

"Where's Megan?" I ask.

"Jim's got the kids."

"All of them?" I say, my eyes bulging. Megan and Ben are

barely five, and David's a toddler, Charlie a baby. "Where did she find Jim? And can he be cloned?"

"Karen's parents are with them, too, but they're slowing down," Ellen says. "The way I look at it, it's like Jim is watching out for six people, not four."

"What about your parents? Do they watch Megan much?"

"Not much. I don't want Megan around Ed too much. Too much danger of contamination."

Ellen and I move through the house, trying to stay out of the way of the movers, and the captain and XO of the venture: Laurie and Karen. We bypass the kitchen, just off the foyer at the front of the house, and move through the family room at the back, but that's a busy room, Karen directing the placement of the lawyer's bookcase against a wall. We finally find our way out the sliding glass doors to the backyard. There are pine trees and orange trees scattered on the lawn, all circling a rectangular pool holding center stage. Along the back wall of the property is a row of red hibiscus bushes. It's like a tiny Eden.

We look around at the yard, at the birds singing in the pine trees, at the cool blue appeal of the pool, at the long, low profile of the house, at the shake roof, at all the bustle seen through every window.

"We'd better find a better place to hide. They'll find us if they look," Ellen says.

"I'm too tired to move. If they come and get me, it's going to be a fight to the death. I'll hold this ground till my blood runs red, or out, or something equally gruesome," I say.

We sit on the edge of the pool, resting our feet on the steps in the shallow end.

"It's a nice house—gorgeous, in fact," I say. "Now all she needs to do is learn how to pick men."

"Look who's talking."

We both snort. It's true. I can't pick 'em. I don't even try anymore.

"Aren't there plenty of guys in the navy?" Ellen says.

"You know how that went. I don't want to dance that dance again. Plus, I outrank most of the single ones. The pool's closed, if you know what I mean."

"*I feel no love for you* was an aberration, like the plague," Ellen says. "You can't give up just because he got to you first."

"Sure I can," I say. "You want to know a secret? I've never been all that great with guys. Oh, I can flirt with them, but I can't get much beyond that. I'd like to think it was because I was a late bloomer, got such a late start at it, but I don't think that excuse works anymore."

"You give a good imitation of a girl who's good at it."

"Thank you. I think."

We sit in silence. I can hear the girls talking; Karen laughs at something. Then I see her looking at us through the sliding door, doing the military move of pointing two fingers at her eyes, then at us. I elbow Ellen, she looks, and then we both cover our faces with our hands, *you can't see me* kid style.

"What's the real reason?" Ellen says.

I cast a glance at her, sitting so prettily on the edge of the pool, her legs tanned and toned, her hair still beautifully and almost naturally blond. Ellen's looks have become more chiseled with age; she has a sharper, cleaner edge, though the skin on her neck is looser than it was at twenty-five.

"I'm not pretty anymore," I say. "Like it's a news flash."

Ellen snorts and bursts out laughing. "You're so full of shit."

"Like a sack of shit is so pretty."

Ellen turns to look at me, her eyes wide. "You're serious? You don't know you're gorgeous? When did that happen?"

"When I lost my looks."

"God, you are so stupid. I had no idea. Is our country even safe?"

"Shut up."

"Come on, seriously—you can't be serious." I just stare at the pool. I've lost it. It comes, it goes, and mine went. It was fun while it lasted. "Diane, you are a goddess of beauty," Ellen says.

"Will you knock it off? You're not helping."

"Diane, really, don't you know you're still a pretty girl?"

"Not like I used to be," I say. Yes, it sounds vain and petty when I say it out loud. It just figures that Ellen would be the one to make me say it out loud.

"Nothing's like it used to be. Thank God," she says on a belt of laughter, throwing her arm over my shoulder. "You don't need a Halloween mask, Ryan. You need a good prescription from a slightly shady doctor."

"I just live in fear of being that ugly kid again," I say. "I thought I was past it. I thought that I was all 'live in the moment' and 'take whatever comes,' wring the juice out of it, keep moving. But I liked being pretty. I really, really liked it."

"Who wouldn't?"

"It seems shallow, though, doesn't it?"

"As long as you're as deep as the rest of the world," Ellen says with a shrug, "who's going to notice?"

"Oh, that was deep," I say, feeling a knot unloosen in my chest.

"Was that supposed to be a pun?"

"I can't remember what a pun is, so you figure it out."

We stare into the pool, at the distortion of our feet on the step; we both have painted toenails. Ellen's are blush white and mine are cardinal red.

"Do you get pedicures?" she asks.

"No, I figure I can bend over and paint my own toenails. I'm in the military, you know."

"Hoo-ah," she says, grinning.

"Do you ever think about Mike?" I ask.

"Only when I realize how happy I am that he's gone," Ellen says.

"What was wrong with that guy?"

"You know how everyone thinks Peter Pan is so damn cute? Well, I don't. I never did. Here's this eternal kid who gets in trouble all the time, who is always running away from good things to chase bad things, who bullies everyone around him to do the same, but boy howdy, does he like Wendy taking care of him and sewing on his damn buttons and making sure he's got something to eat. He even treats Tinker Bell like shit. The only thing I ever liked about that movie was Tiger Lily. I don't know how I ended up married to a guy like that."

"Peter Pans are good at convincing people that naughty is cute," I say. "And Mike had a very sexy edge. That's hard to resist at twenty."

"If he'd only said, 'I feel no love for you,' it would have been the perfect ending."

"You jerk," I say. "You can't make that a good story for me."

"I can keep trying, though," Ellen says. "Am I getting a tan line?" She lifts the sleeve of her shirt and peers at her skin. "Shit. I am. Let's go in and convince Laurie to give a party, a house-warming party."

"When?"

"Well, now," Ellen says, grinning. "I mean, we're here and you're flying out tomorrow night. No time like the present, right?

We'll just call everyone, get pizza and submarine sandwiches, lots of Coke; then we'll all put her stuff away and she'll have no idea where her towels are tomorrow."

"You are the goddess of evil plans."

"Thank you. I like you, too."

"I want to watch you convince her of this," I say, getting out of the pool.

"Oh, I'm not going to bother convincing her. I'm just going to do it. You watch; she'll thank me later."

"She might, but only because she's so damned polite," I say.

Karen

— Summer 1992 —

"Hurry up. I want to get there before the beach traffic," I say.

"Then we should have left in January," Ellen says, hauling out a bulging lime green beach bag with a dark blue *Little Mermaid* beach towel poking out of the top. "Megan! Will you get the cooler?"

"We have a cooler," Charlie says.

"Everybody gets a cooler," I say.

"We're not sharing?" David says.

"We're sharing. We're just starting with a lot of coolers and a lot of food, and we'll see how we end up," I say.

"I'm hungry," Ben says.

"We'll eat when we get to the beach," Ellen says, loading her beach bag into the back of my minivan. "Who's got to go? Go now!"

"I don't have to go," Charlie says.

"Go anyway," I say.

"I'll go in with them," Laurie says. "Come on, boys. Let's go."

"I don't have to go either," Ben says.

"Go anyway," I say.

"Heck, you keep talking about it and I'll have to go. And I just went," Megan says.

"Let's all go," I say, unbuckling my seat belt and following the parade into Ellen's house in Encino.

"It shouldn't be this much trouble to go to the bathroom," Ellen says. "I can almost remember when I did it without any thought or any plan at all. I was so innocent then."

"Weren't we all?" I say, herding the kids from behind toward the bathroom.

"I'll use the one in my room!" Megan shouts, running down the hallway.

"Me, too!" Ben yells, charging after her.

"We just lost fifteen minutes," Ellen says.

"Since we didn't start for the beach in January, it may not make a difference," Laurie says.

"I remember when driving to Malibu from the Valley was a simple little thirty-minute drive through a canyon. Now it's *Road Warrior*," Ellen says.

"Hey, so, do you love your new couch as much as I told you you would?" I ask. Ellen's house is a sprawling ranch with a front rose garden tumbling through a wooden fence. It has the kind of charm that houses don't seem to have anymore, a sort of quiet homeyness and informal elegance. It's a beauty, even if the kitchen and the baths needed remodeling when she bought it. The house has good bones. Everything else is just cosmetic.

"Yes, Mom. Thank you so much for making me spend my money on furniture," Ellen says to me over her shoulder. "Flush!" she says to David. David, age almost-seven, flushes and pulls his bathing suit up, catching his wing wang in the process until it slips inside. David starts to run out of the bathroom until Laurie says, "Hands!" David sighs and washes his hands. Charlie, age just-turned-five, pushes his bathing suit down, aims, and then looks over at David at the sink. "Eyes front!" I say. Charlie and his wing wang are aimed in the proper direction again. David runs out of the bathroom, hands dripping, and I hear a bathroom door slam down the hall.

"Hands!" Laurie calls out.

"Did it!" Megan yells as she runs past me.

"Close the door!" I yell to Ben.

The sound of the toilet flushing, and then Ben yells, "I did!" which I know is a lie since I heard the toilet flush.

"Isn't this fun?" Ellen says. "Don't you just love going to the beach?"

"I do," Laurie says. "It's the most relaxing way to spend a Saturday."

"So I figure we need to leave Paradise Cove by three so we can get to Diane's dad's house by four or so," I say. "Jim said that he'll be there by four for sure and get the grill going. Pi, Holly, and Bill are going to get there by five at the latest; then at seven we'll call Diane and yell obscenities at her—"

"What's *abscenties?*" David asks, pulling at his swimsuit. I kneel down and pull it up evenly, giving him a kiss on the forehead.

"It's what you say to friends who are in the navy," I say.

"That'll come back to haunt you," Ellen says.

"Then after we talk to Diane and clean up—" I pause to yell, "Charlie, let's go! Ben? Megan? Come on! Get in the car! After we clean up," I say, holding Charlie by the hand and pushing David in front of me, "you guys will be on your own. Girls' night, just you three. How I'll envy you in my house of men."

"You want to borrow a toothbrush?" Ellen says. "I've got a couch you can sleep on."

"As if I'd contribute to ruining that gorgeous couch," I say. "So, Ellen's with me and the boys. Laurie and Megan in Laurie's car."

"Why isn't Mom riding with us?" Megan says, staring at me.

Megan, nine years old, has the blond hair of her mother and the pale blue eyes of her father; that's all she has of her father. It was a nice contribution and clearly all he was capable of.

"I'm going to make sure that Karen knows how to get there, and you're going to make sure Laurie knows how to get there," Ellen says. "Okay?"

"Don't they know how to get there? They've been to Paradise Cove before," Megan says.

"Yeah, but it's better safe than sorry," Ellen says. "I'll see you there, kid. You can trust her, Laurie. Megan could lead you there blindfolded."

"I'm counting on it," Laurie says, climbing behind the wheel of her Mercedes. Megan gets in with a wave to us and fastens her seat belt. "Let's lead, shall we? You can guide us all."

"Okay," Megan says, waving to us out of her open window.

"You're a nice mom—you know that?" I say to Ellen as we back up out of her driveway.

"Don't let word get around. It will destroy my street cred," she says.

"What's *street cred*?" Charlie asks.

"Something that navy people want and can't get," Ellen says.

"Please, let me be there when those words come back to haunt you," I say, laughing.

I forgot the cooler," Megan says.

"That's okay," Ellen says. "We'll hit Gammi's house if we find ourselves close to starvation or anything."

"Let's get the blanket spread out, and the towels!" I say as the boys run for the water. They make a U-turn, throw their towels on the sand in huge clumps of twisted terry cloth, and run off again. "Well. That was helpful."

"The little darlings," Laurie says with a smile.

We're about fifteen feet from the foam, a disorganized pile of towels, a blanket that's already half-covered in sand, a lone cooler and three beach bags, one lime green, one dove gray and white stripes, and one hot pink with orange trim. Mine is the pink-and-orange one. I figure that if the boys wander while hunting sand crabs, I want them to be able to find their way back to my spot on the beach quickly. It's kind of insulting how much I must look like all the other moms wearing one-piece bathing suits and huge black sunglasses.

Megan is knee deep in the water already, Ben diving under the waves five feet in front of her. Charlie and David are watching some older kids play Frisbee at the water's edge. I watch it all, keeping them in sight while I swish out the blanket, fold the towels, and set them in a pile neatly on top of it. I flip open my towel with military precision and sit on it, my beach bag next to me, the cooler on the other side.

"Ready for liftoff?" Ellen says, looking at me.

"Let's not forget who forgot her cooler," I say. "You're going to want to be nice to me."

"There must be other options. Oh! I know! I'm going bodysurfing," Ellen says. "I'll be with Megan and Ben."

"Roger," I say. "Liftoff."

Ellen chuckles as she runs between our two nine-year-olds and dives into the waves. Ben whoops and follows her, Megan dips her head under the next wave, and they all swim out to the breaker line together.

"How was the drive?" I ask Laurie.

Laurie is wearing a navy blue one-piece with a crisscross back. She's also wearing a big straw hat and huge tortoiseshell sunglasses. She looks like an ad for a weekend at the Riviera. I'm wearing sturdy black sunglasses and a turquoise blue racer-back one-piece. I don't know what I look like, but whatever it is, it's more utilitarian than glamorous.

"Fine," she says. "She's a great girl, isn't she?"

"Adorable," I say. "A chip off the old block, don't you think?"

"You mean, like Ellen."

"Yeah, not like Mike. I don't see Mike in her. Do you?"

"Only the eyes," she says. "Or maybe sometimes in the look she can give you, kind of a daring, *are you looking at me?* kind of look."

"Yeah, I can see that. Ellen's look is more *who are you looking at?* Subtle, but definitely a difference," I say.

We stare at the water, watching Ellen bodysurf with the two older ones, watching the two younger boys build a sand castle with two plastic buckets.

"They could use a shovel," Laurie says.

"They lost it the last time we went to the beach. No more shovels until next summer."

"Is that a parenting thing?" she asks, gazing over at me.

I sit up and cross my legs. "Yes, I guess it is." Then I laugh. "I make up the rules as I go, figuring that my love will be enough to make up for all my mistakes along the way."

Laurie keeps her eyes on the ocean, her expression hidden by glasses, hair, and hat, and by Laurie's natural composure. I turn my face out to sea and watch Ellen coaching the kids on when to catch the wave, when to start swimming toward shore, timing it so that the wave will lift them up and propel them forward. They listen to her, heads glistening, mouths open, eyes wide as they tread water next to each other. I watch them, leaning back on my elbows, letting the sun bake into me, easing me to the marrow.

"Then what about my parents?" Laurie says.

"What about them?"

"Did my parents not love me? Is that really it? I guess that must be it, after all. Three years of therapy, what a waste of time."

I swallow hard. I'm so glib, so easy with advice and comforting words. What an idiot.

"I think they did love you, Laurie. I just think that," I say, trying to find the exact right words, "maybe they didn't love you the way they should have, the way you needed. I think that's always the risk. That you do your best, you love the best you can, but it's just not right somehow. Sometimes."

"Then love isn't enough."

"When it's the best you can give anyone, and it's all you can give, then it should be enough. It has to be enough, doesn't it?"

"What are you guys talking about?" Ellen says, dropping down to her knees on the blanket, getting sand all over it.

"Love," I say. "And whether it's enough. Or when it's not enough. Or something."

"Are we talking about *I feel no love for you*, because if we are, I have some rare words on that topic," Ellen says, toweling off her face and then dropping to the middle of the blanket between us.

"I've heard all your words on that topic. They're not that rare," Laurie says.

"We're talking about her parents," I say.

"Mom! Look at my bridge!" Charlie shouts to me, waving his little sandy hands.

"It's amazing!" I shout.

"No! Come see!" he says.

"I'll be there in a few minutes, I promise," I say. I don't want to leave Ellen and Laurie. I scan the water; Megan and Ben are still bodysurfing, their lean, tanned bodies glistening. "Why don't you build a turret to go with the bridge," I say to Charlie. He turns his sandy body back to his brother and they start digging deep for wet sand.

"So, what's the deal about your parents?" Ellen says. "Mitchell, hand me a Coke."

I reach into the cooler and fish out a Diet Coke, getting one for each of us. We pop the tops, the fizz sounding cool and refreshing. We're Pavlov's dogs around Diet Coke.

"You know what the deal is," Laurie says.

"Then why are we talking about it?" Ellen asks, looking over at me.

"Well, we're kind of talking about being parents," I say. "About—"

"Love is all you need," Laurie inserts.

"God, not the Beatles. You know how I hate the Beatles," Ellen says. "And what a crock. Love, yeah, it's important. It's essential, but it's not all you need. You need to be tough. You told me that yourself, Karen. Remember?"

"Yeah," I say, taking a swallow of Coke, willing the conversation to stay on track.

"I'll tell you something I learned from being a parent," Ellen says. We're all looking out to sea, at the kids and the sun and the moving sparkles on the water, at the crash of the waves and the foam and the endless movement and thunderous sound of it all. "Love is the gas that powers everything, every middle-of-the-night fever and every annoying parent/teacher meeting, but toughness is the vehicle."

"A car metaphor?" I say.

"Shut up, Mitchell. I'm trying to be profound," Ellen says. "Your parents . . . I don't know what the hell their deal is. I don't know if they're missing the gas or the car, but they're dead by the side of the road. Do I think they love you? Yeah. Sure. They love you. Let's go with that. But do they have the vehicle? Maybe a moped. With kids, you need to be a tank. You have to be tough. You have to grit it out. You have to be strong enough to do whatever needs to be done while they're weak. And, news flash, you're the toughest girl I know, McCormick. Why do you think I picked you for Megan? Besides your awe-inspiring bank account, which I assume will go to my kid someday." Ellen chuckles and nudges Laurie with her elbow. "And I know you know I'm not kidding about that."

Laurie is shaking her head, her mouth pulled down in a frown.

"What?" Ellen says.

"Come on," Laurie says. "I'm not tough."

"Yes, you are, Laurie," I say.

"Listen," Ellen says sharply. "You raised yourself, Laurie. You've been on your own your whole life. The only thing you didn't need to worry about was where your next meal was coming from, but other than that, you're practically an orphan. And look at you. You were a great student, make a great friend, have a great job, and live a great life. Except for your taste in men, which is lousy, you turned out great. And you did it yourself. You do whatever it takes, Laurie, and you always have."

I'm crying. I can't help it. I don't think I should have to try.

Laurie turns to Ellen and they hug, tanned arms wrapped around each other. They separate, smiling wobbly smiles.

"You forgot to tell her that she doesn't have split ends," I say when we've all gotten a bit of our composure back.

"I was trying to keep it short," Ellen says.

"So," I say. "What kind of mom am I? I'm not really up to being compared to a tank, but I wouldn't mind being a Porsche."

"You are kind of low to the ground," Ellen says on a chuckle, digging her hands into the sand, her eyes reflecting the deep blue of the ocean.

"Hey, I'll take it," I say.

We stare at the water and at the kids, sipping our Cokes while the sun beats down. Everything as it should be.

You take David. I'll get Charlie," I say, opening the rear door of the minivan.

"Got it," Jim says, coming around his car, telling our oldest son, "Ben, will you help your mom with the beach bag? Just put it in the kitchen."

"Quietly," I say. "I don't want your brothers to wake up."

Ben complies without a word, nodding his acquiescence. Jim bends and lifts David out of the backseat; David mumbles something and puts his arms around Jim's neck. I do the same with Charlie, but he doesn't put his arms around my neck; Charlie is dead to the world.

"He weighs a ton," I say, walking behind Jim up the garage steps to the house.

"It's been a long day for them," Jim says.

"It's been a long day for everyone," I say. "Fun, though."

The house is dark except for the lights on timers, at the kitchen desk, the front door, and the master bedroom. Dark and quiet, the sound of crickets muffling all other noises. We're still in our newlywed house in La Crescenta; we've outgrown it and there's no room to add on and I don't want to add a second floor and ruin the lines of the house, but still, we're staying. This is home.

"They don't need a shower?" Jim whispers, nudging open the boys' bedroom door with his foot.

"They took a shower at Gammi's in Paradise Cove," I say.

Jim and I strip the younger boys and get them in pj's, urging them to go to the bathroom one more time. It's a long drive from Camarillo to La Crescenta.

"I don't have to," David murmurs.

"Try," I say. Standing at the toilet, his eyes closed, he manages a twenty-second dribble. Hands on his shoulders, I walk him to bed. He and Charlie share a bedroom; Ben has a room of his own. I tuck David in, pulling the blankets up to his chin, kiss him on the cheek, and then switch places with Jim and do the same thing to Charlie. Charlie turns on his side and sticks his thumb in his mouth.

"I can't wait to see our orthodontic bills," Jim says.

"You do like to live for adventure," I say as we walk into the hallway. I leave the door open a crack, a very precise one and a half inches. David likes it just so.

Jim's arm over my shoulder, we walk to Ben's room. He's in bed reading a book. "Lights out, buddy," Jim says. "You can read it tomorrow."

"I'm not that tired," Ben says, his dark brown eyes pleading.

"Well, I am," I say. "Night, night. The book will wait for you." I tuck him in, give him a kiss, watch Jim ruffle Ben's dark hair, and as Jim passes me, I say, "I love you, honey."

"Love you, too, Mom," Ben says as he turns his blankets into a tight cocoon.

"I love you, too, Mom," Jim says as we walk to our room, his hand trailing down my back to rest on my butt.

"It works better if you don't call me Mom," I say, flipping on the overhead light.

"I'm all for whatever works," Jim says.

"You know what?" I say, pulling off my cotton shirt over my head. "It all works."

Jim grins and his brown eyes twinkle, and my heart flip-flops just like it did when he showed up looking for Helen. "You are one lucky guy," I say, wrapping my arms around his neck. He lifts me up and carries me to the bathroom, my toes a few inches off the carpet.

"Don't I know it," he says. "But you got a little sunburned. Let me get some vitamin E on that."

I sit on the edge of the tub while Jim soothes vitamin E oil across the tops of my shoulders. I watch him in the mirror, his hands so large and gentle, his head bent down, concentrating on making sure my skin is taken care of, that I'm not going to be in pain tomorrow. He's got a few gray hairs now, just a few near his temples. I wonder if he'll ever seem old to me. Diane's dad seems old now, old and a little frail, a little lost.

"How did Diane's dad look to you?" I say.

"Oh, same as ever, I guess," Jim says.

"How was he when you got there? Was he expecting you?"

"Sure." Jim straightens up, putting the oil away in the medicine cabinet. "Why? How did he seem to you?"

"Well," I say, loading my toothbrush and then Jim's with toothpaste, "he seemed older to me. I mean, when we had the Exclusives over for Memorial Day, he seemed perkier than he did today."

"It was probably all the kids combined with the heat. That can wear anybody out."

"I guess," I say over the toothbrush in my mouth. We brush,

rinse, floss. I wash my face and pat on my very expensive eye cream. Jim clips his fingernails while sitting on the toilet seat.

"I looked at his lawn mower before you got there," Jim says. "I think he needs his blades sharpened. We could drive over there next Saturday, bring your mom with us. I'll do the upkeep on his lawn mower while you do what you do to his bathrooms, and your mom'll keep him entertained. How does that sound?"

I look at this man, this wonderful, selfless, loving man, and a big grin blooms on my face. "I think that sounds perfect. My mom needs an outing anyway. She doesn't get out enough since Dad's gone. We could take them all out to eat, just pizza. But a nice pizza."

"Nice pizza," Jim says, nodding, walking to the bedroom. I follow him, rubbing in my hand cream. "I'm always up for nice pizza, but I think you know that I never met a pizza I didn't think was nice."

Jim climbs in bed, turns back my side of the covers, and pats the sheets.

"Subtle," I say, climbing in.

"Hey, whatever works," he says, sliding me to him, leaning over me, and smiling down at me.

"Hey," I answer, pulling his face down to mine, "with you, it all works."

Laurie

– Spring 1995 –

"What?" I hold the phone in my hand, pressed painfully tight against my ear. "No. No. No, I'll be right there. I'm on my way. Yes, I'm on my way. No. I'm fine. I'm on my way."

I hang up, dropping the phone in the cradle like a live rat.

"Madeline? Call Karen," I say to my assistant. "Call Diane. Call Pi. Call Holly. Call Candy and Cindy. . . . No, that's too much; never mind. Just call Karen."

"I was just finishing that deposition—" Madeline says from the outer office.

"Call Karen!" I shout. "Call *Karen*!"

I hear a pile of papers fall on the floor and then Madeline's shaky voice. "Yes, right away." I should have made the call myself. It's more personal. How horrible of me to have my assistant do it, but my hands are shaking so much. . . . "She's on the line," Madeline says.

"Karen," I say. "Karen, Karen."

I can't think of what else to say; I simply can't make any words come out. There are no words in my brain, just a long, slow scream.

"Laurie," she says. "What happened? What's wrong?"

I can hear kids in the background. I glance at my watch; it's just after four o'clock and the boys will be home from school or on their way to baseball practice or tennis. . . . What season is it? Isn't it too early for tennis? Baseball. It must be baseball season.

"*Laurie!* What's wrong?" Karen shouts, jerking me out of my stupor. "What is it?"

"It's Ellen," I say. My voice sounds fine, strong and clear; I'm a little breathless, I think. My brain is tingling. Is this what it feels like to faint? "It's Ellen." I keep repeating words. I've got to stop that. That doesn't help. That doesn't do anyone any good. "Karen," I say, starting to cry, "it's Ellen."

"Where are you?" Karen says, her voice strong and clear and firm. I want to sound like that. "Where should I go?"

"Go to the hospital. Can you go to the hospital? Can you?" I say. My words are sloppy with tears. I can't breathe. I can't pull it to-gether. I'm falling apart, every seam, every line.

"Yes. Yes, I'll call Jim. He'll do the kids. I'm leaving now. The Encino hospital? That one?"

"Yes. Please hurry. I'm on my way. Please hurry," I choke out, barely able to take a breath over my tears.

"I'm coming. I'm coming. Oh, Laurie," Karen says, starting to cry. I can hear Charlie in the background: "Mom, what's the mat-ter? Mom, why are you crying?" "Oh, God, Laurie," she says to me. She takes a hard breath. "I'll meet you there. I'll be there."

Ellen's funeral is closed-casket. Her body was too badly man-gled for anything else. It was a seven-car pileup at the Ventura/Sepulveda intersection; a seventy-two-year-old man driv-ing a white Cadillac Seville had a massive heart attack and plowed through the light without stopping. It was determined that he died before crashing into the first car. Ellen's car was the fourth car struck in the collision and she was jackknifed into the fifth and sixth cars. Three people died and five were injured.

I like to think that she didn't know what hit her; if she did, she would have been really pissed off.

I nearly smile thinking that, and I look down at Megan at my side. Megan insisted on wearing a bright yellow sheath dress with a little black cardigan. She and Ellen had just bought the dress for a piano recital a week prior to the accident. I think the yellow dress is the perfect choice. I put my arm around Megan and she allows it, but she doesn't lean into it. I don't expect her to. I don't expect anything, anything beyond the fact that I will love her and cherish her for the rest of my life. What she feels for me is out of my hands.

She is almost twelve years old and she has to start over with a new mother, a mother who has no idea what to do or what to say.

"Are you going to say something?" Karen whispers. She's at my side. She's been at my side almost constantly since the hospital. What will happen to me when she leaves my side to return to her own life? More important, what will happen to Megan?

I nod. I squeeze Megan's hand just before I rise. Megan allows it, but that is all. I think that is very gracious of her.

I stand in front of the crowd, picking out Karen, Diane, Jim, and Pi in a row. Behind them are Holly and Bill, Lee from Phoenix and Candy from Hawaii and Cindy from San Diego and Joan from New York, their respective husbands beside them. Karen's kids are here, as is Karen's mother and Diane's dad, and Ellen's parents, of course, and Ellen's sister from Kentucky and her kids. Mike is not here. I am so relieved he is not here.

A few throats clear and I pull my thoughts away from Mike and onto Ellen.

"Ellen was always telling me what to do," I say. There is a stunned silence and then titters of laughter. "And she usually did it in a loud voice, shouting advice or encouragement, telling me to see things as they are and not as I wished them to be. I have to be honest. It was annoying."

The crowd, those who knew Ellen well, is relaxing against the pews. Those who did not know Ellen well, those who worked with her at Dean Witter where she was an investment broker, look very uncomfortable. Oh, well. This is for Ellen. This is for *us*.

"But I listened to her," I say. "She made it very difficult not to listen to her, didn't she?"

Megan is looking at me, her pale eyes cautious. Karen is smiling at me and nodding encouragement. Diane is grinning and making a rolling sign with her hand.

"I dated a very bad guy once—I suppose we all have at least one of those—and she was on my side even when she hated my choices; she was loudly and violently on my side. She was my counselor of war and she made me laugh about things that should make you weep.

"And Karen, sitting there with her lovely husband and three sons, she is my surrogate mother. In fact, she is probably everyone's surrogate mother. She makes us all feel safe and warm and loved. Especially me. Ellen knew that, by giving me the gift of Megan in my life, we would be well tended with Karen at our beck and call."

Karen laughs and reaches over to put an arm around Megan. Megan relaxes just a bit, and so do I.

"I don't know what other people say at memorial services. I only know what I want to say. Ellen, and the other Exclusives, taught me about love. I didn't know what love felt like before I became a Beta Pi; I didn't know what it looked like. These girls taught me, showed me, year after year, heartache upon heartache, laugh upon laugh; they taught me that love is tough. It endures tragedy and joy and monotony. Love makes you laugh. Ellen told me something once—actually, she yelled it at me." The faces in the church laugh at me, all eyes alight and glowing with the joy of remembering Ellen and her inexhaustible fire. "She said that there was no fairness in love. That love is never concerned with what's fair or 'never having to say you're sorry' or all the other things we learn about love from songs and romantic poetry and Mother's Day cards. No, she said, love is not rational and it is not just; it is not evenhanded and it is not balanced; it is not gentle or soft. Love brawls. Love consumes. Love inspires. Love gives life its shape and form and meaning. But it is not fair."

Megan is crying, burying her face in Karen's shoulder.

"Do you know when she told me that, Megan?" I say. Megan lifts her head and looks at me, her eyes red-rimmed. "When you were about a year old. When I asked her what it was like to be your mom. I didn't truly understand what she meant then. But I do now. Love consumes and love inspires. Love stands when everything else falls apart. I love you, and I loved her. I will always love her. I will always love you. Your mom believed in that love, and because she did, I know we're going to be okay."

Later that day, I look up and see a face I haven't seen in almost twenty years.

"Lavender Barrette," I say. "I'd know you anywhere. Thank you so much for coming."

He looks the same. His eyes are just as vivid a blue, his hair just slightly thinner, his waist just slightly thicker, but he's just the same. He's the smiling, jovial man I remember.

"I haven't been called that in years, I'm happy to report." He grins. "It's good to see you, Laurie," he says. His voice is deeper than it was, a bit more gravelly; it's a man's voice. "I saw it in the newspaper, about the accident. I'm so sorry. Ellen was one of a kind, wasn't she?"

"She was," I say. "That's her daughter, over by the buffet table. In the yellow dress."

"She looks a lot like her mother," he says. "She's a beautiful girl. Is there a father around?"

"They were divorced before she was born, so, no, there is no father around, and in case you didn't guess from my eulogy, I'm the stand-in mother."

I don't know why I'm telling him this, and in such an adversarial manner. I don't know what's wrong with me. I used to be so easy in Matt's company; he was the man I'd be with when I couldn't bear to be with the man I was in love with. I hope he didn't realize that. What an uncomfortable thought.

Before he can respond to my awkward remark, I say, "So, do you have kids? Are you married?"

Matt smiles and takes a step back, his hands in his pockets. "No kids, though I wanted kids. I'm divorced."

"Oh, I'm sorry. Was it amicable?"

"Very. She got the house, the furniture, and the dog. I just got out. We both got what we wanted."

"Oh. I'm sorry," I say again. "You should have had a better attorney."

"Like you?" At my stunned expression, he says, "I talked to

Karen and met Jim before I came over to say hello to you. I do my homework. I've learned it's the key to everything."

There are so many undercurrents in those remarks that I pursue the one that's the safest. "You've met Jim. Isn't he a great guy?"

"He seems very nice," he says. "I'd like to get to know him better. Maybe a double date?"

"What? I'm sorry. Excuse me?"

"Double. Date," he says. "Though I can fly solo, but I thought you'd feel more comfortable with backup."

"I'm sorry. . . . What?"

"Laurie," he says, looking deeply into my eyes. What on earth is he going to see in my eyes? "I want to take you out. I've wanted to take you out since 1975."

"This is Ellen's funeral!"

"I remember Ellen well. I don't think she'd mind," he says.

"Wait. . . . You've wanted to take me out since 1975?"

"Is there any other reason for my letting you girls get away with calling me Lavender Barrette?"

"What?"

I've been shocked before in my life, but never quite like this. Everything is being turned on its head, and I've had more than enough of that lately.

"I'm sorry," I say before he can get a word out, "but this is a difficult time for me. In fact, your timing couldn't be worse." Which is putting it mildly.

"I know, and I'm sorry for that, but I've learned that my timing with you is always going to be bad, so I just have to ignore that." He leans toward me, his shoulder brushing the wall. I find myself backing up a step and stiffening my neck. "I know that Megan is going to be taking all of your time for the next few months."

"Until she's eighteen, and that makes it the next six years," I say.

Matt swallows and tilts his head at me. He's a very nice-looking man; I've always thought so, but I never thought anything more than that. I can't imagine why not.

"Six years is a long time, and I think you're overstating it, but even during that six years you're going to have a free lunch hour or a free Friday night, and when you do, I'll be there."

"Now, wait a minute—this is feeling very uncomfortable to me. I don't like the idea of you . . . Well, it sounds almost like I'm being stalked."

"If I'm a stalker, I'm the laziest stalker in the world. Since 1975, Laurie. That's twenty years of waiting."

"You were married in there somewhere," I say.

"I was killing time," he says, and then he winks.

"You know," I say, starting to smile, "that sounds suspiciously criminal."

"Anything's better than Lavender Barrette. Call me Stalker. See if it helps."

"I don't think that will help," I say, really smiling.

"I don't either," he says, and then he leans forward and kisses me on the cheek. "I'm very sorry about Ellen. You'll be hearing from me." He walks out of the room before I can collect a single thought.

"Who was that?" Megan says at my elbow.

I jerk at the sound of her voice and put my arm around her shoulder. She leans into me slightly and I take a full, deep breath. "Just an old friend from college. He knew your mom and really liked her."

"He really liked you, too," Karen says at my back. "Didn't Matt Carlson grow up beautifully?"

He certainly did.

Summer 1995 –

"I don't think having a Fourth of July party is in the best of taste," I say. "It's too soon after Ellen. I think it will upset Megan."

"Flossing her teeth will upset Megan," Karen says. "She's going to be upset about everything and nothing for a good long time. You have to give her life structure and make things as normal as they can be. We always do a Fourth of July party. That's normal. Don't take that away from her."

"But why do I have to host it?"

"You have the biggest yard and the biggest pool," she says. "And the best parking. Plus, it's your turn."

I sigh into the phone. "Fine. But I'm going to keep it small, no inviting everyone."

Everyone came, including people I hadn't invited but Karen clearly had. Matt Carlson, to be precise. I hadn't seen him since Ellen's funeral, though he'd called and asked me to dinner. We hadn't been able to set a date yet though. Yes, I've been stalling. It's too soon since Ellen for me to entertain ideas of dating. I need to establish a pattern of normalcy between Megan and me first.

"I brought enough potato salad to feed fifty people. Do you have enough room in your fridge for it?" Karen says, her arms cradling a huge Tupperware bowl.

"You also brought Lavender Barrette," I say, opening the refrigerator door and moving a gallon of milk, a pack of Diet Coke, and a jar of dill pickles. Karen slides in the potato salad. "What were you thinking?"

Karen leans against the kitchen counter, her arms crossed, staring at me. "I actually don't have an ulterior movie, Laurie. It's the

Fourth of July, a time when Americans have parties. He's divorced and alone. I think he's a nice guy; I've always thought he was a nice guy. Why not invite him? Including kids, there are going to be about fifty people here today. What's one more? You'll barely notice him."

"You know that's not true."

"Really?" Karen stands up straight and grabs me by the arms, smiling into my face. "You're going to notice him? What are you going to notice about him? His great sense of humor? That killer smile? Those fabulous blue eyes? All of the above?"

"You're right. I won't notice him," I say, walking past her and out of the kitchen.

But, of course, I do notice him.

My backyard is quickly filling up with people. Some are coming through the front door and depositing food in my kitchen, but most are entering straight through the side gate into my backyard. I have a table with an umbrella set up by the pool, and a small outdoor sofa and loveseat with two matching chairs on the covered patio running along the back of the house, and Jim and Diane's dad are opening up old-fashioned webbed lawn chairs on the pool deck. Karen's mom is spreading a vinyl red-checked tablecloth on the long picnic table near the barbeque, and Ellen's parents are coming through the gate, Lavender Barrette holding Ellen's mom's elbow as she negotiates the switch from the paved walkway to the lawn.

Megan sees her grandparents and runs over to them, her blond hair swinging from a messy ponytail, her arms wrapping around Ellen's mom in desperate vitality.

"Does she see them often?" Karen murmurs.

"Once a week," I say. "Sometimes twice a week. Sometimes I wish it could be more, and sometimes I wish the exact opposite."

Karen slides a glance at me, our eyes meet, and we do not say the things we think about Ed, about what he did to Ellen when he endlessly criticized her weight and her fair, freckled skin. I walk over to greet them, smiling.

"Hello! Happy Fourth of July!" I say. "Did you bring chairs? I have enough, I think, and I do think you'll find the chairs on the patio the most comfortable. May I get you a drink?"

I keep talking, faster and faster, throwing hospitality over them with so much force that they won't have a chance to say a word. Mrs. Olson smiles and enfolds me in a hug. Mr. Olson, who has never invited me to call him Ed and who I nevertheless think of as Ed, stands behind his wife and smiles stiffly at me. They were surprised, to put it mildly, at Ellen's decision to give me custody of Megan. In the normal course of things, Megan would have gone to Ellen's sister, but Megan has seen her aunt exactly eight times since she was born for a total of fifteen days out of her life. It wasn't enough. It wasn't even close to being enough. Megan understands that better than anyone.

"That sounds lovely, Laurie," Mrs. Olson says, her arm around Megan's shoulders, clutching her to her side. "Thank you. What a lovely day for a party."

I don't look at Matt, standing to one side of Mrs. Olson. I don't look at Megan, her slender body pressed tenaciously to her grandmother. I don't look at Ed, who is looking at me and looking at Megan and seeing too many things I don't want him to see, seeing that we aren't a family, not yet.

"Come on, Megan," Karen says, tugging on her ponytail, "let's round up the boys and make sure you guys all get sunscreen before you jump in the pool."

"Sunscreen," Ed snorts, sticking his hands in the pockets of his khaki shorts. "In my day no one wore sunscreen. Having a tan makes you look good, healthy. Megan could use some color."

"Sunscreen," I say to Ed, "is not optional."

There is a moment of awkward silence. These moments with Ed are fairly routine, I understand that now, but I never find them any less awkward.

"Ben!" Karen calls out, breaking the moment. "Where'd your dad put the beach bag?"

"I think it's in the car!" Ben yells back, hanging upside down from a branch of an orange tree.

"That's where I need it," Karen says. "In the car. Jim? The beach bag?" she calls out.

Jim, standing and staring at the barbeque with three other men, two of them Exclusive husbands, looks up. "Last I saw it, it was on the kitchen table."

"I'm going to kill someone. Probably myself," Karen says.

"I've got sunscreen," Matt says. "I keep some in my glove box. I've watched too many movies where some innocent city slicker is stranded in the desert because he runs out of gas or has a flat tire and his face is one giant blister by the time the evil trucker finally gets around to killing him."

"Where in this scenario does sunscreen save the day?" I ask.

"Well," Matt says, grinning, "it can't hurt."

Mrs. Olson laughs. I laugh. Karen laughs. Even Ed chuckles. That's what I remember about Lavender Barrette; he always made me laugh.

"I'll go get it," he says.

"That's okay; I have some in the house. We can all share," I say. "Megan, will you please go get the sunscreen? It's with the first aid supplies, on the third shelf in the pantry."

"It's not even that hot out," Ed says, but Matt is already leading Ed toward the barbeque, the group of men surrounding it already having grown to six.

Two hours later and half of the group, and all of the children, are in the pool and the other half, all men, are still staring at the barbeque.

"Do we need more hamburgers?" I ask Jim. "I have another pound thawed and in the fridge."

"I think we're fine for now," Jim says, turning a hot dog. "I talked to Matt."

"About?"

The other men drift away, eyes averted, until only Jim remains, and Jim is staring at the barbeque.

"About you. About him. About . . . his intentions," Jim says.

"Oh, my God," I say, plopping down on a lawn chair. Jim hands me a Diet Coke from the cooler at his feet.

"It wasn't that bad," Jim says.

"What did you say to him? *Why* did you say anything to him?"

Jim shrugs and looks at me, his brown eyes glowing with compassion and with just the slightest glimmer of territorial male. "Just making sure, that's all."

"Making sure of what?"

"That you don't get hurt."

I look across the yard to where Matt is standing on the edge of the pool, his hair dripping wet, his bathing suit molded to his body. He's grinning and talking to someone in the pool; someone splashes him and then he does a cannonball into the pool, shouting a challenge as he leaps. I smile just watching him.

"I'm so embarrassed," I say. "He must have been so embarrassed, not to mention bewildered."

"I don't think so," Jim says, spearing one hot dog after another and putting them on an empty plate. "He said he was glad to know that, after all this time, someone had your back."

"Really?" I say, looking first at Jim and then at Matt climbing out of the pool, the water sheeting off of him. He must feel my gaze because he looks at me then and I can't make myself pretend that I wasn't watching him. Matt smiles at me. And I smile in return.

"Really," Jim says smoothly. "Have a hot dog. I'm overstocked in hot dogs."

Matt stands next to me as I wave good-bye to the last guests. His car stands alone on the street, looking forlorn. I can feel Megan at my back, standing in the doorway, watching us. Matt should go. I don't have the words, or the will, to make him go.

"That was fun," Matt says. "You do this every year?"

"Yes, but we take turns hosting," I say.

His car sits, waiting for him. Megan silently waits for me.

"Even Diane?" he asks.

"Absolutely. One year we did the Fourth in Memphis. Of course, not many of us could make it, but we did it. It was her turn to host," I say, grinning. I haven't smiled this much in months. "Thank you for coming. I guess you've got a long drive?"

Matt nods. "Palos Verdes. It's not that bad. I could come out here once a week and not complain. Even twice a week. I'm tough."

We are facing each other on my driveway, our bodies angled toward and away, toward and away, our eyes meeting and then darting out to the street. Or mine are. His eyes are fixed on me; I can feel that. I smile, feeling that, and I'm almost ashamed of myself for how giddy I feel.

"Laurie?" Megan says from the doorway. "Are you coming in now?"

If I go in this will end, and I'm not ready for that yet.

"Yes," I say to her, turning back to the house. "I'm coming. Would you like to come in? I'd offer you coffee, but—"

"But you don't drink coffee," he says. "I'll take whatever you're offering."

My pulse races and my grin widens, and I lead the way into my house past my twelve-year-old daughter.

"Aren't we going to bed?" Megan asks.

"Pretty soon," I say. "Why don't you get ready for bed? I'll come tuck you in in a few minutes."

"Okay," Megan says, staring at Matt. "Good night."

"Good night, Megan. Thanks for the best Fourth of July I've had in years," Matt says.

"Night," she says, her gaze flicking between the two of us. I feel as guilty as if I were in a police line-up.

"This probably isn't one of my better ideas," I say when Megan is out of sight.

"Don't grade yourself until the exam is over," he says. "You two are just starting. Give it time."

"I didn't mean Megan," I say. "I meant . . . this. Us."

"There's an us? Already? Damn, I'm good," he says, smiling down at me, his arm slipping around my waist as casually as if he'd been doing it for twenty years.

I step away from his touch and walk through the kitchen toward the refrigerator, opening it up, peering inside, pretending that none of this affects me. "I can offer you Diet Coke, Diet Sprite, Diet Dr. Pepper, orange juice, V-8, or milk."

"Milk. Straight up," he says.

I get out the gallon jug, still surprised by the heft of it; until Megan came to me, I existed on a quart of milk every two weeks, just enough for a dribble on my oatmeal. Megan goes through a gallon of milk every three days.

"A glass?" Matt says as I pour the milk into a cut glass tumbler. "I'm used to drinking milk from Mom's fridge out of an old jelly jar. Remember those Flintstones jars?"

"Sorry," I say. "I'm sadly short of Flintstones memories. I was terribly abused as a child."

"You must have been, no Flintstones," he says, taking a healthy swallow of his milk. "Quick, what's George Jetson's wife's name?"

"Sorry, no Jetsons either."

"Okay, now you're scaring me," Matt says, but he says it in such a silly way that I laugh. Matt drains his glass and puts the empty glass on the kitchen counter. "Now that I've got milk breath, kissing you is going to be a challenge. But I'm up for it."

"What?" I say, jerking upright and backing up a step. "Why would you kiss me?"

"The very fact that you asked me that just proves how much you need to be kissed."

Matt hasn't moved, but I take another step backward, crossing my arms over my chest.

"Let me rephrase that," he says, walking toward me, a gentle smile on his face. "I need to kiss you. I've got to kiss you. I'm not going to let another five minutes go by without kissing you." Taking my face in his hands, he says, "I'm going to kiss you right now. Ready or not."

Tipping my face up, leaning down to me, he kisses me lightly on the corner of my mouth, nibbling my lower lip, breathing softly on my jaw, taking my mouth in his and teasing a kiss out of me.

His is a kiss of tenderness and happiness and hope. Euphoria swells, and with it, joy so bright that I am blind with it.

I didn't know. I didn't know kisses could be anything but passionate and desperate. I didn't know kisses could be a gift, something bestowed.

My arms wind around his back and I sigh into his kiss, pressing into him, and then straining away from him, embarrassed, exposed, afraid.

"I don't know how to do this," I say, my forehead resting on his chest, my hands on his torso, holding open a space between us.

"I know you don't," he says, wrapping his arms around me and pulling me firmly against him. "That's why I'm going to do everything. Try to relax and enjoy it."

I chuckle and nuzzle my face against his neck.

"I wish I'd done this twenty years ago," he says, his mouth brushing my hair. "I was young and stupid."

"Weren't we all," I say.

"You definitely were, not to know that I was in love with you. I thought it was obvious."

I lean back and look at his face. He's serious. "You were in love with me?"

"I not only was," he says, tilting my face with his hand, "I'm almost a hundred percent sure I still am."

"Oh, Matt . . ." I say, ducking my head, horrified and mortified.

"Worse yet, I'm starting to get the idea that I always will be."

"Matt—" I say, pulling away from him.

"I know, right?" he says, interrupting me before I can even begin to voice all my many objections to what has to be blatant exaggeration. "How pathetic can you get? I think I've got the un-requited love routine nailed."

"No, don't," I say. "Please stop. You're not pathetic."

"The way I see it," he says, kissing my brow, my nose, my cheek, my neck, "it's only pathetic if I sit back and don't do anything about it. So I'm not going to do that. Now that I'm older and wiser, I'm going to do a lot about it. I'm going to give you my best shot."

He kisses my mouth, a searing kiss and leaves me shaking from my soul out to my skin.

"I figure you're going to go down like an enraged rhino," he says lightly, his hands wrapped almost casually around my waist. "But you will go down," he teases.

I burst out laughing, his arms around me, his smile lighting up my house, and my life, like a beacon.

"Laurie?" Megan says.

I jerk away from Matt. "Yes. Megan." I run a hand through my hair; my hands are shaking. "Are you ready to be tucked in?"

"I don't need you to do that," she says, her eyes as cold as ice chips. "I can see you're busy."

I've just been slapped, and I feel slapped. Before I can order my thoughts, Matt steps in.

"She's never going to be too busy for you, you can count on that," Matt says. "I've known Laurie a long time. In fact, I've known her for as long as I knew your mom. Your mom, she was something. Definitely unforgettable."

Megan is standing in the doorway, her bathrobe wrapped around her, her hair tumbling around her face, her expression carefully neutral. I never noticed before how a carefully neutral face on a child practically shouts terror.

"You knew my mom?" Megan asks, coming into the kitchen half a step.

"I met her in college. In fact, I met her the same night that I met Laurie. That was quite a night," Matt says, leaning against the kitchen counter near the table. "Can I get a refill?" he says to me, indicating his glass. I nod and give him more milk. He takes the glass and sips it, looking at Megan. "You look a lot like your mom, but I guess you know that. I was always sorry we lost touch."

"How did you meet?" Megan asks, taking another step into the kitchen.

Matt sits at the kitchen table and leans back, stretching his legs out. The light over the kitchen table illuminates him, creating a glow like a fireplace in a cold room. Matt is holding center stage and beckoning us to join him with every word he speaks. "It was at a party. No one loved a party like your mom. I guess you like parties?"

"They're okay," Megan mumbles.

"Now you sound like Laurie," Matt says with a grin. "She was never the party animal your mom was."

"I like parties," Megan says, lifting her chin. "Today was a party and I had fun today."

"Me, too," Matt says. "Thanks for letting me come, and for letting me stay. I had such a good time that I don't want to leave. Laurie's good company. I lost touch with her, too, and I've missed her. I hope I don't have to miss her anymore."

Megan shifts her weight from foot to foot, looking down at the kitchen table. Matt sips his milk. I am afraid to move, afraid to break this moment.

"You can stay. I don't care if you stay," Megan says.

Matt pushes a kitchen chair out with his foot, toward Megan. "Have a seat and I'll tell you how I met your mom and about how she gave me the worst nickname a guy could ever have."

"She did?" Megan's eyes light up and a smile touches the corner of her mouth. She sits in the chair and leans her elbows on the kitchen table, staring at Matt, and then staring at me. "Did she? What was it?"

I smile. "I'm not sure it was Ellen who did it. It might have been Karen."

"It might have been you; you were there too," Matt says, "but it was Ellen. You think I'd forget that? I haven't forgotten anything. Not anything." He's staring at me, his eyes so blue and so gentle and so full of meaning.

"Tell me!" Megan says, grinning. "What was it? Was it really bad?"

"As bad as it gets," Matt says, grim faced.

"Come on!" Megan says, laughing.

"Well," Matt says, looking at me, "I guess I can tell you. As long as it doesn't leave this room and as long as I have a big bowl of popcorn to go with my milk . . ."

"I'll make the popcorn!" Megan says, leaping up to run to the pantry.

"And you're going to have to promise!" Matt calls after her.

I walk over to him and lay my hand on his shoulder; he looks up at me and it's all there in his eyes, everything.

"Thank you," I whisper.

"For what? Sharing my humiliation with the next generation?" he says.

I lean down and kiss him quickly on the mouth, before Megan comes back into the room, struggling with the cellophane covering the popcorn package.

"See how easy I am?" he says, laughter shining out of his eyes. "Why didn't you take advantage of me twenty years ago?"

But I did. I did take advantage of him.

"Okay, what was it?" Megan says, putting the popcorn in the microwave and setting the time.

"I don't have my popcorn yet," Matt says.

"Stall tactic," I say, shaking my head. "Time to man up."

"Going for irony, huh?" Matt says, winking at me. "Okay, here goes." He leans forward and Megan leans toward him; the microwave whirs, the sound of popcorn popping an intermittent backdrop. "Lavender Barrette. Your mom called me Lavender Barrette."

"She did?" Megan squeals. "Really?"

"Ask around," I say, pouring Megan a glass of milk and setting it in front of her. "There are a million witnesses."

"Unfortunately, that's true," Matt says, sighing.

"And now," I say, leaning down swiftly to kiss Megan on the top of her head, "a million and one."

Spring 1997 —

"Laurie?" Megan calls.

"Yes?"

"Laurie!" Megan says, louder, her voice strident and shocked.

I get up from the kitchen table and the Sunday paper and my fresh cup of coffee and my bagel with cream cheese and walk toward Megan's bedroom. "What is it?"

By the time I get to the closed door of Megan's bedroom, I can hear her muffled crying. When I open the door, I can see why. Chester, the black Newfoundland-Lab mix we picked out from the pound together, the dog that was going to make us a family, the dog that would turn my pristine house into a hairball-covered home, the dog that would be someone for my new daughter to love in a strange home, is lying at the foot of Megan's bed, taking up more than half of it. Chester, his eyes shut and his head resting on one extended paw, is still. He's too still.

I look at Megan, her back pressed against the closet door, her hand over her mouth, her eyes shedding tears.

I look at Chester, at his rib cage, and I confirm what Megan already knows. Chester is dead.

"Oh, no," I say. "Chester. Oh, God, Megan." I hold out my arms to her and she rushes across the room into them. I can't make myself go to Chester. Megan clearly can't either.

We hold each other, crying. I rub her back and she grips me tighter.

"I was just talking on the phone," Megan says over her tears. "I was walking all around him and he was alive; I know he was. And then I hung up and I asked him if he wanted to go outside." She cries harder. "And he didn't move. So I said it again and I rubbed his head, and he didn't move. He was stiff. He's dead. What are we going to do? Oh, Mom."

She stiffens in my arms, but I hold her just as I did before, just as tightly; my breath does not change and my heart does not stop, but this is the first time she's called me Mom.

"We're going to call the Exclusives, and we're going to bury Chester in our own backyard, and we're going to send him off the way he deserves. Don't you think? Don't you think he'd like that?"

She loosens her hold on me and looks up into my eyes. Her light blue eyes are red and puffy and her nose is swollen and drippy, and she's the most beautiful girl I ever saw.

"Yeah. I do," she says, her voice small and tight. "I can't touch him. Can you? I can't do it."

"Neither can I. We need a man. Let's go call one, okay?"

"Okay."

We walk out of her room together, arms around each other, sniffing in perfect harmony.

* * *

I know I dug a hole here once already, to plant that Japanese maple," Jim says, stepping on the shovel and pushing it deep into the earth. "The next time I dig this same hole, just throw me in it."

"You want to trade jobs?" Matt says. Matt is carrying Chester out of Megan's bedroom in her comforter, slung over his back like Santa Claus. Chester weighed one hundred and twenty-eight pounds.

"Just bury him in the blanket," Megan says. "He loved that blanket."

"He's sure going to love being buried here, isn't he?" Karen says. "It's so beautiful."

"Is this a catered funeral? Because I'm starving," Pi says.

"Touching," I say. "Always the heartfelt comment at the precise moment."

"Believe me, it's heartfelt. I left before I ate. Because you called," Pi says, staring at me.

"Okay, fine, let's just turn it into a party," I say, looking into Megan's eyes, getting her silent approval. "First order of business: who's calling Diane?"

"I will," Megan says, "but don't bury Chester without me." Megan runs through the backyard to the house.

Matt says, "She wants to be a mourner. She couldn't have volunteered to be a pallbearer?"

"You want to be a pallbearer, but you can't pitch in and be a gravedigger?" Jim says to Matt.

"That about covers it," Matt says, handing Jim a beer.

The hole is dug and Jim climbs out of it, my Japanese maple sitting off to one side, its roots looking naked and vulnerable.

"Boys, get over here and lower Chester into the ground. After the service, you guys will be in charge of covering him over," Jim says.

"Okay, Dad," Ben says. "When are we doing that?"

"As soon as Megan gets off the phone," Jim says.

"You ever notice how girls are always on the phone?" Ben says.

"Every day of my life," Jim says.

"Honey, that Japanese maple can't have its roots exposed for too long, and I was thinking that, as soon as Chester is buried, could you dig a hole right behind him and a little to the left for the tree? That way, it's almost in the same place and it will be a nice grave marker for Chester. Plus, it was too close to the fence before. This spot will be better," Karen says.

Jim looks at her, one arm resting on the shovel handle, dirt on his knees and his hands, and says, "Are you sure Chester died of natural causes? Because I'm starting to think this was all a ploy to get me to move that tree."

Matt clinks his beer can against Jim's with a grin, and they both upend their cans in unison.

The boys have dragged Chester in his blanket over to the edge of the hole.

"Do we just push him in or what?" David asks.

"Oh, something more tender than that," Karen says.

"Push him quick, before Megan gets back. Chester won't know the difference," Jim says. David, Charlie, and Ben look at me. I nod, and, enshrouded in a cream-and-blue paisley comforter, Chester tumbles into the dirt.

"Well, that was heartfelt," Pi says.

"Here comes Megan," I say. "Nobody tell her about the shove!"

"Diane says she wishes she could be here for the service, but that she'll play 'Taps' at six o'clock, her time, and we should all salute the grave in unison then," Megan says. She looks a little better, a little more of the sparkle back in her eyes. This was such a good idea.

"Okay, so who's going to say the words over Chester?" Karen says.

"I will," Pi says. Pi gets up and walks toward the grave, looks into it, says, "See ya, Chester," and walks back to her lawn chair. "When are Holly and Bill due to show up? It's so rude, being late to a funeral."

"Pi, you have the soul of a Mongol," Karen says.

"We Hawaiians are a sturdy breed," Pi says. "Is it time for the luau?"

"I just want to say," I say, holding Megan's hand, "that my favorite memory of Chester is when we first brought him home and he hid his head behind the couch and he thought we couldn't find him. Remember when we called his name, standing right there, and his black butt just wagged and wagged? He really thought he'd outsmarted us."

Megan smiles, tears forming in her eyes.

"My favorite Chester memory is the time we took him to David's soccer game and he broke the leash and ran off with the soccer ball in his mouth," Ben says. "That was a good game."

"My favorite is when he walked me home after I fell off my bike and hurt my knee," Charlie says.

"What about when he picked up that box turtle and dropped it on your foot?" Jim says.

"That was a moment, all right," I say. "What about you, Megan? What's your favorite Chester moment?"

"When we first saw him and picked him out," she says. "When he wormed his way onto my lap on the drive home from the animal shelter, so warm and happy. And then he peed on my lap as we pulled into the driveway."

We all laugh, even Megan. No, mostly Megan.

I put my arm around Megan and she wraps an arm around me. "Are you okay?" I ask.

"No," she says. "But I will be. Thanks for this. Mom."

I hug her close and we watch in silence as Karen's sons fill in the grave.

Thank you, Chester.

Spring 1999 –

"I'm so glad I reached you. I don't know what to do!" I say. "Maybe nothing, maybe doing nothing is best, but I can't quite believe that. I feel like I need to *do* something."

"What happened?" Diane says.

"I'm sorry. I should have asked—are you busy?" I move the phone to my left ear.

"No, it's okay. Go ahead."

"No, really, are you busy?"

"Will you just spit it out?"

"Well, it's about Megan."

"Obviously. You never get this upset about yourself."

"This boy Colin, who's a year ahead of her, asked her to the spring dance, and then when she wouldn't let him touch her breast on a date, he told her that he was asking someone else. And she already has the dress. And it's been altered. But of course, that's the least of it, but you know how excited you get when you already have the dress, and all her friends know about her going, and now this. I could just kill that rotten little kid!"

"Laurie, can I just say that being Megan's mom is the best thing that could have happened to you? Your volcano has finally exploded."

"That sounds awful," I say, "but what should I do about Megan? The poor girl is just moping around, and she's so embarrassed. She feels like she did something wrong when we both know it's this horrible boy who's entirely at fault."

"Completely. No discussion required," Diane says. "But I have to say, it's impressive as all hell that Megan told you about the breast thing. I would never have told my mom anything like that. How'd you get it out of her? Rubber hose? Nyquil?"

"The poor thing was just hysterical. I think she told me without meaning to."

"That sounds normal."

"What should I do? Anything? I would just love to call this boy's mother."

"Well, you know you can't do that."

"I know, but it's tempting."

"Yeah, but there are other ways to get revenge. I say fight fire with fire."

"Diane, I honestly don't see how that would work. . . . Wait. . . . You mean make him suffer?"

"Absolutely. Have you talked to Karen about it?"

"Not yet. She's working on a design project in Pasadena and it's hard for her to find a free minute."

"Call her. She's got a few boys lying around that you could use," Diane says. "Call me after you call her. Let me know the scoop, okay?"

"Roger that," I say, laughing for the first time in two days.

"Roger and out," Diane says, hanging up.

I'm pacing in the kitchen, which was redesigned by Karen

three years ago. Actually, Karen is responsible for an entire rework-
ing of the space, knocking out a wall, adding windows, putting in
a new kitchen and all new baths, refurnishing. She even had ideas
about the landscaping, beyond the location of the Japanese maple.
She has a nice business doing that for people; she calls it *design
problem solving*. She calls what I do *marriage problem solving*. She
calls what Diane does *naval personnel problem solving*. I think she's
in love with the phrase *problem solving*.

"Karen?" I say. "Do you have a minute?"

"Sure. What's up?"

"It's about Megan. This boy at school, a year older—"

"Older men, always trouble," she says.

I tell her the story as briefly as I can, and before I even get to
the part about how I need a solution, Karen is offering one.

"Okay, here's what I think we should do. We'll get Ben to take
her to the dance. No one at her school knows him, so they won't
know that he's practically her brother. They'll look cute together
and he'll play it like he's dippity-do over her, and Colin can be the
one looking like a douche, God willing."

"Really? Do you think Ben would mind?"

"Well, I'll ask him, but I think he'll do it. If I can explain it
just right, he'll be overjoyed."

"What will you say?"

"Something about how some jerk is trying to make Megan
miserable. That should do it," Karen says. "If he knows he's riding
to the rescue, the hero of the story, he'll be dying to do it."

"Do you want me to ask him?"

"No, I'll do it. I'll call you back. Bye."

The phone rings while it's still in my hand.

"Did you talk to Karen?" It's Diane.

"Yes, and she thinks Ben will take Megan to the dance and

shove Colin's face in it," I say. "I probably shouldn't say things like that about another child, but—"

"But yeah, who cares. This is our girl we're fighting for. Colin's mom is on her own," Diane says.

"Hey, that's my other line. Let me call you back."

"Roger."

"Hello?"

"Did you talk to Karen?" It's Matt.

"I did, after I talked to Diane, who advised me to talk to Karen," I say, walking through the great room to sit on the patio in the backyard.

"Karen's the one with sons just hanging around doing nothing," Matt says.

"That's what Diane said."

"Is Ben going to do it?"

"Karen's asking him now," I say. "You know, do you think it might actually take a village to raise a child?"

"It may not take a village, but it does take the Exclusives," Matt says, chuckling. "Am I going to see you tonight?"

"I'll have to see how this goes. Let me get back to you, okay?"

"If Ben comes through, I want a picture of me pinning her flowers on, or whatever they do nowadays."

"I think Megan would like that. Oh, there's my other line. Let me call you back."

"Got it."

"Hello?"

"Okay, so I talked to Ben and he wants to know what color Megan's dress is so that he can buy her a matching corsage. Is that the sweetest thing?"

"I'm going to kiss that boy the next time I see him. Fair warning."

"David was so upset when he heard about it that he offered to take Megan. He said that he's tall enough to pass for sixteen and that no one would have to know he's in eighth grade. Charlie's so mad that he's not big enough to take her that he talked about rocking Colin's mailbox. I didn't put much effort into talking him out of it," Karen says, laughing.

"So you'll bring Ben here? It's this Saturday. I'll drive them. I'll buy the corsage."

"Are you insane? Ben would die of shame if he didn't pay for the flowers himself. I'm trying to raise a chivalrous bunch here, Laurie. Don't get in my way. What color's the dress?"

"Purple."

"Like a lavender or a royal or what?"

"Lavender with white accents. She'll be wearing white shoes," I say.

"Okay, so does she want the flowers to match the dress or does she want contrast?"

"I have no idea."

"Is she there? Put her on."

"She's at drill team practice," I say. "I think she'll trust your judgment on the flowers. I know I do."

"Okay, and speaking of lavender, how's Lavender Barrette?"

"The same," I say, getting up from the love seat on the patio and walking over to the pool.

"You mean the same level of impatience that you finally get married or the same level of patience in dealing with the neurotic Ms. McCormick?"

"You're so pushy," I say.

"Somebody has to be since Matt's clearly falling down on the job. Look, I've got to go. Somebody's trying to call. Call me back with a time!"

I hang up and look around the yard. I wanted a garden wedding once, a wedding like Karen and Jim had at the Bel-Air Country Club. I wanted that wedding with Doug. I never even think of Doug anymore, and in not thinking of Doug, I realize that I've left my self-destructive dating patterns in the past. I thought I was choosing the man to love so perfectly, each time so perfectly, but it's obvious I wasn't. I was repeating a pattern of emotional distance that I learned from my parents. I loved men who kept me out of their lives. But I don't do that with Matt. At least, I don't think I do.

The phone rings in my hand.

"Hello?"

"God, what a prick," Pi says. "I just heard about Megan and Colonoscopy from Diane. What are we doing to make him suffer?"

I laugh. "His name is Colin."

"Not as far as I'm concerned. So I hear the plan is for Ben to take Megan and push Colonoscopy's face in it. How's that going?"

"Everything's in place. Ben has agreed; he's buying her flowers with his own money—"

"Sweet kid!"

"And all that's left is for Ben to formally ask Megan to go."

"She'll say yes, right? I mean, she's not going to feel weird going with Ben."

"I don't think so." But I have to admit, I haven't put much thought into it. I've been too busy rescuing her. "I'll talk to her as soon as she gets home."

"Call me back and tell me what she says, what he says, the whole thing."

"Okay," I say. "I'll call you later tonight."

"Smell ya," Pi says and hangs up.

I walk back in the house and put the phone in the charger. It rings a few seconds later. I barely have time to pop my Diet Coke before it's about to shift to the answering machine.

"Hello?" I say, taking a sip.

"I just heard," Jim says. "First, can I say a big congratulations that your daughter told you about the whole going-to-second-base thing? Wow. I'm not sure if I should be grossed out, but it seems like a wow to me."

"Thanks," I say, taking another sip.

"Second, Ben only has his driver's permit and he can't legally drive at night with a passenger, but I was thinking that, if it's just a few blocks, maybe he could drive them into the hotel parking lot and do the whole valet thing, make a big deal out of it. That would totally mess with Colonoscopy's head."

"Colonoscopy?" I say, nearly choking on my drink.

"Pi called."

"I figured. Listen, I don't know about driving the car. That seems a little dangerous, not to mention illegal."

"Try to stop being a lawyer for just fifteen minutes. I'd be in a car right behind them," Jim says. "But if you agree to this, don't tell Karen."

"Right. That's going to happen," I say, starting to laugh.

"Narc," Jim says. "Hey, before I let you go, it's time for you to rotate your tires. I'll be over sometime on Saturday."

"Okay. See you Saturday."

"See ya, narc," he says and hangs up.

I have just enough time to use the bathroom before the phone rings again.

"Hey, I just heard."

"Hi, Cindy. What did you hear?"

"The whole thing, plus how you might need a great car for Ben to drive Megan in. Bob's brother just bought a classic Mustang with a perfect paint job; I think it's a 'sixty-six, blue, but I can't really remember. Anyway, I've already talked to Bob about it and he talked to his brother and they are totally up for a road trip to LA if you want that car for Megan to arrive at the dance in. I talked to Jim already and he said that Ben is totally capable of driving it, and it would only be for a few blocks anyway, so, should I tell Bob he can go?"

"I don't think Karen is going to agree to let Ben drive. I just got off the phone with her and we agreed that I'd be driving," I say.

"Really? How long ago did you talk to her, because things may have changed."

"Well, true. Let me call her and then I'll call you back."

"Okay. Bye."

The phone rings almost immediately and I can hear the *warning: low battery* sound chirping.

"What the hell?" Diane says. "I thought you were going to call me right back? I've heard from Pi and Cindy and Jim already! Way to leave me hanging, McCormick."

"I'm sorry! I've barely been off the phone since we talked. Let me fill you in—"

"Oh, I'm all caught up, but you could have called. The guys here are all atwitter over the whole Colonoscopy debacle. They're taking bets on how soon he flees the scene. So, what's Megan wearing? All I got out of Jim was that it was a dress. Idiot."

"It's lavender," I say, "with white trim, white shoes."

"Speaking of lavender, how's our buddy Lavender Barrette? Is he still hard on the scent?"

"Classy," I say.

"McCormick, you're too old to have to worry about being classy. You either got it or you don't, and you've got it, so live a little."

"What are you saying?"

"I'm saying marry the poor bastard. He deserves it."

"Diane, be serious."

"I am being serious. What the hell are you waiting for?" When there's only silence on my end, she says, "Sweetie, really, what are you waiting for? Isn't he the guy you always dreamed of? Isn't he the guy who makes every wish come true?"

I sigh and say, "Let me call you back on my cell. This thing's about to go dead."

"Roger that."

I call her back on my cell a few seconds later. "The thing is," I say, without any preamble, "is that he's not the guy I always dreamed of. The guy I always dreamed of was never this involved in my life. He was always on the outside, or I was on the outside, but there was always this space between us. I never dreamed of a guy who would be close, you know?"

"Okay, McCormick, scratch that. Your dreams suck. Matt's the guy you should have been dreaming of, right? We can agree on that, right?"

"Yeah," I whisper, staring out the kitchen window to the massive sycamore trees. "He's dreamy; that's for sure."

"Then what are you waiting for? This is the first guy who's gone after you like he means it. Do him a big, fat favor and let him catch you. How hard can it be?"

"I guess not that hard," I say, starting to laugh.

"Well, hell, no, it's not hard at all. Now, go fall at his feet and let him do the rest. Call me back with the full scoop! I mean it! I don't want to hear it from Cindy; she always misses essential details."

I hang up feeling a bit giddy. I sit down at my kitchen table and stare out at the trees, at the dappled light on the dappled bark, and I think of nothing at all. I am simply happy.

The phone rings.

"Hello?"

"There is no way Ben is driving Bob's brother's Mustang," Karen says.

"I've been telling everyone that," I say.

"What is Cindy thinking? Just because her son is old enough to drive, she thinks everyone is old enough to drive?"

"Well, don't forget, she used to be an Omega," I say, grinning, feeling euphoria taking over every cell.

"Okay, just making sure we're on the same page. Have you talked to Megan yet?"

I glance at the microwave clock. "I leave to pick her up in fifteen minutes. I'll tell her what's been happening, and then, what? Let Ben call her with the formal invite?"

"Yeah, that sounds good. I'll have him call her at about seven, okay?"

"Okay," I say. "And, Karen? I told Matt I'd call him back, and after I talk to him, I'm going to be calling you later today. Be available!"

Karen starts laughing. "Okay. I'll be here. Call him right now, okay? I can't wait to hear back. I'm going to want every detail! No skipping the juicy parts."

I nod and start to laugh. "You just got off the phone with Diane, right?"

"Roger that."

Karen

"Down in front!"

"Are we getting popcorn at this premiere? A bling bag? Anything?"

"Somebody shove a bag of popcorn in the microwave for Candy before she passes out from hunger," I say. The whole room looks at me expectantly, so I get up off the floor with a huff and say, "Fine. I'll be your server today. Is there anything I can get you?"

"Finally, we're getting some service in this dump," Pi says.

"I'd like my popcorn with just the barest drizzle of butter, salted butter," Diane says primly, "and then just keep drizzling until it's sopping wet. Got it? Thank you."

"Fine, you get drizzled if we get a movie out of you," I say, heading for the kitchen. "Megan has a schedule to keep and we can't sit here all day while you mess with the DVD player."

"McCormick's DVD player is completely uncooperative," Diane says, going back to punching buttons, "and does not know how to play well with others."

"Or it could be operator error," Pi says.

Laurie's house is magnificent, sprawling, and homey. All three at the same time. It's minutes from LA (usually) and yet it seems like it's on the edge of the magic forest. It's a pretty place, *a place to call home*, as Laurie has said more than once, once too often according to Ellen. Oh, Ellen . . . Anyway, where was I? Right. La Cañada. Laurie's house was looking pretty good when she bought it, but once Megan took up residence, Laurie went full tilt and full out. The house looks fantastic. The kitchen is all white marble with heavy veins and white cabinets and dark wood floors. It looks elegant and warm, high-end and comfortable.

Laurie and Megan don't look up as I walk in, so I study them for a second before I say anything. Laurie's hair is a pale champagne blond that makes her eyes look more blue than gray; she wears it shorter, to the chin, blunt cut, no bangs. She looks both very professional and very feminine. Laurie is still slender and still Laurie, but only around the edges. At her core, she's soft and squishy.

Megan. Megan is Ellen all the way with a sugar coating of Laurie on top. Megan is . . . one of us. Megan is *not* a placeholder for Ellen—that would be disgusting—but she's not only Laurie's kid; she's our kid, too. To a much lesser degree, naturally, but still, *ours*.

"I have an order for popcorn from the peanut gallery," I say, walking in fully. They look up in tandem, this mother and child who found each other like two lost survivors of a shipwreck.

They don't look alike, not really, but they dress alike and they move in the same way sometimes, a lifting of the head with a simultaneous flick of the hair, the way they root around in their purses, like a careful archaeological dig, the way they use a pen, from the grab all the way to the tossing discard. Laurie is still that blue-blood beauty, and Megan bears the hot, glowing imprint of Ellen's red-blooded femininity. I still remember that so clearly, my first impression of both Ellen Olson on one side of me and Laurie McCormick on the other. I don't know what I was then, except slightly desperate, anxiety and confusion coming out of me with every breath.

"I'm on it," Megan says, turning from whatever she and Laurie were doing to pull a microwave bag out of the cupboard next to the refrigerator and pop it into the microwave. Megan's blond hair, long and loosely curled, swings with each movement. She looks like a palomino in motion, young and vital and fearless.

"With butter," I add. "Real butter. I hope you have it or Diane will stage a mutiny. And she's the one to do it."

"I know who I'm dealing with," Laurie says, pulling a stick of butter out of the stainless steel fridge.

"What are you guys doing?" I say, coming closer.

"Time traveling," Megan says, her bright blue eyes sparkling.

"Without a net," Laurie says, smiling up at me. "Look at this, Karen. Look at how young we all were."

The photo album is something from the ULA student store; red leather, gold embossed with the ULA emblem, and gigantic. It's a scrapbook, not a photo album at all; do they even sell scrapbooks anymore? Does anyone, anymore, keep the scraps, the paper bits of life that mark large moments and small, the ticket stubs, the theater programs, the letters of acceptance, the transcripts?

There's a photo of Laurie in her white dress at Presents, holding her yellow and white bouquet on the gold-carpeted stair of the Beta Pi house, her light brown hair swept back behind her shoulders in a smooth, straight fall, her smile picture perfect, frozen and held while the photographer clicked and saved the moment. At the bottom of the picture, *Beta Pi Presents 1975*, in gold letters.

I look up at Laurie, tears in my eyes, smiling, and say, "Just like yesterday."

"I know," she says.

"Enjoy every minute!" I say to Megan, who has come back to stand next to Laurie. "It flies by! You think it will never end, and then, bam, it's over."

"That's what I've heard," Megan says with a grin. She has a beautiful smile; Ellen's perfect white teeth in a perfect row.

I flip the pages, past Christmas parties and Hawaiian luaus in some Beta Pi parent's backyard, to all of us, Candy and Holly and Missy and Pi and Cindy and Joan and Lee and Ellen and Diane and Laurie, and I, arms around one another, grinning, mouths open in a whoop of joy, cuddled next to dates who sometimes turned into husbands and sometimes did not.

Greg is there, looking stiff in the photographs. Why did I never see how stiff and solemn and stern he was? Doug is there, of course, with Diane, and he is still the most handsome man I've ever seen. And it doesn't mean a thing, or nothing important.

When I think back on the parties, on all the times a photographer was hired and went hurrying through the party, taking photographs as quickly as he could, I think of my date, our dates, the boy/girl-ness of those nights. But when I see these pictures, I realize that it's us, the women, the Beta Pis hugging and laughing and posing against a dark sky, that dominate the shots. It was *us*. We were the party; we were the center of it all. The very purpose of the party was to hold us and bind us, to remind us of who we were to one another. We must have known it, deep down, in that silent place where a twenty-year-old girl never looks, because we are all together in these pictures. It's us. Photo after photo of us, arm in arm, side by side, looking so ready and so prepared.

"I've got it!" Diane yells from the family room.

"Thank *God*," Pi says.

"Showtime," I say.

The microwave beeps; Megan grabs the bag and opens it; Laurie puts the butter in a glass measuring cup and sets it in to melt for thirty seconds.

"Come on! Where are you guys?" Holly calls.

"Slaving over a hot microwave!" I yell back. "Popcorn doesn't just magically appear, you know." Then I look at Laurie and Megan and say softly, "Except, yeah, it kind of does."

Megan chuckles as Laurie stirs the melted butter over the popcorn.

"What are you *doing*?" Diane calls.

"Drizzling!" I shout back.

"Oh. Okay. Carry on," Diane says.

Megan splits the popcorn into six small Fiesta ware bowls, the kind Diane's mother used to have, because Diane made a point of telling us so, and so we all bought a piece of anything Fiesta ware, just to shut her up, we told her, but really, because if Fiesta ware means so much to Diane, then Fiesta ware will mean so much to me. Between the three of us, we carry the bowls into the family room and pass the bowls out to the girls sprawled in luxurious abandon around the luxurious room. The floors are the same dark-stained oak as the kitchen, the walls are burnt caramel with caramel velvet floor-length drapes to match, drapes that I've never once seen closed, and the long, slim sectional is in mocha wool that has a hint of lavender in the weave. The throw pillows are all muted lavender, each pillow a different shape and texture. I love this room. It throws off a great, if silent, cue to snuggle in and relax.

"I still want my bling bag," Pi says over a mouthful of popcorn.

"Yeah, yeah," I say.

"Is everybody set?" Laurie asks. "Okay, then, this is for you, Megan, from us. It's a kind of going-away gift, and a graduation gift."

Megan is sitting next to Laurie in the corner of the sectional, their shoulders bumping.

"I still get to keep the diamond studs, right?" Megan asks, nudging Laurie's shoulder to show she's joking.

"Oh, she's a smart one," Holly says. "Way to keep your wits about you, kid."

"Idiot child," Laurie says, laughing.

"Hey, can we just show this thing? You can talk afterward," Diane says. "I'm hitting *play* now."

The video starts. Diane and Laurie and I did most of it, with a little help from Pi since she is the PR person and has an opinion on things like this. Okay, Pi did most of it, but Laurie, Diane, and I supplied most of the content. Who knew that we were the historians of the group? The title comes up . . . *Tales of Megan the Kid*; there's a tumbleweed rolling down an empty street in the background.

"What is this, a Western?" Diane says.

"I was going for atmosphere," Pi says. "Cretin."

"I'm calling you John Ford from now on," Diane says.

"Down in front," I say, trying to get them to shut up. I'm sitting next to Megan on the couch, Laurie on the other side; Megan smiles and crosses her legs, Indian style. Getting in the mood and grabbing the theme and running with it, right into the desert.

The first shot is a photograph of Laurie and Ellen, each of them wearing a black evening gown, their arms bare, their smiles wide, arms around each other in a two-armed hug, cheek to cheek. In fact, that old song "Dancing in the Dark" starts to play, music, no lyrics. As the music continues, there are photos of all of us, usually

in black evening wear, always smiling, always hugging one an-
other. One of Missy and Ellen, holding drinks aloft, Missy looking
completely plastered. One of Ellen in her senior year, sitting on
Mike's lap in someone's living room. Then another of Ellen, Diane,
Laurie, and me in a semicircle, arms raised, our fingers in the
ULA victory sign, and the music switches briefly to the ULA fight
song played by the ULA marching band. Then there's a picture of
Sammy Spartan on the white horse, reared on his hind feet, on the
ULA Coliseum football field.

As the image fades, the music continues, softly and strangely
melding into "Both Sides Now," and photos of Ellen's wedding to
Mike. Mike and Ellen cutting the cake. Mike and Ellen walking
down the aisle. Ellen with the Exclusives in our wedding outfits;
we look so young, so unscathed, which is an illusion. Even then,
we had our scars.

I have to admit, Mike was a very good-looking guy. He really
did have that James Dean thing going for him. Of course, that only
works when you're young. Nobody wants a fifty-year-old James
Dean loitering about.

Then the true videos start, the age of photography as the best
way to capture a moment changing abruptly to video with sound
and movement. A few hours after Megan was born, while Ellen
was still in the hospital, and the music switches to "You Must
Have Been a Beautiful Baby."

"I look like crap. Put that camera down," Ellen says to the camera, her hair flat and the whites of her eyes red with broken blood
vessels, a shapeless hospital gown hanging askew on her shoulders.
She looks young and happy and exhausted. Megan is in her arms,
a tiny bundle in a plain hospital receiving blanket.

"Will you shut up and try to act maternal? Good grief, Olson,
I'm trying to immortalize you!" Pi says, off camera

Laughter erupts beyond the camera lens and the camera turns. Laurie and Diane and I look at the camera innocently, shaking our heads in confusion.

"What?" Diane says. "Don't film me; get the kid!"

"Do something interesting," Pi says, the camera shaking slightly.

Diane flips a double bird to Pi, down at her hip level. "How's that?"

Pi laughs and swings the camera back to Ellen and Megan.

"You keep moving that camera around like that and we're all going to puke when we watch it," I say on film.

The camera starts to move toward the Karen in the film, and I say, "Just hold it still!"

"She's so bossy," Ellen says. "Motherhood has done something to her."

"You wait," the filmed Karen says, laughing.

The newborn film stops just as suddenly as it started, and a video of Megan and Ellen at Paradise Cove in Malibu comes up, the pier just to the left; the music switches to "Surfer Girl" by the Beach Boys.

"I love this song," I say.

"Shh!" from around the room.

Megan is about three years old and is wearing a tiny little hot-pink one-piece with double pink ruffles on the butt. She looks completely adorable, her white-blond hair gleaming in the sun. She's standing on the shore, the foam from the breaking waves just covering her toes, and every time a wave comes up to her, she stamps her feet in the sand, pushing against the foamy water. Ellen is standing at her side and holding her hand, staring down at her, smiling, looking back at the camera once with a big, white grin on her tanned face, then looking down at Megan again, talking to her.

The Beach Boys keep singing, but it's switched to "Little Deuce Coupe" and it's coming over the car radio. Ellen is driving, her face half-hidden by sunglasses; I'm filming Megan in the back-seat, in her car seat, bouncing her legs, her pink Nike sneakers the closest thing to the camera lens, her whole body vibrating to the beat of the music, her little pink mouth in an O of sound as she sings along.

"Rock on, kid!" Ellen says from the front seat, just before she turns on her blinker.

I remember that day. We were driving out to Camarillo to visit Diane's dad.

The next film cut is Megan getting off the school bus from her first day of school, Ellen whispering as the bus brakes to a stop: *"Megan's first day!"* Megan, her little legs negotiating the big bus steps one by one, and then she was down and running across the road, and then from behind the camera, very loud, Ellen's voice: "Both ways!" Megan jerks to a halt and looks right, left, right, and then runs to her mom, her little face beaming with pride and ac-complishment; then the camera jolts and we see only the top of Megan's head, her arms wrapped around Ellen's legs.

I look over at Laurie and Megan. They are holding hands. Laurie is silently and slowly weeping. Megan is simply smiling.

The music stills and the light fades, and when the focus returns, it's Ellen behind the camera again and Megan is in the distance, walking away down the street in Encino where Ellen used to live. "Bye, Megan," Ellen calls out. Megan turns around and glares at the camera. "I'm really leaving, Mom!" she calls back. Megan must be about eight years old, her little body so taut with anger, her hair thin and slightly tangled, the seat of her pants loose and dirty. "Okay, well, take care of yourself," Ellen calls out. Megan turns stiffly and walks a few more steps. "I mean it, Mom!" she says, turning around swiftly to throw this latest threat. "I know you do, kid," Ellen says softly to the microphone. "I'm here if you change your mind!" she calls out. Megan keeps marching until she's lost to the dusk and the distance the camera can manage.

Megan, next to me, sniffs.

"How long were you gone?" I ask.

"Maybe fifteen minutes," she says. "She didn't say a word about it when I sneaked in the front door, just, 'Glad you changed your mind.' "

Then there's Megan at a swim meet, a row of kids racing down the lanes doing freestyle, all glistening bodies and swim caps, impossible to tell one kid from another, parents shouting from the edge of the pool, the teammates swinging white towels, the timers looking at the kids so seriously, stopwatches and clipboards proclaiming their official duty. The camera swings slowly from one kid to another, trying to focus in on *the* kid, the one kid that this camera should be paying attention to. The microphone picks up Ellen breathing, "I forgot her lane number!" Then the swimmers touch the wall and look up at the face of their lane timers, panting, asking, "Time?" their faces covers by goggles, water sliding down their bodies as they climb out, a wash of clear water covering them, like walking through a waterfall. Still, the only difference between these kids is the team color of their swimsuits and whether they're boys or girls. Finding Megan in that pack of eight swimmers is impossible. Then one of the young swimmers comes over to the camera, her goggles pushed up to rest on her cap, impossibly long legs toned and tanned, breasts just starting to bud, and she says, "Did you see me, Mom? Did you see me? It was my best time ever!" And Ellen answers, "I was watching you the whole time. You looked amazing! Like a shark!"

Then we're at Ellen's funeral service and Laurie is speaking about Ellen, about how bossy she was and how much of a fighter she was and how she wouldn't put up with anything from anyone and was willing and eager to take all comers. And how she transformed and enriched all our lives. It wasn't very long ago; we all remember so clearly that day and that moment, and we didn't really need to include it in this video, but it seemed wrong not to include it. It seemed that, if we didn't put it in, it would be as if Ellen simply disappeared and we just didn't take note of it. So it's in. Because nothing could be further from the truth.

The sound comes up slowly, Pearl Jam's "Smile," and there's Megan, flashing a big grin full of braces, and next to her is Laurie, flashing her own braces at the camera. They stand side by side, arms around each other's shoulders in front of an orthodontic office, but not Ed's because he retired in 1995, right after Ellen died.

The music shifts to "Heartbreaker," and Megan and Ben are standing in front of Laurie's fireplace, Megan in her lavender gown, Ben in formal wear and looking more handsome than usual. Ben has a wrist corsage of deep pink roses with a purple ribbon and is putting it on Megan's wrist. They look solemn and a little nervous, and then Jim says off camera, "You could have had a 'sixty-six Mustang to go with those flowers!" Ben smiles and then I say off camera, "No, he couldn't!" and then Ben starts to laugh. Megan smiles at Ben, and she leans toward him to whisper something, and Ben grins and looks at the camera. "Are you really marrying a guy called Lavender Barrette?" And then Laurie starts laughing and the camera bounces around a bit, and then Matt's face appears right in front of the camera, really close, and he says, "No. She's marrying the Lazy Stalker. There is no Lavender Barrette. There *is* no Lavender Barrette." And he makes that move with his hand that Obi Wan did in *Star Wars*. The power of the force isn't working for Matt, because to us, he'll always be Lavender Barrette. And you know what? I think he secretly loves it.

I hope he loves it because he's stuck with it.

The video closes in on the roses of the corsage, fades out, and then fades in on a cluster of red roses: Laurie's bridal bouquet. It's Laurie's backyard and it's Laurie's wedding to Matt Carlson. One of the most romantic songs of all time—"If," by Bread—is playing softly, and there's Laurie, walking down a grass aisle to marry Matt.

We're all there in this video; everyone came. Candy and Steve have just moved back to California from Hawaii, Cindy and Bob from San Diego, Joan and Benedict from New York, Holly and Bill, Lee from Arizona . . . all the Exclusives we see as often as we can, but as often as we can sometimes stretches for a decade or two. My kids are there, Ben, David, and Charlie. One of Laurie's nieces came, Bond, who's twenty-three and going to grad school at UCLA, the only one of her family to come. Except for us, of course.

The video shows us all as we sit under the trees, the pool sparkling off to the right. Megan is standing next to Matt, waiting with him as Laurie comes down the garden aisle. I haven't seen this video before; it was taken by a professional videographer, and it's nice to be able to see the wedding from this point of view, almost omniscient.

Laurie looks beautiful, of course; she is the bride. Matt looks like a guy on his first date, so nervously excited that he looks close to throwing up. He leans in and says something to Megan, and Megan smiles at him. Then they both turn to smile at Laurie just as she joins them at the rose arbor altar. I remember that moment from the wedding, that leaning in, smiling, sharing moment, and it warmed my heart then as it warms my heart now.

They've found each other, these three; they've made a family.

"He looks so happy, doesn't he?" Laurie says softly, next to me.

"He does," I say. "He always did. He was always such a happy guy."

"It's a rare trait. I appreciate it more now," Laurie says.

"Words of wisdom there, Megan. Listen up," I say.

Megan nods and says, "Mom's got a good one."

Laurie beams at me and presses Megan to her side.

The music becomes "Brick House," and Diane says, "Really? 'Brick House'? That's what I get for my wedding segment? Who put the fix in on me?"

"Laurie paid me off in Girl Scout Thin Mints. *I'll never go hungry again*," Pi says, fist raised to the sky.

"Okay, Scarlett. At least we know your price now," Diane says.

"Hey, at least no one played it at your *actual* wedding," I say.

The camera focuses on Diane at her dad's house in Camarillo. Diane in a dress of oyster silk, belted at the waist and slightly off the shoulder. She's standing in the living room, the view of the green hilltops and a distant slice of ocean. Her dad is in a wheelchair next to the stone fireplace and the guests, all thirty of us, are sitting on her mom's old beige couch and nubby green chairs. (Diane did get her dad to agree to throw out the old blue accent pillows, but Diane and I, on a shopping trip that will live in infamy, chose the same shade of light blue, only with a checked pattern. Her dad was relieved; you could actually see it on his face.)

Standing next to Diane is her soon-to-be husband, Mac. Captain Diane Ryan met Captain Jeff MacKay in New Orleans, about a year before she retired in February 2000 (we all went, including

Megan, and we were all overwhelmed by the Change of Command and Retirement ceremony; I wasn't the only one who cried). So Diane did, after twenty-five years in the navy, fulfill her dad's command that she not "shit where she eats." Megan is standing next to Diane wearing a pale turquoise silk sheath dress.

"I knew I was being upstaged," Diane says now. "The kid gets blue and I get *been there, done that* white."

"You reap what you sow," Pi says.

"Oh, nice," Diane says.

Megan laughs and leans forward; Laurie reaches out and runs a hand down her daughter's hair.

Diane's segment only shows the part where Megan, Diane, and Mac are all standing, Megan taking Diane's bouquet from her when the rings are exchanged, and then it fades out, taking "Brick House" with it.

The next photo is of Megan in a two-piece bathing suit, sitting around the pool with three of her high school girlfriends, all of them with earbuds and cell phones in pretty cases, talking to one another and to the thousands of people trapped in their cell phone memory cards. Megan looks at the camera and scowls, "What is it, Mom?"

"Just wanted to get this on tape for you," Laurie's voice says from behind the camera.

"It's not tape! It's a disk!" Megan says in annoyance. One of the girls chuckles, the one with really big, fake boobs.

"Sorry. Right. Disk," Laurie says, tightening the focus on the camera, showing us Megan in all her youth and anger and misdirected frustration. Megan looks wonderful, of course, even in her teenage rage; she has a lot of Ellen in her, the same hair, the same tendency to freckle, the same full bust.

The view of Megan around the pool fades out and then fades in to a picture of Ellen at the beach with Laurie, both of them propped on their elbows, lying on their bellies, their bikini tops outlining the shape of their breasts like an old *Playboy* cartoon.

The music is "If I Only Had a Brain," from *The Wizard of Oz.* Pi starts laughing. So do I.

"What's so funny?" Diane says. "I don't get it."

"Why's this in here?" Megan asks.

"Think about it for a minute," Laurie says, motioning for Diane to put the tape on hold.

"I wish *I* had a brain," Diane says. "Maybe then I'd know what's going on."

Megan's face clears in understanding and then she looks embarrassed. "Oh," she says.

"What?" Holly says.

"I wanted my breasts done," Megan says in a muted voice. "For a graduation present. Mom and I had a fight about it just before my friends came over."

"You mean, made bigger?" Diane says. And then she starts laughing. "What is it with these Olson girls, never happy with their boobs? It has to be genetic, some sort of mutation, right?"

"You know your boobs are just the same size as Mom Number One's, right?" Pi says. "And you know that she hated her boobs because she thought they were too damn big, right?"

"Could you please stop calling Ellen Mom Number One? I really don't like being referred to as Number Two," Laurie says.

"Luck of the draw, McCormick," Pi says.

"Anyway, you, with the same boobs, think yours are too small," I say. "What does that tell you?"

"I know," Megan says, "but—"

"No buts," Laurie interrupts her. "What was too big in 1976 is too small in 2001? That's nonsense. Don't fall for it."

"You're a beautiful girl," I say. "Don't let anyone make you think you're not."

"Hear, hear," Diane says, nodding.

"Let's finish this tribute," Pi says. "I'm out of popcorn."

Diane hits *play* again and we all snuggle into a cozy position, the bittersweet moment of seeing Ellen again and her own, and our own, self-loathing pushed behind us.

The next video clip is of Megan onstage in her high school's production of *Guys and Dolls* (she played Adelaide and really rocked it); the video is of her singing "Take Back Your Mink," and it segues beautifully into her being given the mobile home in Malibu.

"That was amazing! How did you do that, Pi?" Candy says. "I didn't know you were that good."

"Gee. Thanks," Pi says.

"It's the irony of the juxtaposition that I love," I say.

"Yeah, I'm all about the juxtaposition," Pi says.

"Anybody else notice how it sounds dirty when Pi says it?" Diane says.

The music becomes "California Girls" by the Beach Boys, and Megan is standing with her Olson grandparents at Paradise Cove, Laurie next to her. They're on the road that's in front of the trailer, the ocean in the background, a bed of red geraniums in the foreground. Mr. Olson, Ed, stands stiffly next to Laurie and Megan, looking both grim and worn down by life. Life will do that to you. He looks at the camera and says, "This was Ellen's favorite place, and since she's gone, I think you should have it." He hands the key to Laurie, who gives it to Megan. They both look at him, and at the camera, and then Megan grins and waves at the camera (Gammi) and the camera goes dark.

"You'd never know, from looking at that, that I bought the

place from him," Laurie says. "Of course, he might have been able to get more if it had actually gone on the market."

Megan chuckles and lays her head on Laurie's shoulder.

The next scene is of Megan's high school graduation. "Pomp and Circumstance" is playing. We're all there, of course. We'll always be there. Megan's name is called and she strides across the stage, picking up her diploma, a big smile on her face as she walks back to her seat.

Megan Olson McCormick.

The music shifts to Alice Cooper's "School's Out for Summer," and Pi is filming Megan, Laurie, Diane, and me walking around the ULA campus not long after Megan got accepted in March. It's changed since 1978. It looks prettier, cleaner, more organized, and there are more buildings. It seems to have grown, spread out. The video shows us, like the old broads we've mysteriously become, pointing out all the changes to Megan.

"This was never here!"

"They built a new bookstore!"

"That fountain never worked once, the whole time we were here."

"This street is closed to traffic now?"

"Megan, that was my dorm! That's Birnhaven. I was on the eighth floor."

"You were in Birnhaven? So was I!"

"Me, too! I had no idea! I wonder if we ever saw each other in the cafeteria. I gained five pounds my first semester, all on mac and cheese. Megan, step away from the mac and cheese!"

"We had to have seen each other there, but how would we have met? There were—what?—two thousand women in that dorm? This was back when they had women's and mens's dorms, kid, the dark ages."

"No, there's no way we could have met in the dorms, not unless we were roommates."

"What floor were you on?"

"Sixth."

"I was on the fifth. What time did you eat dinner?"

"Bigger than a bread box. How the hell am I supposed to remember that after all these years?"

"Somebody's getting cranky about her Alzheimer's diagnosis."

The camera follows Megan as she walks across the quad, looking at the massive sycamores, smiling back at us as we follow her, these women who've been with her from the start, who've loved one another and loved her for as long as she can remember. I know this is what Ellen wanted for her. I know we've done our best for her. For them both.

I also know that, in giving Megan to Laurie, Ellen gave Laurie exactly what both Megan and Laurie needed.

The sunlight hits Megan's hair, and in a brief second of profile, she looks exactly like Ellen. I feel my heart stop, and then I smile, the bittersweet joy of this day washing through me. I have a lot of bittersweet days now.

Megan is a freshman at ULA and today, an hour from now, we're driving her down to campus for Rush. We're all going, of course. She's ours. Whether she pledges Beta Pi or not, that's her choice; she's a Beta Pi legacy, but if Beta Pi doesn't suit her, we won't care. She'll find her way.

After all, she'll always be an Exclusive.

Readers Guide for

Sorority Sisters

by Claudia Welch

DISCUSSION QUESTIONS

1) Why do you think the author chose to use alternating voices? Which character do you identify with the most?

2) Each character, to some degree, feels her self-worth is determined by what a man thinks of her. Do you think this is a true reflection of life as it was then or is now?

3) Do you get the sense that the sisterhood bonded these women or do you think they could have befriended each other independently of the sorority?

4) Do you think the women ever recovered from the emotional scars their past loves caused them?

5) Laurie ponders: *Does a true bad boy know he's bad? Isn't he just being himself?* What do you think?

6) Karen's mother is the most loving and involved of all the mothers represented, yet she reinforces the message that girls are judged by their appearance. Was this kind of her or cruel? What was her motivation?

7) Laurie's decision to date Doug created tension within the group. How would you have treated Laurie and the situation if you were Diane? If you were Karen? Have you ever had a man impact your female friendships in this way?

8) Which character surprised you? Which character disappointed you? Which character did you feel most sympathetic toward?

9) What kind of portrait do these women paint of a sisterhood? Does it resemble what you know or believe to be true of sororities?

10) What do you think keeps these women (and their families) so close years after their days in the sorority house?